In early twentieth-century San Francisco, a cardsharp and a casino bouncer must rescue an Indian woman before she receives an unjust punishment in **Ed Gorman**'s "The Old Ways."

Al Sarrantonio recounts the adventures of an outlaw's lover in "The Stories of Darlin' Lily."

In **Tom Piccirilli**'s "The Day Lamarr Had a Tall Drink with His Short Daddy," a plantation owner's bastard son seeks a reckoning with his father.

AND FOURTEEN ADDITIONAL STORIES OF . . .

Desperadoes

Desperadoes

Edited by
Ed Gorman
and **Martin H. Greenberg**

BERKLEY BOOKS, NEW YORK

These are works of fiction. Names, characters, places, and incidents are
either the product of the authors' imaginations or are used fictitiously,
and any resemblance to actual persons, living or dead, business
establishments, events, or locales is entirely coincidental.

DESPERADOES

A Berkley Book / published by arrangement with
the authors

PRINTING HISTORY
Berkley edition / June 2001

All rights reserved.
Copyright © 2001 by Tekno Books and Ed Gorman

A complete listing of the individual copyrights and permissions
can be found on page 277.

This book, or parts thereof, may not be reproduced in
any form without permission.
For information address: The Berkley Publishing Group,
a division of Penguin Putnam Inc.,
375 Hudson Street, New York, New York 10014.

The Penguin Putnam Inc. World Wide Web site address is
www.penguinputnam.com

ISBN: 0-425-18008-5

BERKLEY®
Berkley Books are published by The Berkley Publishing Group,
a division of Penguin Putnam Inc.,
375 Hudson Street, New York, New York 10014.
BERKLEY and the "B" design
are trademarks belonging to Penguin Putnam Inc.

PRINTED IN THE UNITED STATES OF AMERICA

10 9 8 7 6 5 4 3 2 1

Contents

Introduction

Martin H. Greenberg

THERE WERE PROBABLY never any Western gunfights that happened the way Hollywood later depicted them. For outlaws of ordinary stripe, the old West was a place of drunken brawls, ambushes, and back-shootings. It was only the robber barons, land tyrants, and mine owners who could take lives and still ride in the silken comfort of their personal railroad cars.

Read Fredric Remington's notebooks sometime. Or check out a collection of newspaper stories published during the times of Billy the Kid, Wild Bill Hickok, and Butch Cassidy. A night spent with such stories will disabuse you forever of the "romance" of the frontier. For most desperadoes, life was hard, dirty, treacherous, and brief. If the law didn't get you, a bounty hunter would. Sometimes they were the same person (lawmen of the time were nothing if not duplicitous).

Which brings us to this book.

This is a cross-section of stories of men in trouble. Some of them are victims of circumstance; some are pretty bad people. You'll find violence, sorrow, and some occasional humor, probably in about the same proportions you'd have found back then. One thing that good Western fiction always does—it reminds you that the people then were just as we are now, with the same aspirations, hopes, and fears.

One thing all these tales have in common is excitement. Despite any number of attempts to bury Western fiction, it is still being read and enjoyed by millions of people around the world. And for a damned good reason. It's fun to read.

The Town No Guns Could Tame

Louis L'Amour

Chapter 1
TOWN TAMER WANTED!

THE MINER CALLED Perry stepped from the bucket and leaned his pick and shovel against a boulder. He was a big man with broad shoulders and narrow hips. Despite the wet, clinging diggin' clothes, he moved with the ease and freedom of a big cat. His greenish eyes turned toward Doc Greenley, banker, postmaster, and saloon man of Basin City, who was talking with the other townsmen.

Perry's head and arms were bare, and the woolen undershirt failed to cover the mighty muscles that rippled along his back and shoulders. One of the men, noting the powerful arms and the strong neck, turned and said something to the others. They nodded, together.

"Hey, Perry," Doc Greenley called, "drift over here, will you? Me and these two gents want to make a proposition to you."

Casually, Perry picked up the spare pick handle leaning against the boulder and walked over, his wet clothes sloshing as he moved. He stopped when he reached the trio, and his eyes studied them, coldly penetrating. The three men shifted uneasily.

"Go ahead with it, then," Perry said shortly.

"It's like this," Doc explained. "Buff McCarty"—he nodded toward the larger of his two companions—"and Wade Manning, here, and myself have been worried about the rough element from the mines. They seem to be taking over the town. No respectable citizens or their womenfolk are safe. And as for the holdups that have been raising hell with us businessmen . . ." Doc Greenley mopped his brow with a fresh bandanna handkerchief, letting the sentence go unfinished.

"We want you to help us, Perry," the heavyset, honest-faced McCarty put in. "Manning, here, runs the freight line and I have the general supply outfit. We're all substantial citizens and need a man of your type for town marshal."

"As soon as I heard you were here, I told the boys you were just the man for us," Greenley put in eagerly.

Perry's green eyes narrowed thoughtfully. "I see." His gaze shifted from Doc Greenley, the most prominent and wealthiest man there, to the stolid McCarty, and then to the young townsman, Wade Manning. He smiled a little. "The town fathers, out in force, eh?" He glanced at Wade, looking at him thoughtfully. "But where's Rafe Landon, owner of the Sluice Box Bar?"

"Rafe Landon?" Doc Greenley's eyes glinted. "Why, his bar is the hangout for this tough crowd! In fact, we have reason to suspect—"

"Better let Perry form his own suspicions, Doc," Wade Manning interrupted. "I'm not at all sure about Rafe."

"You may not be," Greenley snapped, "but I am! Perry, I'm convinced that Landon is the ringleader of the whole kit an' caboodle of the killers and renegades we're trying to clean out!"

"Why," Perry said suddenly, "do you choose this particular time to pick a marshal? There must be a reason."

"There is," Wade Manning agreed. "You probably know about the volume of gold production here. Anyway, Doc has better than two hundred thousand in his big vault now. I have about half that much. There's a rumor around of a plot to loot the stage of the whole load."

"It's Landon," Greenley said, "that's who it is! An' do you know what *I* think?" He looked from one to the other, pulling excitedly at his ear lobe. "I think Rafe Landon is none other than *Clip Haynes*, the toughest, coldest gunman who ever pulled a trigger!"

Perry's eyes narrowed. "I heard he was down in Arizona."

"But I happen to know," Greenley said sharply, "that Clip Haynes headed this way—with the ten thousand he got from that stage job near Goldroad!"

Perry looked at Doc thoughtfully. "Maybe so. It could be that way, all right." He glanced at Buff McCarty, who was watching him from his small blue eyes. "Sure, I'll take the job! I'll ride in tonight, by the canyon trail."

The three men walked to their horses, and Perry turned abruptly back to the mine office to draw his time.

∽∽∾

THE MOON WAS rising when the man called Perry swung onto his horse and took the canyon trail for Basin City. The big black stepped out swiftly, and the man lounged in the saddle, his eyes narrowed with thought. He rode with the ease of one long accustomed to the saddle, and almost without thinking kept to the shadows along the road, guiding his horse neatly so as to render it almost invisible in the dim light.

From the black, flat-crowned hat tied under his chin with a rawhide thong to the hand-tooled cowman's boots, his costume offered nothing that would catch the glint of light or prevent him from merging indistinguishably with his background. Even the two big guns with their polished wooden butts, tied down and ready for use, harmonized perfectly with his somber dress.

The trail dipped through canyons and wound around lofty mesas, and once he forded a small stream. Shortly after, riding through a maze of gigantic boulders, he reined in sharply. His keen ear had detected a sudden sound.

Even as he came to a halt he heard the hard rattle of hooves from a running horse somewhere on the trail ahead, and almost at the same instant, the sharp *spang* of a high-powered rifle.

Soundlessly, he slid from the saddle, and even before his feet touched the sand of the trail, his guns were gripped in his big hands. Tensely, he ran forward, staying in the soft sand where his feet made no noise. Suddenly, dead ahead of him and just around a huge boulder, a pistol roared. He jerked to a halt, and eased around the rock.

A black figure of a man was on its knees in the road. Just as the man looked around, the rifle up on the mountainside crashed again, and the kneeling figure spilled over on its face.

Perry's gun roared at the flash of the rifle, and roared again as a bullet whipped by his ear. The rifle fired once more, and Perry felt his hat jerk on his head as he emptied his gun at the concealed marksman.

There was no reply. Cautiously Perry lifted his head, then began to inch toward the dark figure sprawled in the road before him. A match flared suddenly up on the hillside, and Perry started to fire, then held it. The man might think him dead, and his present position was too open to take a chance. As he reached the body, the rattle of a horse's hooves faded rapidly into the distance.

Perry's lips set grimly. Then he got to his knees and lifted the body.

It was a boy—an attractive, fair-haired youngster. He had been shot twice, once through the body, and once through the head. Perry started to rise.

"Hold it!" The voice was that of a woman, but it was cold and even. "One move and I'll shoot!"

She was standing at one side of the road with a pistol aimed at Perry's belt line. Even in the moonlight she was lovely. Perry held perfectly still, riveted to the position as much by her beauty as by the gun she held so steadily.

"You murderer!" she said, her voice low with contempt. "Stand up, and keep your hands high!"

He put the boy gently back on the ground and got to his feet. "I'm afraid you're mistaken, miss," he said. "I didn't kill this boy."

"Don't make yourself a liar as well as a killer!" she exclaimed. "Didn't I hear you shooting? Haven't I eyes?"

"While you're holding me here," he said gently, "the real killer is making his getaway. If you'll put down that gun, I'll explain."

"Explain?" There was just a hint of hysteria in her voice. "After you've killed my brother?"

"Your brother?" he was startled now. "Why, I didn't—"

Her voice trembled, but the gun was unrelenting. "You didn't know, I suppose, that you killed Wade Manning?" Her disbelief was evident in her tone.

"Wade Manning?" he stepped forward. "Why, this isn't Wade Manning!"

"Not—not Wade?" her voice was incredulous. "But who is it then?"

He stepped back. "Take a look, Miss Manning. I don't know many people around here. I met your brother today at the Indian Creek Diggin's. He's a sight older than this poor youngster."

She dropped to her knees beside the boy. Then she looked up. "Why, this is young Tommy McCarty! What in the world can he be doing out here tonight?"

"Any relation to Buff McCarty?" he asked quickly.

"His son." Her eyes misted with tears. "Oh, this is awful! We—we came over the trail from Salt Lake together, his folks and mine!"

He took her by the shoulders. "Listen, Miss Manning.

I don't like to butt in, you knowin' the lad an' all, but your brother came out here to see me today. He wanted me to be marshal here in Basin City. I took the job, so I guess this is the first part right here."

She drew back, aghast. "Then you—you're *Clip Haynes!*"

It was his turn to be startled now. "Who told you that?" he demanded. Things were moving a little too fast. "Who knew I was Clip Haynes?"

"Wade. He recognized you today. The others don't know. He wanted to see you tonight about something. He said it would take a man like you to handle the law job here."

Frowning thoughtfully, he caught up the boy's horse, grazing nearby, and lashed the body to the saddle. Then he mounted the big black, and the girl swung up on her pinto. Silently they took the trail for Basin City.

Despite the fact that she seemed to have accepted him, he could sense the suspicion that held her aloof. The fact remained that she had found him kneeling over the body, six-gun in hand. He could scarcely blame her. After all, he was not a simple miner named Perry. He was Clip Haynes—a notorious gunman with a blood price on his head.

"Who'd profit by this boy's death?" he asked suddenly. "Does he have any enemies?"

"Tommy McCarty?" her voice was incredulous. "Goodness no! He was just sixteen, and there wasn't a finer boy in Peace Valley. Everyone liked him."

Carefully, he explained all that had happened, conscious of her skepticism and of the fact that she rode warily, with one hand on her pistol. "But who'd want to kill Tommy?" she exclaimed. "And why go to all that trouble? He rides alone to the claim every morning."

Except for the glaring lights of Rafe Landon's Sluice Box Bar and Doc Greenley's High-Stake Palace, the main street of the town was in darkness. But even before they reined in at the hitching rail of the High-Stake, the body had been seen, and a crowd gathered.

They were a sullen, hard-bitten crew of miners, gamblers, freighters, and drifters that follow gold camps. They crowded around shouting questions. Then suddenly Wade Manning pushed through, followed by Buff McCarty.

One glance, and the big man's face went white. "Tommy!" His voice was agonized, and he sprang forward to lift the boy from the saddle.

He stared down into the boy's white, blood-stained face. When he looked up his placid features were set in hard, desperate lines. "Who did this?" he demanded.

With the crowd staring, Clip quietly told his story, helped by a word here and there from the girl, Ruth Manning. When the story was ended, Clip found himself ringed by a circle of hard, hostile eyes.

"Then," Buff McCarty said ominously, "you didn't see this feller up on the hill, eh? And Ruth didn't either. How do I know you didn't kill Tommy?"

"Yeah," a big man with a broken nose said loudly. "This stranger's yarn sounds fishy to me. The gal finds you all a standin' over the McCarty kid with a gun, an'—"

"Shut up, Porter!" Manning interrupted. "Let's hear him out."

"Why should I shoot the boy?" Clip protested. "I never saw the kid before. I don't shoot strangers."

"You say you heard shots, then rode up to him." Buff rested his big hands on his hips, his eyes hard. "Did anybody but you an' Ruth come nigh him?"

"Not a soul!" Clip said positively.

"Then," Buff's voice was harshly triumphant, "how d' you account for *this*?" He lifted an empty leather poke, shaking it in Haynes's face. "That there poke held three thousand dollars when my boy left town!"

The broken-nosed Porter crowded closer to Clip. "You dirty, murderin' coyote!" he shouted, his face red with anger. "Y' oughta be lynched, dry-gulchin' a kid that way!"

"That's right!" another voice yelled. "Lynch him!"

"Hold it!" Clip Haynes's voice was hard. His greenish eyes seemed to glow as he backed away. Suddenly, they saw he was holding two guns, although no man had seen him draw. "Manning, you an' McCarty ought to know better than this! Look at those wounds! That boy was shot with a rifle, not a six-gun! He was shot from higher up the mountain. You'll find both those wounds range downward! You come out to Indian Creek to offer me the job of lawman around here. Well, I took it, an' solvin' this murder is goin' t' be my first job. But just to clear the air, I'm a-tellin' all of you now, my name ain't Perry— it's *Clip Haynes!*"

He backed to his horse, stepped quickly around, and threw himself into the saddle. Then he faced the crowd, now staring at him, white-faced. Beyond them, he saw Doc Greenley. The banker-saloon man was smiling oddly.

"I'll be around," Haynes said then, "an' I aim to complete the job I started. You all know who I am. But if anybody here thinks I'm the killer of that boy, he can talk it out with me tomorrow noon in this street—with six-guns!"

Clip Haynes wheeled the big black and rode rapidly away, and the crowd stood silent until he was out of sight. Then quietly they walked inside.

"What d' you think, Wade?" McCarty asked, turning to the tall, silent man beside him.

Manning was staring up the road after Haynes, a curious light in his eyes. "I think we'd better let him handle it," Wade said, "at least for the time. There's more in this than meets the eye!"

Doc Greenley walked up, rubbing his hands with satisfaction. "Just the man!" he said eagerly. "Did you see how he handled that? Just the man we need! We can make our shipment now when we want to, and that man will take care of it!"

Chapter 2
MAN-BAIT FOR THE BUSHWHACK BROTHERS

Dawn found clip Haynes sitting among the boulders beside the trail from Indian Creek. Below him was the spot where Tommy McCarty had fallen the previous night. Opposite him, somewhere on the hillside, was the place where the murderer had waited. The very place of concealment was obvious enough. It was not a hundred yards away, in a cluster of boulders and rock cedar, not unlike his own resting place. That the murderer had waited there was undoubted, but why?

Clip Haynes pushed his hat back on his head and rolled a smoke.

First, what were the facts? McCarty, Greenley, and Manning, three of Basin City's most reputable businessmen, had hired him as marshal. But Rafe Landon, owner of the biggest mine, and the most popular saloon and dance hall, had not come along. Why?

Secondly, someone had killed and robbed Tommy McCarty. Obviously, the killer had not robbed him, for both Clip and Ruth Manning had been too close. Then, the obvious conclusion was that Tommy had been robbed before he was killed!

Clip sat up suddenly, his eyes narrowed. He was remembering the chafed spot on Tommy's wrist, dimly seen in the light from the High-Stake Palace. Chafed from what? The answer hit him like a blow. Tommy McCarty had not only been robbed, but had been bound hand and foot! He had escaped, and then had been shot.

But why shoot him afterward? That didn't make sense. He already had lost the money, and if the thief had any doubts, he would have killed him the first time. The only answer was that Tommy McCarty had been mistaken for somebody else!

But who? Obviously, whoever had waited on the hillside the previous night had been expecting someone to come along. So far, Clip knew of only three people besides McCarty who might have come along. Wade Manning, Ruth Manning, and himself. But wait! What was Wade doing on the road so late? And why was Ruth traveling alone on that lonely trail?

There was always the possibility that Wade Manning, knowing Perry actually was Clip Haynes, had planned to kill him for the reward offered in Arizona. However, Manning didn't look like a cowardly killer, and the theory didn't, somehow, fit the facts.

Clip Haynes shook his head with disgust. If it was just a matter of shooting it out with some tough gunman, he was all right, but figuring out a problem like this was something he had not bargained for. It was unlikely, however, that anyone would want to shoot Ruth, or that anyone guessed she was on the road that night. That left Wade and himself as the prospective victims of the killer, for by now he would know his mistake.

Three men had known that he was taking the canyon trail to town—Doc Greenley, Wade Manning, and Buff McCarty. Clip's eyes narrowed. Why, since he had been riding slowly, and Tommy McCarty probably at a breakneck speed, hadn't Tommy passed him? Obviously because Tommy had come out on the trail at some point between where Clip had first heard his running horse and the point where he had seen the boy killed.

Mounting, Clip turned the big black down the mountainside to the trail. As he rode along he scanned the edges carefully. Suddenly, he reined in.

The hoofprints of the big black were plainly seen, but suddenly a new trail had appeared, and Clip could see where a horse had been jumped from the embankment onto the trail. Dismounting, and leading the black, he climbed the embankment and followed the trail. As soon as he saw it was plainly discernible, he swung into the saddle again and followed it rapidly.

Two miles from the canyon trail, at the end of a bottleneck canyon, he found a half-ruined adobe house. Here the trail ended.

Dismounting cautiously, Clip walked up to the 'dobe. The place was empty. Gun in hand, he knelt, examining the hardpacked earth of the floor.

The earth was scuffed and kicked as though by a pair of heels, such marks as a man might make in a struggle to free himself. But there were no ropes in sight, nothing. . . .

He froze. A shadow had fallen across him. He knew a man was crouching at the window behind him. His own gun was concealed from the watcher by his body. Apparently studying the earth, he waited for the first movement of the man behind him.

It could only have been an instant later that he heard the click of a cocking gun hammer, and in that same flashing split second, he hurled himself to one side. The roar of the gun boomed in the 'dobe hut, and the dirt against the wall jumped in an awkward spray even as his own pistol roared. Clip leaped to the door.

A bullet slammed against the doorjamb not an inch from his head, as he recklessly sprang into the open, both guns bucking. The man staggered, tried to fire again, and then plunged over on his face.

For a moment, Clip Haynes stood still, the light breeze brushing a lock of hair along his forehead. The sun felt warm against his cheek, and the silent figure on the sand looked sprawled and helpless.

Automatically, Clip loaded his guns. Then he walked over to the body. Before he knelt his eyes scanned the rim of the canyon, examining every boulder, every tree. Satisfied, he bent over the fallen man. Then his eyes narrowed thoughtfully. It was the big man who had been so eager to see him lynched the night before, the man who had joined Porter in his protests.

Clip's eyes narrowed thoughtfully, then he got to his feet. He turned slowly, facing the shack. He stood there a moment carelessly, his thumbs hooked in his belt.

"All right," he said finally, "you can come out from behind that shack. With your hands high!"

Wade Manning stepped out, his hands up. His eyes glinted shrewdly. "Nice going," he said. "How did you know I was there?"

Clip shrugged, and indicated the big black horse with a motion of his head. "His ears. He doesn't miss a thing." He waited, his eyes cold.

"I suppose you want to know what I'm doing here?"

"Exactly. And what you were doing on the canyon trail last night. You seem to be around whenever there's any shooting going on."

"I can explain that," Wade said, smiling a little. "I don't blame you for being suspicious. After we talked to you at the mine that day, I decided I'd better go back out there and tell you I knew who you were, and to be careful around the men at the mine. And I didn't want you to jump to conclusions about Landon."

"What's Rafe Landon to you?" Clip demanded.

Wade shrugged, rolling a smoke. "Maybe I know men, maybe I don't," he affirmed, running his tongue along the paper. "But Rafe sizes up to me like a square shooter." He glanced up. "And in spite of what Ruth says, I think you are, too."

"Know this hombre?" Clip indicated the man on the ground.

Wade nodded. "Only to see him. He worked for Buff McCarty for a while. Lately he's been hanging around the Sluice Box. Name's Dirk Barlow. He's got a couple of tough-hand brothers."

Mounting, they started down the trail together. Clip Haynes glanced out of the corner of his eyes at Manning. He was clean-cut, smooth, good-looking. His actions were suspicious, but he didn't seem the type for a killer.

Clip frowned a little. So Ruth didn't like him? Something stirred inside him, and he found himself wishing she felt differently. Then he grinned wryly. A hunted gunman like Clip Haynes getting soft about a girl! There wouldn't ever be any girls like Ruth for him.

He looked up, his mind reverting to the former problem. "How about this gent Porter back in town—the one who was so sure I shot Tommy McCarty. Where does he fit in?"

"A bad hombre. Gun-slick, and tough. He killed a prospector his first night in town. About two weeks later he shot it out with a man named Pete Handown."

"I've heard of Handown. This Porter must be fast."

"He is. But mostly a fistfighter. He runs with the surviving Barlow brothers—Joe and Gonny. They're gunmen, too. They've figured in most of the trouble around here. But they've got a ringleader. Somebody behind the scenes we can't decide on."

"Greenley thinks it's Rafe, eh?"

"Yes. I'll admit most of the gang hang around the Sluice Box. But I'm sure Rafe's in the clear." Wade looked up. "Listen, Clip. If you ride with the stage tomorrow, watch your step. There's three hundred thousand in gold going out."

Doc Greenley was standing with Buff McCarty on the walk in front of the High-Stake Palace when they rode up. He glanced swiftly at the body slung over the lead horse. Then he smiled brightly. "Got 'em on the run, boy?" he asked. "Who is it this time?"

"Dirk Barlow," Buff said, his eyes narrowing. "You'll have to ride careful now, Haynes. His brothers will come for you. They're tough as hell."

Haynes shrugged. "He asked for it." His eyes lifted to Buff's. "I back-trailed Tommy. I knew he cut in ahead of me last night, and if you looked, there was a chafed spot on his wrist. I knew he'd been tied, so I looked for the place. I found it, and this hombre tried to kill me."

"You think he killed Tommy?" Buff demanded.

"I don't know. He hasn't the money on him." He turned his head to see Ruth Manning standing in front of the post office. Their eyes met, and she turned away abruptly.

Clip swung down from the saddle and walked across the street. When he stepped into the Sluice Box he saw Rafe Landon leaning against the end of the bar.

He was a tall man, handsome, and superbly built. There was an easy grace in his movements that was deceptive. He was wearing black, and when he turned, Clip saw he carried two guns, tied low.

"How are you, Haynes?" he said, holding out his hand. "I've been expecting you."

Haynes nodded. "What do you know about this McCarty killing?" he asked coolly. He deliberately ignored the outstretched hand.

Landon smiled. "An accident, of course. Nobody cared about hurting Tommy. He was a grand youngster."

"What d'you mean—an accident?"

"Just that. They were gunning for somebody else, but Tommy got there first." Rafe looked down at his cigarette, flicked off the ash, and glanced up. "In fact, it would be my guess they were gunning for you. Somebody who didn't want Clip Haynes butting in."

"Nobody knew I was Haynes."

Rafe shrugged. "I did. I'd known for two weeks. Manning knew, too. Probably there were others." He nodded toward the street. "I see you got Dirk Barlow. Watch those brothers of his. And look out for Porter, too."

"You're the second man who told me that."

"There'll be more. Joe and Gonny Barlow will be in as soon as they hear about this. Joe's bad, but Gonny's the worst. Gonny uses both hands, and he's fast."

"Why tell me this?" Clip asked. He looked up, and their eyes met.

Rafe Landon smiled. "You'll need it, Haynes. I'm a gambler, and it's my business to know about men. A word of friendly advice never hurt anyone—even a gent like you. Joe Barlow's never been beat in a gunfight. And like I said, Gonny's the worst."

"Porter? What's he like?" Clip asked.

"Maybe I can tell you," a harsh voice broke in.

Clip turned to see Porter standing in the doorway. He was big, probably twenty pounds bigger than Clip, and his shoulders were powerful.

"All right," Clip said. "You tell me."

Chapter 3
THE BARLOWS STRIKE

PORTER WALKED OVER to the bar.

Glancing past him Clip could see the room filling with men. Come to see the fun, to see if the new marshal could take it. Clip grinned suddenly.

"What's funny?" Porter snarled suspiciously.

"You," Clip said shortly. "Last night I thought I heard you say I needed lynching. I suggested anyone who wanted to debate the matter could shoot it out with me in the street. You weren't around. What's the matter? Yellow?"

Porter stared, taken aback by the sudden attack. Somebody chuckled, and he let out a snarl of rage. "Why, you—!"

Clip's open palm slapped him across the mouth with such force that Porter's head jerked back.

With a savage roar, the big man swung. But Clip was too fast. Swaying on his feet, he slipped the punch and smashed a vicious right hand into the man's body. Porter took it without flinching, and swung both hands to Clip's head.

Haynes staggered, and before he could set himself, Porter swung a powerful right that knocked him sprawling. Before Clip could get to his feet, Porter rushed in, kicking viciously at Haynes's face, but the young marshal jerked his head aside and took the kick on the shoulder. The camel boot sent pain shocks through his body.

It knocked him rolling, but he gathered his feet under him and met Porter's charge with a jarring left jab that

set the bigger man back on his heels and smashed his
upper lip into his teeth.

Porter ducked his head and charged, but Clip was stead-
ying down, and he sidestepped suddenly, bringing up a
jolting right uppercut that straightened Porter up for a
crashing right that knocked him reeling into the bar.

He grabbed a bottle and hurled it across the room, but
Clip ducked and charged in, grabbing the big man about
the knees and dropping him to the floor. Deliberately, Clip
fell with him, driving his head into the man's stomach
with all his force, and then spinning on over to land on
his feet.

Breathing easily, he waited until Porter got up. The big
man was dazed, and before he could assemble his facul-
ties, Clip walked in and slapped him viciously with both
hands, and then snapped his fist into Porter's solar plexus
with a jolt that doubled the bigger man up with a groan.
A left hook spun him half around and ripped the skin
under one eye. As he backed away, trying to cover, Clip
walked in and pulled his hands away, crossing a wicked
short right hook to the chin. Without a sound, Porter
crumpled to the floor.

Turning on his heel, Clip walked quickly from the
room, never so much as glancing back.

It was almost noon when he rode slowly down the
mountain trail and tied his horse in a clump of mesquite.
He glanced at the sun. In about fifteen minutes the stage
should be along, and if it was to be held up, it would be
somewhere in the next two miles. Carefully, he walked
ahead until he found a place among the boulders, and then
settled down to wait until the stage came along. From
there on he could follow it.

Suddenly, he noticed a cloud of dust above the trail in
the distance. The stage. He got up, and stood watching it
as it drew nearer. He could see that everything was as it
should be, and turning, he walked back to his horse. When
he was about a dozen steps away, he halted in midstep,
and drew back. There on the ground, over one of his own

tracks was a fresh bootprint, one heel rounded badly, and a queer scar across the toe!

His hand shot to his gun, but before he could draw, something crashed down over his head, and he tumbled forward into blackness. . . .

It was hours later when he opened his eyes. When he tried to lift his head a spasm of pain shot over him, and he groaned desperately. Then for a long moment he lay still, and through the wave of pain from his throbbing head, he remembered the stage, the bootprint, the gold.

Desperately, he got to his hands and knees. On the ground where his head had lain was a pool of blood, and when he lifted one hand, he found his hair matted with it and stiffened with sand. Crawling to his feet, he had to steady himself against a boulder. Then he retched violently, and was sick.

After he staggered to his horse and took a drink from his canteen, he felt better. Summoning all his resolution, he went back and examined the ground. The man had evidently followed him, waited behind a boulder, and as he returned to his horse, knocked him over the head. Quite obviously, he had been left for dead.

Clip walked back to his horse, checking his guns. They hadn't been tampered with. When he swung into the saddle and turned the big black down the trail, his lips were set in a tight, grim line. He loosened the big guns, and despite his throbbing head, cantered down the trail.

He didn't have far to ride. Only about three hundred yards from where he had waited, he found the coach, lying on its side, one wheel smashed. A dead horse lay in a tangle of harness, and sprawled on the ground was the stage driver. He had been shot between the eyes with a rifle.

About twenty yards away, evidently killed as he was making for the shelter of a circle of boulders, was the messenger.

❧❧

IT WAS TWO hours before Clip Haynes rode up in front of the High-Stake Palace and tied the black to the hitching rail. His head throbbing, he stepped in.

At once the hard round muzzle of a gun jammed into his spine.

Clip stopped, his hands slowly lifting.

"Back up, an' back careful!" he heard Buff McCarty saying, his voice deadly. "One false move an' I'll drill you, gunman or no gunman!"

"What's the matter, Buff?" Clip asked. His head throbbed and he felt his anger mounting.

"You ask what's the matter!" Wade Manning snapped. Stepping up he jerked Clip's guns from their holsters. "We trusted you, and then you—"

"We found the money, that's what!" Buff snarled, his voice husky with rage. "The money you took off Tommy! We shook down your duffel bag an' found it there—the whole three thousand dollars you murdered him for!"

"Listen, men!" he protested. "If you found any money there it was a plant. Why—"

"I'm sorry, boy," Doc Greenley interrupted, shaking his head gravely, his usual smile gone. "We've got you dead to rights this time!"

Clip started to protest again, and then his jaw clamped shut. If they wanted to be like that, argument, he figured, was useless. He turned to walk out, and found himself facing Porter.

The big man sneered, and, for just an instant as Clip watched him, he saw the man's eyes flash a message to one of his captors. Then Porter was past, and Clip was being rushed to jail.

When the cell door clanged shut he walked across the narrow room, dropped on his bunk and was almost immediately asleep.

It seemed a long time later when he was awakened. It was completely dark, and listening, he knew the jail was deserted.

Clip walked across to the window, and took hold of the bars.

Then he heard a whisper. "Haynes!"

"Who is it?" he asked softly.

"It's me—Rafe. Stick your hand through the bars. I've got a key!"

Clip Haynes thrust his hand out, and felt the cold metal of a jail key in his hand. Then he heard Rafe speaking again. "Better make it quick. Porter's got a mob about worked up to lynching you."

In two strides he was across the cell. The key grated in the lock, and the door swung wide. Then he turned and stepped back, throwing the blankets into a rough hump to resemble a sleeping figure. Going out, he locked the door after him. His gun belts were on the desk in the outer office, and he swept them up, hurriedly checking the guns as he stepped outside.

Rafe Landon was waiting there. Surprisingly, Rafe had the black horse with him. Without a word, Clip gripped the gambler's hand, and then swung up.

"Listen," Rafe said, gripping his wrist. "Whoever robbed that stage today kidnaped Ruth!"

"What!" Clip jerked around, his jaws set.

"She rode out along the trail just before the stage left town. She told me she wanted to watch you. She hasn't returned yet, and Wade's just found out. There's only one place she can be—with the Barlows!"

"You know where they hang out?" Clip snapped.

"Somewhere back of the Organ. There's a box canyon up there, that might be it. Take the west route around the Organ and you'll find the trail, but watch your step!"

Clip looked down at Rafe in the darkness, his eyes keen. "Just what is Ruth Manning to you?" he demanded.

Clip thought he detected the ghost of a smile. "Does it matter? The girl's in danger!"

"Right!" Clip swung his horse. As he did so he heard

someone shout, and glancing back, he saw a crowd of
men spew from the doors if High-Stake.

The big black stretched his legs and sprang away into
the night, swinging around the town to the trail in tireless,
space-eating strides.

Chapter 4
GUN LAW COMES TO BASIN CITY

THE HUGE PINNACLES of rock known as the Organ
loomed ahead. For years during his wanderings, Clip
Haynes had heard of them. Some queer volcanic effect
had shot these hollow spires up into the sky, leaving them
thin to varying degrees, and under the blows of a stick or
rock they gave forth a deep, resonant sound. Around them
lay rugged broken country.

For a half hour he cut back and forth through the rocks
before he located the box canyon. And then it was the
horse that found the narrow thread of trail winding among
the boulders. A few minutes of riding, and he sighted the
dim light that came from a cabin window.

He dismounted and slipped a gun into his hand. Then
he walked boldly forward, and threw the door open.

A startled Mexican jerked up from his seat on a box
and dropped a hand for his gun, but at the sight of Clip,
he reached for air. "Don't shoot, señor!" he gasped. "Por
dios, don't shoot!"

Clip stepped in and swung his back to the wall.
"Where's the girl?" he snapped.

"The señorita, she here. The Barlows, they go."

Clip stepped quickly across the room and spun the
Mexican around. Picking up a handful of loose rope, he
bound the man hand and foot. Then stooping, he untied
Ruth.

"Thanks," she said, rubbing her wrists. "I was beginning to think—"

"No!" he exclaimed dryly.

Her face stiffened abruptly. Clip grinned at her. "You had that coming, lady. Let's get out of here!"

Suddenly, he stopped. In the corner was a heap of sacks taken from the stage earlier that day. Pausing, he jerked the tie string. The sack toppled slowly over. And from its mouth spilled nothing more than a thin stream of sand!

"Why—!" Ruth gasped. "Why, where's the gold?"

"I'll show you later!" Clip said grimly. "I suspected this!"

There was no talk on the ride homeward. Clip rode at Ruth's side, seemingly intent only on reaching town. It was almost daylight when they rode swiftly up the dusty street.

"Should you do this?" she protested. "Aren't they looking for you?"

"If they are, they better not find me!" he snapped. "I'm doing some looking myself. You ride to your brother, quick, and tell him about that sand. Tell him to bring Buff McCarty to the High-Stake just as quick as he can make it!"

His eyes narrowed. "And you," he went on grimly, "will have a chance to drop by the Sluice Box and see your precious lover, who didn't have guts enough to come after you himself!"

Her eyes widened with amazement, but before she could speak, he wheeled his horse and rode rapidly back up the street and dismounted. Then he walked into the Sluice Box, his face dark with rage.

Rafe Landon stood just inside the door. He walked up to Clip, smiling gravely. "I heard what you said to Ruth," he said. "I want to tell you just two things, Haynes. The first has to do with my want of—guts—as you put it. Once I offered you my hand, and you refused it. Will you take it now?"

Something in his manner seemed strange. Clip glanced down at the gloved hand. Then he took it. Amazement came into his eyes.

"Yes," Rafe said, "you're right. It's iron. The blacksmith in Goldfield made it, several years ago. I lost both my hands after a fire."

Clip looked up, his face tight. "Rafe, I—"

"Forget it. As for Ruth—"

The doors burst open, and Clip wheeled. Wade Manning stood in the door, Buff McCarty beside him. "The Barlows are coming!" he exclaimed, his face tense. "Both of them, Clip, and they've been bragging all morning that they'll kill you on sight!"

He stepped into the street, his steps echoing hollowly as he stepped across the boardwalk. He stopped in the edge of the dusty street and looked north.

The Barlows, Joe and Gonny, were standing on the porch in front of the old hotel building. Then they saw him, and started toward the steps.

Somewhere a horse whinnied, and in the saloon, a man's nervous laughter sounded strangely loud. Clip Haynes walked slowly, taking measured steps.

Joe Barlow's hand was poised over his gun. Gonny waited carelessly, slouching, a shock of hair hanging down over his eyes.

When they were fifty feet apart, the Barlows stiffened as though at a signal, and drew. Joe's hand moved; Clip Haynes shot.

The street broke in a thundering roar through which he found himself walking straight toward them, his guns hammering. He knew the first shot he had taken at Joe had been too quick. Suddenly it seemed as if a white hot branding iron had hit his left shoulder. He dropped that gun, feeling the warm blood run down his sleeve. His arm was useless—but his right gun kept firing.

Suddenly, Joe was falling from the steps, and almost as in a dream Clip saw the man straighten out, arms widespread, blood staining the dust beneath him.

Clip started to step forward, and realized suddenly that he was on his knees. He got up, feeling another slug hit him in the side. Gonny was facing him, legs spread wide, a fire-blossoming gun in either hand. A streak of red crossed his jaw.

Clip started toward him, holding his last bullet. Something slanted a rapier of pain along his ribs, and one of his legs tried to buckle, but still Clip held his fire. Then, suddenly, about a dozen feet away from Gonny, Clip Haynes turned loose his gun.

Almost before his eyes Gonny's gray flannel shirt turned into a crimson, sodden mass. The gunman started to fall, caught himself, and lifted a gun. They were almost body to body when the shot flamed in Clip's face. Something struck him a terrific blow on the side of the head, and he fell. . . .

Actually it was only a minute, but it seemed hours. Men were running from every direction, and as Clip Haynes caught at somebody's leg and pulled his bloody body erect, he heard Wade gabbling in his ear. But he didn't stop. It was only a dozen feet, but it seemed a mile. Step by step, he made it, fumbling shells into his gun.

Weaving on his feet, he stopped, facing Doc Greenley. His eyes wavered, then they focused.

Doc's face went sickly with fear. He opened and closed his mouth, trying to speak. Then suddenly he broke, and went for his gun.

It was just swinging level when Clip shot him. Then Clip pitched over on his face, and lay still.

He must have been a long time coming out of it because they were all there—Ruth, Rafe Landon, Wade Manning, and Buff McCarty—when he opened his eyes. He looked from one to the other.

"Doc?" he questioned weakly.

"You got him, Clip. We found the gold in his safe. He never moved an ounce of it, just sand. We made Porter confess. He robbed Tommy of the three thousand dollars, and later Doc Greenley made him plant it on you. One of the Barlows slugged you.

"We found the note you left in the jail. You were right.

It was Doc who killed Tommy, trying to kill you. He didn't know you were Clip Haynes at first.

"I told him," Wade continued, "never suspecting he was the guilty one behind all this. He knew he couldn't fool you. Felt he'd given himself away somehow. He confessed before he died."

Clip nodded. "At first—at the mine. He said Clip Haynes got ten thousand. Only the law and the bandits knew it was that much." Clip paused, a wan smile twisting his features. "He was the one planned that job—not Haynes. I was the law. The express company hired me. When he said that, I was suspicious."

Clip closed his eyes, and lay very still. When he opened them again everyone was gone but Ruth. She was smiling, and she leaned over and kissed him gently on the lips.

"And Rafe?" he questioned.

"I tried to explain, but you ran away. He's my uncle— my mother's brother. He started Wade in business here, but no one knew. He thought it might hurt Wade if people knew a gambler backed him."

"Oh," he said. For a moment he was silent. Then he looked up, and they both smiled.

"That's nice," he said.

A Simple Trail to Silver

Trey R. Barker

For V. Evans

"COMIN' BACK," THE boy said.

He began to whistle, like Daddy had taught him. By the time Daddy got back, he'd whistle better than Daddy.

"Comin' back with the silver."

From Daddy's porch chair, he watched the sun disappear behind the mountains. Tomorrow was a new day, like somebody went and bought it at the A&P. And he would have only two toes left.

"What I'm gonna do when I run outta toes?"

One finger, and then one toe, for every day Daddy had been gone.

"Comin' back?"

THE IMPERIAL PALACE Theatre.

At three stories, it towered over the town. Gold leaf trimmed its edges and red velvet curtains hung in the windows. The doors were etched glass, male and female figures carved into one another. Next door loomed the Hotel

Baghdad, equally adorned. A balcony ran the length of the second floor, connecting the two buildings.

Tethering his horse, Holloway checked the Schofield's load and ran a hand over his sweaty face. No amount of righteous anger was going to dispel his fear. He thought of his son, alone in the cabin for better than two weeks. Scared, low on food, maybe still crying about Daddy leaving.

Holloway reholstered his Schofield and headed inside.

Music poured out as though the notes were a river full from winter runoff, crashing through the mountains. Violins and a piano, a banjo and a drum. Voices carried over the music. Laughing voices, crying and shouting, whispering.

Whispering like when Buckie had come to help Daddy work at the general store. Or when Buckie had come to help Daddy work at the feedlot. Whispering like they always did when Buckie came to help his Daddy work.

The sound hit Holloway hard, a cheap gut punch.

"Help ya?" a hostess asked.

"Looking for a man."

"Me, too. Maybe you're him."

When she winked, regret strummed his insides. Eight years and still Holloway missed Esther. She had winked her beautiful green eyes at him all the time. "Don't think so," he said tiredly. "Calls himself Villard. Two gold teeth right in front."

The woman's eyes widened and Holloway's insides tightened. "Mr. Nash? He's always here. You a friend of his?"

"I know him."

She squealed. "He rich as they say? I hear he's got mines and railroads and mills and such. Got more money than he'll ever spend." She pointed at a flower pinned to her breast. "Picked this himself. Second floor, first box." Her face flushed with excitement. Villard had obviously gotten to her as deeply as he'd gotten to Holloway.

"I get to that balcony from up there?"

"Sure. Customers like to repair to the hotel after shows. I'd love to have dinner with Mr. Nash."

Holloway's sigh was a deep rumble. "If you're looking for a man, look somewhere else. Ain't no man in his suit."

She frowned. "You're wrong, mister, he's a great man. He's building a race track here, gonna let me manage it."

"Uh-huh." Holloway headed up the stairs. The music was muffled now, hard to hear through the walls. It seemed as far away as Villard's—Nash's—promise of riches last spring.

At the box door, he stopped. His hands shook. He wasn't at all sure he'd be able to hold the gun long enough to get his deed back. But it had to be done. Holloway made the mistake and Buckie was paying for it. But when it was fixed, he and Buckie would head east and when they got there, Holloway could rest until the exhaustion infecting his bones was gone.

Swallowing a wad of fear, Holloway drew his Schofield, opened the door, and stepped into the box.

∾∘∾

"GOOD SHOW?" HOLLOWAY asked.

Villard stiffened. The man at his right started.

"Not a word, Sheriff," Holloway ordered. "Just want Villard." Holloway jammed the gun tightly against Villard's neck. The silver chain around it twinkled in the dim light.

"Please, Sheriff," Villard said expansively. "A man I knew back in the day, a gambler who couldn't keep up."

The sheriff, a tubby man with a drinker's map covering his nose, nodded.

"Have no fear and leave us for a moment, would you?"

"But, Mr. Nash, what if he—"

Villard cut the sheriff off. "Nonsense, sir, I will be most fine."

His eyes on Holloway, the sheriff left the box and scuttled down the stairs.

"You found me."

"Where's Eve?"

Villard laughed. "Under wraps for a few nights."

Eve had been a hard woman with a surprisingly compassionate streak in her. A streak that had allowed her to apologize to Holloway as she and Villard had ridden away.

"I didn't understand her apology until four months later."

Villard nodded. "Eve can be most difficult at times. Now she wishes to retire from our enterprise."

"Give," Holloway said.

"So much trouble for a sheet of paper?"

Holloway pressed the gun deeper into Villard's neck.

On stage, the music continued. Two dancers accompanied the small orchestra, filling the stage with beads and bits of clothing.

"It'll save my boy. I want it back."

"I must point out that you sold me that deed."

"Damn you," Holloway hissed. "That's a good mine. Your boys work it every day. I want it back."

Villard looked at Holloway, his face punctured by surprise. "Drawing ore? Making a profit? Damn." His lips curled into a snarl before he shook his head dismissively. "I stole nothing, sir. You were adequately reimbursed with Midland-Odessa Railway stock."

"Ain't no such rail," Holloway said. He slapped Villard's face. "Damnit, I need that money."

Angrily, Villard stood, his face inches from Holloway's. "Or what, you sad excuse for a man. You'll send that simpleton after me?"

When Villard laughed, Holloway jammed the gun's barrel down the man's throat. Villard gagged, his eyes wide with shock.

"Your choice," Holloway said. "The deed or an extra mouth in back of your head."

Villard grinned and backed away from the gun. He nodded to Holloway as Holloway let him go.

Holloway hesitated. Somewhere inside him, he wanted to simply end it now. Shoot and let whatever happened happen. But where would that leave Buckie? Alone in Lamar, just enough food for a few more days and then what? He'd get a job? Sweeping the courthouse? Cleaning the livery?

Buckie couldn't work. He would sit in that lonely cabin. He'd run out of food but still get well water until he was too weak for that. Then he'd lay on that bed, calling for his daddy, until he died.

"Let's go," Holloway said, pointing toward the door with the gun.

"Thank you, no. I'll wait for the sheriff. No doubt he's bringing a number of men to see to my welfare. You, however, will go to jail. What of your retard then?"

Holloway fired.

The bullet punched through Villard's thigh, leaving a bloody hole and smoking fabric.

"Son of a bitch," Villard screamed. He doubled over. "You shot me."

On stage, the music halted abruptly. Patrons turned to see. Voices rose.

"Ain't nothing up here," Holloway called to the patrons. "Just a little misfire." He waved. "We're fine. Thanks for worrying."

The music lurched forward again. The dancers, frowning, danced. Some patrons continued watching them, some went back to watching the show.

Holloway grabbed Villard around the chest and dragged him from the box. They went together, one man carrying the other, to the balcony. Outside, night had settled in comfortably.

"What room?" Holloway asked.

Villard cursed and struggled. Blood stained his pin-striped pants, decorated his white spats and black shoes.

"Damnit," Holloway said. "Which room or I'll finish it here and get on outta town."

"I . . . no room . . . here."

Holloway clapped him on the head with the butt of the Schofield hard enough to get his attention. "You wouldn't stay anywhere but the Baghdad. Which room?"

Villard didn't answer.

Holloway clapped him again. Blood leaked down Villard's cheek.

"Don't," he sputtered. "Please, don't hit me again. It's two-ten, two doors down."

When they were nearly there, Villard called out. "Get the gun! He shot me!"

Holloway clapped Villard again, hard this time, knocking the man unconscious. Villard went limp as Holloway burst through the door.

She was in bed, her dress tattered, her face bruised. She gripped a small pistol tightly.

"Don't," Holloway whispered.

When he slammed the door, she looked at him long and hard. "Dunstan Holloway," she whispered. "Didn't think I'd see you again."

He dumped Villard to the floor. "Neither did he."

∽∾∾

"YOUR BOY." HER voice shook as badly as her hands. "He still—uh, I mean—"

"Alive? Yeah, he is."

"He was a good boy, Dunstan."

"Is a good boy," Holloway corrected. "Where is it?"

She frowned. "What?"

"Eve, I want the deed. Give it to me and I'll leave."

"Dunstan, please. He doesn't have it."

He'd expected her to say that. But he hadn't expected her tone: regretful, sad, apologetic.

"He doesn't have it anymore, he—"

"Listen to me, woman." Holloway slammed his gun down on the dressing table. "I ain't got the money. Buckie needs that school and they're hauling tons of ore outta that hole. Now where is it?"

"What?" Her eyes brightened as she laughed. "Somebody's working it? Ain't that just the way. Nicky slicks it to someone else and they hit it rich. And I'm here trying to keep my dress together with stolen thread. Wait a minute. What school?"

Holloway held his hands together tightly. "Back east. Buckie and I can move there. I can get some help with him but I got to pay. That's what the mine was for. I was going to pry open that vein and suck it dry."

"Oh, Dunstan, you are a noble man. But what were you going to do? Dig it by hand? You got no tools and Buckie cain't help. I don't care what they're pulling out of it, for you, that mine was a pipe dream."

"No," he shouted. "That shaft is full of silver. I just need a few weeks there and then Buckie and I can go east. I could get some . . ."

"What?"

He stared coldly at her. "Some rest, Eve. I'm tired."

"He's a handful, huh?"

Eve was mostly a good woman who'd gotten locked in a cage with the wrong man. Even when she and Villard had been conning him, she had treated Holloway decently. Their conversations had been easy and comfortable. "Yeah. Too hard to do it alone anymore."

On the floor, Villard stirred slightly. The blood on his cheek had dried to a rusty brown. "And he stole the only chance I had."

"The railroad stocks were fake."

"I know," Holloway said. "I tried to cash them in and got laughed at. Midland-Odessa Railway." He snorted. "And I fell for it."

"There is no deed, Dunstan," she said. "He used it to prop up some cheap card game and then used that money to finance some other thing and then something else and now here we are."

"Conning the whole town."

She shook her head. "It look like it? We're falling faster than a rock slide. There ain't anything left. We eat every couple of days unless somebody treats us. Stole a horse in Denver, cleaned out a tiny bar in Leadville. My clothes are wearing thin and I cain't even go on jobs now because I look like a cheap burlesque girl."

"What happened to your face?"

She averted her gaze and he knew. He had known it when she and Villard had been conning him out of his mine deed. He'd heard Villard yelling one morning about runny eggs.

Holloway tried to ignore it and concentrate on Buckie. "There is money here," he said. Quickly, he rifled the drawers of the dressing table. There was money. If not Holloway's deed, then someone else's money. He didn't care where it had been, only that it would leave with him.

"Dunstan, there isn't—"

"There has to be." His voice filled the room, banged against the walls and ceiling. The bits of patched clothes he found he threw on the floor. The trunk held only worn shoes and stockings. "Where is it?" He moved violently toward her.

"Dunstan," she yelped. She pushed away from him, her face terrified.

He stopped cold. "I'm sorry, I won't hurt you, you don't gotta worry about that. But I need that money." Or Buckie would die, he realized quietly. The farm had never made it and when he sold it, the money was gone fast. He hadn't been able to work in town because Buckie needed so much watching. "He's got no clothes, he's got hardly any food. What am I supposed to do? I love my boy."

"Dunstan, I'm sorry. We've hit the skids, bad luck, I guess. Nicky's trying to impress the people around here into buying some mining company stock."

"Midland-Odessa Railway Mining?" Holloway asked bitterly.

"Might as well be. But ain't hardly anybody taking it. He can't sell anymore, Dunstan, he's lost his touch."

How could it all have gone so wrong? Esther wasn't

supposed to die in her childbed. Buckie wasn't supposed to be simple. Holloway wasn't supposed to be jobless with an empty wallet.

Daddy wasn't supposed to be two hundred miles from his son.

Holloway lowered his head, tried to swallow his anguish. "Shoulda done better, Buckie, I'm sorry."

"You do what you can do," Eve said. "I wish I could help, Dunstan, truly I do. But there is nothing here." She moved to his side. "I know how you feel, at least on some level. I'm exhausted, too. This whole thing, money and the traveling and parties and society people. It's got no sparkle left. It used to shine, when we were in San Francisco and New York and Richmond." She rubbed her dingy dress. "Looks like a rusty can now. I just want to sleep for a few weeks and then have an omelet."

He chuckled in spite of the depression filling his insides. "An omelet?"

"Isn't this precious?" Villard asked. He rolled over and Holloway saw pain etched on his face. He pulled a gun from his waistband.

Holloway eyed his own gun, six feet away.

"Certainly, Dunstan Holloway, make your move. No one will fault me with your killing. You broke in here. You shot me. You assaulted Miss Eve. Yes, yes, the two of you, falling into the love of the desperate, the love of the lonely and unwanted. I should have seen it back in Lamar."

Eve snorted. "Him? Fall for him? His kid's a retard."

Villard frowned. "But I heard you—"

"Keeping him busy until you decided to join us."

Holloway stared, the empty hole inside him growing larger. She was no different than Villard, ran the same cons. And Holloway had swallowed it just like an ignorant fish going after fake worms.

"Now, sir," Villard said. "There is this little matter of you having shot me and accused me of theft."

"I need that money," Holloway said. "And I want your chain."

It hung lightly around Villard's neck, a decorative chain with small links.

"Why, this wasn't even yours to begin with."

"Buckie liked it. Call it an apology to the boy."

Eve caught Holloway's gaze and winked.

"I shall call it no such thing. I shall—"

When Eve sneezed and startled Villard, Holloway sprang. He hit Villard with his full body, diving into him as though into a pool. The men thudded to the floor. Holloway banged Villard's <u>gun</u> hand against the iron bedpost until the gun clattered away.

Villard's fists, little balls of iron, pounded at Holloway's gut. A flurry of punches battered his head. He howled and covered himself with one hand while punching at Villard with the other. Fist connected with nose and Villard rolled away.

Holloway scrabbled for the gun, but Eve held it. Her hands shook, tears on her face.

"Eve," Holloway said. He held his hands out, palms up. "Don't do anything crazy."

"By all means," Villard sputtered, blood coming from his nose. "Do something crazy, just make sure it's the right crazy thing."

"I'm tired, Nicky," she said. "I told you that."

Villard stood slowly. "Yes, you did."

"But you don't listen. I don't want to wear church charity clothes. I cain't even take a good bath or get a good haircut. I'm tired, I want out." She swung the gun slowly toward Villard. "And you hit me."

"I'm sorry about that, baby," Villard said. "I'm a little high-strung right now. I got everything riding on this last deal. One last deal and we'll be rich. Everything'll be fine. But there is no out in this business, honey, you got to keep going."

She laughed sadly and shook her head as Holloway

took the gun from her. "You fouled up again, Nicky. You shoulda kep' the mine."

"I want my money," Holloway said. "Give it or I'll—" His eyes were on Villard and Eve, but his head was full of his son.

"Kill me, then," Villard said.

When Holloway fired, Eve cried.

∽◦∾

"COMIN' BACK," THE boy shouted.

After hitching his horse, Holloway hugged his son furiously. "Buckie, I missed you, boy."

"I can whistle, but I ran out of toes," Buckie said.

"Whistle for me."

The boy whistled a few notes before they dissolved beneath his grin.

The bruises on Eve's cheek were fading, gone from purple to a sickly yellow.

"They know it was you," she said, hitching Villard's horse.

"Yeah."

"They thought he was a good man."

"Their mistake."

"They'll come after you. We're gonna hafta go somewhere."

"Mexico, maybe."

She shrugged. "Makes no difference to me."

"You gonna get some sleep tonight?" he asked.

"We all are. Then maybe we'll have an omelet."

"Omelet?" Buckie asked.

"Eggs," Holloway said.

"I like eggs. Wanna hear me whistle?"

Holloway looped the silver chain around Buckie's neck. The boy's fingers pranced through its links. "Yeah, Buckie, you whistle."

The Way to Cheyenne

James Reasoner

My dearest Cora,

These words addressed to you find me in Kansas City, a bustling, cosmopolitan community despite the fact that it is perched on the very brink of the frontier. So far, my journey westward has proven to be both tremendously exciting and quite educational. One can see all types of people here in this city: cavalrymen, dashing in their blue uniforms with the yellow stripes down the legs of their trousers; sturdy townsmen in sober suits; buffalo hunters, gigantic in their coats made from the hides of the very animals they have slain; wild-eyed, big-hatted cowboys up from Texas; and even an occasional buckskin-clad red Indian (although they are all tame now, I am told). I am so glad that we decided to buy the store in Wyoming. I think I am going to enjoy living in the West.

The train for Cheyenne leaves tomorrow morning. I shall travel on and, once I reach that no doubt fair city, conclude the agreement with Mr. Hargraves and turn over to him the purchase price. Then, as soon as I am settled, I will send for you and you can put the crowded environs of Philadelphia behind you for all time. I am certain you will very much enjoy living in the wide-open spaces of Wyoming, as I know I am going to.

For tonight I am staying at a small traveler's hotel, and there I met the most intriguing gentleman who has visited here in Kansas City on many previous occasions. He is quite the raconteur, and he has promised to show me some of the town's more interesting sights. I am looking forward to our outing this evening.

By the time this letter reaches you, I will most likely be in Cheyenne, making all the arrangements for our new life there. Until I set pen to paper again, I remain

> *Your loving husband,*
> *Henry*

From *The Kansas City Times*, May 5, 1878:

The body of a grievously wounded man was discovered early this morning in an alley behind the Great Western Saloon. The man had been stabbed several times and was taken to the clinic of Dr. Joshua Pendleton, where he remains in grave condition and is not expected to survive.

Authorities stated that the man carried no identification and had no money in his pockets, so they speculate the motive for the attack upon him was robbery.

Salina, Kansas
June 21st, 1878

My darling Cora,

I thank the Good Lord you were spared knowing
the travails that have befallen me these past six
weeks. Surely you have been quite worried that you
received no further epistles from me until now, and
for any concern I have caused you I am utterly,
abjectly apologetic. I was unable to write because
I was badly injured and have been until recently
recuperating at a private medical facility in Kansas
City. I hasten to assure you that I am completely
recovered from my wounds and there is no need for
you to concern yourself with my health at this time.
Unfortunately, the fault for my mishap lies entirely
at my feet.

You see, my dearest, I made a terrible error in
judgment by befriending Mr. Jud Grissom, of whom
I spoke in my previous letter. Far from being the
jovial sort he appeared on first acquaintance, he
proved on further association to be a violent sort
with an inordinate fondness for liquor and abso-
lutely no scruples. Instead of escorting me on a tour
of Kansas City's cultural attractions, as he had
promised to do, Mr. Grissom instead took me to a
saloon, the sort of place the likes of which I hope
you never have the misfortune to visit, nor would
you have any reason to, being as you are a good
and pious woman, unlike some of the females whose
behavior I reluctantly witnessed in the Great Western Saloon. As soon as I saw what sort of debauch-
ery was going on, I implored Mr. Grissom that we
should leave, but he insisted that I remain and have
a drink with him. As you know, I take an occasional
glass of port, so I thought perhaps to mollify him
and have one drink. He was still reluctant to depart,
however, so, being unfamiliar with the city as I was,

I judged it prudent to stay at his side for the time being, rather than risk getting lost on the way back to the hotel. This proved to be a mistake.

When we finally left the Great Western, Mr. Grissom, who had imbibed quite heavily, claimed to know a different route that would take us back to the hotel much more quickly. He led me into a dark, narrow, squalid lane behind the saloon, and then . . . it is difficult still to write about this . . . and then he viciously attacked me with a knife he took from under his coat. I thought that I was slain. When I awoke, I was under the care of Dr. Pendleton, who is a good man though overly fond of the grape himself.

Cora, wonderful Cora, the light of my life, I fear I must confess to you that all the money we saved to buy the store in Cheyenne, which I had in a money belt worn under my clothing, as you know, is gone. Undoubtedly, Mr. Grissom stole it when he attempted to murder me. So I was left not only badly wounded but destitute. Dr. Pendleton, in his generosity, cared for me without compensation these past weeks, and all he required was a note stating that I would pay him the sum of a hundred and fifty dollars once I am back on my feet financially. I hope that will be soon, because, you see, I am now well enough that I have been able to secure employment.

I am traveling west with a group of men who are bound for Cheyenne, as am I, of course. I still hope to make arrangements to purchase Mr. Hargraves's store. In the meantime, I have fallen in with my current boon companions, a cheerful, rugged lot of Westerners. I have agreed to cook for them and care for their horses during our journey (though my culinary skills are not much and I lack a great deal of experience with horses, as you know), and in return they have offered me a mount to ride and their protection on the journey, as well as a share in the

*profits of their business venture, the exact details of
which are still unknown to me. We have already
reached the town of Salina after leaving Kansas
City two days ago.*

*I hope to make Cheyenne in a week or possibly
two. Until my next opportunity to write, I remain*

> *Your loving husband,*
> *Henry*

From the Russell, Kansas, *Gazette*, June 27, 1878:

> A westbound Union Pacific train was stopped
> and robbed between Russell and Hays City
> yesterday. The bandits blocked the track by
> prying up a section of the rails, then took
> command of the halted train at gunpoint. The
> desperadoes, who were all masked except one,
> broke into the express car and took the mes-
> senger's pouches, in addition to looting what-
> ever valuables they could find amongst the
> train's passengers and crew. There was a brief
> bit of gunplay when one of the passengers at-
> tempted to oppose the robbers, but no one was
> seriously wounded. The bandits fled on horse-
> back to the north. Officials of the Union
> Pacific Railroad have promised that these mis-
> creants will be tracked down and brought to
> justice.

Dear Cora,

*Once again it seems that I have made a terrible
mistake. The companions I judged to be so friendly
and helpful have proven to be anything but. I cannot
tell you where we are as I write this letter, because
in truth I do not know. Nor am I certain of the date,
since for several days we have been fleeing through
a Godforsaken wilderness from a posse of men who*

wish to apprehend us and hang us. I apologize for any shock this news may cause to your delicate nature. I miss you terribly and wish I was back home with you in Philadelphia.

To summarize the misadventure that led me to this abject state: For several days I continued to travel west with the group of companions I mentioned in my previous missive. The long hours on horseback were quite grueling and caused a painful condition which I will not offend your sensibilities by naming or describing. I was, however, beginning to grow accustomed to this arduous means of travel.

Then, the leader of our jolly little band, a man who calls himself Teague, told us to halt next to the railroad tracks which we had been generally following ever since we left Kansas City. To my great surprise, several of the men took sturdy iron bars from their packs and began to pry up one of the tracks. I could see no reason for this wanton bit of destruction, and when I asked Mr. Teague, he merely rubbed his jaw (which was covered with several days' growth of beard by this time) and said to me, "You'll find out, Henry." He then handed me a colorful bandanna and told me to tie it around my neck. "Pull it up over your face when I give the word," he told me, and that should have alerted me to what he and the others intended to do. However, in my naïveté, I was merely puzzled, not alarmed.

A train began to approach from the east, and when I pointed out to Mr. Teague that, given the damage to the tracks, it could hardly proceed on its way, he merely laughed and said that was the general idea. Then, he and the other members of the group concealed themselves in a nearby dry ditch they called an arroyo. I should say that we concealed ourselves, since I was among them. Mr. Teague insisted that I accompany them. To my surprise and trepidation, he took a pistol from his belt

and pressed it into my hand. "Just in case any of
them passengers get spooked and go to throwing
lead," he told me.

While I was attempting to decipher both his
grammar and his meaning, the train came to a stop,
and Mr. Teague and his companions rushed up out
of the arroyo and pointed their guns at the engineer
and the fireman in the locomotive. I came along
behind them, hoping there would be no violence.
The others had covered their faces with their bandannas, but Mr. Teague had forgotten to tell me to
do so, and I had neglected the matter. I did not
realize my face was uncovered until I saw several
of the men on the train staring at me. Then, feeling
guilty about it, I raised my bandanna so that the
lower half of my face was concealed, but it was too
late, of course. My features had already been seen.
What the long-term results of that carelessness on
my part may be, I have no way of knowing.

It pains me to say it, but Mr. Teague and my
other companions are thieves. They robbed the train
and everyone on it. Mr. Teague even shot a man
who tried to resist having his money stolen. Having
lost all of our carefully saved funds to Mr. Grissom
back in Kansas City, I can certainly sympathize with
the unfortunate gentleman. He tried to take a gun
from under his coat, and Mr. Teague pointed his
pistol at him and shot him. The noise of the gun was
quite loud, and the smoke that came from its barrel
smelled bad. The passenger was struck in the shoulder by the bullet and bled, as Mr. Teague put it
later, "like a stuck pig." But I think he will be all
right with proper medical care.

When my companions were finished looting the
train, they took their horses (I had been holding the
reins, since that is my job, though I neglected to
mention it until now) and rode away swiftly. I
deemed it wise to join them. The mood of the pas-

sengers on the train was an ugly one, and I thought
that they might not be too inclined at the moment
to listen to my explanation that I am not really a
robber, but rather as much an innocent victim as
they themselves were.

I had thought to leave the group later and take
my chances on traveling alone across the frontier,
as frightening a prospect as that may be, but Mr.
Teague seems to think that I am one of them now
and has indicated that he would be reluctant to see
me go. For one thing, the horse I have been riding
is not my own but belongs to the group. For another, Mr. Teague says that if the posse that is following us was to catch me alone, they would "string
me up." That means they would hang me, although
I am not sure how that would be possible since trees
are so uncommon in this desolate landscape. Mr.
Teague says they would find a way, though.

I can write no more. I humbly beg your pardon,
my dear wife, for inflicting this sordid tale upon you,
but I felt that I would surely go mad if I could not
share some of my burden with someone. If we come
to a settlement where mail service is available, I
will post this letter to you in the sincere hope that
by the time it reaches you, I will find myself in much
more favorable circumstances. I would still like to
reach Cheyenne and become the simple storekeeper
that I hoped to be.

                                        Your husband,
                                        Henry

From the diary of Harriet Poe:

July 15. On way back to ranch from shopping trip
in Wichita.

July 16. Stagecoach busted an axle. Had to wait
four hours for it to be replaced.

*July 17. Stagecoach held up by outlaws. Only one
I got a good look at was a scrawny fellow called
Hank by the others. I'll remember him.*

Dear Cora,

*We're somewhere in what they call the Badlands.
Sorry I haven't written for a while. Teague keeps
pushing us north. We got away from that posse of
railroad detectives, and the next thing I know, we're
holding up a stagecoach. An old woman on there
glared at me like she was a buzzard and I was a
fresh-killed carcass. Then we stopped in a little
town in Nebraska and Teague and the boys went
into the bank and came back out yelling and shooting. I had the horses ready for them, so we were
able to get away without anybody getting killed.*

*Don't tell your parents, but it looks like I've be-
come an outlaw, whether I want to be or not. When
we got up here to the Dakotas, Teague showed me
a piece of paper that one of the boys found tacked
up on a building in some wide place in the road.
He called it a reward dodger, because it promised
a reward for anybody who helped catch the man
whose picture was drawn on it. That man, I hate to
say, was me. The authorities must have gotten my
description from somebody on that train we
stopped.*

*I swear to you, Cora, I never meant for this to
happen. All I wanted to do was go to Cheyenne, buy
that store from Mr. Hargraves, send for you, and
then start our family and our new life in the West.
Instead I have made mistake after mistake that has
led me to this dreadful situation. I would turn myself
in to the law, but Teague says those star-packers
would never believe my claims of innocence. They
are convinced I'm just as big an outlaw as he and
the others are.*

I don't know what to do, Cora. I thought maybe writing it out like this would help me get my thoughts in order so that I could see a way out of this dilemma. However, all my alternatives seem undesirable to me. I suppose I'll have to wait for a better time to leave the gang. If I could just make it to Cheyenne . . .

Your husband,
Henry

From the Deadwood *Enterprise*, September 7, 1878:

DUNLEAVY GANG SCOURGE OF THE BLACK HILLS
ORE SHIPMENTS HIJACKED; MURDER IN DEADWOOD
NOTORIOUS BANDIT LEADER HANK DUNLEAVY STILL AT LARGE

Dear Cora,

Whatever you read in the newspapers back East about me, don't believe it. This reporter from Deadwood has been spreading all sorts of lies about me, and I hear that some of the stories have made their way to the eastern papers and Harper's Weekly *and the like. You know me better than that. You know I'm not a criminal and a murderer, like they say.*

It's true that I had to shoot Teague, of course. I've been practicing a lot with a pistol ever since we got to the Dakotas, and I'm better with it than I ever thought I would be. It turns out that I have a natural aptitude with firearms, a talent I surely never would have discovered had I stayed in Philadelphia. Teague thought he could ride roughshod over me, and he got proddy when I told him I wanted to do more than just hold the damned horses. (Please pardon my language. I fear that my

*current companions have been a bad influence on
the manner in which I speak.) Anyway, I think
Teague just planned to pistol-whip me, but when he
drew his gun I naturally drew mine and there was
some shooting, I'm afraid. After that, the rest of the
boys seemed to think I ought to have a turn at running things, so I decided we would move over to
the Black Hills and sort of help ourselves to some
of the gold that's being carted around over there.*

*I would depart for Cheyenne now, this very min-
ute (I have enough gold to pay Mr. Hargraves for
his store), but I cannot leave the boys in the lurch.
They look to me for leadership. Besides, there are
those reward dodgers out on me, and the law in
Cheyenne might not take kindly to it if I showed up
there. I'll have to wait a while, until everybody has
forgotten about all the unfortunate events of the past
few months. Then I'll send for you, and we'll be
together again at last, darling.*

Henry

Cora,

*I don't hardly know how to tell you this. I met a
gal when the boys and I rode down to Belle Fourche
for a few days, and we wound up getting hitched.
Her name is Sally, and while she's hardly the same
sort of lovely, genteel woman that you are, she's a
better shot with a rifle than I am and can cuss like
a bullwhacker. Plus her amatory skills are far from
insufficient. I can only apologize for succumbing to
the temptations of the flesh. It's not a real marriage,
of course, since legally you and I are still wed, but
Sally doesn't know that. If you want to begin di-
vorce proceedings against me, I completely understand, but I implore you to be patient with me. I still
plan to leave this gang of ruffians as soon as the
time is right, and my fondest hope is that when I*

*finally arrive in Cheyenne and send for you, you will
be a welcome recipient of that summons and will
join me as soon as you can.*

*Yours truly,
Hank*

*P.S. While it is true that we shot up a bunch of
Pinkerton agents, they were laying for us and had
it coming. I wouldn't want you to think that we're
really as bad as we're painted.*

From the Laramie *Sentinel*, October 20, 1878:

> The infamous bandit Hank Dunleavy was
> wounded near here yesterday in a gun battle
> with Federal marshals. Dunleavy, who is
> wanted in several states and territories on
> charges of murder and robbery, was wounded
> but escaped before he could be taken into cus-
> tody. Two members of his gang were killed
> in the fighting, as was one of the marshals.
> Authorities promise a redoubled effort to
> catch the notorious bandit who has burst into
> prominence in the Western states over the past
> few months.

Dear Cora,

*I don't know why I'm still writing to you. You
probably tear up these blamed letters as soon as
you see my scrawl on the envelopes and never even
read them. But somehow it makes me feel better,
and I don't like the thought of you believing all the
bad things they say about me. Those Federal marshals are all corrupt and little more than outlaws
themselves. A man has a right to defend himself
from such rascals, and that's all I did in Laramie.*

I was on my way to Cheyenne when they jumped

*us, Cora. You know what that means. I was ready
to put the bandit life behind me at last. These past
few months seem more like years as I have toiled
to escape the clutches of outlawry. But the damned
lawmen won't let me quit.*

*I miss you a lot. I reckon we're still married,
since I haven't heard any different. Or maybe the
news just hasn't caught up with me yet. Sally came
down with a fever and died sudden-like, so you
don't have to worry about my affections being divided any longer. I would love to be with you again
and share my life with you as we planned from the
start, but I reckon maybe that can't happen now.*

*I got a bullet hole in my arm, but it didn't bleed
much and it's healing up all right. It was my left
arm, thank God. If it had been my gun arm, I
might've been in trouble.*

Hank

From an advertisement:

*The Outlaw's Fate; or, Bloody Hank Dunleavy's
    Last Raid*
(Published by Beadle's Frontier Library, New York.
    Price 10 cents.)

Cora,

*If you ever read this, I reckon I'm dead, because
we're holed up in this old line shack on Prophet
Mountain with a posse outside and I don't figure
we'll ever make it out alive. I'm sorry, I really am.
Six months ago I never figured on being an outlaw.
I never figured on being anything except a storekeeper and your husband and the father of our children. Life takes a few funny turns here and there.*

*I never made it to Cheyenne. We hit the bank in
Rawlings instead and would have gotten away clean*

with a good bit of loot if not for some bad luck. My horse got hit and went down, and when I fell I lost the sack of money we'd taken out of the bank. The boys came back for me. They're a loyal bunch, fine lads each and every one. I wish they hadn't got shot up so bad by the law. The ones of us that were left got out of town two jumps ahead of a posse.

I got hit a couple of times, once in the leg and once in the chest. I'm mighty afraid that second bullet got a lung, because I've been coughing up blood the last hour or so. Feel pretty weak, too, which is why my writing looks a mite spidery. It doesn't really matter, though, because those possemen are getting ready to rush the place, and I'd rather go out quick than cough up the rest of my life for hours and hours. As long as I've got a gun in my hand, I feel pretty good.

I'm sorry, Cora. I wish things had been different. Yet there's a part of me that doesn't. Folks never respected me back in Philadelphia, but they do out here. I'm Hank Dunleavy, the famous outlaw. Sure, they're scared of me, but they look up to me, too. I never knew what that was like—

Asa says they're coming now. I love you, Cora.

SEE THE GRUESOME REMAINS OF THE FAMOUS OUTLAW HENRY DUNLEAVY, SHOT OVER ONE HUNDRED TIMES IN THE FAMOUS BATTLE OF PROPHET MOUNTAIN! PERFECTLY PRESERVED! COLONEL ARTEMUS FRANKLIN'S TRAVELING CARNIVAL AND EXPOSITION OF WILD WEST MEMORABILIA!
CHEYENNE FAIR GROUNDS—ONE DAY ONLY

Posse

C. Hall Thompson

BILLY REO WAS dreaming again. The pain in the small of his back where buckshot had riddled the intestines seemed far away now, and he was not lying in the loft of an abandoned barn; he could not smell the hay nor hear the rats squealing in the empty stalls below.

He was back in a town in the Panhandle and he was nineteen and had never watched a man die. A mob jostled along the main square. He could see the red, mustached faces of furious men and hear them yelling, "Lynch the murdering greaser! Bust into the cell and string him up!"

Then he saw two townsmen come out through the jail door, dragging the Mexican boy between them. He heard the boy praying and moaning, and followed the mob across the dusty wide square to the big oak. The boy was crying softly and someone larruped the flank of the pony and it jolted out from under and the boy screamed only once before the hemp snapped his spine.

And, here in the barn loft, Reo could see the boy's face, twisted at a crazy angle by the knot under the left ear. Only now it was his own face; it was Billy Reo who danced there above the stiff white masks of the mob.

"No!"

He lurched to a sitting position.

The stab of fire along his back brought him full awake. Sweat wilted the blond bristles of his jaw. It stung his eyes. He sank back, breathing too hard.

Get hold of yourself, he thought. *Let them form their damned posse. They'll never find you here.*

They had never caught him before. In the ten years since he had drifted north into the territories, Billy Reo had killed four men. Riding from one gun town to the next, he had learned the lightning downsweep and rise of hand that could put three slugs into a man's belly before he sprawled in the dust. And the killing had been a safe, secret thing. People had looked at him and wondered, maybe, but no one had ever been able to prove his suspicions.

Safe and easy, his mind said. And this time was no different.

Only this time *was* different. This time it had been in a grubby saloon in Alamosa with a mob of witnesses right on the spot.

He hadn't figured the greenhorn to call his bluff. The greenhorn, a spindly kid named Reckonridge, had looked as if he never left Mama's side. Reo and Jack Larnin had idled into the bar to wash the red dust out of their tonsils and had seen this kid sporting a load of double eagles. It wasn't hard to talk up a game of deuces wild. It should have been easy to slip that deuce off the bottom when the pot was at its peak.

But Reckonridge had a quick eye and a temper to match. He had cursed and dropped one hand below the table. Reo never stopped to argue. A beer-blown blonde had screamed. The shots had sounded very loud and Reckonridge had gone over backward, still seated, with two small holes in his chest.

The saloon crowd had not moved. Elbow to elbow, guns level, Reo and Larnin had backed through swinging doors to the ponies at the hitch. They had swung up and wheeled west, and in that moment Reo had seen the long, loose-limbed man come running through the moonlight, glimpsed the lifting shotgun, the flash of a metal star against a black vest.

"Ride, Jack! Ride like hell!"

Slapping heels to the roan's flanks, he had bent low. But not low enough. He had felt the fire needles burn into his back almost before he heard the slam and echo of the double barrels. Somehow, he had kept the roan haunch to haunch with Larnin's pinto. Somehow, he had ridden.

Reo was sweating again. The blood-wet flannel shirt stuck to his back. His legs had a numbness that frightened him. Witnesses, he thought. This time there was proof. This time, the man in the black vest would talk. The citizens of Alamosa would swear in as deputies. Before daylight, the posse would lead out. Maybe even now . . .

"Damn," he said hoarsely.

His head rolled from side to side. He could see the Mexican boy very clearly; the hard, implacable faces of the mob, the sudden, singing wrench of the rope.

"Billy."

His body stiffened. A hand clawed for the pistol that lay by his hip. He caught the scrape of boots on the ladder; a light shaft cut up through the loft trap. Then the lean, flat-planed face and narrow shoulders came into view, one fist holding high the lantern, and Jack Larnin said, "Easy, Billy. Just me."

The gun hand relaxed.

Larnin set down the lamp. It was hooded so that only a thin yellow beam broke the darkness.

Reo's eyes narrowed. "Well?"

Larnin stood tall above him. A rat rustled in the hay. Light shimmered on the dainty needlework of a spider's web. Larnin said, "How's the wound?"

Reo looked at him. "The wound's all right. I'm not thinking about the wound."

The silent question hung between them. Reo felt sweat cold along his ribs.

Finally Larnin looked away, said, "I went up along the rise. You can see Alamosa from there. It don't look good, Billy. They started already. I seen torches moving out of town; high, like they were carried by men on horseback."

"Posse," Reo whispered.

Larnin's boots shifted. "You better let me take a look."

"The hell with the wound!"

Reo hauled himself to one elbow. The effort cost him plenty. There was a red-brown stain where his back had crushed the hay.

"What're the chances?" he said.

Larnin shook his head. "We got three, four hours on them, Billy. But we was riding too hard to cover trail. We left signs a blind man could follow."

Reo wet his lips. In the dark stillness now, a wind was rising and he could hear a voice praying high and shrill in Spanish and then cracking to dead silence.

Reo set his elbows, shoved himself erect. His teeth shut hard against the pain.

Larnin helped him. The numbness made his legs heavy and awkward. His insides burned. He held the pistol in a white-knuckled grip. He leaned against the wall, coughing for breath.

Larnin's face went uncertain. "Listen, Billy."

Pale eyes swung up. "I'm listening."

A minute passed. Their glances held. Then Larnin said, "Maybe it'd be better if you didn't run. You need a doctor, Billy. If you just waited here . . ."

"For the posse?" Reo said. "Sit here and wait for the mob to drag me out?" Fever made his stare too bright. "Wait for the rope?"

"I'm only saying . . ."

The gun hand lifted a fraction. "You said it. Now forget it."

"Sure, Billy, but . . ."

"But—you'd like to back down?"

"Billy, you got me wrong."

The gun was level with Larnin's belt buckle now. "Maybe," Reo said. "But you get me right. We're going to move. We're going to keep moving. They won't get me. Remember that, Jack. No mob'll ever get me."

Wind soughed in the stalls below. A rat skittered into the hay.

Larnin nodded. All he said was, "You still need a doctor."

"We'll head for Monte Vista. There's old Doc Carson."

Larnin frowned. "We ain't got much money. The doc mightn't want to . . ."

Billy Reo's hands moved light and smooth with the gun, broke it, and checked the cylinder, snapped the breech shut again. He looked at the gun for a long time, then said, "He'll want to."

∽∽∽

SHADOWS FOLLOWED THEM. The moon was high and cloud-pierced and, behind them now, the pale meadows were restless with shadows that might have been wind bending the tall grass, or the groping movements of a posse.

Reo tried not to look back. Turned north and west toward the far reaches of the San Juan range, his face set rigid against thought and the memory of a sun-bleached Panhandle town. The jogging of the saddle played hell with his back. He could feel the wounds seeping slowly; hot fingers clawed up from his belly and made breathing a torture.

Lifting gradually under them the land climbed toward distant foothills. The horses were wearing thin. The moon went down and winking stone-cold stars gave little light. Larnin took to shifting against the pommel, peering over his shoulder. Reo had drawn the Winchester from its saddle boot; he held it ready across his lap. Under the muffled dusty beat of hoofs, a Mexican tongue whimpered, *Madre de Dios, socorro*, save me. *Madre de . . .*

"Shut up," Reo said aloud. "Shut up."

Larnin glanced at him sharply. A white edge fringed Reo's lips. He shook his head dully.

"Nothing. I was . . . Nothing."

Dawn was a pearl-gray cat paddling down from the westward mountains. A ground mist swirled rump-high to the ponies, made a cottony haze along the rim of Monte Vista. They reined in at the east end of the main street.

Reo felt dizzy. The numbness of his legs was worse.

"Jack. The poncho. In case we meet somebody."

Larnin unstrapped the latigos and slipped the oilskin over Reo's shoulders. It hid the dark, clotted stain of the shirt.

"All right," Reo said. "Let's go."

They didn't meet anybody. Monte Vista was curled up in sleep. A memory of stale beer and bought laughter drifted through dim saloon doorways. Even the red lights of the western skirt of town had gone dead. A dog high-tailed across a side lane. Morning wind stirred the lazy dust.

The riders swung south along Don Paulo Street. Doc Carson's house was at the far end, gray, sand-eaten, set back in weeds. They hitched the ponies in the shelter of a sad willow and walked around to the kitchen door.

Reo moved slowly. Each step sent pain splintering through his chest and stomach. In the shade of the back stoop, he leaned against the wall, sucking deep lungsful of air. Larnin waited.

Finally, Reo said, "Now."

They didn't knock. The latch was up. The kitchen smelled of rancid coffee grounds. They went down the side hall. A thick, wet snoring led the way to the bedroom. Reo stopped on the doorsill. His palm rested lightly on the low-slung pistol.

The doc lay among crumpled quilts, fully dressed and booted. His string tie was undone and gray stubble matted his sunken cheeks. His mouth hung open. When he breathed out, a stink of whiskey tainted the air.

Reo made a sign. Larnin crossed to the window and drew the blind. In the dark now, Reo leaned at the foot of the bed. Larnin stood just beside the pillow. Reo nodded. Larnin lifted the Colt and pressed the small muzzle under the hinge of Doc Carson's jaw.

Long bony fingers knotted in the patchwork. The doc's eyelids twitched and opened very slowly.

"Quiet," Reo said. "Nice and quiet, Doc."

Carson sat up carefully, drawing back from the touch of the gun. "Reo. What is this?"

Reo set a smile against the biting twinges of the wound. "A professional visit, Doc."

Carson let out a long sigh, but he kept watching the gun. Some of the liquor-haze cleared from his eyes. "Law on your tail?"

The smile faded. "A misunderstanding," Reo said flatly. "There was a kid. He didn't trust me. I don't like it when people don't trust me."

The doc's stare wavered. The voice went shrill. "Well, what do you want with me? I can't . . ."

Reo turned around and pulled aside the poncho. Carson whistled, swung his feet to the floor. "Sit down," he said, "I'll look."

For a second, Reo didn't move. Finally, he sat on the bed.

Carson said, "I'll need light."

Larnin looked at Reo and then brought a lamp from the washstand and set fire to the wick.

The doc peeled off Reo's shirt. Flesh tore where flannel stuck to the edges of the wound. Reo sat still, head down, sweating. Carson's fingers prodded; his loose mouth pursed. He straightened.

Reo said, "So?"

Doc Carson scratched his jaw. "It won't be no cinch, Reo."

"You can do it?"

"There'll be a lot of pain."

Reo said, "You can do it."

The doc went to the clothes chest. He uncorked a bottle, drank, and swabbed his mouth with a shirt sleeve. At last, he said, "This is against the law. I never handle these things, unless . . ."

Reo said, "You'll be paid."

A smile cracked wet lips. "Five hundred?"

Larnin's gun started to lift. "You lousy cheating . . ."

Reo shook his head. Larnin stood still. Reo looked at the doc.

"All right. Five hundred."

The smile broadened. Carson took a step forward.

"Not now," Reo said flatly. "Later. When this blows over."

Carson said, "Maybe you better get somebody else. I got nothing to ease the pain and . . ."

Abruptly, Reo stood up. His insides twisted and burned; nothing showed in his face. His hand hung over the thigh-thonged Colt. Carson went back a step.

"Like I told you," Reo said, "I don't like it when people won't trust me."

The lamp wick flickered. Morning was a pale yellow crack fringing the dark blind. Somewhere, a rooster crowed the day.

Doc Carson again tilted the bottle. The drink was a long one. He punched the cork home with his palm and said, "I'll get the instruments ready."

Reo sat down heavily. His head throbbed. He shut out the buzzing of his ears and looked up at Larnin. "Circulate," he said. "Ride out a ways. See if you can get wind of the posse."

Larnin flicked a glance at Doc.

Reo said, "I'll handle him."

Carson kept working over his leather case. The instruments chinked as if his hands were trembling.

"How long?" Larnin asked.

Reo swung his gaze to Carson.

"An hour," Carson said. "Maybe two."

Reo's square face tightened. "That long?"

"I told you. Probing for that shot won't be no picnic."

Reo's breathing had picked up a beat. He managed to steady it and then he nodded at Larnin.

Larnin sheathed the gun and crossed to the hall. "I'll be back." The door closed.

The room was quite still. Reo could hear the rasp of his own lungs. He sat there, watching Carson spread bright tools on a towel on the bedside chair. Carson turned up the lamp wick and filled the washbasin with water from a cracked ewer. He rolled back his sleeves.

"On the bed," he said. "Belly down."

Reo sat still. Their eyes held. Reo drew the Colt and lay down, right arm stretched wide, the gun in his fist. His cheek pressed the greasy pillow, eyes turned toward the lamp. Carson's hands moved over the instruments, forced a thin wood splint against Reo's lips. "Bite when it gets bad." Carson lifted a needle-fine probe, bent over the bed. "This is it."

The probe went deep. The splint snapped between Reo's teeth.

◦◦◦

THEY WERE COMING. The posse was riding down on him and he could not move. He lay there, watching the hoofs rear and crash down at his face. They did not hang him at once. They drove white-hot pokers into his back and dragged him over live coals and then the rope burned his neck. He was praying in broken Spanish and the mob laughed when the knot jerked taut under his ear . . .

It lasted an hour and twenty minutes. Then the blackness went away. He could see the lamp, made pale now by the blaze of sun against the blind. The splint was gone. He tasted salt where his teeth had dug into the lower lip.

Stitches and plaster held him in a vise. Far off Monte

Vista stirred with morning life. On the main drag, a pian-
ola wrangled.

Doc Carson sat in the rocker by the window. "Sixteen
buckshot," he was saying. "Don't know how you ever got
this far."

Reo's lips burned. He licked them with a dry tongue.
"Jack?"

"Yeah." Spurs chinked. "Here, Billy." Larnin brought
him a tumbler of whiskey.

"Watch it," Carson said. "Watch them stitches."

Reo gained one elbow. His back seemed to tear apart,
but the liquor helped. He looked up at Larnin. "Any
luck?"

Larnin took the glass and refilled it. "If you'd call it
that."

He drank. Reo waited.

"I was up to the saloon. Ran into this Express rider.
He'd passed a party on the east road."

"And?"

"Posse," Larnin said. "Pony-boy says they was riding
down a gunny. Lost his trail back in the meadows, then
picked it up again. They're heading this way, Billy."

"How far behind are they?"

"Twenty miles when he saw them; moving slow, asking
questions at every cabin they passed."

"Then we got time." Abruptly, Reo swung his legs out
of bed. His mouth twitched with pain.

Doc Carson jumped up. "God A'mighty, man! Easy!"

Reo sat there, head low, hands clutching the mattress
edge. "We ride," he told Larnin. "We make the mountains. They'll never track us through shale and rock."

Larnin said, "Billy, maybe . . ."

"We won't go over that again," Reo said thickly. "We
ride."

"Ride?" Carson shrilled. "Are you loco? Half an hour
in the saddle and them stitches'll bust wide open. Your
back'll be a sieve. And if you hemorrhage inwardly . . ."

Reo said, "Shut up."

"I tell you, it's one sure way to die."

Reo's mouth paled. "I can think of worse ways."

"But, my money . . ."

"Shut up!" Reo caught hold of the bedstead and rose very slowly. The room pitched wildly, but he did not fall. "I'll need a clean shirt, Doc."

It took a long while to get dressed. Finally teeth set against a rising inward ache, Reo faced Larnin. "The horses?"

"All ready."

Reo lifted his pistol from the tangle of red-flecked covers. He turned to Carson. His eyes showed no emotion at all.

The doc's loose mouth went to pieces. "Listen, Reo." It was a dry whisper. "No hard feelings, eh? You know me. I'm a businessman. It ain't that I didn't trust . . ." Carson swallowed noisily and forced a smile. "Ain't that right, Reo? No hard feelings?"

"Yeah."

The gun went up fast and down. Carson saw it coming. He sidestepped too late. The barrel got him along the ear. He went down headfirst against the bed.

"Sure," Reo said softly. "No hard feelings."

Larnin wet his lips. "Look, Billy . . ."

The eyes stopped him. They were too brilliant and hard. "It gives us time," Reo said. "It'll remind him to keep his lip buttoned."

They went out through the kitchen. Reo waited in the warm shade of the stoop. Far up the street, a Mexican woman was stringing out wet wash. She did not look their way.

Larnin led the horses around. They had been fed and watered, but they didn't look rested. Reo frowned. There was no helping it. Trading for new mounts would only attract attention.

He caught the roan's stirrup and stepped up. The skin of his back stretched tight. Plaster cramped his ribs and he felt a wet ribbon run down his spine. He told himself it was only sweat, but he knew it was fresh blood. His jaw muscles corded. He gave Larnin the nod.

They rode along an alley to the south edge of town, then swung west. Reo sat with one hand resting on the butt of his Colt. Morning sun struck fire from the watchful slits of his eyes. They did not pass anybody. Far away, at the center of Monte Vista, a school bell chimed, clean and cool sounding.

When they hit open ground, Reo turned once. He saw the main drag, pale and dusty under a yellow sky. Wagons rumbled up with kegs from the brewery. Grangers lounged and smoked outside the barbershop and a fat woman waddled home with a basket of greens. There was no sign that anyone had noticed the passing of two strange riders.

The pain was a network of burning wires that jerked taut with every roll of the saddle. The wetness was thick along Reo's back now, soaking slowly into the bandages. He cursed Doc Carson for a bungler; he cursed a quick-tempered greenhorn and a man with a star pinned to his black vest. A nerve twitched his mouth.

"The hills," he said. "We make the hills and we're safe."

Larnin frowned. "It's a rough climb."

Reo seemed not to hear.

"We make the hills and we're all right," he said.

Larnin's frown deepened, but he didn't speak again.

Just before noon, they hit the first spur of the San Juans. Larnin hadn't been wrong. The going was steep and treacherous with tangleweed and shale. The horses didn't help. Reo's roan was whiteflanked and frothing at the bit. It walked head down, laboring against sun and the steady rise. Its feet were no longer sure.

Larnin was in the lead when they came onto the ledge. The pitching trail hung like the rungs of a ladder to the mountain face. The ledge was less than five feet wide with sheer wall to the left and, on the right, a drop of jagged rock to the next bench, thirty feet below.

Larnin heard the sudden slither of hoofs. Behind him, the roan shrilled and Reo yelled, "Jack!" He swung in the saddle, saw the roan already plunging over the rim, pawing for a grip. Reo twisted violently, trying to jump clear, but his right boot heel snagged the stirrup.

Man and horse went down together. Their screams echoed high above the rattle of shale, pierced the billow of rising dust. A few pebbles danced in their wake and the screaming stopped.

Larnin backtracked on foot. It took time. Dust had settled; the lower bench lay still under the blistering sun. He saw the roan first. It had struck the ledge head-on; its neck was snapped and twisted at a foolish angle.

"Jack."

It wasn't more than a whisper. Reo lay against a boulder, legs stuck out straight before him, arms folded hard across his belly. The tear wasn't only skin-deep anymore. There was a hot, wet feeling in his chest.

The grit-streaked face went crooked when Larnin tried to lift him. The legs wouldn't move at all. He tried to speak and the wetness welled into his throat. A bubble of red broke past his lips, trickled down into the blond beard. Larnin let go of him. Reo sat there, choking back the wetness, his eyes on Larnin. After a long time, he said, "So this is it."

Larnin did not answer. Uneasily now, his glance moved down the long ramp of the spur. He took a deep breath. "Listen, Billy . . ."

The pale eyes didn't blink. "Go on. Say it."

Larnin's mouth worked. "I didn't have nothing to do with this, Billy. I never done no killing. We were friends. All right. I helped you while I could. But now . . ." The narrow jaw tightened. "Now I want out, Billy." He started to turn away.

"All right," Reo said. "You want out."

Larnin stared at the gun in Reo's fist. "Billy, you're crazy."

"I told you once. Whatever happened, it'd never be the posse. The mob'll never take me."

Slowly, the meaning got to Larnin. He shook his head. "I don't like it, Billy. I don't want your murder on my hands. You got a gun. You can do it yourself."

"Maybe," Reo said. "Only I can't be sure. It ain't easy to put a bullet through your own head. At the last minute, I might lose nerve." His gaze switched down to the blanched eastward flats. His voice went sharp. "Then they'd come with their goddamn rope. They'd . . ."

It ended in a coughing fit. Bright red drained down his chin. The gun hand didn't waver.

"I'm not sure, Jack. You're going to do me a favor. You're going to make me sure."

"Billy . . ."

"That's how it is." The muzzle came belly-high on Larnin. "It's me or you, Jack."

They looked at each other. Then Larnin's bony fingers went down and closed on the Colt butt and the long barrel came up, clean and shining in the sun.

∞∞

THE POSSE CAME into Monte Vista at high noon. They rode wearily. Stetsons tilted against the glare, wetting grit-caked lips. The tall loose-limbed rider sat straight, scanning the dusty main street. The silver star winked against his black vest.

They were passing the telegraph office, when a man came running out. He wore a deputy's star. He waved a slip of yellow paper.

"You Rob Tucker? Sheriff down Alamosa way?"

The tall man nodded.

"Still riding the tail of that Reo fella?"

Tucker's eyes narrowed. "You got news?"

The man held out the yellow slip. "They sent that on for you. Said you'd pass this way, maybe want our help."

Tucker smoothed the paper on his thigh. Riders nudged close. "I'll be damned," Tucker said.

The deputy laughed. "That's what I says to my wife, 'That Reo's did it again.' Looks as if your hunting party's over, Sheriff. Seems like that Reckonridge boy is going to live, after all. Come to, early this morning, and said he wouldn't press any charges. Admitted he was starting to draw when Reo fired. Ain't much use arresting Reo when the victim hisself says it was self-defense." The grin widened. "Honest boy, that Reckonridge. Sounds like a nice kid."

"Yeah," Tucker said. "Nice kid."

The riders were silent, then something like a sigh of relief went among them. They hitched ponies and ambled off to the cool shade of the nearest saloon. Tucker dismounted and lit a cigarette. For a long moment, he stared at the match flame. He flung the match to the dust. "The luck of some sidewinders!"

The deputy nodded. "You had a long ride. You're wore thin."

"Can you figure it?" Tucker shook his head. "Here's this Reo, suspicioned of murder in four counties and just when we think he's pinned down, ready to bring to trial, out he slides by the skin of his teeth."

The deputy frowned. Then a thought made him smile. "Say, I got some stuff up to the office. Curl the hair on your chest."

Tucker stared at the dead match. "The luck," he said. "The luck always rides with him." Then he shrugged and grinned back. "Like you say. It was a long ride."

They went off along the dry, hot boardwalk. The sheriff's office was at the east end of the main drag. Their backs were turned to the distant San Juan range. They didn't notice the shadows against the sun, the black, picket-winged birds that hovered for a long time above a mountain ledge and then circled down with a slow final grace.

Gold Men

Marcus Pelegrimas

THE THREE LITTLE ladies sitting with the six of hearts and five of spades looked so good to Jim Mathers, he would have sworn they winked at him. It was the first decent hand he'd been dealt since he sat down more than two hours ago. Trying to maintain a poker face behind his scruffy, brown beard, Jim wondered how much he could bet without giving anything away.

"Are you going to bet, or are you just gonna sit there grinning?" asked the slender man who sat directly across from Mathers.

Jim glared at the lanky, ash-blond gambler who sat confidently behind the largest stack of chips at the table. Suppressing a smirk, Mathers threw in thirty dollars. "Just shut up and play, will ya!" By this time, he had become sick of the constant flow of comments and jibes coming from the winner's mouth.

"Let's not get sore here, Jim," said Henry Whiteoak,

who sat to the cowboy's left. "This is a friendly game, remember?" Henry knew what would happen if Jim got out of line: a fight between the cowboy and the pale man opposite him . . . a fight Jim would surely lose.

Satisfied that the situation had cooled down after a moment of tense silence, Henry, a twenty-eight-year-old snake-oil salesman, threw in his thirty dollars. He thought he could smell a bluff coming from the drunk cowboy and had enough confidence in his pairs of aces and threes to stay in the game.

The winner of the night was next to bet. After downing a swig of whiskey, the man cleared his throat and threw in his chips. "I'll probably regret this, considering your skill at card handling," he said with a thick Southern accent, "but I'll call you."

Bud Jenkins, the bearlike blacksmith of the town, just shook his head and threw down his cards. Although it had taken him two hours to figure it out, he finally realized this table was no place for amateurs, unless they had a strong desire for poverty. "I'm out."

Unable to suppress his smile any longer, Mathers answered the expectant looks of the other men by proudly laying down his hand. The lovely women painted on the cards smiled back at him and him alone.

"Beats me," said Whiteoak.

The man across from Mathers shifted in his seat and raised a handkerchief to his mouth to catch the wheezing coughs that suddenly wracked his body.

Sick of this man and his coughing, Mathers just wanted to win his money. "C'mon, Holliday! Let's see what you got!"

The cards fell to the table from John Holliday's hand to reveal three jacks and a deuce. As his coughing subsided, he moved the deuce aside, uncovering the fourth jack. "Oh come now, Jim. I think I've taken enough of your money by now for you to call me Doc."

"You cheatin' sonuva bitch!" Pushing away from the

table, Jim Mathers's hand fell down to the Colt tucked under his belt.

Bud Jenkins slid back from the table as well. Whiteoak, a veteran of the gambler's circuit, was confident in the accuracy of Holliday's pistol. He saw no need to desert his money to the fiery temper of a dumb cowboy.

Doc just sat there looking at Mathers's attempt at bravado and smiled. "You sure do have pluck, suh. However, your words have too much wind," he drawled while his right hand flicked above the table, clutching his nickel-plated .45, ". . . and not enough thunduh." The casual expression dropped from Holliday's face as he thumbed back the hammer of his pistol.

"Hold it, Doc!"

The gambler's eyes didn't budge from the cowboy. "That you, Creek?"

Turkey Creek Jack Johnson, looking every bit as scruffy as his name would imply, strode into the hushed room and put a hand on his friend's shoulder.

"We got a meeting to get to," he said. "Finish this later . . . after business is taken care of."

Doc reholstered his gun and stood up from the table. Seeing this, Jim Mathers regained some of his courage.

"We *will* finish this later, you lyin' bastard," said Jim, while trying to look mean. In response, Doc coughed, collected his winnings, and walked outside with his friend.

As though the incident was completely forgotten, the odd-looking pair discussed the business at hand, while heading toward the town's biggest hotel.

Creek, six-foot-one, muscular, and covered in scraggly hair, spoke in fluid, animated gestures that gave away his energetic character. He may have looked like an average trail-rider, but the big man was a skilled gunman and experienced businessman. Many times, that "business" took place on the wrong side of the law.

Much of his skill was acquired from the man who walked beside him. John Henry "Doc" Holliday stood an inch shorter than his companion, but his reputation as an outlaw and gambler loomed miles above him. His ash-blond hair peeked from under a black hat that matched the rest of his fancy black suit. Although he looked like a dandy, the blue eyes glaring intently out at the world challenged anyone to take him so lightly.

Suffering from consumption, the man's face was pale and drawn, matching his frail physique. The rasping cough that periodically shook his body was one of the grim trademarks of the infamous dentist-turned-gambler. The other was the small, deadly arsenal he always carried. Under his fancy gambler's suitcoat was his nickel-plated .45, a second pistol, and a knife kept in his breast pocket.

By the time they had reached the small restaurant in the hotel's lobby, their plans were straightened, their lines rehearsed, and the deal was ready to go.

"Doc," said Creek as they approached a small man sitting at a table along the back wall of the room, "meet Mr. James Hudson. He's a banker from Ohio and he's interested in hearing us out."

"Pleased, suh," Doc said while shaking the banker's extended hand with a strength that took Hudson by surprise.

After seating themselves, Creek took the initiative and addressed the timid-looking banker. "I'm sure you know about the robberies going on lately . . . the coaches filled with gold?"

The banker nodded and wiped a bead of sweat from his balding head. "Well, my partner and me . . . we're gold men. We're the ones who took that stage out of Deadwood last month.

"We took a whole load of gold bricks off that stage and brought it all here when we saw they were all marked as United States property. The government'll have all the numbers and weights on record, so we can't rightly sell it through our normal people."

After hacking into a white handkerchief, Holliday added, "That's where you come in."

The banker appeared more and more nervous as he sat

with the two outlaws. So far, the man hadn't said a word. Actually, Holliday was surprised the Ohio man was there at all. The meek little businessman in the conservative brown suit looked more like a school teacher than the type that would deal with the likes of him and Creek.

Creek spoke up again, drawing Hudson's eyes over to him. "We'll sell you the whole load for twenty thousand dollars. It's worth a lot more than that, but you can get it melted down and out of sight better than we can. We just ain't got the people to handle that much gold . . . you do."

"Yes, I do," squeaked Hudson. He took a second to think before answering. "I want to see the gold first . . . and test it, of course."

"Of course," said Doc.

⌒◦⌒

THE LITTLE LAKE had no name. Situated just behind a small log cabin, the standing brown water only appeared on a few maps, where it was still hard to find. That made it perfect for the stage robbers to keep up appearances of hiding a legitimate stash of gold.

What rested on the gravelly bottom of that lake was only gold to the fool's eye. In reality, Creek had found the load of iron sulfide in the fireplace of the abandoned cabin next to the lake. After telling Doc about it over cards some time ago, Holliday came up with the idea of turning that fake gold into some real money.

Stripping down to his long johns, Creek made his way to the lake, dove in, and fetched one of the metal bars from the muddy depths.

"Here y' go," he said, dropping the brick at the banker's feet.

Hudson stooped to pick it up while Doc looked on, lighting a cigarette. Turning the rectangle of glittering ore in his hands, the banker examined the phony treasure . . . and didn't look impressed.

"I still want to test it."

"Oh, by all means, Mistah Hudson . . . test away."

Hudson glanced over at Doc, wondering if he had upset the Georgian. Knowing the full extent of Holliday's reputation, the banker was deathly afraid of getting on the man's bad side. He tried to cover this by looking aloof and nonchalant. It didn't work.

Creek, soaking through his dirty trail clothes, followed the others to the cabin and watched Hudson's shaky movements while handling the heavy brick. The banker retrieved a black satchel containing the acid and droppers used to test gold from his saddlebag.

Johnson laughed quietly to himself as he saw the nervous glances being thrown toward Holliday. He could smell the fear coming from the little man and it was obvious Hudson was trying to avoid direct eye contact with Doc. Creek knew Doc was staring the man down with those fiery, determined eyes of his. Those eyes belonged to a strong-willed, dangerous man and looked somewhat out of place in the head of a scrawny victim of tuberculosis.

The trio had just reached the cabin as sunlight began to fade in the western sky. Inside, it was too dark to see clearly, so Doc lit a lantern to illuminate Hudson's workspace.

Removing a small knife from its scabbard, the little man trimmed off some shavings from the brick of fool's gold. As he did, Creek admired the job he and Doc had done a week before of forging the United States Government stamp and serial number on the brick's long face. Just for authenticity, they had taken the time to imprint every brick with a seal and number. The next step was to make sure the gold managed to pass its upcoming test.

Hudson approached the glittering splinters laying on the table and nearly jumped out of his skin at the sudden sound of someone roughly knocking on the cabin's door.

"Aw, shit," whispered Creek. "We can't let anyone see that gold. Cut the light, Doc."

Holliday blew out the flame while Creek stomped over

to the door. "Who's out there?" Johnson barked. Between the raised voices, stomping feet, and sudden sense of urgency, Hudson's attention was divided more ways than he could keep track of.

In that time, Doc made the switch.

With the practiced motions of a professional card cheat, Holliday whisked the shavings off the table and into his coat pocket. After replacing them with a handful of real gold shavings he had been palming since he entered the cabin, the gambler began relighting the lantern.

"Who was it, Creek?" Doc asked nonchalantly.

"Just some stranger wantin' some food. I told him to get his ass off my land before I shot it off. Now, Mr. Hudson, where were we?"

"I uh . . ." The banker's eyes quickly adjusted to the returning flicker of light. "I was just going to test this gold. Here we go . . ."

The gold men watched intently as the little banker went about his task. They looked for any sign of trouble . . . any hint that the switch had been noticed.

It hadn't been.

The distraction had worked . . . the test was passed.

"Everything seems to be in order," said the banker.

Creek nodded.

Doc coughed.

"I'll have to take the gold back to Ohio. However, I'll want one of you to come with me, at least as far as Chicago. I have some friends there, and that's where you will get your money . . . after the rest of the gold is tested. If there's any . . . trouble along the way, my escort is dead. That's my insurance."

Laughing from the bottom of his gut, Creek Johnson walked over to Hudson and slapped the small man on the back. "We won't try to grab the gold back from ya! Hell, we just want our money." He looked over at Holliday, who was now sitting in a rocking chair in the far corner of the cabin. His tuberculosis had been acting up, draining much of the energy out of the lanky gambler.

"I'll go with ya," Creek continued. "How's that . . . all right?"

Hudson didn't try to hide his relief. He still hadn't made prolonged eye contact with Holliday since his first look into the killer's eyes.

"He's got some good common sense for a banker, huh, Doc?"

Holliday cleared his bloody throat as he answered, "The man's no fool, that's for sure."

With that, the two gold men laughed. Although he didn't get the inside joke, Hudson laughed, too.

◆◆◆

THE TRAIL FROM Leadville to Chicago was a well-traveled one due to the Colorado town's recent popularity on the gamblers' circuit. The four men riding on the battered stage with a payload of fake U.S. gold were feeling every bump on the muddy path.

The men (Creek, Hudson, the driver, and a man riding shotgun) all wore the alert, determined faces of those protecting a valuable cargo across a rough land. Even though one of those men knew the cargo to be just as worthless as the beat-up coach carrying it, he knew rumors of a load of gold were enough to bring trouble.

Creek stuck his head out of the stage's window and yelled at the driver over the noise of rattling wheels, managing also to get a look at the armed escort sitting beside the driver. Johnson had seen the banker pay the guard a large sum of money before the trip began and knew that was to make sure Creek was the first man killed in the event of a double cross.

"Hey, driver! Where are we?"

The man holding the reins turned his dirty, annoyed face down to Creek. "We're just east of the Missouri River . . . headed for a trail stop at a town just a few miles off."

Turning his gaze to the trail ahead, Creek strained his

eyes for any sight of the promised town. Although an experienced rider, Johnson hated stages with a passion. While searching the horizon, instead of civilization, Creek spotted a cloud of dust being kicked up by an approaching group of horses.

They were closing fast.

Johnson felt the twinge of worry bite into his gut. He and Doc had toyed with the idea of having the stage robbed to repeat the gold trick on another pigeon, but eventually ruled it out. Creek knew if those boys were stage robbers, they were real ones.

That was the first problem. The second was the shotgun bearer up front. Undoubtedly, the man would earn his money by blowing Creek's head off if a robbery started.

"What's that noise?" Hudson asked in a shaky voice when the thunder of approaching horses and gunfire reached his ears.

"Robbers," said Creek. Without another word, Johnson slid his Peacemaker from underneath his long riding coat and leaned out of the window to face the gunmen. Just as his head cleared the coach, it was met by the muzzle of a shotgun being swung around in his direction.

The man sitting next to the driver almost got the chance to pull his trigger before Creek put a piece of hot lead between his eyes. The body twitched once before dropping out of the seat, onto the road, and under the heavy wooden wheels. Johnson was safe . . . for the moment.

The four gunmen were still drawing closer.

Having plenty of experience, the driver knew not to pause to cry over his fallen comrade. He was doing his damnedest just to keep the stage ahead of the raiders.

As the bandits passed by the dusty body of the coach's hired protector, they began their assault in force. Whoops and hollers accompanied the cracks of gunshots as the raiding party spurred their mounts to close the distance between them and their prey.

Creek took careful aim at the lead robber as he caught up to the stage, and fired. As though yanked from the saddle by a rope, the scruffy man jerked backward and hit the ground, clutching the fresh wound still smoking in his chest.

At that point, the other three men turned their fire on Johnson, sending bullets flying past his head. Outnumbered and outgunned, Creek decided to try and end the battle quickly before the bandits got the upper hand.

James Hudson cowered on the floor of the stage, covering his head with his hands as though they would stop a bullet from shattering his skull. "Are those your boys?" he shrieked.

"Oh, hell yeah. My boys love shooting at me like this. We're roughhousing, is all." A piece of the wooden frame just two inches from Johnson's head caught a bullet, sending splinters raining down on Creek's hair and Hudson's back. All suspicions of the battle being a setup suddenly left Hudson's mind.

Johnson took the initiative by aiming his pistol out the window and wildly squeezing off the remaining bullets left in his revolver.

Two of the shots found their mark. Unfortunately, both of the marks were on the same man. A fine, red mist sprayed from the second robber's shoulder wound as the bullet tore through. The slug following the first made a dull, meaty slap as it buried itself deep into the man's gut. A dark, moist stain spread across the bandit's stomach as he swayed and fell to the dirt.

Creek had managed to down two of the men, but now he had to reload and get the last two before they pulled up close to the coach and tore into the flimsy vehicle with pistol fire. Even as he pushed out the gun's cylinder and dumped the bullet casings onto the floor, Creek was doubtful he'd live long enough to slap it shut again.

Johnson's whole body shuddered at the sound of a shotgun blast from outside. Expecting to feel buckshot ripping him in half, Creek looked down at the expected injury. He saw only his sweaty shirt . . . blood-free. His eyes flicked back to the action outside just in time to see a bandit's riderless horse and two other men behind it, one with smoking shotgun in hand.

In open-mouthed surprise, Creek and Hudson gaped at the new riders. At first, due to the dirty bandannas covering their faces, the strangers looked like more outlaws. Creek's sharper eyes caught the glint from the sun off of the badges pinned to the men's chests, and that was the best thing he'd seen all day.

The remaining bandit was not as pleased to see new arrivals. Turning slightly in his saddle to aim his pistol at the shotgun-bearing deputy, the thief's trigger finger just started to tense as the other lawman's hand flashed upward and fired off two shots from a pistol that found their way to the bandit's head and chest.

Thanking whatever stars that looked over him, the driver reined the team to a halt and slumped forward with head in hands for a moment to catch his breath.

"Thank God . . . thank God you boys got here" was all the old driver could get out.

The young deputy rode up closer to the stage while replacing the spent shell from his shotgun. After removing the bandanna from his face, Creek saw the deputy's sturdy coolness betraying his experience in this type of work.

"Is everyone all right?" the lawman asked.

Peering from the floor of the coach, James Hudson shakily surveyed the scene. "Is it over? Are they gone?"

"Yeah, yeah, they're gone! Hell, that was some ride!" Johnson said, reveling in the thrill he felt from cheating death. "I wanna shake your hand, boy!"

As Creek began to open the stage door, the deputy rode up and held it shut with his foot while raising his shotgun to cover them both. "Sit back down, there, and throw your guns out the other window."

The thrill left Creek's soul as quickly as it had arrived. "What? What for?" he asked.

"We heard these bandits were gonna rob this stage of its gold . . . that's how we knew where to get them. We also heard the gold on this here stage was stolen government property . . . that's how we knew where to get you, Creek."

Glancing over the deputy's shoulder, Johnson saw the second lawman covering his partner with the pistol that had just shot a man dead out of his saddle. He then took a good look at the badge on the young man's chest. U.S. MARSHAL. "Aw shit," he grumbled while chucking his guns out the window as ordered.

"Where's Doc?" the deputy asked.

Creek just stared straight ahead . . . straight into the wide-eyed, panic-stricken face of James Hudson.

∽◦∽

OF ALL THE humiliating things that had ever happened to James Hudson, being arrested and handcuffed to a ruffian like Turkey Creek Jack Johnson topped the banker's personal list. It did, that is, until they reached the grimy town of Chicago when Creek spoke up to the young deputy facing the two prisoners in the commandeered stage.

"Hey, boy, I gotta take a piss."

"We're almost there," he said. "Just hold it."

Shifting uncomfortably in the stiff wooden seat, Creek winced at the lawman. "I been holdin' it for the whole ride and we're comin' up on a saloon. Let us out, so I can take care of business. You can even watch if you want," Johnson added sarcastically.

The deputy leaned his head out of the window to confer with his superior, who rode alongside the coach. With a curt nod of approval from the marshal, the stage was brought to a stop and Johnson, dragging the banker behind him, was escorted to the outhouse.

"Hurry up, now," grunted the deputy as he shoved the two men into the foul-smelling confines of the wooden shack.

As Creek tended to his business, he leaned over to Hudson. "I got an idea," he said.

"What?"

"I think we can get out of this if we act now, before they lock us up."

"I don't want to make this any worse." Hudson's voice trembled. "Any more shooting, and we'll be hung. I just wish to . . ."

"No, no shootin'. You still got that money in your suitcase, right? The money you was gonna pay us for the gold?"

"Yes."

"Use that to buy our way outta here. Hell, twenty thousand dollars is enough to turn a U.S. marshal's head long enough for us to escape. If not, we're no worse off. If they go for it, we'll cut out and settle up later."

The idea of jail time did not sit well with the timid man and he gingerly agreed to the scheme. "That's my money. You pay me back half and it's a deal."

"Fair enough."

～○～

THIS TIME, WHEN the young deputy glanced back for approval from his superior, the other man, still fresh from the trail and covered with grit, shifted his gaze from side to side, making sure there were no witnesses to his next act. Comfortable that nobody was watching the group behind the saloon, the marshal nodded and tossed the handcuff keys to his young deputy.

"You say the money's in the leather case on top of the stage?"

"Y-yes, sir," Hudson stammered nervously.

The deputy scrambled to the cash while his boss kept watch. Opening the case, the young man quickly counted the bills, shut the case again, and handed it over to the marshal. After a hushed conference between the two lawmen, the deputy returned to Creek and Hudson.

"We gotta keep the gold, but you two . . ." He shrugged to himself while removing the cuffs from their hands. "You somehow escaped."

Turning his back on the two escapees, the deputy didn't
have to wait more than one or two seconds before the
sound of scurrying feet on the dirt road faded from ear-
shot.

After putting some distance between themselves and
the two lawmen, Creek and Hudson stopped to regain
their breath. They decided to split up to make the job
harder for the posse that was sure to form once the marshals reported the "escape." The plan was to meet again
in Leadville a week later where the banker would be re-
paid for Creek's half of the marshals' bribe.

Hudson made his way to the home of his Chicago contact, while Creek headed back to the saloon to get his
money. After all, he did his part to earn that cash, and he
was going to get it; one way or another. Approaching the
head marshal, Johnson stealthily crept up behind the man
and pounced just as the horses began to stir.

Creek's right hand shot out to grab at the marshal's leg.
As he made contact, the rider jumped in surprise while he
instinctively pulled his .45 from its holster. The shiny barrel just touched Creek's forehead as the marshal's eyes
caught up with his reflexes.

"Jesus, Creek. You neahly met your makah," drawled
the man on the horse.

"Aw, you couldn't shoot me. You're the law."

The marshal pulled down his bandanna to reveal the
pale, sunken face of Doc Holliday. Doc put his nickel-
plated .45 back in its place as he extended a hand to
Creek. Taking it, Johnson climbed onto the horse as a
smile found its way to his battered face.

"Where's your deputy?"

Motioning toward the outhouse, Holliday said, "We
might have to use him again. He can play deputy and
knock on cabin doors like a professional. Anyway, I gave
him his share, so I suggest we take ours and put this town
behind us. Our banker friend may not be a genius, but
he'll wise up when he's alone in Leadville long enough.
And God knows we'd be in trouble if his Chicago friends

inspected the gold they paid twenty thousand dollars for."

After picking up fresh horses and a trail heading west, the gold men paused to split up their hard-earned money.

"I'll be laying low in Cheyenne for a piece, Doc. At least, long enough for this to blow over. We should get together for a drink to celebrate our little gold strike. Where should I look?"

"Dodge City," Holliday said, turning to cough into a white handkerchief. The gambler's spirit rustled under his skin, fueled by the sack of money in his saddlebag. For a brief second, Doc thought he could actually hear the poker tables calling to him from the Long Branch Saloon back in Kansas.

"I'll be there for a while. I believe I feel a winnin' streak comin' on."

(This story is based on true events as told by John M. Myers in his book *Doc Holliday*.)

Gambler's Luck

❦

Bill Gulick

J EFF KANE HAD come a long way across the desert
country that night, pushing his horse hard so that he
would reach the mountains while there was yet time to
utilize the light of the dying moon. He crossed the icy
stream, left his horse ground-tied in the deep shadow of
the valley, and climbed upward afoot to the ledge which
he remembered from so long ago.

He inched his way carefully along the sheer face, circled a protruding rock, then, just as the last rays of the
moon failed, came to the entrance of the hidden box canyon he sought.

He paused there, taut as a fiddle string, and stared into
the darkness ahead. At first he saw nothing, then his
straining eyes caught a faint reddish glow. He let his
breath out in a long sigh and drew the single-action Colt
from its holster.

He had been right. When he lost the trail in the desert
west of Cottonwood City two days ago, he'd made a guess
that Steve Burgess would hole up here. Ten years might
change the way a man lived, but the years didn't change

a man's habits of thought. And Jeff knew the way Steve Burgess's mind worked, knew it as well as he knew this canyon.

Quietly Jeff moved toward the dull glow of the fire. He was very close before he saw the blanket-wrapped figure of the sleeping man.

So Burgess considered himself safe here, he mused. Burgess must have forgotten that there was one person other than himself who knew the existence of this place.

A loose rock rolled under Jeff's foot. He froze as it made a small rattling sound. Till now, he had forgotten about the slide. He could not cross that jumble of loose rock without awakening Burgess, and he could not risk a fight in the dark.

He thrust the Colt back into its holster and sat down. Dawn would come in two hours. He could wait. He sat staring fixedly at the sleeping figure, and because there were memories here in this canyon his thoughts circled unwillingly back into the past, the strange patterns of his own life and that of Steve Burgess weaving themselves before his mind's eye.

Two men were once again in the canyon where they had lived together in their youth, ten years ago. Two men, one an officer of the law, the other a killer. He, Jeff Kane, wore the badge; the sleeping man yonder, Steve Burgess, had blood on his hands and murder on his soul.

Yet—and this was the thing that tormented Jeff Kane—but for the quirks of fate, the forks of an old trail, the fall of a tossed coin, he might be that sleeping figure and Steve Burgess the one sitting here waiting for the dawn.

But for the forks of an old trail, the fall of a tossed coin . . .

∽∘∾

THE EARLY SPRING sun hung in the center of the sky when the two young men came out of the desert and reached the hilltop where the trail forked. They reined up.

"This is it," Steve said. "Here's where we split up."

Jeff nodded without looking at the man who had been his partner for nearly a year of gold panning back there in the mountains. They were heartily sick of each other's company, sick the way men get when they share the same cabin, eat the same food, think the same thoughts for too long.

It might have been different, Jeff supposed, if they'd struck it rich. But they hadn't. They'd worked hard for a long year and now each of them had only a meager year's wages—slightly under a thousand dollars apiece.

Long ago, they had agreed to part company when they got back to civilization. The gold dust, the food, the equipment were already divided. All that remained now was deciding which trail each was to take.

The lefthand trail led northward to Cottonwood City and the prosperous ranching country that surrounded it.

The righthand trail led southward into barren, less inviting country. Steve looked at Jeff and said shortly, "I suppose you're wanting to take the lefthand trail, too."

"I'd sort of figured on it," Jeff said.

"We agreed to split up here."

Jeff nodded wearily. The direction he rode didn't matter, just so he put distance between himself and his ex-partner—quick.

Steve took a silver dollar from his pocket. "Shall we settle it the usual way?"

"Good enough," Jeff said.

"Heads I take the left-hand trail, tails you take it," Steve said, and tossed the coin into the air.

Jeff watched it spin over in a high, glittering arc. It landed on the ground and both men leaned down in their saddles to look at it.

"Heads," Steve said. "My luck's holding."

"Yeah," Jeff said, then he wheeled his horse about and set off at a jog-trot along the right-hand trail, without so much as a backward glance at the man who had once been his friend. . . .

∽⚬∾

THE MAN LYING by the fire moved slightly and Jeff's hand went to the butt of his gun, remaining there until the sleeping form grew quiet once more. The hand relaxed slowly.

That's where it began, he thought, back there where the trail forked. He had learned, later, by the rangeland grapevine, what had happened after Steve Burgess went riding up trail to Cottonwood City.

He'd done a thing natural enough for a young man eager for life and hungry for the pleasures of civilization after a long year in the wilderness. He'd got drunk that first night in Cottonwood City, gloriously, roaringly drunk. He'd bought liquor for everybody in the house, danced with the girls there in Blackie Dunnevan's Emporium, then wound up the wild night by losing all his remaining gold in a card game.

It was a thing any young fellow might do. Jeff himself might have done it if he had had the opportunity. But there were no roaring boomtowns along the southbound trail, no dancing girls, no high-stake card games. There was only the parched, barren range, the scattered trading posts, the occasional ranches stocked with scrubby cattle.

He'd felt bitter about his prospects in the country when he rode tired, dirty and hungry into the yard of the J-6 that evening, bitter at himself for being such a fool as to let the toss of a coin send him into this Godforsaken place. . . .

He reined up in the yard in front of the grimy frame house and called, "Howdy. Anybody home?"

A mongrel dog barked at him from the safety of the porch. After a moment, a thin, stooped, tired looking old man came out.

"Howdy, stranger. Get down and come in."

"Don't want to trouble you," Jeff said. "I need water and grain for my horse. Be glad to pay you for it."

"Get down, get down!" the man insisted. "We ain't got much here at the J-6, but you're welcome to it. And no more of your insults about paying."

Jeff dismounted and introduced himself. The old man's name was Jennings and he informed Jeff that everybody called him Pop. He said he lived alone on the J-6 and worked it alone, which was evident enough to Jeff when he saw the rundown condition of the house and outbuildings.

Pop Jennings took care of the horse and then warmed up a pot of beans and a panful of bacon for Jeff. After Jeff had eaten, the old man looked at him with shrewd, twinkling eyes and asked, "Are you ridin' or lookin'?"

"I'm not headed any place in particular, if that's what you mean," Jeff said.

"Then you're lookin'. There's only two kinds of people. One kind is always ridin' over the hill to a place where the grass is greener. They never find it. The other kind is lookin' for a place to settle down and it don't matter much to 'em where that place is. I figure you're the lookin' kind."

"How can you tell?"

"It's in a man's eyes, youngster. You can always see it in a man's eyes." Pop started clearing away the dishes. "Reckon you're tired. I got an extra bed and you're welcome to it. We can talk tomorrow."

Jeff had a good night's rest. He'd planned to move on the next day, but in the morning Pop said he was going out to mend a drift fence and asked Jeff to come along, and because he was hungry for talk Jeff went. Then something else came up to delay him the next day, and the day after that, till suddenly a week had gone by and he found himself not wanting to leave at all.

Pop offered him a job at forty a month and Jeff took it as a matter of course. The weeks drifted by pleasantly and swiftly, and by spring roundup time he felt as though he had never known any other home but the J-6.

He noticed during the round-up that Pop was cutting

out cattle for market that were too young to sell profitably
and he protested against it. "You're selling off all your
breeding stock, Pop. Keep those beeves another year or
two and you'll make some real money. Sell them now
and you'll barely break even."

Pop nodded wearily. "I know. But it ain't a question
of what I want to do. The J-6 is mortgaged to the nub. I
got a payment to meet and no way to raise the cash except
selling some beef."

Jeff looked at him closely and said, "This payment—
how much is it?"

"Fifteen hundred dollars."

"I've got a thousand of it."

Pop shook his head. "You're a fool to offer a loan to
a washed-up cow outfit like mine."

Jeff stared out across the sunlit expanse of range. A
recent rain had turned the dry, dust-gray grass a fresh
green. Cattle grew fat on that kind of grazing land, he
knew. If a man could hang on another season, if a man
would buckle down and do some honest-to-God work
here . . .

Suddenly he felt a sense of power and strength. *He*
could do it. If Pop would give him a chance, he could
make something of this place.

"Who said this outfit was washed up?" he demanded
belligerently. "Look. I'll loan you the thousand and we'll
keep the cattle till they're prime. When we sell you pay
the thousand back and we'll split the extra profit two
ways. How does that sound?"

Pop rubbed a tired hand across his chin and smiled.
"That's what I like about you youngsters. Think you can
whip anything. Okay, it's a deal."

That had been the beginning. Jeff had worked hard,
harder than he had ever worked at anything. And the J-6
gradually came back to life. Pop said it was the new
blood, the young blood, that accomplished the miracle.

Every now and then during those harsh years Jeff heard
bits of news about Steve Burgess. He was still hanging

around Cottonwood City. He worked first at this job, then at that, never staying long with one position.

A brief, bloody range war flared up between two of the big cow outfits near Cottonwood City and rumor had it that Burgess drew gunman's wages to ride for one of them for a while. There was an unsavory tale, too, concerning Burgess and a girl who danced in Blackie Dunnevan's Emporium, but Jeff discounted it because he knew how gossip spreaders loved to enlarge on such things.

His intense hate for Burgess lessened with distance and years. He began to see that what had happened during those long months in the mountains was only natural. The fault had been as much his own as his partner's. With his new perspective, he remembered again those qualities about Burgess that you couldn't help liking—the easygoing manner, the willingness to take hardship without complaint, the skill with horses.

You had to admire Steve's gambling heart, too. There was never an argument that he wasn't willing to settle by the mere toss of a coin. . . .

∽◦∾

THE FIRE WAS completely dead now. Jeff Kane shifted his cramped limbs carefully, shivering with the night chill. Dawn was not far away. Already a faint tinge of gray lightened the eastern sky and within the hour the sleeping man would waken.

A predawn silence held the mountains in a breathless hush, as if the vast wilderness were standing on tiptoe watching for the first glimpse of the sun. Sitting there in the silence, Jeff Kane felt that human life was a small, pitiful, tragic thing. Why was it that the breaks fell wrong for one man and right for the next? Why was it that he should have a comfortable home, a fine wife, two children that he loved, while Steve Burgess yonder had neither home nor peace nor a living soul to care for him?

Why had the luck been all on his side? Pop Jennings's

dying and leaving him the ranch; Linda's coming into the community as a school teacher; meeting him, marrying him; his appointment as United States Marshal—all had been breaks that went his way.

But Steve Burgess had received only bad breaks. Certainly his falling in love with the dancehall girl hadn't been his fault. He had not been to blame for the fight with Blackie Dunnevan, if you could believe the tales you heard. And each bad break that had piled remorselessly one upon another to set him off on the road of crime— they could have come to any man.

They could have happened to himself, thought Jeff Kane. He shivered with something more than cold and for a moment wished that he had sent one of his deputies to do this job.

The darkness lessened gradually. Jeff took the Colt from its holster and checked it for the last time. Burgess had sworn he would not be taken alive.

Daylight came. The sleeping man stirred lazily, pushed the blanket aside, and sat up. Jeff leveled his gun.

"Get up, Burgess," he said coldly. "You're under arrest."

Steve Burgess froze with complete surprise. Slowly he turned his head and looked at Jeff. His hair was matted and dirty. A week's stubble of brownish beard covered his face. His eyes were bloodshot.

But something of the old devil-take-it light twinkled in them now and he smiled. "Hello, Jeff. How'd you know I was here?"

"I remembered the place, too. You should have thought of that."

"To tell the truth, I didn't think a United States Marshal would waste his time on me. I thought you'd send a deputy."

"This was one job I had to do myself," Jeff said.

"For old times' sake?"

Jeff shook his head. "Pack up your things, Steve. We're going back."

Burgess stood up. He'd slept with his gun and belt on but he kept his right hand carefully away from his side. The smile left his face and his eyes grew cold.

"You're wrong, Jeff. *I'm* not going back—alive. Might as well shoot me and get it over with."

Jeff looked at him steadily. He knew Burgess wasn't bluffing. He knew that it would be impossible for him to tie the outlaw and carry him along the narrow ledge that offered the only exit to the canyon—a man needed both hands free on that dangerous trail.

Slowly he holstered his gun. "If that's the way you want it, Steve. I'll give you an even break."

"I didn't think you were that much of a gambler."

Jeff shook his head and did not answer. To him, it wasn't a gamble; it was a sort of justice. In a way, it was an attempt to make up for the cruel tricks an erratic fate had played on the man before him, an attempt to give him one last make-or-break chance.

He waited patiently for the outlaw to make the first move. But Burgess kept looking at him, smiling. "Mind if I smoke?" he said.

"Go ahead," Jeff said.

Burgess took the makings from a shirt pocket and slowly built a cigarette. Not until he had lit it and taken a deep pull did he speak. Then he said, "Jeff, you're a square hombre. You're too white to die."

"I don't figure on dying," Jeff said.

Burgess made an impatient gesture with his hand. "None of us do. But you got to admit that when lead starts flying somebody gets hurt. It might be you. Now, suppose we say each of us has got a fifty-fifty chance. If you kill me, then your job is done, justice is done, and you go back to your wife and kids. But if I kill you, what does anybody gain? I go free, just as I was till you found me here, but you're dead. And I'm *still* free."

"What are you driving at?" Jeff asked stolidly.

"I'll make a deal." Burgess took a silver dollar from his pocket and held it in the palm of his left hand. "I'll toss this coin. If it comes down heads, you go back home and forget you ever saw me. If it comes down tails, I'll go back to Cottonwood City with you."

Jeff stared at the silver dollar and the years rolled back to a day when the trail forked and a glittering coin spun into the air.

"That dollar," he said huskily, "is it . . . ?"

Steve Burgess grinned. "Yeah, it's the same one we used to settle our arguments with. Fact is, I use it to settle all my problems. Sort of a good luck piece." He tossed the coin up and caught it carelessly in his left hand. "What do you say?" he said. "Heads I go free, tails I go back to Cottonwood City."

Jeff shook his head. "Sorry. That's a thing I can't gamble on."

Steve Burgess looked at him steadily for a moment, then his eyes went cold and he snapped, "Well, gamble on this!" and he reached for his gun.

Jeff's hand automatically dipped down and up. Two shots sounded in the narrow canyon, roaring almost as one. Jeff felt a slight tug at his shirt sleeve as a slug singed him but he barely noticed it. Steve Burgess stood rigid for a moment, then fell to the ground clutching at the red stain spreading on his chest.

Jeff holstered his gun and ran to the wounded man. When he turned him over on his back he saw that there was no chance to save him. Steve Burgess was dying.

He seemed to realize it. He opened his eyes as Jeff put an arm under his shoulders and a faint flicker of the old light came into them. "You always were a better shot than me, Jeff," he breathed.

"I'm sorry," Jeff said. "I'm sorry it had to end this way."

Burgess shook his head slightly. "No. This is the best way. You're white, Jeff, all the way through. Me—hell, I never was any good."

Suddenly a great bitterness against the injustice of life, the unfairness of life, the cruelty of a fate which would not allow a man to fight back, overwhelmed Jeff Kane.

"It wasn't you," he muttered thickly. "It was the breaks. You got the bad ones, I got the good ones. Like the time you tossed the coin back there where the trail forked. If it had fallen the other way, I might be in your place."

"No, Jeff." The voice was weaker now but there was peace in it. Peace and a touch of regret. "No, you wouldn't, Jeff. A man makes his own breaks. It's what he's got inside that counts, not the way the trail forks, nor the way the coin falls. . . ."

He paused, as if to gather the last of his ebbing strength, then he whispered weakly, "If you don't believe me, look at the coin, Jeff. . . ."

The body in Jeff Kane's arms stiffened, then relaxed. Gently he eased the fingers apart and picked up the silver dollar lying in the palm. He stared at it, turned it over.

It was heads on both sides.

The Old Ways

~⌖~

Ed Gorman

For Norman Partridge

THERE HAD BEEN a gunfight earlier in the evening, but then, in a place like this one, there usually were gunfights earlier. And later, for that matter.

The name of the place was Madame Dupree's and it was one of the big casino-drinking establishments that were filling the most disreputable part of San Francisco in this year of 1903. The Barbary Coast was the name for the entire district and, yes, it was every bit as dangerous as you've heard. Cops, even the young strong ones, would only come down here in fours and sixes, and even then an awful lot of them got killed.

The way I got this job was to get myself good and beaten up and tossed in an alley behind the Madame's. One of her men found me and brought me to her and she asked me if I wanted a job and since I hadn't eaten in three days I said yes and so she put me to work as a floater in her casino. What I did was walk around with a few hundred dollars of Madame Dupree's money in my pockets and pretend to be drunk. Inevitably, rubes would spot me as an easy mark and invite me into one of their

poker games. Thanks to a few accoutrements such as a
holdout vest and a sleeve holdout, I could pretty much
deal myself any cards I wanted to. Eighty-five percent of
my winnings went back to Madame Dupree. The rest I
kept. Not bad pay for somebody who'd been raised on an
Oklahoma reservation and seen three of his brothers and
sisters die of tuberculosis before they reached eight years
of age. I'd gotten my memory back and wished I hadn't.

What Madame Dupree didn't say—didn't need to say,
really—was that an Indian was a perfect mark because he
was held to be the lowest form of life in these United
States, even below that of Negro and Chinaman. What
rube could possibly resist taking money from a drunken
Indian? Or, for that matter, what Indian could resist? You
saw a lot of red men along the Barbary Coast, men who'd
worked or stolen their way into some money and now
wanted to spend it the way white men did. The Barbary
was about the only place in the land where no distinction
was made among the races—if you had the money, you
could have anything any other man could have. This in-
cluded all the white girls, some of whom were as young
as thirteen, though this particular summer a wave of various venereal diseases was sweeping the Barbary. More
than six hundred people had died so far. A Methodist
minister had suggested in one of the local newspapers that
the Barbary be set afire with all its "human filth" still in
it. I wasn't sure that Jesus would have approved of such
a proposal, but then you never could tell.

Tonight's gunfight pretty much started the way they all
do in a place like this.

On the ground floor, Madame Dupree's consisted of
three large rooms, the walls of which were covered by
giant murals of easy women in even easier poses. As you
wandered among the sailors, the city councilmen, the
crooked cops, the whores, the pickpockets, the professional gamblers, the farmers, the clerks, the disguised
ministers and priests and even the occasional rabbi, the
slumming socialites, and the sad-eyed fathers looking for

their runaway daughters, you found gambling devices of every kind: faro, baffling board, roulette, keno, goose-and-balls, and—well, you get the idea.

Tonight a drunken rube suspected he'd been cheated out of his money. And no doubt he suspected correctly. He got loud and then he got violent and then as he was being escorted out one of the side doors by a giant Negro bouncer with a ruffled white shirt already bloody this early in the evening, he made the worst mistake of all. He pulled his gun and tried to shoot the bouncer in the side. And the bouncer responded by drawing his own gun and shooting the man's gun away. And then the bouncer threw the man through the side door and went out into the dark alley.

Everybody who worked here knew what was going to happen next. Every bouncer at every major casino in the Barbary had a specialty. Some were especially good with knives and guns, for instance. This man's specialty was his strength. He liked to grab the top of somebody's head with his giant hand and give the head a violent wrench to the left, thereby breaking the neck. I'd seen him do it once and I couldn't get the sight out of my mind for a couple of weeks afterward. The funny thing was he was called Mr. Stevenson because late at night, at a steak house down the street, he read Robert Louis Stevenson stories out loud to anybody who'd listen. Mr. Stevenson told me once, "I was a plantation nigger and my master thought it'd be funny to have a big buck like me know how to read. So he had me educated from the time I was six and a couple of times a week he'd have me come up to the house and read to all his friends and they just couldn't believe I could read the way I did." That gave us something in common. An Oklahoma white man who ran the town next to my reservation put me through two years of college. I probably would have finished except the man dropped straight down dead of a heart attack and his son wasn't anywhere near as generous.

That was how Mr. Stevenson and I were the same, the

education. How we were different was his physical strength.

After Mr. Stevenson finished with the rube, I got myself a good cigar and wandered around in my good clothes, weaving a little the way I did to let people know that I was a drunken Indian, and I got pulled into three different games in as many hours. I won a little over four hundred dollars. Madame Dupree would be happy—at least she would be if she'd gotten over her terrible cold, which some of us had come to suspect was maybe something more than a cold. Be funny if one of the owners died of venereal disease the way their girls and their customers did.

Around ten, I saw Mr. Stevenson working his way over to me. He wore his usual attire, a bowler perched at a rakish angle on his big head, his fancy shirt with the celluloid collar, and a sparkling diamond stickpin through his red cravat.

"You catch a drink with me?" he said as he leaned over the table where I was playing.

"Something wrong?"

He nodded. He had solemn brown eyes that hinted at both his intelligence and his anger.

"Five minutes."

"You know that coon?" one of the rubes said after Mr. Stevenson had left.

"Met him a little earlier. Why?"

The rube shook his head. "Scares the piss out of me, he does. I heard about how he snaps them necks." He shuddered. "Back in Nebraska, you just don't see things like that."

I finished the hand and then joined Mr. Stevenson at the bar. As always, he drank tea. He took his job very seriously and he didn't want whiskey to make him careless.

I didn't much worry about things like that. I had a shot of rye with a beer back.

"What's up, Mr. Stevenson?"

"Moira."

"Oh."

There was a group of reservation Indians who had collected in the Barbary over the past two years or so. Maybe a dozen of us, all employed in various capacities by the casinos. One was a very beautiful Indian girl who'd been called "Moira" by the Indian agent where she'd grown up. Mr. Stevenson was sweet on her, and in a terrible way. He'd go through periods where he couldn't sleep: you'd see him standing in front of her cheap hotel, staring up at her window, doing some kind of sad sentry duty. Or you'd see him following her. Or you'd see him sitting alone in a coffeehouse all teary-eyed and glum and you knew who he was thinking about. Or I did, anyway. I'd gone through the same thing with Moira myself. I'd been in bitter love with her for nearly a year but then I'd passed through it. Like a fever.

Not that you could blame Moira. She was as captivated by another reservation Indian named Two Eagle as we were captivated by her. Did all the same things we did with her. Followed him around. Bought him gifts he didn't want. Wrote him pleading little notes.

Then they got a place and moved in together. Moira and Two Eagle, but word was things weren't going well. He was one of those Indians too fond of the bottle and too bitter toward the white man to function well. Kept a drum up in his room and sometimes in the middle of the night you'd hear it, a tom-tom here in the center of the Barbary, and him yowling ancient Indian war cries and chants. He was fierce, Two Eagle, and he seemed to hate me especially, seemed to think that I had no pride in my red skin or my ancestors. I returned the favor, thinking he was pretty much of a melodramatic asshole. I was just as much an Indian as he was. I just kept it to myself was all.

Only time I ever liked him was one night when I ran into him and Moira in a Barbary restaurant, real late it was, and Two Eagle gentle drunk on wine, and him telling her in great excited rushes about the old religions of ours, and how only the red man—of all the earth's peoples— understood that sky and sun and the winds were all part of the Great God spirit—and how a man or woman who knew how to truly speak to God could then address all living creatures on the earth, be they elk or horse or great mountain eagle, for all things and all creatures are God's, and thus all things in the world, seen and unseen alike, are indivisible, and of God. And he spoke with such passion and sweep and majesty that I could see tears in his eyes—as I felt tears in my own eyes . . . and I saw that there was a good side to his belligerent clinging to the old ways. But his bad side . . .

Moira liked white-man things. Back when she'd let me take her to supper a few times, we'd gone for a long carriage ride by the bay and she'd enjoyed it. Then we went up where the fancy shops were. She made a lot of little-girl sounds, pleased and cute and dreamy.

This was the part of her Two Eagle hated. By now he'd got her to dress in deerskin instead of cloth dresses, her shining black hair in pigtails instead of tumbling tresses, her face innocent of the "whore paint," as he pontifically called it. He worked as a bouncer in a place so tough it might have given Mr. Stevenson pause, and she worked behind the bar in the same place. Pity the man who got drunk and started sweet-talking Moira. Two Eagle would drag him outside and make the man plead for a quick death.

Now that I was over Moira, I didn't especially like hearing about either of them. But you couldn't say the same for Mr. Stevenson. He was as aggrieved as ever, all pain and dashed hope.

"She went out on him."

"Oh, bullshit."

"True," he said. "Few nights ago. They got into a bad fight and he kicked her in the stomach. He didn't know she was just startin' to carry a baby. Killed the baby and nearly killed Moira, too."

"The sonofabitch. Somebody should kill that bastard."

"You haven't heard the rest of it."

"I'm not sure I want to."

"He wants to cut her."

"Cut her?"

"The old ways, he says. What the Indians used to do back when I was on the plantation. When a woman went out on a man like that. You know—her nose."

"That's crazy. Nobody does that shit anymore."

"He does. Or at least he says he does. You know how he is. All that warrior bullshit he gets into."

"Where's Moira?"

"That's the worst part. She thinks she's got it coming. She's just waitin' in her room for him to come up and cut her. Says she believes in the old ways, too."

I shook my head. "That sounds like Moira." I took my pocket watch from my breeches. "I've got some time off coming. I can tell Madame Dupree I'm going for the rest of the night."

"You're tough, man, but you aren't that tough. Two Eagle'll kill you." He showed me his hands. How big they were. And strong. And black. "Fucker tries to cut her, I'll take care of him." He nodded to the front door, his bowler perched at a precarious angle. Sometimes I wondered if he had it glued to his bald head. "Let's go."

We went.

Making our way along the board sidewalks this time of night meant stepping over corpses, drunks, and reeking puddles of vomit and blood from various fights. Every important casino had a band of its own, which meant that the noise was as bad as the odors.

It was raining, which meant the boards were slick. But we walked fast, anyway. Two Eagle had a couple of rooms on the second floor of a livery stable. Moira lived there, too. She'd waited a long time for him to marry her. I figured she'd wait a lot longer.

A drunken rube made a crack about Mr. Stevenson, but if the black man heard, he didn't let on. Just kept walking.

Real quiet and real intense. Like he had only one thought in the entire world and everything else just got in the way. Moira can make you like that.

The Barbary looked pretty much as usual, a jumble of cheap clothing stores for drunken sailors, dance halls where the girls were practically naked, and signs that advertised every kind of whore anybody could ever want. There was a new one this month, a mulatto who went over four hundred pounds, and a lot of Barbary regulars were giving her a try just to see what it'd be like, a lady so fat.

Half a block away you could smell the sweet hay and the sour horseshit in the rain and the night. Closer, you could hear the horses roll against their stalls, making small nervous sounds as they dreamed.

We went up a long stretch of outside stairs. The two-by-fours were new and smelled of sawn wood, tangy as autumn apples on a back porch.

Stevenson didn't knock. He just kicked the door in and stepped over the threshold. The walls inside were stained and the floors so scuffed the wood was slivery. She'd put up new red curtains that were supposed to make the shabby room a home but all the curtains did was make everything else look even older and uglier.

Moira, sad beautiful Indian child that she was, sat in a corner with her head on her knees. When she looked up, her black eyes glistened in the lantern light. She wore a deerskin dress and moccasins. The walls were covered with the lances and shields and knives and arrows of Two Eagle's tribe. He liked to smoke opium up here and tell dream-stories about ancient days when the medicine men said that the bravest warriors had horses that could fly. But the toys on the wall looked dulled and dusty and drab. Every couple of weeks he had his little group of Barbary-area Indians up here, Moira had told me once. The last stand, I'd remarked sarcastically. But she hadn't found it funny at all.

"This is crazy shit, Moira," I said. "We're gonna get you out of here before he comes back."

She had wrists and ankles so delicate they could make you cry. She stood up in her red skin, no more than ninety pounds and five feet she was, and walked over to Mr. Stevenson and said, "You don't have no goddamn right to come here, Mr. Stevenson. Or you either," she said to me. "What happens between Two Eagle and me is our business."

"You ever seen a woman who's been cut?" I said. I had. The man always took the nose, the same thing the ancient Egyptians had taken, just sawed it right off the face, so that only a dark and bloody hole was left. No brave ever wanted a woman who'd been cut, so many of the women went into the forest to live. A few even drank poison wine to end it quickly.

She looked at Mr. Stevenson. "We don't have no whiskey left."

"So the nigger goes and fetches you some, huh?" he said in his deep and bitter voice.

"I need to talk to Jimmy here, Mr. Stevenson, that's all. Just ten minutes or so."

He brought up his big murderous hands and looked at them as if he wasn't quite sure what they were.

"Rye?" he said.

She smiled and was even more beautiful. "Thanks for remembering. I'll get some money from Two Eagle and pay you back."

"I don't want any of his money," Mr. Stevenson said, and fixed her with his melancholy gaze. "I just want you."

"Oh, Mr. Stevenson," she said, and gently touched her small hand to his wide, hard chin. Sisterly, I guess you'd say. She was like that with every man but Two Eagle.

"You don't let him lay a hand on her," Mr. Stevenson said to me as he crossed the room to the door.

I brought up my Colt. "Don't worry, Mr. Stevenson."

He glanced at her one more time, sad and loving and

scared and obviously baffled by his own tumultuous feelings, and then he left.

"Poor Mr. Stevenson."

"He's a decent man," I said.

"Kinda scary, though."

"Not any more so than Two Eagle."

"I just wished he understood how I felt about Two Eagle."

"Maybe he finds it kind of hard to understand a man who kicks a woman so hard she loses the baby she's carrying—and then wants to cut her nose off."

"He didn't mean to kick me that hard. He was real sorry. He cried when he saw—the baby."

I went over to the window and looked out on the Barbary Coast. One of the local editorial writers had estimated that a man was robbed every five minutes in the Barbary. At least when it rained, it didn't smell so bad.

I turned back to her. "I want to put you on a train tonight. For Denver. There's one that leaves in an hour and a half."

"I don't want to go."

"You know what he's gonna do to you."

Her eyes suddenly filled. She padded back to her corner and sat down and put her head on her knees and wept quietly.

I went over and sat down next to her and stroked her head as she cried.

After a time she looked up, her cheeks streaky with warm tears that I wiped away with my knuckles.

"He caught me."

"It's not something I want to hear about."

"I was so mad at him—with the baby and everything— that I just went out and got drunk. Didn't even know who I was with or where I was."

"Moira, I really don't want to hear."

"So he came looking for me. Took him all night. And you know where he found me?"

I sighed. She was going to tell me anyway.

"Up in some white sailors' room. There were two of them. One of them was inside me when he came through the door and found me."

I didn't say anything. Neither did she. Not for a long time.

"You know what was funny, Jimmy?"

"What?"

"He didn't hurt either one of them. Didn't lay a hand on them. Just stood there staring at me. And the guy, well, he pulled out and picked up his clothes and got out of there real fast with his friend. It was their own room, too. That's what was real funny. By then, I was sober. I tried to cover myself up but I couldn't find my clothes, so I went over and held Two Eagle just like he was my little boy, and then he started crying. I'd never heard him cry before. It was like he didn't know how. And then I got him over to the bed and I tried to make love to him but he couldn't. And he hasn't been able to since it happened, almost a week now. He's not a man anymore. That's what he said to me. He said that he can't be a man ever again after what he saw. And it's my fault, Jimmy. It's all my fault."

I wanted to hate him, or her, or myself, I wanted to hate some goddamned body, but I couldn't. It was just sad human shit and at the moment it overwhelmed me, left me ice cold and confused. People are so goddamned confusing sometimes.

She laughed. "You and Mr. Stevenson must have some conversations about us, Jimmy."

I stood up, reached back down, and took her wrist. "C'mon now, I'm taking you to the train."

"You ain't takin' her nowhere."

A harsh, quick voice from behind me in the doorway. When I turned I was looking into Two Eagle's insane dark eyes. I'd never seen him when he didn't look angry, when he didn't look ready for blood. He wore a piece of leather tied around his head, his rough black hair touching his shoulders, his gaunt cheeks crosshatched with myriad knife slashes. His buckskin outfit gave him the kind of Indian ferocity he wanted.

He came into the room.

"Why can't you be true to our ancestors for once, Jimmy?" he said, pointing his Colt right at my head. "Cutting her is the only thing I can do. Even Moira agrees. So why should you try to stop it? It's our blood, Jimmy, our tribal way."

"I don't want you to cut her."

His hard face smiled. "You gonna stop me, Jimmy?"

He expected me to be afraid of him and I was. But that didn't mean I wouldn't shoot him if I had to.

And then Mr. Stevenson was in the doorway.

Moira made a female sound in her throat. Two Eagle followed my gaze over his shoulder to the huge black man in the doorframe.

"You're smart to have him around, Jimmy. You'll need him."

Mr. Stevenson came into the room carrying a bottle of rotgut rye in one hand and a single rose in the other. He carried the flower to Moira and gave it to her. Then, without any warning, he turned around and backhanded Two Eagle so hard the Indian's feet left the floor and he flew backwards into the wall. The entire room shook.

Mr. Stevenson wasn't going to bother with any preliminaries.

He went right for Two Eagle, who was trying to right his vision and his breathing and his ability to stand up straight. He'd struck his head hard when he'd collided with the wall and he looked disoriented. Bright red blood ran from his nostrils.

Mr. Stevenson grabbed him and it was easy to see what he was going to do. Maybe he thought that this would ultimately give him his first real chance with Moira, killing Two Eagle by snapping his neck.

"No!" I shouted.

And dove on Mr. Stevenson's back, trying to pull him off Two Eagle.

But it was no use. I clung to Mr. Stevenson like a child. I could not even budge him.

By now he had his hands in place, one on top of Two Eagle's head, the other on the bottom of his neck—ready for the single wrench that would kill Two Eagle.

Two Eagle used fists, feet, even his teeth to get free, but Mr. Stevenson paid no attention. He was setting himself to perform his most magnificent act . . .

Moira shot him once in the side and then raised the gun and shot him once on top of the head. His hair flew off, a bloody black coil of curls affixed to the wall by pieces of sticky flesh and bone.

The funny thing was, he kept right on going, as if he refused to acknowledge what Moira had done to him.

Getting ready to snap Two Eagle's neck—

And then she ran closer, shrieking, and shot him again, and this time not even Mr. Stevenson could refuse to acknowledge what had happened. Blood poured from his ears.

An enraged Two Eagle was now able to bring his hands up and seize Mr. Stevenson's throat, holding tight, choking him, as the big black fell over backwards, Two Eagle riding him down to the floor and then grabbing the gun from Moira's hand.

Two Eagle put the barrel of the .45 to Mr. Stevenson's forehead and fired three times. Didn't seem to matter to him that Mr. Stevenson had died a little while ago.

With each shot, Mr. Stevenson's head jerked upward from the coarse board floor and then slapped back down.

Two Eagle was calling him nigger and a lot of other things in our native tongue.

Then he was done, Two Eagle, pitching forward and lying facedown on the floor, very still for a long time.

I got up and straightened my clothes and picked up my gun from the floor where it had fallen when I'd jumped on Mr. Stevenson.

Moira said, "You two shouldn't have come up here."

"I guess not." I nodded to Mr. Stevenson. "He was trying to help you was all."

"It wasn't none of his business and it ain't none of yours, either."

"I guess he didn't see it that way. Seeing's he loved you and all."

"A nigger," Two Eagle said, getting up from the floor suddenly. "A nigger, lovin' Moira. Maybe you think that's all right, Jimmy, but then you give up bein' a true man a long time back."

And then he went for me. Couldn't help himself. He still had all this fury and it had to light somewhere.

Some came at me, but he was stupid because he didn't look at my hand.

I felt his powerful arm wrap around my neck. I smelled his sweat and whiskey and tobacco.

He pushed me back against the wall.

And that was when I raised my Colt and put it directly to his ribs and fired three times.

He was dead before he hit the floor.

She was screaming, Moira was. That was about all I can tell you about my last few minutes in the room. She was screaming and Two Eagle had fallen close by Mr. Stevenson and then I was running. That's about all I can remember.

Then there was the night and the rain and I was running and running and running and tripping and falling and hurting myself bad but no matter how far or how fast I ran, I could still hear Moira screaming.

◦◦◦

WEEK LATER IT WAS.

I was back doing my nightly turn at Madame Dupree's, winning upwards of five hundred dollars this particular night, when I saw Lone Deer come in the side door by the faro layout.

She looked frantic. I figured it was me she wanted.

Being's as we were waiting for some liquid refreshments at our table, I got up and went over to her.

When I reached her, she said, "She's goin', Jimmy. Leavin' us. Twenty-five minutes, her train leaves. I didn't find out till half an hour ago myself. Thought I'd better tell you."

"I appreciate it."

I suppose, like Mr. Stevenson, I'd had the idle dream that Moira and I would be lovers now that Two Eagle was gone. I didn't have to worry about any recriminations from the law getting in my way. A dead nigger and a dead Injun on the Barbary Coast don't exactly turn out a lot of curious cops. They're just two more slabs down at the morgue.

I'd figured I'd give it a few weeks and then go see her, tell her how what I did was the only thing I known to do—kill him to save my own life. And then I'd gentlelike invite her out for some dinner and . . .

But that wasn't to be. Not now.

Moira was leaving.

"You'd better hurry," Lone Deer said. And then took my arm and drew me closer. "There's something else I need to tell you."

❧

LESS THAN TWO minutes later I was running toward the depot. It was crowded and the conductor walked up and down all pompous as he consulted his railroad watch and shouted out that there were only a few minutes left before this particular train pulled out.

I found her in the very back of the last coach. The car was barely half full and she looked small and isolated there with the seats so much taller than she was. Moira. She'd always be a child.

I dropped into the seat next to her and said, "Lone Deer told me what you did."

"I wish she wouldn't have. I didn't want nobody to see me off."

"I love you, Moira."

"I don't want to hear that. Not with Two Eagle barely a week dead. Didn't I betray him enough?"

I'd seen the soldiers drag my grandfather from the reservation one day when I was very young. They were taking him to a federal penitentiary where he would die less than two months later at the hands of some angry white prisoners. I could still feel my panic that day—panic and terror and a sense that my own life was ending, too.

That's how I felt now, with Moira.

"But I won't betray him no more," Moira said. "You can bet on that."

"Is that why you did it?"

"Why I did it is none of your business."

I looked at her there in her black mourning dress and black mourning hat and black mourning veil, a veil so heavy you couldn't make out anything on the other side.

"No man'll ever want to bother me again. I made sure of that."

I was tempted to lift the veil quickly and see what she looked like. Lone Deer had said that Moira had used a butcher knife on her nose and that nothing remained but a bloody hole.

But then I decided that I didn't want to remember her that way. That I always wanted her to be young and beautiful Moira in my mind. Every man needs something to believe in, even if he knows it's not true.

"You got a ticket, buck?" the conductor asked me. Ordinarily, I'd take exception to his calling me "buck," but at the moment it just didn't seem very important.

I leaned over and kissed Moira, pressing her veil to her cheek. I still couldn't see anything.

"Hurry up, buck. You get your ass off of here or you show me a ticket."

I squeezed her hand. "I love you, Moira. And I always will."

And then I was gone, and the train was pulling out, all steam and power and majesty in the western night.

Then I walked slowly back to Madame Dupree's where I got just as drunk as Indians are supposed to get.

A Friend in Deed

Morris Hershman

I've got good reasons to think I know more than most about that particular trouble, more than almost anybody else in the county or the state itself. I'm the one who can tell you what happened when that hombre you ask about came to town and what took place while he stayed among us. If you really want to know about this, put down those greasy cards of yours and listen in.

MONROE SMALLWOOD—THAT was his handle—was riding a tawny path of land not far from a creek that had been briefly gilded after an early spring rain. No sooner had he come near a cluster of sagging willows than his animal tripped on who-knows-what and threw him. Monroe by himself could've got up and stumbled out of sight of anybody in the outskirts of town, but a careful touch of his downed roan's neck told him that the groaning beast's neck was shattered.

And in less time than it takes to tell, a good number of

townsfolk swarmed all over the area. I, myself, still re-member following the pack and listening. The stranger didn't like questions and hardly said a word.

Which was fine with the vet who hurried out. Doc Garber told him plain that the horse had to be sent, as he put it, to a better place. The stranger slowly took out his Colt Pocket pistol. He was raising the weapon at long last when Del Webster snarled and did the chore. The stranger did bury his animal, I have to say that much, but it wasn't easy for him.

So he carried his shabby Hamley saddle into the town of New Dundy, which was no different from hundreds of other towns he had passed through or lived in. When he had to, he wrote with his left hand, which the clerk of the New Dundy Hotel knew couldn't be natural to him. He scorned the form in that register book to write that his home city was Venice, Nevada. Believe that, and I've got an acre of mud I'll sell you real cheap.

Monroe Smallwood brushed the sporting ladies aside and waited in his room till the surroundings were quiet. Only then did he walk out to Commerce Street. Moseying through a clot of cicadas he passed the clothing store, the hardware emporium, the Presbyterian church, and the sa-loon. He alighted in the last of these, called—this was in the seventies—the Other Meeting Hall.

Inside, standing next to the free lunch, he brought out money enough for one beer. Asked about his plans, he said flatly that he was expecting to leave soon as he could. Without money and unable to afford a stage trip, let alone another horse, he had a problem for himself.

Which is when Del Webster, who had brusquely fin-ished off Monroe's animal and who had owned the Other, as it was known since God was in short pants, made an offer. A few careful looks at Monroe had helped him de-cide that the stranger was in decent physical condition and could be taken advantage of.

"I might hire you for a few days' work if you don't mind not gettin' much pay."

Monroe had to agree to Del Webster's brutal financial terms, but insisted on getting his money after every day. I think he liked inconveniencing Del, if only a little bit.

But he did a barman's grueling work without complaint, and handled the donkey jobs that Del had been putting off to give to some day worker. Monroe was very good at putting together anything that broke. He fixed things for a few customers, insisting on pay for those chores. Del realized that it would be bad business to hold out on Monroe's salary, even for ten minutes.

Monroe stayed on the job till Arnie Molodetsky, the one-armed barman, came back from seeing his wife through her last sickness. By that time, he had grown a mustache—which shifted attention from his thin face— what my dad called facial foliage. He wore it from then on.

It was Hector Goldthwait who saved Monroe's scrawny rump by drawing him aside on his last working afternoon. An overweight smoker who'd been wounded during the war at Piney Ridge in Arkansas, Hector and his missus owned and ran New Dundy's hardware store. Made a good thing out of it, too, everybody said.

"I'm going to need a temporary assistant till I can find somebody permanent," he told Monroe. "Have we got a deal?"

∽∾

MONROE SETTLED INTO the new job. He might not have been the world's number-one store clerk, but he could demonstrate awkward-to-use items for customers and make everything look easy. He could install some items skillfully, too. Your ma's iron wouldn't work after she'd brought it home? Bring it back to Hector, who'd send Monroe out to the house. Bet your last buffalo nickel it would be working in no time. I know because I was a goggle-eyed witness to one of those small miracles.

Hector's weakened heart gave up on him one late af-

ternoon while he was selling a paint roller to Dora Kenall.
Monroe turned Dora away, called for help, made sure that
it came quickly, and went down to the basement to locate
a dozen horse muzzles that had been sent to the hardware
store instead of the blacksmith.

It wasn't long before Del Webster was offering to buy
out the store for much less than it was worth. Dorryce
Goldthwait, Hector's spunky widow, made it clear that
she would stay as long as Monroe was willing to work
there. Monroe would have resumed his travels after a decent interval, but said he'd be only too glad to see Del
disappointed and unable to push a widow and her small
son out of their home and livelihood.

It wasn't long before Dorryce was seriously suggesting
that Del buy the business, goodwill and all.

"Sorry," he said, refusing the offer of permanence and
security. "I always did hate to tie myself down."

ⅽ◦◦ⅽ

HE REMAINED THE prime worker he had been from the
start. Dorryce was taking inventory one afternoon in October—this will give you an idea how effective Monroe
could be—when she noticed a gap on one of the lower
shelves toward the back.

"The small meat cutters are gone," she said wonder-
ingly to a relaxed Monroe. "Not even Hector could sell
those things and the wholesaler went outta business before
they could be sent back."

"I sold 'em all. Meant to tell you I'd done it."

"You can tell me *how* you did it."

"Well, I've got good reason to know from working at
The Other that some of the card players are very quick to
take advantage."

"Quick to cheat is what you mean," said Dorryce, who
looked facts in the eye.

"True enough. Well, I offered the small cutters at what
I called a sale price and told each one on the side that

they were made to slice the tips of cards when the players wanted to locate those certain cards at any time during a game."

Dorryce Goldthwait said at the time that she didn't know whether or not to laugh at Monroe's being so resourceful. "The money will be useful," she told Monroe finally. "Besides, anybody who plays cards at Del's place deserves what he gets."

Chad Goldthwait, Dorryce and Hector's son, no more than ten years old at the time, talked to Monroe very often. He was at an age (and I'll bet every man in the room remembers it!) when a fella who mentions fillies refers to horses and not some member of the fair sex.

Chad, at that time, was taking chances on animals it could be dangerous to ride. Monroe didn't offer advice, not being a believer in sticking his nose in other people's business.

A fidgety Dorryce, hurrying downstairs to the basement stockroom after Chad had gone thundering out of the store, brought up the matter. "I can't let my son take his life in both hands with horses he's too young to handle," she said, looking keenly at Monroe for a way out of this dilemma, like he'd handled so many other worries in the last months.

Monroe could've told her that she wasn't able to keep a halter on the boy. But he talked neutrally, as he nearly always did when asked about some problem about human beings.

He liked breaking rules that any self-appointed authority had set up, though, and had to force himself against advising the boy that some friend's father might lend him a horse for a free hour or so.

Chad said suddenly one afternoon to Monroe, "Del Webster took me aside yesterday and told me what I really need to know about handling bad horses and buyin' 'em cheap later on."

Do the opposite of what Webster says and you'll live a

long and happy life. Monroe was sorely tempted, for once, to offer a sliver of advice.

Chad talked a while longer before Monroe doused his cigar and went back to work. Dorryce had made it clear she didn't want that odor on her business premises, but Monroe always took a smoke as close to the store entrance as he could manage.

He happened to be smoking one afternoon just before Thanksgiving. Dorryce, who had taken time to start a holiday dinner, which Monroe eventually agreed to share, was out of sight. He heard a sharp indrawn breath through the opened kitchen window, he was sure. He doused the cigar, then made his way to the kitchen to see if anything was wrong.

He found Dorryce controlling herself while she talked to the sheriff, who at that time was Alva Pennymore, with that unshined sheriff's badge over his heart. Somebody said at Alva's funeral not long ago that he was one of those men who never hurried. The truth is that Alva could dawdle lazily when he was on the run.

It seemed, according to Pennymore's usual drawl, that Chad had borrowed a horse from Del Webster, one of those intractable beasts that Del was always buying for no money to mention in order to resell to the unwary. The boy hadn't been seen since.

Chad wasn't back in time for the big dinner. Dorryce served it for herself and Monroe, not being the one to look in a mirror and see how unhappy she was. There wasn't much talk between them, as you can imagine.

Monroe was getting ready for one last smoke outdoors before going up to bed when a cart pulled up and two hefty cow-waddies eased Chad out. The sheriff's first and only deputy told Monroe afterwards that Chad had been found at the creek bottom and just in time, because his head was already in the muddy water. The black Suffolk punch stallion, uninjured, had run off. The deputy said that if Monroe put an ear to the ground he'd be able to hear Del Webster complaining that Chad had cost him a valuable animal and he'd be expecting to be paid by Dorryce.

Doc Tiverton and his leather bag came by in minutes and the doc hurried upstairs. Monroe finished his cigar and looked in for a few minutes.

Chad seemed bandaged almost to the nostrils, with broken legs, arms to match, and trouble in several ribs that would give him hard times in the future.

Dorryce told her son determinedly that he'd feel better before too much longer. There was a grit in her voice that Monroe recognized, not to mention Chad and the doc.

"Will my boy need surgery?" she asked in Chad's hearing rather than softening blows, rather than pretending.

"I think so," Tiverton said, pulling at his Abe Lincoln beard. "I can't be certain till another day or two at the most."

"I'll pay you in time," Dorryce promised.

"I know that Hector's widow will take care of any obligations," Tiverton said easily, but with a sudden note of warning in his voice. "What he'll need after that is a schedule of exercises to be done under the supervision of an expert. There's a man in Tookaway who will work with him till he's as good as can be."

"Have you any idea—" she started.

"I can't tell you what it'll cost."

"What I meant to ask was how long my son will have to work at that."

Tiverton flushed to the tips of his ears. "I couldn't tell you that, ma'am."

What the practical Dorryce actually did later on was to hurry out to the Other Meeting Hall and talk to Del. Over the heated sounds of a poker game in progress at a round rear table, they talked. Del refused to lend money, but offered once again to buy the hardware store if Dorryce would throw in goodwill, that is, introduce the new proprietors around and say how glad she was to be leaving the business in the hands of such fine people. She refused. Del swore he'd hire some folks to open a hardware store down Commerce Street and drive Dorryce out of business, but Dorryce guessed right away that he wouldn't put up money on a gamble like that.

His current and more miserly offer for the business came to less than he wanted to put up in the past ("I'm subtracting costs of the horse that your son lost for me") and amounted to a lot less than Dorryce desperately needed.

She left without another word and went home, where she saw to Chad's immediate needs and then worked next to Monroe Smallwood.

At one point Monroe put down the insides of a clock he had been repairing for fun, and said, "Wouldn't it be fitting and proper to get the money you need out of Del Webster without giving away the place? He caused Chad's accident in the main because he wanted to tie you up so you'd have no time to take care of Chad and the store, both."

Dorryce nodded, attracted to the notion of plucking Webster in the pocketbook, where he lived, so to say.

"Would it be possible to do that?"

"To get at that weasel," Monroe said, "I'll be glad if it meant doing the foot soldier's work, but I'd need a smidge of help."

"You can have it," Dorryce said firmly.

∽◦∾

THE NEXT MORNING, a cloudy Sunday, Dorryce changed from her black clothes to the spry going-to-church outfit she favored. Downstairs, she opened the outside door on Lew Grassley, whose burly body fitted nearly all the space in front of her.

"Is Smallwood here? Oh, yes," he added as Monroe in weekday clothes came up behind his boss. "If you want to bring anything with you, Smallwood, I'll go upstairs with you while you fetch whatever it is."

"Why should I do anything you say?"

"Sheriff Pennymore wants to talk to you."

It crossed Monroe's mind to say he wasn't sure that the lazy Sheriff Alva Pennymore was energetic enough to move his jaw in talking.

Lew Grassley added, "And the sheriff ain't the only one who'll talk—not by a long sight."

Dorryce turned immediately to Monroe. "I'll come with you."

"I can't see why you should," Monroe said pointedly. "Thanks for the generous offer, though."

The sheriff's department wagon took him and Grassley out past the end of Commerce Street, where one small stone building held the local jail along with the sheriff's office. Pennymore was always ordering somebody to put duckboards in front of the place, but he wouldn't do it himself and it never got done. It took time to wipe mud off his boots when he got inside.

Pennymore, who resented coming to the office on Sunday, sat with his hands in back of his head and his feet on the desk. His unshined badge was also on the desk. His Sunday clothes hadn't developed any fresh folds because he'd moved so little.

He did open one eye resentfully as Monroe walked in before the deputy, but said nothing.

Lew Grassley did some talking. "Why did you steal the money out of Del Webster's safe early this morning?"

Isn't that one dumb question! "I had no idea somebody done that."

Del Webster, who had been making sure his horse was fed and complaining about the cost of oats, hurried importantly into the office. At sight of Monroe, the heavy but quick-moving saloon boss started to rush at him.

Lew Grassley, with a body that people said wasn't much smaller than a covered wagon, stepped in front of them. Monroe had been reaching for one of the chairs to defend himself.

"He's the one who did it, all right," Webster snarled, not pausing to wipe foam off the corners of his thick lips.

"Who else in New Dundy knows enough to open an up-to-date safe without leaving any sign it's even been touched? That devil is smooth as paint and he can work on all sorts of mechanical things."

Monroe didn't really care if Webster knew who'd been responsible, and the saloon boss had shrewdly assumed the job had got done by the only man in town who could manage it without smashing the door, at least, to bits.

"He can't prove I did anything," Monroe snapped.

"I can tell the sheriff that Vint Larrabee saw a wagon parked across from my place of business very early this morning, probably to carry a bag of money away. What's more, the initials H. G. were on both sides of it, length-wise."

"H. G. for Hector Goldthwait," said the deputy, while Pennymore repeated the letters under his breath. "That much, and his smoothness with all kinds of tools is evidence enough for anybody that he stole one week's earnings from my business."

"It's a shame the money hasn't turned up to make everything definite," Pennymore remarked, girding his energies for a massive shrug.

Webster, urged ahead by the sheriff's lackadaisical attitude, insisted, "My money has to be found."

Pennymore looked resentful.

"It's in that thief's room and you've got to get it out."

The sheriff had seen that suggestion coming. Now he pursed his lips.

Monroe put in, "I think it's a good idea, Sheriff, for you to search my room."

"If he's so anxious for you to do that, Alva Pennymore, you can bet the money isn't there," Webster snapped. "My week's receipts has to be someplace else in the house where this thief can reach it."

Which was true enough. Monroe had taken out a space in the elm flooring of the cellar, put the money in under it, and returned the wood so neatly that no one would know what he had done if that person didn't look very closely. Dorryce had helped him and she'd know where to reach money that might be needed to help Chad if Monroe himself wasn't available.

Pennymore turned his head to the deputy. "Lew, as soon as possible, you're to go to the Goldthwait store and make a careful search. Very careful, like I would do if I had the time to do it. I don't want nobody in town saying that the members of this here department don't get their job done."

Monroe, looking across at the saloon owner, who had to keep his rage muffled, found himself able to keep from grinning.

Webster asked suddenly, "And what about him? What'll you do with Smallwood in the meantime? Give him a medal or what?"

Pennymore drew himself up as much as he could while sitting, and turned away. "Lew, I want you to tellygraph Sheriff Knott in Rimson."

Webster was first to ask the question that had surged to Monroe's lips as well. "Where does the county seat come into this?"

"This here is a case of grand theft," Pennymore remarked.

"That's true enough," Webster said. "He worked his way into my saloon early this morning and stole twenty thousand dollars, my month's earnings."

Monroe almost gave himself away, knowing very well that only a little less than ten thousand dollars had been in the safe at the Other Meeting Hall.

"So it's grand theft, so Smallwood has to be tried at the county seat," Del said, and pointed toward Grassley this time instead of bothering to turn his head. "Let Knott know what happened and he'll send a deputy to pick up Smallwood. Sheriff Knott will want the job done right away, Sunday or no Sunday."

"And after the trial I hope he goes to prison for a good long time," he added after a moment.

"Prison?" Monroe, who had been enjoying the spectacle

of Del Webster's angry hatred, looked upset. "I've always lived free and had my roaming legs and a horse carry me everywhere. I don't think I'd do good in prison if I fetched up in one of those places."

It was Del Webster's turn to look satisfied.

Lew Grassley had tapped out the message on the telegraph equipment in the northeast corner of the room. The answer came only moments later, and Grassley told the sheriff what had been communicated, knowing better than to push a piece of paper under Pennymore's nose for him to take the trouble to read it.

"A deputy will be here in two hours," he said.

"Good. In the meantime, Lew, you can look over those reward posters." He pointed to the sheets on the spike in one of the empty chairs. "Find out if anybody is wanted who is the least bit like Smallwood here."

Monroe said truthfully, "He won't find nothin'."

"Do that chore, Lew," Pennymore ordered. "Sheriff Knott's deputy will want that information soon as may be."

Monroe was looking out at brass-colored clouds and wondering what it would be like to have his vital freedom taken away. He suddenly spun around to see Dorryce Goldthwait hurry into this room, determination written plainly on her strong features.

"Sheriff, there's something you have to know," she began.

"It's already been decided 'round here that I'm guilty," Monroe said quickly before she could take some of the blame on her sturdy shoulders. She might have admitted that she'd been the lookout for Monroe during the safe robbery and had promptly hidden herself when Vint Larrabee started to walk along Commerce Street. "I'm going on trial in the county seat and if I'm found guilty I'll be sent away."

As he was talking he looked pointedly in Dorryce's direction. She had stared, then gasped. Only when he winked did she understand that the man who was so good

at handling all sorts of objects wasn't going to be detained
for long against his will. He'd be able to open a lock in
any tin can he might be put into.

And then he'd resume his wanderings. No matter what
the law might try to do, Monroe Smallwood was forever
going to remain a free man. As Dorryce herself remarked
some years afterwards, a little sadly, Monroe Smallwood's
freedom was the man himself.

Assassin

∽○∽

Frank Gruber

THE TRAIN SCREECHED to a stop and Billy Mason swung up to the engine platform. He thrust his Frontier Model Colt into the face of the engineer and said, "Throw up your hands!"

Dick Small, a moment late as usual, came up from the other side and covered the fireman. "And damn quick about it!" he snarled.

The fireman's teeth chattered, but the engineer was made of sterner stuff. He raised his hands slowly. A scowl twisted his face.

He looked from Dick Small to Billy Mason and asked, "Which one of you is Jess Carney?"

Dick Small swore and struck at the engineer with the long barrel of his Colt.

Billy Mason struck out with his left hand and knocked the gun down. "Cut it!" he snapped. "You know the orders."

From the direction of the express car, a voice roared, "Open up, or we'll blow it open."

A gun roared; another. A man screamed in pain. Dick Small's face showed fright.

"Easy," Billy Mason cautioned.

The sharp, spiteful crack of a rifle was followed by a half-dozen duller reports, then Jess Carney's triumphant voice rang out: "All right, Sam!"

Billy Mason knew Jess was talking to Charley Ford, who was using the name of Sam, according to pre-arrangement. Billy knew, too, that the ring in Jess's tone indicated that the express messenger had surrendered.

Boots clattered alongside the engine and Billy risked a glance to the side. He saw the bearded face of Jess Carney and nodded.

"Another minute!" Jess said.

Charley Ford appeared carrying a half-filled wheat sack. "All right, Tom," he said to Jess.

Jess Carney cried out, "You, engineer, start up. And if you stop inside of a mile I'll blow your head off."

The engineer said sullenly, "Which one of you is Jess Carney?"

Jess Carney snarled. "You think Jess Carney's the only man who can stick up a train?"

Billy Mason clambered down from the cab. Behind him came Dick Small. They lined up beside Jess and Charley Ford.

"Get going!" Jess ordered.

Steam hissed and the wheels of the engine began moving. The four bandits waited until the engine had gone perhaps fifty feet, then, as if by a signal, they turned and plunged into the thick brush that lined the roadway.

"Tom!" a voice called softly from ahead of them.

"All right," Jess replied.

They found Ed Mitchell already mounted on his horse, holding the reins of the other four. The men mounted swiftly and headed their horses in a northerly direction.

"Whew!" Ed Mitchell exclaimed in relief. "When I heard that shootin' I thought sure—"

"You think too much!" snapped Jess Carney. "I told you nothing would happen."

Ed Mitchell subsided, but after a moment Billy Mason asked quietly, "What happened, Jess?"

Jess Carney turned his head in the gloom. Billy could not see his features, but he sensed that the outlaw chief was trying to see his expression.

Finally Jess said, "The conductor opened on us with a rifle."

He did not add, "So I killed him," but Billy Mason knew that. When Jess Carney fired, he shot to kill. He had always done so. He was a killer by instinct.

Billy Mason had never killed a man, but now the stigma was on him. He was tarred with the same brush that had blackened Jess Carney these many years. If he was captured he would receive the same treatment as Jess Carney.

Well, he had thought of all that before he had thrown in with Jess Carney. He had weighed everything and made his choice. Yet he had not thought it would feel—like this!

They came to a small stream and halted. "In a couple of hours everybody in fifty miles is going to be on the lookout for four or five men. I think we'd better break up here and meet again later on."

"Sure," said Dick Small, "but let's divvy up first."

"Why?" Jess Carney asked softly.

"Because—" Dick Small stopped short. He cleared his throat. "No reason at all."

"Anybody else wanta divvy now?" Carney went on.

"Whenever you say the word, Jess," Charley Ford said quickly.

Jess Carney snorted. "All right then, we'll split here. Billy, you come with me. The rest of you go east. We'll meet tomorrow night at your place, Charley. And now, remember—don't take any chances. I mean that particularly for you, Ed—don't get drunk!"

Jess Carney waited until the three men had gone off before he fell in beside Billy Mason. He said then, "Why

I ever picked up a bunch of fellows like that, I don't
know."

"Don't you think it went all right?" Billy Mason asked.

Jess Carney snorted. "The conductor killed and the express messenger wounded. Hell, there'll be plenty of noise
over that. But you're all right, Billy, I was watching you.
You were a lot cooler than Dick Small or Charley Ford."

Billy Mason said nothing.

Jess Carney peered at him and asked, "Well, how do
you like it?"

"I don't know," Billy Mason said truthfully. "I hadn't
counted on anyone being killed."

"It couldn't be helped. With Charley, Ed, and Dick so
jittery, they got me nervous." He sighed wearily. "If I only
had a bunch like we had in 'seventy-six—Frank, Cole,
Clell. Well, let's go on."

'Seventy six, Billy thought. Yet that was the year the
powerful Carney Federation had suffered its severest de-
feat. Eight of them, probably the outstanding outlaws of
the day, they had descended upon Northport in Minnesota.
Three had died and three had remained there, behind
bleak, dank walls. Only two of the eight, Frank and Jess
Carney, had escaped.

And now Frank Carney, in poor health, had gone into
retirement and Jess Carney had gathered about him a new
band, an inferior one, he said. It was the second job for
Dick Small, Ed Mitchell, and Charley Ford, the first for
Billy Mason. A hefty wheat sack on Jess's saddle was the
result. And one man dead, another wounded.

They would howl about that; the newspapers and the
law-enforcement bodies. Jess Carney, the terror of the
countryside, outlaw and killer. He must be exterminated.

Billy Mason was riding with Jess Carney now. He had
crossed his Rubicon, headed up the road from which there
is no turning back. He was an outlaw, a member of the
notorious Carney gang.

They rode through the woods and came out upon a
narrow country road. Ahead and to the right, a tiny square

of light showed in a larger rectangle of blackness. A dog barked.

"Easy, Billy," Jess Carney said quietly. But Billy Mason was not skittish. He had been cooler than Charley Ford and Dick Small back there on the train. Jess Carney himself had said that.

He rode beside Jess and said, "Do you suppose it's really safe to go back there to Ford's place?"

"It's as safe as anywhere" was Carney's reply. "The Fords have a bad reputation in their own neighborhood and people let them pretty much alone. They've got the local law bluffed."

"But what about the Wilkinsons?"

Jess Carney snorted. "Since 1875 Mr. William hasn't stepped out of his house in Chicago without a couple of bodyguards. He's afraid I'll get him. He does a lot of hollering but he does it at a distance. Shucks, Billy, I've been at this a long time. A long time."

He shook his head and went on: "I never really came in. I went out in 'sixty-three and this is 'eighty-two. Nineteen years and I'm only thirty-four now." He laughed harshly.

There were questions in Billy Mason's mind. He wanted to ask, Do the faces of the men you've killed ever haunt you in your dreams? Do you ever wish you could look at a policeman and not be afraid? Don't you ever— ever yearn for peace?

Billy wanted to ask those questions, but he didn't. Because he was riding beside Jess Carney, now. And soon he would learn the answers himself.

Morning. A golden sun creeping up over the freshly plowed farmlands. Smoke coming lazily from a chimney; a rooster crowing.

Jess Carney said, "Milltown's just ahead, but we'd better get some breakfast here."

"Here?"

"Why not? They don't know us. We are stock buyers.

This sack"—he slapped it—"might contain grain for our horses."

They had thrown their linen dusters away during the night. They were now wearing broadcloth suits, with rather long coats, sufficiently long to conceal the pistols strapped about their waists. Many men dressed like this. Jess Carney was tall and slender. His beard, neatly trimmed, gave him a dignified appearance. Some might even mistake him for a minister. Certainly he didn't look like Jess Carney.

Jess Carney was a hulking, beetle-browed man with a ferocious black beard and blazing black eyes. Women and children quailed when he looked at them, strong men trembled. That's what people said.

They rode into the farmyard.

"Hello!" Jess called.

A man carrying a milk pail came out of the log barn. "Morning, strangers," he said cheerfully.

"Good morning, sir!" Jess Carney replied heartily. "We were just riding by and we wondered if we could beg a bite of breakfast."

"Why, certainly," the farmer replied. "I imagine Florence is just about settin' the table. Light, won't you?"

Jess Carney swung easily to the ground. Billy Mason dismounted rather stiffly. He turned toward the door of the house—and stopped.

A girl had come out, a tall slender girl with chestnut-colored hair. She wore a gingham dress, and there was flour on her bare forearms and a spot of it on the tip of her nose, but her features were finely chiseled, her complexion smooth and fresh. Her eyes smiled a welcome.

"I've just taken the biscuits out of the oven," she said. "Won't you come in?"

"We certainly will," said Jess Carney. "Allow me to introduce my assistant, Billy Mason. My own name's Tom Howard."

"Howdy, Mr. Howard," said the farmer, "and Mr. Mason. I'm Jim King and this is my daughter, Florence. Traveling men, aren't you?"

"Something of the sort," Jess Carney shot a quick glance toward the small log barn, then added, "I'm a stock buyer. You haven't got fifteen or twenty good head you want to sell, have you?"

"Gosh, no!" exclaimed Jim King. "I've got two cows, that's all."

They went into the house and sat down at the table in the kitchen. Florence King set out plates, poured coffee, and brought crisp bacon, eggs, and fresh biscuits.

"Pitch in, gentlemen," said Jim King.

Jess Carney reached for the plate of biscuits, took one, and passed them to Billy Mason. Billy took a biscuit and broke it to apply butter.

Jim King said, "Heard about the holdup?"

Billy Mason's teeth closed on the biscuit. A ripple ran up his spine, paralyzed him. Then Jess Carney's matter-of-fact voice broke the spell. "What holdup?"

"Train holdup, over near Black Cut, last night. Jess Carney's gang."

"Doggone!" exclaimed Jess Carney. "So he's done it again. I don't see how he gets away with it."

"Neither do I," replied Jim King. "Except that everyone's so scared of him, they don't even chase him much. Paul Potter was by here a half-hour ago. He told me about it. Carney got $50,000 out of the express car and the whole train crew was afraid to go after him."

"Fifty thousand!" exclaimed Jess Carney. "That is somethin'. Almost makes a fellow want to turn train robber, doesn't it?"

From near the stove, the voice of Florence King said crisply, "Why should it?"

Jess Carney turned. "Fifty thousand dollars is a lot more'n most people make in a lifetime of hard work."

"That's true," conceded Florence King. "But I don't imagine Jess Carney gets much enjoyment out of his

money. He can't lie down in a bed at night and know that
he'll still be in that bed in the morning."

"Why not? Your dad himself said folks are so scared
of him they don't even dare go near him."

Florence King came a step closer to the table. "But
what about his own men? Can Jess Carney trust them?
With the huge reward the governor's placed on Carney's
head, can Jess Carney go close his eyes at night and be
sure that one of his own men won't creep up on him and
send a bullet through his head?"

The light went out of Jess Carney's eyes. Billy Mason,
sitting across from him saw that. He saw, too, the slight
twitching of the muscles about the mouth, and he guessed
suddenly that sheer nerve was carrying Jess through these
days. The chase had been too hard, too long for Jess Carney. He was scared stiff—and as dangerous as death.

Billy said quickly, "I imagine Jess has made pretty sure
of his men."

"Has he? No man can trust his best friend—if there's
a huge premium for treachery."

Jess Carney laughed. Was there a slight touch of nerv-
ousness in his laughter? "Well, we don't have to worry
about Jess Carney, do we? These biscuits are mighty fine,
Miss King. Wish I could eat more of them."

He wiped his mouth on the damask napkin, pushed
back his chair. "Thanks, folks. I guess me and Billy have
got to be riding on." He tossed a silver dollar on the table.
"Thanks, folks!"

Florence King came over, picked up the dollar, and
handed it back to Jess. "Sorry, Mr. Howard. We're not
running a hotel."

Jess Carney bowed. He started for the door. Billy Mason followed. At the door he turned.

"Thanks, Miss King—for the breakfast."

She smiled at him. "You're entirely welcome."

He hesitated. "Perhaps we'll be riding back this way in
a couple of days." He knew he shouldn't have said it the
moment the words were out of his mouth. He was Billy

Mason, a member of Jess Carney's gang. A girl like Florence King must always be a stranger to Billy Mason.

But she said, "Stop in and say hello when you come back."

They rode until shortly before noon, when they entered a grove of poplars by a small stream. Jess dismounted and tied his horse to a sapling.

"We'll lay low here until dark."

Billy climbed from his horse and tethered it securely. Then he sat down on the bank of the stream and looked into the water.

"Better get some sleep, Billy," Jess said kindly.

"How about yourself?"

Jess shrugged. "Not sleepy. I'll sit up—and keep watch."

Was he thinking of what Florence King had said? That he couldn't close his eyes even in the presence of his closest friends—

Billy Mason dropped back. He moved his hat so it shaded his eyes. He tried to sleep but sleep wouldn't come. He was relaxed, but deep down in him a bell seemed to be tolling slowly.

Some time later, Jess Carney's voice asked softly, "Sleeping, Billy?"

"No," Billy replied.

"Thinkin'?"

"Yes."

"That you shouldn't have done it?"

Billy sat up. "No, of course not. I knew what I was getting into and I'm not sorry. I'd do it again."

Jess Carney was silent for a moment. Then he said, "How old are you, Billy?"

"Twenty-three. Why?"

"Just thinkin'. When I was twenty-three every sheriff in six states was lookin' for me. Lord, that was a long time ago. Eleven years. Sometimes it seems like fifty. I think I'll quit and go to California."

Billy Mason looked at him sharply. Jess Carney grinned.

"Don't worry, I went to California once before. I didn't stay very long. But I wish Frank'd come back. He was much better at this thinkin' business. He'd figure out a job and we'd pull it without any fuss. Then we'd go somewhere and have a good time."

"But you're married, Jess. What does Mrs. Carney think about it?"

Jess Carney's eyes blinked. "She doesn't say anything—anymore."

Billy Mason dropped back to the grass.

Shortly before sundown they started again. They rode for three or four hours, then Jess halted.

"One shade is up, one down. That means it's all right."

Billy Mason stared at the chink of light ahead of them. "They're here—?"

Carney nodded. "Yep! Now for the squabblin'."

They rode up to the house and Jess whistled. Instantly a door was jerked open and a woman looked out.

"Maggie?" Jess asked.

The woman disappeared and a tall youth appeared in her place. "Jess!" he exclaimed and came out.

"Hi, Bob," Jess said. He turned to Billy Mason. "Shake hands with Bob Ford, Billy. Charley's younger brother. Bob, this is Billy Mason."

Billy swung down from his gelding and Bob Ford's lean hand gripped his own. There was strength in the boy's grip. Billy looked into Bob's eager face. "Howdy, Bob," he said.

"Sure glad to know you, Billy," Bob Ford replied. "The boys were telling me about you."

"Put the horses away, will you, Bob?" Jess Carney asked.

He went into the house and Billy Mason followed. There were five persons in the room into which they entered, four men and the woman Jess had called Maggie.

Charley Ford introduced a vicious-looking man of about fifty. "The old man, Billy. Call him Cap."

"And my wife," Dick Small said, nodding to Maggie.

Billy Mason turned to Maggie Small. He did not even make a mental comparison between Maggie and Florence King.

Jess Carney tossed the wheat sack on a bare table. "There she is, boys!"

Ed Mitchell reached avidly for the sack. Jess Carney lashed out with his fist and knocked Mitchell back. "I'll do the divvying!" he snapped.

Ed Mitchell's eyes glistened. "Some day—" he muttered.

Jess Carney caught hold of Ed's shirt. "What's that?"

"Nothin', Jess, nothin' at all!" Ed Mitchell exclaimed.

Jess released Ed and sniffed contemptuously. Then he upended the wheat sack upon the table. Exclamations of awe and delight went up. Billy Mason saw that young Bob Ford had come in. His eyes were shining as they took in the money on the table.

"Fifty thousand!" exclaimed Charley Ford.

Jess Carney snorted. "We'll be lucky if there's half of that."

"What do you mean?" cried Dick Small.

"You know damn well they always exaggerate the amount we get. If the papers say fifty thousand my guess is twenty thousand."

Ed Mitchell's eyes blazed. "That's what you say, Jess. There'd better be fifty thousand here, or—"

"Or what?"

Jess's words were toneless. His hands remained on the table. But Ed Mitchell looked into Jess's eyes and wet his lips.

"Nothin', Jess. I was just saying those newspapers lie like hell."

Jess Carney stacked the money on the table. His strong, lean fingers counted it swiftly. When he finished, he said,

"They didn't lie so much this time. There's thirty-eight thousand. That's seven thousand apiece."

"Seven times five is thirty-five," said Bob Ford.

Jess Carney straightened. He looked at Bob Ford, then at Charley Ford. "Your kid brother's good at arithmetic."

"I'll crack his teeth in if he don't keep his mouth shut," snarled Charley Ford. He took a step toward his younger brother. But Bob did not retreat.

"Try it some time, Charley," he said. "I'm taller'n you and—"

"Shet yore mouth, Bob!" said old Cap Ford.

"The extra three thousand goes to someone," Jess Carney said. "I told you boys about that. How do you think we know when there's money on a train?"

Bob Ford's eyes glowed. "Say, that's clever. I didn't know that—"

"Shut up, Bob," said Charley Ford.

"What for? I may as well talk now. Jess, I want to join up with you."

Jess Carney cocked his head to one side. "How old are you?"

"Twenty. That's more'n you were when you started."

"Maybe so, but it's too young—these days. Better wait awhile, Bob."

"What for?" demanded Bob Ford. He jabbed a finger at Billy Mason. "He ain't much older'n me. And I bet I can shoot better'n him."

"Can you now, Bob?" asked Jess Carney, showing his teeth. "Billy's the best man in the outfit—after me."

Instantly, Billy felt the hostile eyes of Ed Mitchell, Dick Small, and Charley Ford. Jess did not seem to notice. He divided stacks of bills.

"There you are, fellows. If you're smart you won't spend it all right away. One of these times—"

"When we spend it there's more where this came from," chuckled Dick Small.

Old Cap Ford went to a cupboard and brought out a

bottle and a pack of greasy playing cards. "How about some fun now, boys?"

Ed Mitchell grabbed the bottle and took a healthy swig. "That hits the spot," he said, smacking his lips.

Dick Small was already shuffling the cards. He did it dexterously. "All right, boys, ante up!"

Jess Carney put a hand to his mouth and yawned. "Count me out. I'm goin' to get some sleep."

"I think I will, too," Billy Mason said.

Jess Carney frowned. "Cap'll fix you up with a bed."

"Yep, you c'n use mine," Old Cap volunteered. He gestured toward a cot on one side of the room. Billy Mason looked at the dirty horse blanket that covered the cot.

"You'll need it yourself, Cap," Billy said.

"Naw, I'll prob'ly stay up and play poker with the boys."

Billy regarded the bed with disfavor. "I'd just as soon sleep out in your hayloft—" he began.

Jess Carney cut in, "No, you stay in here." But he moved to the door himself and went out abruptly.

Dick Small dealt cards, then said, "What's the matter with Jess? He afraid to sleep in the same house with us?"

Ed Mitchell sneered. "Maybe we're not good enough to sleep with. On'y good enough to do the dirty work."

"You know that's not so," Billy Mason said quickly.

Ed Mitchell banged his fist on the table. "You callin' me a liar, squirt?"

Billy Mason's hands dropped loosely to his sides. "If you want to take it up—yes," he replied softly.

Ed Mitchell pushed back his chair. Beside him, Charley Ford caught his arm.

"Cut it, Ed. He—he might be outside, listening."

Ed Mitchell's nostrils flared. "All right, Mason—but I'll remember that."

"I don't care if you do," retorted Billy. He walked to Cap Ford's smelly cot and dropped down on it.

But he did not sleep. The others played cards. They bickered and argued. Dick Small's wife wanted him to

stop drinking and he cursed her furiously. Ed Mitchell
picked a quarrel with Dick Small and Charley Ford again
had to intercede to prevent a fight. Then both Mitchell
and Small turned on Charley and it took the combined
efforts of the three Fords to quiet them.

Billy Mason did not sleep. He stretched out on the cot,
his eyes closed. Jess Carney was outside, probably sleeping in the woods. It was true, what Florence King had
said. Jess Carney could not close his eyes in the presence
of his own men. He could not trust them because the State
of Missouri had offered so much money for his body—
dead or alive—that he was afraid one of his men would
make a try for the reward. For the reward and amnesty.

The gambling and drinking continued through the
night. When the lamps were no longer necessary in the
room, Jess Carney came in. Billy Mason looked at his
face and thought that it was drawn. The eyes, he knew,
were bloodshot.

He looked around the room and said, "Dick, get your
wife to make some breakfast. I want to get going."

"Where to?"

"Clay County, first, then home. My advice to the rest
of you is not to hang around here. Scatter and lay low for
a month or so. I'll get in touch with you if I figure out
anything new." He turned to Billy Mason. "What are you
goin' to do, Billy?"

Billy shrugged. "I haven't made any plans. I might run
over to St. Louis for a while."

"Oh, then you won't be coming my way?"

"I will, Jess," said Charley Ford. "I want to see a lady
over near Independence."

"All right, Charley."

Maggie Small cooked breakfast and served it grudg-
ingly. All the men ate, then Jess Carney got up from the
table and nodded. "I'll be seeing you, fellows."

He and Charley Ford went out. Bob Ford followed. Ed
Mitchell glared at the closed door. "He'll be seeing us!"

Dick Small shook his head. "He's gettin' mighty skittish."

"Don't blame him," rumbled old Cap Ford. "Ten thousand dollars is a mighty powerful bunch of money."

Bob Ford came in. His lean face was dark with anger.

"What's the matter, bud?" sneered Ed Mitchell. "Did he tell you you was still wet behind the ears?"

Bob Ford looked coldly at the outlaw. Billy Mason stepped to the door and went outside. There was a heavy dew on the grass and a nip in the air. He shivered.

He looked at the tumbledown log barn and littered, unkempt yard, then turned and regarded the exterior of the house, which he hadn't seen during the day. He sighed and shook his head. The Fords were a disreputable lot, he thought.

He walked through the wet grass to the barn and found his horse inside, his saddle tossed on the floor. He found a bin of oats and gave the gelding a half-measure, while he curried it. Then he saddled up and led the horse out to the yard.

Angry voices reached his ears. He frowned and wondered if it wouldn't be best just to leave without saying a word. But after a moment he shrugged and entered the house.

Dick Small and Ed Mitchell were facing each other in the middle of the room, their faces distorted with anger. Cap Ford and Maggie Small had gone to another room, but young Bob Ford stood to one side, watching the proceedings with a brooding look on his face.

Billy Mason inhaled sharply. "Cut it, fellows," he said sharply. "First thing you know you're going to get into a fight."

"This is a fight!" snarled Ed Mitchell.

"Reach for your gun—if you've got the nerve!" invited Dick Small.

Billy Mason took a step forward. Then he leaped back.

Small and Mitchell had gone for their guns. Mitchell's was out first; it thundered and Dick Small staggered, but then he was firing. The room shook to the deafening explosions.

Billy whipped out his gun, yelled. "Stop or—!"

And then Ed Mitchell pitched to the floor. Dick Small, his left hand clutching his thigh, hobbled forward. "I got him!" he exulted.

Maggie Small bounced into the room, saw Ed Mitchell on the floor and screamed.

Dick Small turned toward Billy Mason, saw the Frontier Model in Billy's hand and hissed, "You sidin' with him?"

"No," replied Billy thickly. He felt suddenly sick with revulsion.

"He had it comin' to him," Dick Small said. "Didn't he, Bob?"

Bob Ford said evenly, "I guess he did, Dick. He wanted a fight and he got it. You hurt much, Dick?"

Dick Small looked down at the trickle of blood on his trouser leg. "Nah, just a scratch. I can hardly feel it." He lifted his head suddenly. "He drew first on me. Remember that!"

"What difference does it make?" asked Billy.

"It makes a helluva lot of diff'rence, if you was figurin' on tellin' Jess about it."

Billy moved to the door. "You tell him about it." He stepped outside, mounted his horse and rode away.

∽⌒∾

CALLING AT GENERAL Delivery in St. Louis for a letter, Billy Mason found one addressed to James Latimer. He tore it open and read:

Dear Jim:

I was talking to Tom Howard the other day and he told me you were looking for a job. Jack Ladd is looking for a man. The pay is good, I understand,

*and the work not too hard. Why don't you go and
see Jack Ladd? Best wishes*

—John

Decoded, the message was to the effect that Jess Carney
had planned another holdup and that he wanted Billy Mason to come to a certain place in Clay County, Missouri.

Billy took the train to Kansas City the same evening.
Arriving at Kansas City in the morning, he bought a horse
and saddle and started eastward. This was familiar country
to him; his own home was not far from here. It was also
Jess Carney's country.

Jess had been born and raised twenty miles from here.
During the war he had skirmished through the entire section, as a guerilla under Quantrell. Even today, hunted
though he was, Jess Carney could always find shelter in
Jackson and Clay counties.

Before he was an hour out of Kansas City, Billy Mason
knew that the grapevine telegraph was reporting the presence of a horseman, riding eastward. His description was
going ahead of him and somewhere along the line someone would identify him as Billy Mason, whose family
lived in Clay County. That he was a member of Jess Carney's gang was not generally known.

He reached Liberty around noon, had a substantial
lunch in a restaurant, and took the northeast road out of
town. A mile, and Billy saw a horseman awaiting him
beside the road. It was Charley Ford.

"Hi, Billy," Charley greeted as he fell in beside Billy.

"Hello, Charley, what's new?"

"Nebraska, I think, although he hasn't made up his
mind definitely. He mentioned Butte, Montana, too, but
that's too far from here. None of us would know our way
around."

"He's here?"

Charley nodded. "He was at his brother-in-law's with
me, last night. Don't know where he'll be tonight. You

know, he never sleeps twice in the same place." He shook his head and shot a covert look at Billy. "He doesn't know about Ed Mitchell."

"How do you know?"

"Bob told me. He told me something else. That Dick Small's scared stiff Jess will find out he killed Ed and kill him. You think it'd be best to tell him?"

"I'm not a squealer, if that's what you mean," Billy replied shortly.

"I didn't mean anything of the kind," retorted Charley. "Only the kid's here and he was there when it happened."

"Bob's here?"

"Yes, Jess may let him come with us on the next job. Especially if one of the others doesn't show up—and Ed won't, of course."

They reached the little country village of Centerville after a while, but rode directly through it. People saw them, but gave no sign of recognition or salutation. That wasn't the custom around Centerville. You nodded at a stranger and he might turn out to be a Wilkinson man— or one of the "boys." Either way, it didn't do you any good.

Three miles out of Centerville, Charley turned in at a lane leading to a house almost out of sight of the road. "This is Hill's place; his sister's married to Jess's step-brother."

A man sat on the doorstep, whittling. He got up when Charley Ford and Billy dismounted.

"Shake hands with Billy Mason, Bud," Charley introduced.

Bud Hill held out a limp hand. "Harya!" He turned and yelled, "Donny! C'mon out here and put these horses away."

A barefooted boy of about twelve popped out of the house.

"I'll take care of my horse," Bill Mason said. He turned—and stopped.

Bob Ford and Jess Carney came out of the woods at

the side of the house. "I see you got my letter," Jess said. He jerked his head to the trees and Charley Ford and Billy Mason followed him. After a moment Bob Ford came along. Jess did not order him back.

"I've got something good figured out," Jess announced. "Soon's Dick and Ed get here we'll start out. Unless I've got a bum steer, it'll make Black Cut look like small potatoes."

"Say, that'll be swell!" exclaimed Bob Ford.

Jess Carney frowned. "I haven't said yet I'd let you come along, Bob."

"But if one of the others don't show up?"

"They'll show up," Jess said confidently.

But Billy Mason knew that Ed Mitchell would not show up. Bob and Charley Ford knew that, too. The two brothers looked at one another uneasily.

Jess Carney said, "Charley, you come with me. The two young fellows can stay with Bud tonight."

Billy would have preferred to go with Jess, but the outlaw chief had not asked him. He turned back to the house, with Bob Ford.

The moment Jess Carney was out of sight, Bob Ford caught hold of Billy Mason's arm. "There's a dance up here at the schoolhouse tonight, Billy. Let's me and you go."

"I've been ridin' all day," Billy said. "I don't feel much like dancing."

"Aw, the exercise will do you good."

"Perhaps—but I don't think we ought to appear in a public place. Someone might—"

Bob Ford snickered. "Around here? Hell, half the people are related to Jess. And the rest'd be scared to open their mouths. Jess goes to these places himself, when he feels like it. Besides—" Bob Ford winked at Billy, "if I'm goin' to be one of the gang, we ought to get acquainted."

Billy Mason had no heart for music and laughter, but perhaps the gaiety of a country dance was just what he needed. It might relieve for a few hours the black oppressiveness that had been with him for days, since—yes, since he'd turned up the road.

He shrugged. "All right, we'll go to that dance."

The Hills were going, too, it seemed. Supper was early and immediately afterward there was a general washing, scrubbing, and dressing. Bud and Mrs. Hill and the three young Hills were all eager for the dance.

When they were ready, Bud Hill caught Billy's eye and walked to one side. "They usually leave their guns at home when they go to the dance. But if you don't want to do that, there's a woodpile behind the schoolhouse where you can stash your'n. Tell Bob."

The schoolhouse was only a mile from the Hill home and they all walked there. Before they reached it, they could hear the wail of a fiddle.

Billy drew Bob to one side and led him behind the schoolhouse. "Bud said to hide our guns in the woodpile."

Bob Ford looked toward the schoolhouse. "But suppose someone in there should try something?"

"If you think there's a chance of that, we'd better not go in."

Bob shrugged. Then he opened his coat and unbuckled a belt from about his waist. He rolled it around a long-barreled Frontier Model Colt and stuck the whole thing deep into the woodpile. Billy did the same with his own Colt.

Then they went to the front door of the schoolhouse where the dance was being held. The little room was crowded with thirty or forty men, women, and children. The desks and benches had been cleared to the sides and a number of couples were dancing to the music of a single fiddle.

They entered. And the first person Billy Mason saw was Florence King. She was standing on the side talking with another girl. When she saw Billy Mason her eyes opened wide and her nostrils flared a little.

Beside Billy, Bob Ford said, "There's a couple of good-looking girls. Let's ask them to dance with us."

Billy walked steadily toward Florence King. When he reached her he stopped and said, "Hello."

For a moment she just stared at him. Then she said in a voice that was strained. "You—"

"Will you dance with me?"

She hesitated, then nodded suddenly. He put his arm about her and moved to the center of the floor.

"I hadn't expected to see you here," he said.

She replied, "Who are you?"

"Billy Mason."

"But that boy you came in with—that's Bob Ford."

"You know him?"

"Yes, of course. You see, I'm visiting my uncle. I've been here before and I've met the Fords. But you—"

"My name is still Billy Mason."

"That man who was with you the other day. He's—"

"I'm sorry," Billy cut in, "but he told me his name was Tom Howard."

She stiffened. He felt it and turned cold inside. She tried to draw her hand away from his.

"Do you mind—?"

"I do," he said quickly. "Won't you step outside a moment?"

"No." But she let him lead her to the door and did not hold back there. He took her beyond hearing, into the shelter of a big oak tree. Her face was just a blur and he hoped she could not see his own distinctly.

He said, "You mustn't get the wrong ideas—"

"I haven't. But I remember now. Both of you were so interested in the Black Cut robbery and there was a wheat sack on his horse. The papers said—"

"No," he cut her off quickly.

In the gloom she laid her hand on his arm. "Look at me and tell me you're not a member of Jess Carney's gang. Tell me the man with you that day was not Jess Carney—or one of his men. Tell me that."

He couldn't tell her that. He couldn't say anything. And his silence told her the answer.

She inhaled slowly. "I must go inside."

"Florence—" he began and there he stopped. There wasn't anything he could say to her. Because he had ridden up the road with Jess Carney. He could never say anything to Florence King. The conductor who had died at Black Cut stood between him and this girl.

Yet he followed her to the schoolhouse. And at the door a hulking man who had inbibed too freely of corn whiskey grabbed his arm and snarled:

"What's the idea takin' Flo outside?"

"Walter!" Florence King exclaimed. "Come inside."

"I will, after I teach this squirt where he gets off foolin' around with my girl."

Billy hit the big man then—hit him squarely in the mouth with all the strength in his powerful shoulders. The man reeled back, hit the door jamb, and recoiled. Billy Mason smashed him again. Behind Billy a man yelped and hit him back of the ear. Another of Walter's friends lashed at him from the side.

"Fight!" someone roared.

Billy Mason took a stiff punch in his stomach, then lowered his head, and swung with both fists. They landed satisfyingly.

Bob Ford leaped through the door of the schoolhouse. "I'm here, Billy!" he cried.

One of Walter's friends smashed Bob in the face and the stripling fell forward. A terrific blow landed on Billy Mason's right ear and he bared his teeth. Walter and his two friends closed in on him. It was a tight spot for Billy Mason.

And then Jess Carney's voice rang out, cold and hard: "Stop that!"

The attackers fell back. Billy Mason looked up and saw Jess Carney standing a few feet away, in the light cast by the open doorway. There was no gun visible on him. Perhaps these men didn't even know him by sight—but they could recognize the glaring eyes and the grim face and the timbre of the voice.

None said a word, but Billy Mason caught a glimpse of Walter's face and saw that it was slack and sickly-looking.

"What's going on here?" Jess Carney demanded.

"Just a little fight," mumbled one of the men.

Bob Ford climbed to his feet, cursing. "Who's the fool that hit me?"

"Shut up, Bob!" snapped Jess Carney. "The fight's over."

The men who had attacked Billy Mason plunged into the schoolhouse. A woman's face appeared in the doorway for an instant, then was jerked back. Jess Carney was alone outside, with Bob Ford and Billy Mason.

"Come over here," Jess said, jerking his head toward the gloom.

The two followed. When they were under the tree where Billy had spoken with Florence only a few minutes ago, Jess said:

"Dick Small's given himself up!"

Billy Mason gasped. "Surrendered?"

"Bob, where is Ed Mitchell?"

Bob Ford stammered. "Ed? Why—why, I don't—"

"Don't lie!"

Billy Mason said, "He's dead, Jess."

Then Bob Ford burst into a torrent of words. "After you left the other day, Dick and Ed got into a fight. Ed drew on Dick and Dick killed him. He was afraid to tell you. I guess—I guess that's why he gave himself up."

"Yes?" snarled Jess Carney. "Or because he expects to get a reward for snitching?"

"I don't know, Jess, honest I don't!" Bob Ford exclaimed. "He left the same morning. I haven't seen him since. Neither has Charley, I know."

Jess turned to Billy. "Why didn't you tell me about Ed?"

"Because I don't play the game that way, Jess."

Jess was silent for a moment, then he said bitterly, "What a bunch of chicken thieves I've picked for men."

Billy said stiffly, "All right, if—"

Jess Carney made a savage gesture in the gloom. "Not you, Billy. You're the only man I've got any faith in. Ed and Dick and—" he hesitated—"that yellowbelly, Dick Small. He'll talk his guts to Wilkinson. We've got to clear out of here."

"We've got our guns in the woodpile," said Bob Ford.

"Get them. No—wait, I'll come with you."

He didn't trust them out of his sight. The finger of suspicion had stabbed at Jess Carney. The thing he had been fearing so long had happened. One of his men had turned traitor. Another might do so. He couldn't trust anyone now.

They walked to the woodpile and Bob Ford got out the two pistols rolled up in their belts. He handed one to Billy Mason.

"All right, Jess."

"You come with me, Bob," Jess ordered. "Billy, you go back to Bud's place. Charley Ford will pick you up there. He'll bring you to St. Joe." He stopped. After a moment he sighed.

"I trust you, Billy."

He didn't. The very fact that he said so proved that. But he couldn't help himself.

Billy Mason walked back alone to the cabin of Bud Hill. It was dark and quiet, but Charley Ford materialized out of the gloom and said, "Billy?"

"Yes."

"Where's Bob?"

"Jess came to the dance and took him off with him. You know about Dick?"

"Yes, I was with Jess at his mother's place when the news came. Damn that dirty Dick. He was afraid Jess would find out about Ed and kill him. So he turned rat and went to the police."

"Who'd he surrender to?"

"Marshall Gray of Kansas City. And Sheriff Liggett."

"How long ago?"

"This morning. The newspapers haven't got it yet, but it came over the grapevine. It's true, all right."

"But if he surrendered this morning, how come—Well, it's strange Liggett and Gray haven't done anything. Dick knew we were gathering here."

"Yes, but the sheriff of Jackson County doesn't come out to Jess Carney's house. A sheriff did that ten years ago. Jess met him up the road. No, they'll get him somewhere else."

"What makes you so sure they'll get him at all? Jess has been around a good long while."

"Yes, but he's been overdue a long time. Up to now, the people've been friendly. He—we could go to any old Confederate soldier and he'd put us up and wild horses wouldn't make him squeal. But since the governor's issued that big reward and offered immunity—"

"Immunity," said Billy Mason softly. "Yes, that's it. Dick was between two fires. The law wanted him for a killing and Jess wanted him. The law offered immunity for turning traitor."

"The yellow dog!" But there was no vehemence in Charley Ford's epithet. It was too dark to see his face.

Charley Ford went into the house and got a lantern. By its light they went to a stable behind the house and saddled horses. It was then that Billy Mason touched the butt of his Frontier Model. He drew it from the holster.

"Bob got our guns mixed!" he exclaimed. He recalled now Bob had dug the two guns rolled up in their holsters from under the woodpile. Billy had taken the one offered him and strapped it about his waist.

Charley Ford looked at the gun. "What's the difference? It's the same model as yours; newer, though."

"Yes, it is." Billy held the butt of the gun under the lantern. "What're these initials on the butt—*H. H. G.*? Where'd Bob get this gun?"

Charley Ford cleared his throat. "Well, I wouldn't exactly want Jess to know, but Bob and Jim Cummings over near Richmond pulled a couple of small jobs. Bob got this gun in one of them—"

Billy shook his head and holstered the gun. "I'll change with Bob when I see him. I'd prefer my own, even if this is newer."

"Yeah, sure."

They mounted their horses and rode into the night. They would always ride in the night, from now on. From now on, it would be dangerous for Billy Mason to show his face in daylight, among men. The finger had been pointed at him by Dick Small. He was known now, as a Carney man. And what did the governor's proclamation say about Carney men?

. . . and five thousand dollars reward for any member of Jess Carney's band, dead or alive.

They rode until morning, then hid in the woods. At nightfall they came out, along with the other beasts of prey. Three days, and on the third night they reached St. Joseph. But they did not go into the city until dawn was breaking.

The house rented by "Tom Howard" was at the edge of the city, on a little hill. It was a white frame building with a large, sagging barn behind it. The closest house was a hundred yards away.

Charley Ford and Billy Mason led their horses to the barn and put them inside. As they came out of the barn, Bob Ford stepped out of the kitchen door, his right hand under his coat.

He exclaimed in relief when he recognized his brother and Billy. "Say, but I'm glad to see you."

"Je————Tom inside?" Charley asked.

Bob Ford shot an uneasy glance over his shoulder, then motioned toward the barn. Charley and Billy followed him.

"What's up, Bob?" Billy asked sharply. "Something wrong with Jess?"

"Yes, he's breaking, I think. Ever since we've been here he's been as nervous as a cat. Stays in the house all day, in his room, then spends half the night prowling around, outside. You can't even talk to him without his snapping your head off."

"Well," said Charley Ford, "he never was very even-tempered. What's Zee—his wife, say?"

"Hardly anything. But she's plenty worried. Wouldn't surprise me if she pulled out with the kids."

It was telling on Jess Carney. He didn't even trust anyone in his own house. He prowled outside at night, afraid of shadows, yet forcing himself to investigate and prove they were only shadows. He was afraid. The accumulated years of outlawry, living in constant danger, had worn his nerves to a frazzle.

Billy Mason could understand that—even though he had been on the dark road for only a few weeks. His nerves were steady, but deep within him, something gnawed at his vitals. In time it would tell on him, too. He had an object lesson in Jess Carney.

"Is he here now?" Billy asked.

Bob Ford shook his head. "No, we went to bed together last night—in the same bed—but inside of an hour he was up and prowling around the house. I went down—to get something to drink—and discovered he'd left the house."

"What's the news of Dick Small? We haven't seen any newspapers in three days."

"Nothing," replied Bob Ford. "Jess's been getting the papers every day and there hasn't been a single word printed about Dick Small. I'm not so sure that Dick gave himself up."

"But Jess said Dick had been seen in Harry Gray's office!" exclaimed Charley Ford.

"Gray?" asked Billy. "Who's Harry Gray?"

"Police Commissioner of Kansas City. Jess had some connection in his office. Don't know exactly what it is."

Harry Gray—was there a middle initial? A chill fell upon Billy Mason. Deliberately, he drew his gun. "Bob," he said, "you mixed up our guns the other night at Centerville—"

"I know it. Discovered it the next morning. Here—" Bob reached under his coat and brought out Billy Mason's own Frontier Model. "They're the same make except that mine's newer."

Billy Mason smiled. "Yes—but it doesn't have your initials, I notice."

Charley Ford said sharply, "I told you about that. What're you trying to do—rub it in?"

"Of course not. I was just—" He stopped.

A tall, slight woman had suddenly appeared in the doorway of the stable. Her face was drawn and her eyes suspicious. "Who are these men, Bob?"

"My brother, Charley, Mrs. Car———I mean, Mrs. Howard. And Billy Mason."

"How do you do, Mrs. Howard," Billy said, bowing. He stared at the wife of Jess Carney. She looked—why, yes, give her a bit more color and take away about fifteen years and she could pass for Florence King's sister.

She was aware of his eyes upon her and, catching his, held them a moment. Then she relaxed. "You're a—friend of Tom's? Won't you come in and have some breakfast?"

"We'd appreciate it, Mrs. Howard."

They left the barn, walked through the little backyard, and entered the house by the kitchen door. Mrs. Carney busied herself swiftly at the stove, while Charley Ford and Billy Mason washed some of the travel dirt from their faces and hands. By the time they were finished Mrs. Carney had set food on the table.

But Billy Mason never ate any of it. Hardly had he seated himself at the table than Jess Carney slammed into the house.

"Billy! Charley!" he cried. "We've got to clear out of here. Dick Small's confessed. Look—!" He threw a newspaper on the table and dashed into a room off the kitchen. "Zee!" he cried from there.

Billy Mason caught up the newspaper. *Member of Carney Gang Confesses!* screamed a headline.

"Read it out loud!" exclaimed Bob Ford, behind Billy Mason.

Billy Mason read:

> "Police Commissioner Harry H. Gray admitted tonight that the mysterious man who surrendered to him last week is none other than Dick Small, lieutenant of the notorious Jess Carney band of bank and train robbers. Small, the commissioner stated, has made a complete confession, which it is believed will result in the eventual arrest of every member of the outlaw gang. The story is an astonishing one—"

Harry H. Gray, Police Commissioner of Kansas City—H. H. G. Billy Mason put down the newspaper and pushed back his chair.

At that moment, Jess Carney, coatless, came out of the bedroom. "Boys," he announced, "we haven't got any time to lose. We've got to—"

"Jess," said Billy Mason. "I must talk to you."

"Later, Billy. We've got to—"

"This won't wait. You've got to hear it now!"

Something in Billy's tone caught Jess Carney's attention. His bloodshot eyes seemed to look right into Billy Mason's brain. He nodded, almost imperceptibly. Billy Mason stepped swiftly to the door and Jess Carney followed.

"Wait, Jess!" exclaimed Charley Ford. "Don't go out like that. Somebody might see your guns. Your coat—"

Jess Carney turned back. "All right, Billy, I'll be out in a moment."

As he walked to the barn, a warning knell struck somewhere deep within Billy Mason. He stopped, turned.

And then a gun thundered in the house.

"Oh, Lord!" cried Billy.

He plunged toward the kitchen door, tore at it, and burst into the house. In his first wild glance he thought the room was empty. But then his eyes went to the floor, beyond the table—and a cry of horror was torn from his throat.

Jess Carney lay there, blood streaming from a horrible wound in his head.

In the front of the house a door slammed. Feet pounded on stairs, and Zee Carney burst into the kitchen.

"Jess, oh, my God!" she screamed and threw herself upon the man on the floor.

Billy Mason leaped past her and tore through the house. He jerked open the front door and sprang out upon the porch. He saw them running, already more than a hundred feet away. He saw, too, in that one glance, a woman and a man in front of the neighboring house. And he knew it was too late—even for vengeance.

He went back into the house and found Zee Carney sitting on the floor beside the body of her dead husband. Jess Carney, dead at the hand of an assassin.

"You didn't do this?" Zee Carney moaned.

"No. The Fords—"

"It was Bob," Zee Carney said dully. "I didn't like him right from the start. His eyes—they couldn't ever face me. He was planning it all along."

"Yes," said Billy Mason. "I knew it. I—I was calling Jess outside to tell him. I knew for days but didn't tumble to the significance of it, until Jess brought in that paper. I was going to tell—" He broke off and his eyes saw the leather belt on the table, the belt with a holster on each side, one containing a Navy Colt, another a Smith & Wesson. "They got him to take off his guns."

"The first time he took them off in years." Zee Carney's face twisted and a bitter, hysterical laugh came from her lips. Suddenly she got to her feet.

"It's all over, the thing I've dreaded and feared for eight long years. He's dead, and—Jesse!" The face of a small boy showed in the door leading to the front part of the house. Zee sprang toward him, shoved him back into the other room. Then she hurried back to Billy Mason.

"You've got to go! The neighbors have heard the shot. The police will be here."

"It's all right," Billy said dully. "I'm willing to surrender. I—I didn't like it, anyway. I'll take what's coming to me."

"You won't have a chance, Billy Mason!" cried Zee Carney. "Dick Small's turned traitor. Bob and Charley Ford will turn against you. You'll take it all alone. You mustn't—"

"It doesn't make any difference. There's no one—"

"No one cares for you?" cried Zee Carney. "You haven't got a sweetheart? There's no one whose heart would break like mine did during these years—no one?"

There was someone.

Billy Mason wasn't an outlaw—not one at heart. He'd known that the moment he had first thrust his gun at the head of that railroad engineer, so long ago. He'd ridden down the road with Jess Carney, but he hadn't thought as Jess Carney had thought.

Billy Mason straightened. He said, "Good-bye, Mrs. Carney!" and leaped to the door. With his hand on it he whirled and said softly:

"Good-bye, Jess Carney!"

The Stories of Darlin' Lily

⎯⎯∞⎯⎯

Al Sarrantonio

SNOOTFUL DIDN'T THINK we should go anywhere near
the place, since Rhett Favors was so dangerous and all.

But I had other ideas.

And that's how Snootful ended up with a bullet in his
brow, and how I ended up as part of the Favors Gang.

There's a lot of stories here, and I'll have to sort them
all out.

There's the story of me and Snootful, for instance, but
I don't think I'll get to that one for a while. We sure had
our good times while it lasted, and we did some damage
along the way, but it all ends the same way, in the ground,
don't it? So I think I'll let that one lie for now.

But the Favors Gang, that was something else. A step
above, as they say.

Rhett himself was real good with a gun, but it was said
he was even better at getting the right people to do what
had to be done. That's a talent, like any other.

A talent I wanted to learn.

Rhett had other talents, too. Like knowing where to put
it, and when. Not many men know that, especially when

it comes to a lady like me, who needs it now and then, and then again. But ol' Rhett was, if I had to choose, even better with his one-gun than he was with his six-gun.

That ain't another story, it's the one I'm telling now, and as good a place to start as any.

❧

IT'S NO EXAGGERATION to say we became fast lovers—I'd heard he liked the ladies since his wife was dead—and it kind of happened the very first night, after Snootful got hisself shot and I joined the gang.

Rhett took me away from the campsite, after giving the wink to the other boys, who nodded back. He couldn't have been so dumb to think I didn't see, but he might have been, the way things turned out later. But there I go again. "One story at a time, Darlin' Lily!" as my grandmom used to say—but heck, that's yet another story, and maybe I'll get to that one, too.

Anyways, I found myself out under the stars with the famous Rhett Favors, in the dark, with the dim lights of Wichita in the distance.

To break the tension, I said, "This ain't much of a hideout, Rhett—ain't you a'scared of the marshal looking for you out here?"

He didn't even laugh like I thought he would, but just grabbed me and put me on the ground, and there we did it for the first time, and the second, kicking up whatever dust didn't stick to our sweat.

"Not bad, for a wanted man," I said, when it was finally all over.

He pulled his pants on before he looked at me again. I was still naked, and I think he liked what he saw.

"You wanted it bad enough," he said.

I shrugged and said, "Somethin' wrong with that?"

His smile got just a little sour around the edges. "You're a strange one, Darlin'. Ain't like the ones at the whorehouse at all."

"Fifty cents gets you a fifty-cent lay," I said, and kept my own smile. "When it's free and you like it, a stageful of money can't match it."

By then he had his pants back off, and, well, we got a little more dust stuck to us.

∞∞∞

THINGS WERE OKAY then for a while. I stayed in the background, and gave Rhett what he wanted when he wanted it—and sometimes when I wanted it, too. It turned out my josh about the marshal wasn't so far off, since one of Rhett's Wichita snitches rode in the next morning to tell us that Marshal Carter was riding into town later in the day, and that a posse was already forming to meet him. Which meant we had to move out as soon as we could.

Which is what we did, and hard. To the point that, after twelve hours in the saddle, I rode up beside Rhett and said, "You afraid of this Carter fella?"

He didn't laugh, but turned his famous cold eyes on me—which I hadn't seen the night before—and said, "Nope."

Which wasn't quite true, as I learned later—but there I go again, telling stories ahead of myself!

I held his hard stare. "Then why we riding so hard?"

"I got a place I want to get to."

And then he kicked his horse and pulled ahead of me, and I drifted back past the other cold stares of the other boys in the gang. One of 'em, Pete Sanders, who had the longest mustaches I've ever seen in my life, shook his head and said, "Not a good idea, Darlin'. Not a good idea at all."

I was gonna ask him why, but since he was staring at my breasts instead of my face, I thought his mind might be on something besides giving me advice, so I let it pass.

Turned out I was right—but heck, the stories are just

piling up for telling! So I kept dropping back, and we kept riding.

Turns out there was a place Rhett wanted to get to, and it was a good one for an ambush. We reached a ravine that dipped between two cliffs, and halfway through this canyon Rhett brought us up to the right into a cut in the right wall, that led back to a nearly perfect ascent to the top. I couldn't help myself and pulled up next to Pete Sanders as we reached the cliffs.

"Won't the marshal see where we went?" I asked.

"Sure. But by then it'll be too late." He nodded up ahead at Rhett, who was already doubling back on our path, only now at the top of the cliff. "We'll catch 'em as they ride in, shoot 'em like fish in a barrel."

I nodded, and then dropped my horse back again, because Sanders's eyes had done their own dropping, back down to my bosom again.

Rhett spaced us out and set us behind good outcroppings. I had a clean view down into the mouth of the canyon and checked my rifle.

Seems Rhett was thinking about his one-gun, since after the others were settled he motioned me back behind a wall of boulders and we did it standing up, right out in the sun.

As I was pulling my shirt back on Pete Sanders appeared, and I knew the other reason he'd come to find us.

After checking me over he looked straight at Rhett and said, "They're coming, Rhett."

Favors had started to look mad but now he was all business.

"We'll drop 'em before they ride twenty yards in."

Pete nodded and the two of them walked away, talking strategy as they went.

I put my duds back on and got into position for the show.

∽∾∽

AND SHOW IT was, though things didn't work out quite
the way Rhett figured.

Turns out the marshal wasn't quite the butter-brain
Rhett hoped he was. My own question would have been:
Why wouldn't anyone coming into a canyon check the
top bluffs first? And that's just what Carter did. He sent
ten of his men up ahead of him, from a back trail, while
his scrubs, posing as the main force, rode straight toward
the canyon mouth but stopping just short of it. By then
Carter and his crack men were on top, and firing at us
from behind.

We got out, and just barely, with only one dead body
left behind. It should have been Pete Sanders, which
would have been better off for him.

But again: another story, even if I'll get to that one
soon enough.

Like I said, we got out, and it wasn't pretty. By the
time the shooting started the scrubs had made their way
into the canyon below, blocking off the path up to the
cliffs we had taken. The back route was taken by Carter's
men, so there was nothing to do but take the third, steep
route right in front of us. It looked like we were going
straight off the cliff, but Rhett found a way down, though
we did lose two horses in the process and little Jake Fla-
vors, Rhett's little brother, caught a bullet with his ticker
(two, to be truthful, which my grandmom always taught
me to be, and another two in his chest and one in his eye,
which I saw later on in the *Kansas City Star* when they
printed his picture, laid out half-naked on a propped-up
board in front of the Wichita sheriff's office, so's the good
citizens could come gawk at him before they threw him
in a pauper's grave) when he dismounted to cover our
retreat.

We made it away, but now there were seven of us—
the two Mason boys, young good-lookin' Davey Sharpe,
Slim Masters, Pete Sanders, Rhett and me—and we were
on the run for two days straight before shaking the posse,
at least for a while but not for good, as I'll tell.

But for now we had a little breathing room—so of course it was time for the Favors Gang to rob a train.

∞∞

IT HELPED THAT we were hid out not two miles from the railroad, in a desolate stretch between Wichita and Caldwell. Grasslands if ever there were grasslands. You'd of thought it would be a good time to keep moving, or lay low—but of course Favors wasn't known for that, which is why I wanted to hook up with him in the first place.

I sure as hell learned what I wanted to know fast enough.

"The railroad paymaster will be on that train two days from now, and we've got a date with him," Rhett said.

I had to give him credit, he'd holed us up in a good spot. Rhett wasn't the type to go running for kin when trouble was after him—not direct kin, anyways, which was what the dumb lawmen would look for first. What he found was the ranch of a cousin of his late wife, name twice removed from his own, but one he'd gambled and whored and drank with and who would just as soon turn him in as cut off his own arm.

"So what did your wife die of?" I asked him that first night, while Peter Sanders was supposed to be out on watch, which he wasn't, which led to the story I can finally tell you now.

His eyes got real wide with surprise, but he had just had his way with me, and was apt to forgive and also talk, which I'd learned by experience.

"How'd you know about Charlotte?"

I grinned in the near dark, under the sickle crescent of a moon, still under him. "I know lots of things. Been studying you for a long time, Rhett."

I couldn't tell if he liked that or not, but the cold left his eyes for a second. "Fever took her. Don't know if I'd be here now if it hadn't . . ."

"I heard you killed her yourself," I said.

As I said it I knew that I shouldn't have.

The cold came back into his eyes real fast. He pulled off me, and I think he might have killed me right there if more pressing business hadn't come up.

It all happened quick. As he stood up there was a sound in the brush to our right, and I learned right there the last thing I wanted to know about Rhett Favors, and why he had lasted so long. I didn't even see him produce his gun, which must have been on the ground next to us all the time. The shot came even quicker, and there was a groan in the bushes, and then something made the last cold drop to the ground.

Rhett was already there, and I was behind him.

"Jackass," Rhett said, spitting down at the now lifeless body of Pete Sanders, a third bloody eye between his two open, startled ones. He turned to me, and just enough of the cold was gone from his own eyes to keep me alive. "I knew that bucko had his eye on you from the beginning. He'd be alive if he'd done what I told him to."

A long moment passed, and his eyes got even colder. "And you wouldn't be. Don't ever mention Charlotte again, Darlin' Lily."

He left me there in the near-moonless dark, mostly naked, and I knew that he'd never touch me again, and that my days in the Rhett Favors gang were numbered.

∽◦◦∾

NOW I CAN tell the rest of the my stories.

The train robbery went like a breeze. I learned a little more about train robbing than I already knew—like locking the paymaster in his car with two lit sticks of dynamite on the floor next to the safe—it opens a lot quicker and neater that way when the paymaster uses the combination and then yells bloody murder to let him out. That was a keen touch, and I liked the way Slim Masters got in there, checked to make sure the paymaster was telling the truth, and then snuffed the two fuses before anything got messy. ("Real slow fuses is the trick," he told me with a wink right after.) I also liked the way the rest of the gang knew exactly what had to be done and did it, all under the cold eyes of Rhett Favors. Rhett had even put in his distant kin in Pete Sanders place, and the man was a pretty good lookout. Which is, of course, yet another story, but that'll probably be just about the last.

So the train robbery went off like clockwork—and gave Marshal Carter time to get on our trail again, which he did. That was Rhett Favors's one flaw, I thought—that he always let the law get too close. I think he did it for thrills, but I'm not sure, and it don't much matter at this point.

I waited till we got back to the hideout, while the rest of the gang was busy splitting up the paymaster's haul (which was a good one, in bills and some gold coin) and then I called Rhett out into the moonlight for the last time.

I don't know what he thought would happen, but I saw he had his one-gun stowed and his six-gun out.

I gut shot him as soon as he stepped off the porch, my Colt aimed from my side and hard to see in the bad light, then I moved up on him quick and shot him again when he overcame the pain and reached for his six-gun on the ground.

It was the same move I'd used on Snootful, when it became clear that he wouldn't fit into the Favors Gang in a useful way, and I was a little surprised that Favors hadn't remembered me using it. I was even more surprised that he'd been carrying a saddlebag with my portion of the train robbery haul in it.

"Time to meet Charlotte," I said and finished it, and then I turned my gun on the open doorway, which was filled now with members of the Rhett Favors Gang.

"What do you say, fellas?" I asked. "Ready to join the Darlin' Lily Gang?"

Two of them said no, one of them with his gun, which he never quite reached. It was Rhett's kin, of course. That made the rest of them think a little harder on my propo-

sition. When Slim Masters stepped forward and said,
"No," his hands open and empty in front of him, I shot
him between the eyes, the way I'd shot my grandmom
two years before, when she'd stopped being useful. I was
sorry to lose Slim's touch, but when you thought about
it, he'd already taught me everything he had to offer anyway. That slow fuse bit is a gem and has come in quite
handy.

"Any more 'nos'?" I asked. "I've found over the years
it's best to deal with things straight out. Folks is either
useful and willin' or they ain't. Anybody here that ain't
useful and willin'?"

I looked the rest of them over, and let my eyes linger
on young Davey Sharpe, who was pretty good-looking
and might fill my bed for a while, when I had a hankering
for it.

There were no more dissenters, at least not that night,
which ended with us ten miles ahead of Marshal Carter,
a gap we just kept widening—

But there I go again, telling more stories!

Sorry, Grandmom!

I did tell the truth, though, all the way through, and she
sure was useful for teaching me that.

Enemies

❧

Daniel Ransom

CEDAR RAPIDS, IOWA, 1893

SPEAKS SHOULD HAVE known better. Hell, he was dealing with Harry Creed, and Harry Creed was one crazy son of a bitch.

"Where the hell you takin' me, Harry?" Speaks said.

"Oh, you'll see, you'll see," Harry Creed said, sounding like a kid teasing his younger brother. But at a hard-lived sixty-three, Speaks sure didn't look like any kind of kid.

The date was September 2, 1893. The place was Cedar Rapids, Iowa.

"We almost there?" Speaks said after they'd walked four more long blocks.

"Almost, almost." Harry Creed laughed.

These days Harry was dressing like a pirate. He wore a bandanna over his head, a golden ring on his right lobe, and he had a wee bit of a knife scar on his right cheek. Speaks wondered cynically if Harry had given himself that scar.

For all his bitching, Speaks was enjoying the day. This

was one of those golden, lazy autumn days when the flat
autumnal light of the sun seemed to penetrate to your core
and warm your very soul. The air smelled of burning
leaves, and there was no headier perfume than that, and
the trees were so colorful they almost hurt the eye. He
wanted to be a raggedy-ass kid again.

And just then, Harry Creed steered them around a corner and down a dusty alley.

Speaks was hot now, in his black suit coat and gray
trousers, sweating. When they got where they were going
he'd take the coat off. He was wearing a ruffled white
shirt. He'd been doing a little gambling this year, and had
decided to dress appropriately. His Navy Colt was back
in his hotel room. Cedar Rapids had a full force of police.
They'd throw your ass in the jug if they saw you sporting
a handgun. The old days were long gone. Long gone.

The first thing he saw was the big red barn that said
BLACKSMITH over the double doors. The first thing he
heard was the shouts and curses of men who'd already
been doing some drinking at ten o'clock on this fine fall
morning. He could also smell blood, but he wasn't sure
if it was human or animal. The scent of fresh blood tainted
the air. He'd been around enough of it to recognize it
instantly.

"You bring me to a cockfight?" Speaks said.

"Hell, no, man." Harry Creed grinned. "Somethin' a lot
better than that."

And he just beamed his ass off right then. Speaks half
expected him to start skipping at any moment. Skipping.
A grown man.

The barn smelled of the smithy's fire and new-mown
hay and horse shit. The smithy, a wiry little bald guy with
a toothless grin and a wary eye, nodded them toward the
back of the barn. His wary eye was fixed on Harry Creed's
pirate getup. "You wouldn't happen to be Captain Kidd,
would you?" he said, and winked at Speaks.

"Asshole," Harry Creed muttered as they walked to the
back where maybe a dozen men stood in a circle, their

hands filled with greenbacks just pleading to be bet. This was Saturday, and Friday, at least in most places, had been payday.

"You get the old Master in here, and I'll bet he gets through three of them little peckers in under a minute." The man speaking wore a cheap drummer's outfit and puffed on an even cheaper cigar. "And I got three dollars here to say I'm right."

Another man, a youth really, dressed in a blue work-shirt and gray work trousers, said, "I'll see that three and make it four."

The other men laughed.

"This ain't poker, kid," one of them said.

Speaks still couldn't figure out what Harry Creed had gotten him into.

The barking dog got everybody's attention. It was a boxer, and a damned good-size one, and when it moved you could see its muscles move in waves down its back. Tear your damned leg off, this one would.

The men made loud cheering noises, as if a favorite politician had just walked into the barn.

"Master's gonna do it, aren't ya, boy?" said the young guy. "You're gonna make me a rich man, ain't ya, Master ol' boy?"

A couple of the men separated then and Speaks got his first look at the ring. It ran maybe three feet high, was metal, and was maybe four feet across. This was the kind of ring cockfighters used.

"Next batch!" a pudgy guy shouted as he came through the back door carrying a round, lidded metal can.

"God, I hate them things," one of the men in the circle said, and shuddered for everybody to see.

"What the hell's in the metal can?" Speaks asked Harry Creed.

But all Harry did was smile that stupid pirate smile of his. "Ain't you gonna be surprised?" he said.

As the man with the can reached the ring and started to pull the lid off, all the men, without exception, moved back. It was clear they wanted no part of whatever was in the can.

Master was in the ring now, crouched low, his eyes mesmerized by the can in the man's hands. Master's jowls flickered and snapped. Master knew what was in that can, all right.

The men got excited, too. Their eyes gleamed. Some of them made eager, lurid noises in their throats. In many respects, they were even more animal-like than the rats. Killing had never been something Speaks cared to see, even if the victim was an animal. In Houston once, admittedly carrying more than a few drinks around in his belly, he'd broken the nose of a hobo who was trying to set a cat on fire for the amusement of his pals.

The man was swift and sure. In a single motion he jerked the lid away and upended the can.

At least eight or nine fat, angry, filthy, tail-twitching rats fell to the floor of the ring. When they hit the floor they went crazy, running around in frantic circles, bumping into each other, trying to cower when there was no place to hide or cower at all.

Master was jubilant with blood lust.

He didn't need any encouragement.

He leapt upon the first rat, seizing the thing between his teeth, catching it just right so that when teeth met belly, blood spurted and sprayed all over Master's otherwise tan face. The way a burst balloon would spurt and spray.

Speaks had enough already.

This little wagering sport was called ratting. You bet on how many rats a dog could catch and kill in a sixty-second period. Ratting was even more popular in the East than out here. Easterners just didn't talk about it much. They always made you think that they were very civilized people and that you, a Westerner, were somehow heathen. But Speaks had been to New York a couple of times and he knew that civilization was not a dream shared by

everybody. He'd seen a man cut out the eye of his op-
ponent with a Bowie knife.

While Speaks was not partial to rats in any way, he still
couldn't see torturing them this way. He didn't like cock-
fighting, either, far as that went.

"Hey, where ya goin'?" Harry Creed said. "Master here
just got goin'."

But Speaks just wanted out. Who the hell wanted to
watch a dog get himself all bloody by killing rats when
it was such a beautiful day outside? Life versus death;
and at this point in Lyle Speaks's years, he always chose
the way of life and not the way of death.

He was just turning around when he felt something
press against the lower part of his back.

"You just walk out of here real nice and easy, Mr.
Speaks," a voice whispered in his ear, "and everything's
gonna be just fine. Just fine. You understand me?"

Speaks was wondering who it was. You lived a life like
Speaks's, it could be almost anybody, anybody from anywhere for almost any reason at all.

"You understand me, Mr. Speaks?" the voice asked
again.

Speaks nodded.

If there was one thing he understood without any dif-
ficulty at all, it was having somebody hold a gun on him
when he was unarmed. He understood it very, very well.

The gun nudged him around until Speaks was facing
the double front doors of the barn. Then the gun nudged
him right on out of the barn.

∽◦∾

HE DIDN'T REALLY get a good look at the guy until they
were almost out of the alley, and the only glimpse he got
then was by looking over his shoulder.

He was a kid. By Speaks's standards, anyway. Twenty-
two, twenty-three at most. One of those freckled frontier
faces with the pug nose and the quick grin that made them

look like altar boys until you noticed the pugnacious blue
eyes. Speaks had seen kids like this all over the West. Not
knowing what they were looking for but somehow all
finding the same thing: trouble. There used to be a lot
more of this kind in the West, self-styled gunsels who
strutted and peacocked all over the place, just trying to
prove how tough they were. But that was the old West,
when there were a lot of bona fide gunfighters roaming
around, and when kids like this one always got themselves
killed in saloons for saying the wrong thing to the wrong
man. This kid was out of place and out of time, a decade
too late to live out his dime-novel dreams.

A couple of times Speaks thought of trying a move or
two on the kid, but he decided against it. These old bones
weren't what they used to be, and his glimpse of the kid
told him that he was dealing with a very serious pistolero,
or whatever the dime novelists were calling punks this
year.

"I'm going to make it easy for you," Speaks said.

"Just keep walkin'."

"I don't have much money, and I don't know where I
can lay my hands on any, either."

"I don't give a damn about money."

"You will when you get to be my age, kid."

"Just shut up and keep walkin'."

Now they were on the sidewalk. In one of the newspapers that he'd read last night, an editorial had boasted
that Cedar Rapids possessed seven hundred telephones,
fifteen blocks of electric streetlamps, and more than a mile
of paved streets. A lot of the sidewalks were still board,
though. Like this one.

"They're onto you."

"Who's onto me?" the kid said.

"The people. They can see you got a gun on me."

"Bullshit."

"Look at their faces, kid. These aren't dumb people.
One of them's gonna get a cop."

The kid went for it, not right away maybe, but after a

minute or so. He started watching the faces of the pas-
sersby, the women in big picture hats, the men in fancy
Edwardian-style duds, the farmers with their sun-red faces
and hat-white foreheads. Speaks could sense the kid's step
falter as he started to watch passing faces closely. Falter,
and make him vulnerable.

Speaks wheeled around. The kid was right-handed, so
Speaks came in left, fast, under the arc of the kid swinging
his gun around.

He got the kid in the ribs with his elbow and in the
groin with his fist. The kid folded in half, and Speaks
ripped the gun out of his hand.

Speaks knocked off the kid's fancy-ass cowboy hat,
grabbed him by the hair, and dragged him all the way
back to the alley.

"My hat!" the kid kept saying, as if Speaks had taken
his magical talisman away. He didn't seem to notice that
in the meantime Speaks was tearing out a good handful
of his hair.

Speaks found a wall and threw the kid up against it and
then, to send him a clear and unmistakable message,
started slamming the kid's head against the wall, never
once letting go of the greasy hair.

Three, four, five times the kid's head came into slamming contact with the wall until finally his eyes rolled
back, and the kid started sliding to the dusty alley,
whereupon Speaks kicked him in the chest for good measure. Holding a gun on an unarmed Speaks was not the
way to curry favor with the big man.

"Who the hell's this?" said the pirate.

Speaks looked over at Harry Creed and sighed. "What's
the matter, they run out of rats?"

Speaks wished his traveling buddy Sam November was
here. He'd be able to shoo Harry Creed away. But Sam
was up visiting a sick relative in the Decorah area, which
was why they'd traveled up the Mississippi from New
Orleans in the first place. So now Speaks was stuck with
a punk who meant him harm, and the antics of Harry

Creed. He'd come here to see an old friend, Keegan, but now he wondered if he should've come here at all. Harry Creed was not somebody he wanted to spend any time with. And the punk just made things worse.

"Them rats really bothered you, huh?" Harry Creed giggled. "You shoulda seen yer face, Lyle boy. You was whiter than a frozen tit."

The kid was just coming around.

"Who's this?" Harry Creed said.

"Don't know yet," Speaks said. "But I sure aim to find out."

∽∘∽

IN CEDAR RAPIDS, the courthouse was on an island in the middle of town. The original inhabitant of the island, back in the Indian days, had been a horse thief whose luck ran out years later in Missouri, where he was hanged. Local folks never tired of telling this tale. When asked if it was really true or not, this unlikely tale, the residents of the town would point you to the public library and tell you to go look it up. And by God, if it wasn't true, as the books verified, a horse thief had been the first resident of what later became the town. How was that for a rough beginning?

A number of taverns lined the streets two blocks north, giving a good view of the island and, farther down, the ice works.

Harry Creed went and got them beers while Speaks shoved the kid into a booth at the back of the place. It was a choice seat. Hot wind carried the smell of the outhouse through the screen door. The men playing pinochle didn't seem to notice Speaks, or the smell.

"Who the hell are you?" Speaks asked.

"None of your business."

"Kid, I don't need much of an excuse to kick your ass, so you'd better start talkin'."

The kid sighed. "My name's Pecos."

Speaks laughed. "Pecos, huh?"

"Yeah, what's wrong with that?"

"Kid you got farm all over your face, and your twang puts you in Nebraska. So how the hell do you get 'Pecos' out of that?"

But before Pecos could answer, Harry Creed sat the beers down and they proceeded to drink.

"Guess what his name is?" Speaks said to Harry Creed.

"His name?"

"Yeah."

"Now, how the hell would I know what his name is?"

"Take a guess."

Harry Creed shrugged. "Jim?"

"Nope."

"Bob?"

"Uh-uh."

"Arnell?"

"Pecos."

"Oh, bullshit," Harry Creed said.

"Ask him."

Harry Creed took another sip of brew. "What's your name, kid?"

"Go fuck yourself."

"I'd be watchin' my mouth if I was you," Harry Creed said. Then he grinned. "With all due respect, I mean, Mr. Pecos."

"You assholes think this is funny, huh?" Pecos didn't wait for an answer. "Well, it won't be so funny when your friend Chris Keegan gets here and I get him in a gunfight."

"Aw hell," Speaks said. "That's what this's all about."

"What's it all about?" Harry Creed said.

"His name and wearin' his holster slung low like it is," Speaks said. "This dumb kid thinks he's a gunfighter."

"Not thinks," Pecos said, "am."

Speaks made a sour face and shook his head. "Kid, there haven't been any gunfighters since they shut down the trail towns ten years ago. And most of what you hear about gunfighters is bullshit anyway."

"Not about Wild Bill," Pecos said.

"Especially about Wild Bill," Speaks said. "And the only reason Chris Keegan ever got into any gunfights was defendin' himself against kids like you who forced him into it."

"He killed twenty-two men."

Harry Creed snorted. "More like four or five, kid, and Lyle's right, he didn't want to get into any of them. Kid came up to him one night in Abilene and called him out. He woulda killed Chris, but he was so drunk he tripped over his own feet and Chris killed him."

"Yeah," Speaks said, "and another time Chris was standin' at the bar and he saw this kid comin' through the batwings and he saw this kid start to draw and that gave him plenty of warning, so he ducked down and turned around and shot the kid before the kid could clear leather. Didn't take a whole lot of brainpower to do that."

"Plus which," Speaks said, "Chris Keegan is a year older'n me, which'd put him right about sixty-four. Even if he used to be a gunfighter, he sure isn't anymore."

"I could still be the man who beat Chris Keegan," the kid said.

"You're a crazy bastard," Harry Creed said.

But a dangerous one, Speaks thought. He said, "That why you put a gun in my back? So I'd be sure to tell Chris about you when we meet his train tonight?"

The kid nodded. "That way he'd know I was serious. Real serious."

Speaks threw his beer in the kid's face.

Even the pinochle players glanced over to watch this one.

"Hey, Lyle," Harry Creed said. "What the hell you do that for?"

"Because I'm sick of this little prick."

The bartender came over. "You got trouble, take it outside."

"No trouble," Speaks said. "I'm just leavin', is all."

He stood up and did just what he said.

"You son of a bitch," the kid said as Speaks walked out the front door. "You son of a bitch."

$\sim\!\!\infty\!\!\sim$

THE TRAIN WAS eight cars long, all passenger cars except for the caboose. Behind the windows Easterners sat staring imperiously at the small train depot. Not until they reached San Francisco would they be able to inhale civilized air again.

Chris Keegan looked fifteen years younger and ten years better than Speaks. They were almost the same age. Keegan had always been something of a dude, and he was a dude still, what with the black silk gambler's vest, the flat-crowned Stetson, and black Wellington boots shined to blinding perfection.

Amy Keegan was a perfect match for her husband, blonde, poised, beautiful in a slightly wan way. Her dark blue traveling dress clung to curves that time had not ruined as yet. There was just a hint of arrogance in her eyes as she beheld Lyle Speaks. Clearly, she considered both her husband and herself his superior. Once again, Speaks wondered why this woman had ever taken up with Harry Creed.

Thinking about Harry Creed reminded him that Keegan was now married to a woman he'd stolen away from Creed. Why hadn't Harry erupted at the simple mention of Keegan? Strange, he thought. Man stole a woman from me, I'd curse every time I heard his name. I surely would.

"How about a drink?" Speaks said.

"I'd really like to freshen up," Amy said.

Keegan said, "Why don't we freshen up a little first and meet you down in the hotel bar? I assume they have one."

"Yeah," Speaks said, "a nice one."

Speaks walked them back to the hotel. The lamplighters were at work, pushing back the night. Player piano music from the saloons. Violins from the Hungarian restaurant down the street. The steady *clop clop clop* of horses pulling fancy carriages toward the opera house. The dusk sky was vermillion and gold and filled Speaks with a sadness he couldn't articulate, not even to himself. Rainy days and dusk skies always did that to Speaks.

When they reached the hotel entrance, passing couples strolling the sidewalks beneath the round red harvest moon, Keegan said, "Oh, hell, honey, why don't I have a drink with Lyle here and then I'll come up to the room."

Speaks expected her to say no, but she surprised him.

"That's a good idea. Then maybe your dear old friend Speaks here can explain what Harry Creed was doing at the depot."

"Harry Creed?" Keegan said.

"He was standing at the west end of the platform," she said. "Watching us."

"Is Harry Creed in town?" Keegan said to Speaks.

"I'm afraid he is. Sam November ran into him up in Dubuque and told him we'd all be down here today."

"He's not exactly Amy's favorite person," Keegan said.

"I don't want to be in the same town with the man," Amy said. "In fact, I think I'll change our plans, Chris. I think we should leave first thing tomorrow."

For the very first time since he'd met her ten years earlier, Speaks felt sorry for Amy Keegan. Tears shone in her eyes, and she looked genuinely frightened. Speaks wondered just what the hell Harry Creed had done to her, anyway.

Then, as if she sensed that this was one of the few times Speaks liked her, she said in a very soft voice, "Oh, why don't you two have your drink. I'll just go on up to the room." Then to Speaks, smiling sadly: "People will think I lead him around by the nose all the time."

"Oh, honey," Keegan said.

She really was crying now, gently.

"See you in a little bit," Keegan said, and kissed her good-bye on the cheek.

The tears had softened her face; and as he looked at her now, Speaks was almost rocked by her beauty.

⟨∽∘∽⟩

"THE LAST NIGHT the bastard raped her," Keegan said. "Then he broke her arm."

For all of Harry Creed's antics, for all of his prairie-boy affability, he was a treacherous and ruthless son of a bitch, part of a lower order of men who had drifted through the frontier scavengerlike, mostly as con artists who unburdened the dumb and the greedy of their money. But they had more sinister sides, too. They were arsonists and stickup men and hired assassins, too. Whatever was needed in a particular time and place, they would be.

"That's why she's the way she is," Keegan said. "Never lets me out of her sight, because she's scared he's going to show up sometime."

"What I can't figure out is how the hell she ever got with a man like Creed, anyway."

They were in the taproom of the hotel. Men in Edwardian suits and women in bustled dresses filled the room. The waiters wore starched white shirts with celluloid collars.

Keegan said, "Her father was a missionary to the Indians. Lutheran. She got some of that from him. She's always trying to save people. When we lived in Kansas City, she spent half her time working at the Salvation Army." He shook his head. "Well, you know Harry. Back when she was living over in Peoria, he met her at a temperance meeting and her husband had just died of influenza and she was very lonely and . . . well, she ended up marrying him. Didn't last long. Four months, I guess." He made a face. "He made her do all kinds of filthy things I'd rather not talk about. And he beat her up all the time, too." He made a fist. "Nearly every night."

"You never went after him?"

"She won't let me. She's afraid he'll kill me. I mean, a fair fight, guns or fists . . ." He shrugged. "But you know

our Harry. It wouldn't be a fair fight. He'd be up to something."

Just then Speaks looked up and saw Amy coming toward them.

"I decided I'd rather be down here with you two," she
explained as she sat down. "I got a little scared upstairs
all alone. Knowing Harry's in town."

Keegan hadn't been exaggerating her fear. She looked
agitated, all right.

Then she said gently, touching Keegan's hand, "I'd really like to leave tomorrow morning."

He nodded. "That's what we'll do, then." To Speaks:
"Sorry, Lyle."

"I understand." Speaks looked at Amy. "I would've run
him out of town if I'd have known what he did to you,
Amy."

"He's always lurking someplace," she said.

"This has happened before?"

"Oh, sure," she said. "He's shown up several places
over the past five or six years, hasn't he?"

"Yeah," Keegan said, "and he always leaves little re-
minders of himself. A note. A photograph of the two of
them. Only time I ever called him on it, he denied it, of
course. You know Harry."

"Yeah," Speaks said, "unfortunately, I do."

They drank through two hours of conversation, good
conversation, fond memories of a good friendship, once
they found out about Harry Creed, anyway. Keegan asked
after Speaks's wife of five years, Clytie, and Speaks told
him they were still very happy together in Montana.
Ranching, he said, was agreeing with him.

Amy contributed, too. The booze took away her slight
air of superiority. She was just a good woman then, and
Speaks could see how they loved each other and took care
of each other, and he was happy for Keegan. Keegan was
one of the good ones. Despite his years as a reluctant
gunfighter, he was a peaceful, fair-minded, and decent

man, and he deserved good things. There was no mean-
ness in him.

Keegan had just ordered another round when Harry
Creed came into the taproom.

Harry's pirate getup was gone. He wore a tweed coat,
white shirt, dark trousers. His hair was slicked back in the
fashion of the day. He actually looked handsome, and for
the first time Speaks could imagine Harry and Amy walking down streets together. He came straight over to the
table, as if they'd been expecting him.

Amy bowed her head, wouldn't look up at him.

But Keegan looked up, all right. "You got sixty seconds
to get out of here, Harry."

Harry Creed smirked.

"You try to do an old friend a favor and look what you
get."

Speaks wasn't sure which old friend Harry was talking
about, Amy or Keegan.

"Sixty seconds, Harry," Keegan repeated.

Amy still wouldn't look up.

"There's a kid, Noonan's his real handle—Lyle here
met him this afternoon—and anyway, he wants to shoot
it out with you, Keegan. Says you're the last gunfighter
and he wants the honor of puttin' you away. I'm tryin'
hard to talk him out of it."

Now it was Keegan's turn to smirk.

"I'll bet you're tryin' real hard, Harry. I'm sure you
wouldn't want anything terrible to happen to me, us bein'
such good friends and all."

"I'm doin' everything I can," Harry Creed said. "I just
thought I'd let you know. I'd be very careful where you
go tonight."

Then he looked at Amy.

"You're lookin' lovely tonight, Amy."

Her head remained bowed, eyes closed. She was trying
to will him out of existence.

The waiter appeared.

"Will you be staying?" he asked Harry Creed.

"No, he won't be," Keegan said harshly.

The waiter set down their beers and left quickly.

"I'm gonna try'n talk him out of it, Keegan," Harry Creed said.

"You do that," Keegan said. "Now get the hell out of here."

"You sure do look pretty tonight, Amy," Harry Creed said. Then he laughed. "Not quite as pretty as when she was with me, of course, but she was a lot younger then." He glanced at Speaks. "By the way, the kid likes ratting a lot better than you do. I can hardly drag him away from the barn." He patted his stomach. "Guess he's a little younger than you are, Speaks."

That was Harry, always getting in the last line.

They sat in silence for nearly two minutes. Amy brought her head up and reached over and touched her husband's hand again.

"Someday you won't be able to stop me, Amy," Keegan said softly. "Someday I'm going to kill him."

"Then they'd hang you," she said. "And he's the one who should hang."

Speaks said, "I'm going to take care of the kid for you. You two just go ahead and have yourselves a good meal."

"Don't get into trouble," Amy said.

Speaks shrugged.

"I've been in trouble a few times before." He smiled. "And I probably will be again before they plant me."

Keegan frowned.

"I wish there was a train out of here tonight. I want to get out of this town."

"Just relax and enjoy yourselves," Speaks said. He took out some greenbacks and laid them down on the table. "The next round's on me."

"Amy's right," Keegan said. "I don't want you to get into any trouble."

"I'll be fine," Speaks said, then shuddered inwardly. He'd be fine except for seeing the rats in the ratting cage. Kinda funny, the way you could feel sorry for something

you hated. Speaks hated rats, and yet now he felt sorry
as hell for them. He wasn't at all surprised that a punk
like Noonan would enjoy ratting. He wasn't surprised at
all.

He said good-bye and set off for the blacksmith's barn.

∽◦∾

TWO BLOCKS AWAY Speaks started hearing the dogs
barking as they went after the rats. This was something
he'd have to keep to himself, feeling sorry for the rats
and all. People would think he was one strange cowpoke
for taking the side of the rats.

The next thing he heard, this a block away, was the
men. This time of night they were drunk, words slurred.
But you could hear the blood lust in the timbre of their
voices. They didn't much care whose blood it was as long
as somebody excited them by bleeding.

Speaks went inside the barn and moved to the far doors
where the crowd gathered.

Harry Creed and Pecos stood together, watching as
more rats were dumped into the ring. They were at the
back of the crowd, which made things easy for Speaks.

Pecos's face glowed with glee. This was something to
see, all right. He even giggled like a little girl.

Speaks moved up carefully behind him, and then returned the favor Pecos had done for him that afternoon.

Speaks shoved his Colt hard against Pecos's back.

"We're going to turn around and walk outside."

Pecos looked over at Harry Creed. Creed saw what was
going on. He nodded to Pecos.

The three of them went outside.

Pecos obviously figured he was going to get it first, but
Speaks surprised him by turning around and kicking
Harry Creed right square in the balls, then slashing the
barrel of the gun down on the side of Harry Creed's head.
Harry dropped to his knees.

"That's for what you did to Amy," Speaks said. "And

this is so you don't get ideas about Pecos here doin' your killing for you." And with that he brought the toe of his Texas-style boot straight into Harry Creed's jaw. Harry had the good sense to scream.

Pecos he just pistol-whipped a little. Nothing special, nothing for Speaks to brag about or Pecos to bitch about, not for long, anyway, just enough so that Pecos had a couple of good-size welts on his face, and one very sore skull. There was a little blood, but again not enough to warrant bringing a reporter in.

Inside, the dogs went crazy. So did the crowd.

Harry Creed picked himself up. He was pretty wobbly. He started to say something, but then gave up. Very difficult to talk with a mouthful of blood.

"There's a train," Speaks said, "and it leaves in twenty minutes. I want you on it." This train was heading in the direction from which Keegan and Amy had just come.

"A train to where?" Pecos asked, trying to stand up.

"It doesn't matter where," Speaks said, "as long as you're on it."

Harry Creed, having apparently swallowed a mouthful of blood, said, "Amy gonna give you some of that nice sweet ass of hers, is she, Lyle?"

One punch was all it took, a straight hard shot to the solar plexus, and Harry Creed was sitting on his butt again.

"Maybe I should break your arm the way you broke hers, Harry."

"It was an accident."

"Sure it was, Harry."

"The bitch didn't appreciate nothin' I did for her."

"The train," Speaks said. "Be on it. Both of you."

"You son of a bitch," Pecos said as Speaks walked away. "You son of a bitch!"

∽◦∾

SPEAKS WENT BACK to the hotel. Amy and Keegan were
gone. Probably up in bed already. He had three brews,
and then he was upstairs, himself.

He stripped to his long johns, the smell of his boots
sour, meaning he'd have to powder them down inside
again, and then he lay on his bed in the darkness, the
front window and its shade silhouetted on the wall behind
him.

He thought briefly of Clytie, waiting for him to return
to their ranch in Montana. He wished Sam November
would finish up his visit to his relatives so they could head
back.

That was the last thing he thought before he fell asleep.

❦

SOMEBODY WAS POUNDING on his door so hard, all he
could think of—now that he was starting to think
clearly—was that there must be a fire.

"Hey! You in there!" a man's voice shouted.

Speaks was off the bed and at the door in seconds.

The man was familiar-looking somehow—then Speaks
remembered. A man at the bar downstairs earlier that
night.

"You know that friend of yours, the one with the pretty
wife?" the man said. He had gray hair and muttonchop
sideburns and a belly bursting the vest of his dark three-
piece suit.

"What about him?"

"He's got trouble downstairs, mister. There's some
punk kid tryin' to get him into a gunfight downstairs in
the street." The man shook his head. "Hell, mister, we
don't have no gunfights here. This is Cedar Rapids. We've
got over seven hundred telephones."

"Son of a bitch," Speaks said. Then: "Thanks."

He got dressed in seconds and hurried downstairs.

❦

PECOS HAD READ way too many dime novels.

He stood spread-legged in the middle of the street, his right hand hovering just above the pearly handle of his Peacemaker.

He'd gotten a crowd surly enough, too. His kind always wanted crowds around. In the electric light of the new lamps, Pecos looked like a raw kid wearing his older brother's duds.

"I'm givin' you ten more seconds to draw, Keegan," Pecos said to Keegan's back.

He was slurring his words. He was drunk.

Speaks looked over at Harry Creed and scowled. No mystery here. Harry Creed had decided to let the kid do his killing. He got the kid drunk and pushed him out on stage.

Amy Keegan grabbed Speaks's arm when he reached the sidewalk.

"You hear me, Keegan?" Pecos said.

"He's callin' you out," Harry Creed said, "fair and square."

"My Lord," said the man who'd roused Speaks from sleep. "This is Cedar Rapids." He didn't mention the seven hundred telephones this time.

"He doesn't want to kill the kid," Amy whispered to Speaks.

Speaks nodded and then looked over at Keegan. He was standing with his back to his tormentor. You could see the anger and humiliation on Keegan's face. Obviously, a part of him wanted to empty his gun into the kid. But the civilized part of him—the part that had changed for the better under Amy's guidance—declined the pleasure.

Without turning around Keegan said, "Kid, I'm going to walk up these stairs and go into the hotel. And if you want to shoot me, you'll just have to shoot me in the back."

"You think I won't?" Pecos snapped.

Keegan couldn't resist.

"Even a punk like you wouldn't shoot a man in the back."

And with that Keegan started up the stairs.

"You think I won't?" the drunken kid called out again. "You think I won't?"

Keegan took another slow, careful step up the stairs to the front porch of the hotel.

"Draw, you bastard!" Pecos shouted, weaving a bit as he did so, the alcohol slurring his words even more now.

"Shoot him, kid!" Harry creed said. "You gave him a chance! Now shoot him!"

Even boozed up the way he was, the kid was passing fair with a handgun.

His gun cleared leather before Speaks even noticed. The kid brought the gun up and sighted in a quick, easy movement and—

Speaks shot the gun out of his hand.

The kid cried out, dropping the gun and looking around, as if some dark demon had delivered the shot and not some mere mortal.

Speaks walked directly over to Harry Creed. Harry turned and started to move away quickly, but not quickly enough. Speaks grabbed him by the hair, got his arm around Harry Creed's throat, and then proceeded to choke him long enough to make him puke.

A few moments later Harry Creed was on his hands and knees like a dog, vomiting up chunks of the evening's repast.

For good measure and because sometimes he was—he had to admit—a mean son of a bitch, Speaks then kicked Harry Creed in the ribs twice.

Harry did a little more throwing up.

Speaks went back to Amy and Keegan and said, "C'mon."

Keegan said, "God, friend, I really owe you one."

Speaks took Amy by the arm and helped her up the stairs. "I want to get you two into your own room and then I'm going to stand guard all night."

"All night," Amy said. "Are you kidding?"

"No," Speaks said, knowing that Harry Creed would try something else later on. "No, I'm not kidding at all."

∽∾∿∾

SPEAKS FOUND A straight-backed chair and hauled it down in front of Keegan's door. He sat down and put his weapon in his lap and rolled himself another one of his sloppy, lumpen cigarettes.

He was just enjoying the first couple of drags when he heard footsteps coming up the hall stairs. Moments later, a cop appeared.

Out west they were wearing those kepi hats, the kind favored by Foreign Legionnaires and other types of fancy-uniform complements. But Cedar Rapids would apparently brook no such foolishness. This hefty Irishman wore a blue coat and a blue cap and a dramatic star pinned on the chest of his coat. He carried a nightstick and wore a squeaking holster filled with a shiny Navy Colt.

"You the man in the gunfight?" he asked Speaks.

"There wasn't any gunfight."

"There almost was."

Speaks shook his head.

"Some punk named the Pecos Kid stepped out of line." The big Mick grinned.

"The Pecos Kid, huh? In Cedar Rapids?"

"That's what he calls himself."

"So it's all over?"

"All over."

"You a Pinkerton man or something?" the Mick asked.

"No, why?"

"You're guarding the door."

"Oh. No, I just want to see that my friends get a good night's sleep."

"You think the punk'll be back?"

Speaks shrugged. "I just don't want to take any chances."

The Mick said, "Pecos, huh?"

Speaks smiled. "Pecos."

"Wait till I tell the boys."

In the silence again Speaks listened to the various sounds of humanity up and down the hall. A few doors away a couple was having enviably noisy sex. Then there was the man with the tobacco hack. And then there was the nightmare-screamer. And then there was the snorer. The guy was sawing logs so loudly Speaks half-expected to hear the door ripped off its hinges.

Every time he got dozy, Speaks rolled another cigarette. By the fourth one, three hours after he'd applied the seat of his pants to the seat of the chair, he was really starting to get the hang of rolling smokes. Imagine, after all these years, he was finally learning to do it right.

He heard the noise then, and he knew instantly that Harry Creed had outfoxed him.

Creed knew Speaks was sitting in the hall. So Harry decided to shinny up the side of the hotel and go in the window.

The bastard.

Speaks burst through the door into darkness. He glimpsed shifting figures in the gloom, but that was all because just then somebody hit him very hard from behind with a gun.

Pain. Anger. Then a rushing coldness. And then—darkness. Speaks was out, sprawled on the floor.

∽∞∽

PAIN.

He wondered what time it was.

The hotel room was empty.

More pain. Then anger again as he remembered how Harry Creed had come up the side of the hotel.

Muzzy streetlight filled the window frame.

The town of Cedar Rapids was quiet.

Speaks pushed himself to his feet. He'd been out long

enough for the blood on the back of his head to dry and scab over a bit.

He poured warm but clean water from the metal pitcher into the washing pan. He splashed water across his face and the back of his head.

Not until now had he seen the small white piece of paper on top of the bureau. He picked it up.

BARN

The one word.

Nothing more.

He wondered what the hell Harry Creed was up to now.

MOONLIGHT LENT THE old buildings lining the alley a shabby dignity. A couple of cats sat atop a garbage can, imperiously noting Speaks's passing.

Only one of the smithy's doors was open now. The interior was completely dark.

A kind of metallic chittering sound reached Speaks's ears.

At first he couldn't fathom what could make such a noise.

But as he pushed into the barn, his gun leading the way, he had a terrible premonition of what he was about to see.

And of what was making that noise.

One of the rear barn doors was ajar just enough for Speaks to see the shape of the ring.

Keegan was in the ring. Or what was left of him, anyway. The rats had eaten most of his face. One of his eyeballs was already gone. They'd probably fought each other for the sake of eating it. Keegan's forehead glistened. Harry Creed had borrowed an old trick from the Indians. Cover a man in honey and let the rats at him. The rats had also eaten out Keegan's throat. They were working on his stomach and groin now. The air stank of fresh blood and feces.

He was about to fire at the rats, drive them away, when he felt a rifle barrel prod the back of his head, the wound inflicted earlier. He winced.

"Kind of makes you hungry, don't it?" Harry Creed laughed from the darkness behind Speaks.

"Where's Amy?" Speaks snapped.

"Ain't that sweet?" Harry Creed said. "He's worried about Amy. I knew he was interested in that sweet ass of hers. I just knew it."

He stepped out of the shadows. He was wearing his pirate getup again. He plucked Speaks's gun from him. "Pecos went and got hisself killed."

"I'm really sorry to hear that."

"Forced Keegan into a gunfight. Guess you were right, Lyle. Keegan killed Pecos right off."

"Then you tied Keegan to the ring."

Harry Creed shook his head.

"I love that woman, Lyle. I purely do. And she was my wife before she was his. I had to teach him a lesson, didn't I?" Then Creed smiled. "He didn't scream for very long. They killed him right off. I mean, there wasn't all that much pain for him, if that's what you're worried about."

"Where's Amy?"

"I guess that's for me to know," Harry Creed laughed, "and for you to find out. Now it's gonna be your turn, Lyle. You always did think you was a little better'n me. Now you're gonna find out otherwise."

Harry Creed nudged Speaks toward the pit.

"You get in there and sit down."

Speaks hesitated a moment. Not until a few minutes before had he realized how crazy Harry Creed really was. Speaks had no doubt that Creed would shoot him right now if he disobeyed.

Speaks looked in the pit at the rats swarming all over poor Keegan. Poor Keegan was going to be poor Speaks in just a few more seconds.

"Climb in," Harry Creed said.

Speaks raised his leg, climbed into the pit. The rats were too busy feasting on Keegan to pay much attention to Speaks.

Speaks saw the honey pot then, stashed over in the shadows near the right side of the pit. It was about the size of a coffeepot.

"Start daubin' that stuff on your face and hands," Harry Creed said.

Speaks thought of refusing, but why die sooner rather than later? But it'd be better to be shot than to have rats rend you. It'd be much better.

The honey pot was a lidded ceramic bowl. Speaks took the lid off and plunged his hand deep inside.

Sticky honey oozed around his hand, sucking it ever deeper into the bowl.

"Now start rubbin' it on your face, Speaks."

For the first time a few of the scrambling rats looked over in his direction. The sweet smell of the honey pot was what did it. There was a whole new feast over here. Their eyes glowed red in the oppressive darkness.

Harry Creed came right over to the edge of the ring now.

"Start rubbin' it on your face, Speaks. You heard me."

Speaks had no choice. His hand dripping honey, he began to wipe the thick stuff on the angles of his face.

Already a few of the rats had drifted over and were starting to climb his legs. At this point, he could still kick them away. But not for much longer.

"Now sit down."

"No."

Harry Creed aimed the rifle right at Speaks's face.

"I said sit down."

Speaks had one chance, and if he muffed it he was going to be eaten alive the way his friend Keegan had been.

Speaks slowly sat down on his haunches.

More and more rats swarmed around him.

"All the way down," Harry Creed said.

Speaks reluctantly sat all the way down.

Now the rats were all over him, on his back and arms and legs. All he could think of was the illustrations he'd seen of *Gulliver's Travels*, a book Clytie had given him to read, all the tiny people walking up and down the giant.

A rat scrambling over his shoulder lashed out at Speaks's honey-painted face.

Speaks jumped half an inch off the pit floor and made a wild wailing sound in his throat.

"Scary little buggers, aren't they?" Harry Creed said. "Now lay down."

"What?"

"You heard me, Lyle. Lay down. Flat. On the floor."

"No way."

The bullet passed so close to his ear, he could smell the metal of it. A few of the rats scattered. Most continued to cling to Speaks. There were maybe two dozen of the things on him now.

"Lay down, you son of a bitch."

So Speaks lay down. The pit was so small that he had to prop his legs up on the edge of the ring.

Then he screamed.

The rats seemed to suddenly triple in number, and they were all over him, especially his head and hands.

The small honey pot was four inches from his right hand. He would have to be quick. And then he would have to roll away from where Harry Creed was likely to fire.

"My, these fellas sure have big appetites," Harry Creed said. "You and Keegan in one night. My, my."

A rat sank teeth into Speaks's left hand. Speaks sobbed with pain and terror and reached for the honey pot.

He caught Harry Creed right in the center of the forehead.

Then he rolled quickly to the right. Harry Creed staggered, then pumped three bullets into the exact spot Speaks had occupied only moments earlier.

Speaks jumped to his feet, rats hanging off of him as he did so, and lunged at Harry Creed.

He tore the rifle from Creed's hand and drove a punch deep into Harry's stomach. Harry doubled over. Speaks took the rifle and started clubbing Harry Creed on the side of the head until the man slumped forward into unconsciousness.

Once he had slapped and shaken the rats off of him the first thing he did was take the rope off Keegan's wrists and ankles and carry the ripped and bloody body out of the pit. Bleeding from his own bite wounds, he found a horse blanket and covered him with it.

His final act was to pick up the honey pot and empty it lavishly over the length of Harry Creed's face and body, back and forth, back and forth, until Harry was saturated with honey.

～～～

A FEW MINUTES later, Speaks found Amy up in the haymow. She'd been bound and gagged.

She was sobbing when she got to her feet.

"I'll never forget the screaming," she said, leaning on Speaks for support. "He died so slowly."

He let her cling to him, let him be her strength for a long moment. He kept seeing how Keegan's face had looked after the rats had finished with it. He wanted to slice a knife blade into his brain and cut out the memory forever.

"Where's Harry?" she said finally.

"Don't worry about Harry."

"You're going to turn him over to the law, aren't you?"

Grimly, with no hint of humor, he said, "Let's just say I've taken care of Harry in my own way."

They went down the ladder to the ground floor and then out the door. He steered her away from the ring so she couldn't see. Being a good Christian woman, she might try to talk Speaks out of what he was doing.

"We'll go to my hotel room and wash up," Speaks said.

"But Harry. Where's Harry?" Amy said. "Shouldn't we turn him over to the law?"

Harry Creed regained consciousness just then. Two, three, even four blocks away they could still hear him screaming.

"Oh, my God," she said. "You put the rats on him, didn't you?"

Speaks said nothing.

Just took her arm a little tighter and escorted her out of the alley.

After a block or so you couldn't hear Harry scream hardly at all.

Double-Cross

❧❧❧
Elizabeth Fackler

THE MAN FELL to his knees, pleading for mercy from Allister's gun. Seth held his own gun as he watched the door while listening to Allister's threats. They were robbing the bank in Quitten, though Seth guessed it'd be more accurate to say they were attempting to rob it because most of the money was in a safe the teller claimed could be opened only by the manager, who wasn't there. The cash drawer had netted a paltry two hundred dollars, and Allister seemed bent on killing the teller if he didn't cooperate.

Seth began edging toward the door. He wasn't above killing for a purpose, but a dead man couldn't open a safe so he was hard put to see any gain in shooting the teller. Besides, Allister had already fired several shots trying to break the lock, and Seth knew the noise hadn't gone unnoticed.

Allister was in a mood, though, and getting more riled at every pathetic plea out of the teller's mouth. When Seth turned around, he saw Allister put the barrel of his pistol to the man's head and pull the trigger.

Seth looked out the door and saw half a dozen men with rifles running up the street. He fired his gun to scatter them and ran for his horse, Allister on his heels. They galloped into the Badlands, following a crevice through the rugged arroyos, then gained a perch from which they could make a good defense. The posse followed in no time, spreading out below.

After spending a hot hour sweating on the rocks, Allister suggested they make a run for it. Seth turned from where he was bellied down over his Winchester and stared at Allister a minute.

"If we run," Seth finally said, "they'll just be on our tails."

"We can lose 'em," Allister argued.

"There's fifteen men down there, and from what I saw their horses are as good as ours. What makes you think we'll lose 'em?"

" 'Cause you're lucky, Seth," Allister said, giving him a teasing smile.

Seth looked away and muttered, "I used to think so before I hooked up with you."

"What's that s'posed to mean?" Allister growled.

"If you hadn't killed that teller," Seth said, flat to his eyes, "those men wouldn't have come after us. Nobody risks their life for two hundred dollars."

"It would've been a lot more if he'd opened the safe."

"Well, he couldn't do it dead, could he?"

"Aw, he was too stupid to live."

Seth didn't answer, watching the rocks below.

Allister said, "If you think you'd be better off without me, go ahead and try."

Without looking at him, Seth said, "You're the one wants to run. Why don't you do it?"

"What're you gonna do? Stand off all fifteen of 'em by yourself?"

"Maybe."

"Maybe, hell! They're prob'ly circling around behind us right now."

"That's why it's good to have a partner to cover your back," Seth said. "But anyone who wants to run may as well do it 'cause he's lost his nerve anyway."

"I'm the one killed the fuckin' teller! Don't tell me I've lost my nerve."

"It's not much of a challenge to shoot an unarmed man."

"He made me mad, is all," Allister mumbled.

Seth didn't say anything, studying the rocks and thinking if he could catch enough of a glimpse to wing one of the posse, it might discourage the others into going home. But from the way they were keeping out of sight, he figured they saw the situation as a standoff, knowing he and Allister were pinned in the sun with a short supply of water.

Allister said, "Don't make no sense to throw one mistake after another, Seth. We gotta get out of here or we won't be going anyplace ever."

"Go ahead and go, dammit!" Seth shouted. "I said you could."

"I don't need your permission!"

"What're you waiting for, then?"

"Maybe I feel responsible for the punk kid I took under my wing."

Seth rolled over and looked at the man he'd followed since he was eighteen. Allister had been barely thirty when they first hooked up, a dangerous desperado who swaggered with grace. Now he was pushing forty and in such a foul mood most of the time that he ricocheted out of control. Softly Seth said, "I was never a punk kid."

Allister scoffed, "You were born with a hard-on, I s'pose."

"I wasn't born to run from no goddamned posse!"

"What d'ya think we were doing all the way here?"

"Getting out of town."

"And the men riding behind shooting guns in our direction didn't have nothing to do with it?"

"They wouldn't've been there if you hadn't killed the teller!"

"So what? He's dead. We ain't yet."

"Maybe I'd rather be dead than ride with a partner who shoots unarmed men just 'cause he's in a mood."

"You think you're better'n me?"

"Right now I do."

Allister kicked at him, knocking the Winchester out of his hands. It flew over the cliff and bounced on the rocks below, going off as it hit and inspiring a fusillade from the posse.

"You sonofabitch!" Seth shouted, dodging bullets as he grabbed Allister and threw him against a huge boulder to pummel his belly. A bullet whizzed past Seth's ear to hit Allister, and they both flattened fast.

Allister put a hand to his shoulder, blood seeping through his fingers. "It's my gun hand, Seth. I can't shoot."

Seth grabbed Allister's Winchester and emptied it into the rocks hiding the posse. As he pulled bullets out of his belt to reload, he saw his own rifle catching sun below. A shadow flitted across its barrel, and he looked up to see a man on the ridge coming around to the left. Seth fired and the man ducked back behind the rocks.

At that point Seth had to admit Allister was right and they'd better get out. With only one shooter, they didn't have a chance where they were. He emptied the rifle at the posse and reloaded again, then crawled across to Allister. "You sorry excuse for a bandit," Seth said. "I oughta leave you to die."

"Go ahead," Allister warned. "I'll haunt you from every campfire and hearth you ever set eyes on."

Seth smiled. "That'd be a fate worse than death. Let's go."

They ran for their horses and rode down a ravine away from the posse, Allister in the lead. Seth knotted his reins and primed their only rifle, looking back in time to see one of the posse gallop out of an arroyo emptying into the ravine. Seth fired and watched the man fall. Cocking the rifle to fire at the next one, Seth saw him stop to help his friend, then looked at Allister. He was slumped in the saddle, about to lose his reins. Seth slid the rifle into his scabbard and urged his horse to take the lead. Grabbing Allister's reins just before they fell, he high-tailed it into the prairie, flat with no cover in sight.

They were kicking up dust visible for miles, but Seth didn't know the country. He had no place to seek sanctuary, nothing to do but push the horses and hope his luck held. The luck Allister was always joshing about, saying it was half the reason he'd taken Seth under his wing. Allister wasn't joshing now. He was losing a lot of blood and would die if the wound wasn't patched up quick. Seth took a chance and stopped. He pulled his extra shirt out of his saddlebag and held it to the wound, pressing hard to seal off the flow of blood, then tied it with the sleeves around the shoulder and lifted Allister's left hand. "Hold it there," Seth said. "Can you do that?"

"Yeah," Allister mumbled.

"Keep the pressure on or you'll bleed to death."

"I can do it," he said.

Seth swung onto his horse, took Allister's reins, and dug in his spurs. When he looked back he could see the dust of the posse still a good piece behind. The first two men must have been circling around to catch their prey in a scorpion's claw. When that didn't work, the others had to scramble for their horses, giving him and Allister time. Still they had maybe as many as thirteen men on their tail. It might be fewer, Seth hadn't been able to tell if he'd hit any from his perch. However many there were, they knew the country and Seth didn't.

He and Allister were riding across a high plateau rimmed with mountains. It was October and the sun would set early but not for hours yet. Their horses were already lathered, and Seth knew he couldn't keep the pace much longer but didn't see as he had any choice. The choice had been back at the rocks. He tried to figure how things had deteriorated so fast into fighting between themselves when they were surrounded by enemies. Allister had been right and they should have run from the start. Make a stand to get the posse off their horses and discourage them a bit, then get the hell out of there. The problem was that Seth had been mad at Allister for killing the teller.

The middle of a skirmish wasn't any time to settle a grievance, though. He should have kept his head clear and dealt with it later. If he hadn't already done that so many times, he might have been able to handle it again. But Allister had started rubbing Seth wrong with almost every move he made. Seth had sloughed it off and let it slide until he'd reached his breaking point. It seemed he spent half his time mopping up Allister's mistakes, and gradually he was beginning to recognize that the power in their partnership had shifted. In the beginning, Allister had been the expert and Seth a novice eager to learn. Now Seth was a seasoned desperado, and the man he had followed so deep into that life was losing the finesse that had attracted him. It made Seth angry to watch Allister fall apart. Angry with Allister for getting old, angry with himself for following a man who blundered as often as not.

Seth kept the horses moving toward the closest ridge of mountains. When a wind came up, obliterating their tracks in the swirling dust of a sandstorm, he chuckled with bittersweet pride that his luck hadn't deserted him. Not that he really gave much of a damn. He could've died at any moment of the years he'd ridden with Allister; if this turned out to be the day his aces were buried, he'd already lived longer than anyone would have given odds on.

Squinting through the cutting dust, Seth saw the faint traces of a trail leading toward the foothills. He followed the trail into the mountains, and after a while he was rewarded with the sight of a homesteader's cabin in the middle of a clearing. A thin wisp of smoke snaked from the chimney into the wind. Seth reined up and studied the cabin, trying to assess the welcome from whoever might be inside.

Behind the cabin was an empty corral built around a natural cave in the mountain. Seth edged forward, thinking maybe he and Allister could hide in the cave without the homesteader suspecting they were there, at least until dark. As he leaned from the saddle to unlatch the gate, he saw a boy come out of the cabin and peer across at him. Seth guessed the kid's age at nine or ten. He was wearing overalls and a bib shirt, his face scattered with freckles and his blue eyes pinned on Allister, slumped in the saddle. The boy ran through the blowing dust of the yard to climb the fence and take hold of the gate from the inside, pulling it open wide enough for the horses to pass.

"Go on into the cave," he shouted. "We got it rigged for a stable."

"Obliged," Seth shouted back, nudging his horse into the vault of the cavern. He swung down and looked at Allister, then at the boy standing silhouetted against the brighter light outside.

"Your friend sick?" the boy asked.

Seth nodded. "Where's your pa?"

"In the hills," the boy answered. "Won't be back till late tomorrow. Ya wanta bring your friend up to the cabin?"

"Is your ma there?"

"Don't have no ma," he said.

"Anybody else with you?"

The boy shook his head. Seth looked around. His eyes had adjusted to the lesser light and he could see into the farthest reaches of the cave. It ended in a scooped-out hollow twenty feet ahead of him, with a thick layer of soft dust against the wall. Allister groaned, out cold, still sitting his horse. Seth looked at the boy. "Your pa got any whiskey?"

"Jug of corn likker," the boy said.

"Would you fetch it for me? And some clean clothes, towel, sheet, something?"

The boy looked at Allister, then at the dark drops now staining the floor of the cave on the far side of his horse. "He's shot, ain't he?" the boy whispered, turning big eyes back on Seth.

He nodded. "I gotta get the bullet out or he'll die."

"Be right back," the boy said, already running across the corral to climb the fence.

Seth untied his bedroll and spread it in the dust against the wall, then led Allister's horse to stand close. Draping Allister's left arm across his shoulders, he dragged him off the horse and let him down easy on the blanket, watching the blood seep through the makeshift bandage tied over the wound.

Seth led the horse away and tethered it with his own to an empty manger. Through the mouth of the cave, he saw the boy coming back, a wad of cloth under one arm and the jug cradled in front of him, telling Seth it was pretty near full. He went out to open the gate for the boy. They walked back into the cave and stood a moment looking down at Allister. Seth fell to his knees and drew his knife.

The boy watched him peel away the shirt to reveal the ragged hole still seeping blood. Seth opened the jug and poured the liquor over his right hand holding the knife, dousing the blade good, then he probed deep into Allister's flesh for the bullet. Allister flinched, though still unconscious. Seth felt his blade scrape against lead. He stuck his fingers into the hole and pulled the slug from the slime of the wound. "Give me the jug," he said. The boy handed it to him and he poured the liquor over the gory hole. Allister jerked, then lay still again. Seth grabbed a small towel, saturated it with liquor, and laid it across the wound. "Can you hold it?" he asked the boy.

His hand came out and touched the towel, already red with blood.

"Press hard," Seth said, tearing strips from the sheet.

He slid around to wedge his knee under and lift Allister's shoulder to tie the bandage. "Get your hand out of the way," Seth said. The boy leaned back, his bloody palm between his knees, watching Seth yank the knot tight. He eased Allister back onto the floor, then stood up, his own hands red with blood as he looked down at the boy. "He's on his own now," Seth said.

The boy studied Allister a long moment, then looked at Seth and asked, "Ya wanta come up to the house and wash?"

Seth looked out at the corral and yard and the cabin with the thin wisp of smoke coming from the chimney. In the corral was a trough. He walked out to it, seeing it was fed by a trickle of water running off the mountain. Leaning low, he scrubbed his hands and dunked his face, washing away the blood and dust. When he stood up, shaking the water free, he saw the boy was watching him. The boy advanced warily and stuck his own hand into the trough. They both watched the red blood swirl away in the now-pink water. The boy dried his hand on his pant leg, then looked up at Seth.

"What's your name?" Seth asked.

"Burford Adams."

Seth smiled. "They call you Burford?"

The boy nodded.

Seth walked past him into the cave, across to where Allister lay. He picked up the jug, hefted it onto his crooked arm, and lifted it to his mouth. As he drank, he watched the boy looking at their horses, still winded and crusted with sweat. Seth set the jug down and recorked it. "I'm in kind of a spot here, Burford," he said. "I don't like asking favors of strangers, but you can see my friend ain't in any shape to travel."

"Your horses neither," Burford said.

"That's true," Seth said. "Think we could hole up here till morning?"

"Whyn't ya come up to the house?" Burford asked.

Again Seth looked across the yard to the cabin. It stood

isolated in the clearing and could be easily surrounded. Not that the cave was much better, but it had the advantage of sheltering the horses nearby. "Reckon I'll stay with my friend," he said.

Burford looked at Allister. "Who shot him?"

"Didn't get a chance to ask their names."

"Why'd they shoot him?"

Seth considered the possible answers he could give, then said, "Posses tend to do that, at least try. They don't usually get so lucky."

The boy looked at the man unconscious on the blanket, then at the two quality horses, then back at Seth. "You're Seth Strummar, ain't ya?" he whispered. "And that there's Ben Allister."

Seth nodded.

"Golly!" Burford grinned. "I sure am pleased to meet'cha, Mr. Strummar."

Seth saw again the terrified eyes of the teller just before Allister pulled the trigger. "Why's that?" he asked.

"You're 'bout the most famous desperados ever was," the boy crowed. "Ain't nobody braver nor deadlier than Strummar and Allister."

The smell of blood was strong in the cave, and Seth could smell his own sweat in his shirt. The sweat of fear and the blood of rightful vengeance. He wanted to tell the boy he was making a mistake, that he and Allister were no heroes, but he needed the boy, so he smiled and asked, "How'd you know it was us?"

"Should've known from the start," the boy said in awe. "All the stories tell how Seth Strummar's got eyes the color of smoke and cold as death. I used to stare into the sun trying to bleach my eyes out so they'd look like yours. But my pa told me I was gonna make myself blind, and that what my eyes see is more important'n what color they are."

Seth lifted the jug and took another drink. He stared down at Allister a moment, then looked back at the boy. "Go on up to the cabin," Seth said, "and cook us some supper. And if anyone comes asking, you say you ain't seen us."

"I'll do that, Mr. Strummar," Burford promised solemnly. "Ya want I should bring your supper when it's cooked?"

Seth nodded, then watched the boy leave, throwing smiles back over his shoulder. Half an hour later, two men scouting for the posse rode into the yard. Seth watched through the sight of Allister's Winchester as Burford talked to the men. They apparently knew him because they accepted his word that he was alone, their cursory glances at the empty corral not penetrating into the dark of the cave. Seth held his breath so the barrel of the rifle wouldn't betray his presence with a flash of light, though he smiled as he watched Burford send the scouts away. The kid was so smart he didn't even look in Seth's direction after the scouts had ridden off; he went straight back inside the cabin and kept working at supper.

By the time he brought a big bowl of black beans and a bunch of hot biscuits wrapped in a napkin, Seth had taken more nips from the jug than he should have. He settled down to eat as the kid watched him, reminding Seth of the dozens of little boys he'd seen over the years, their eyes shining with admiration as they stared at him and Allister riding by. Seth felt sick but kept eating, knowing his inner man needed nourishment even if his soul had died of neglect. When he finished, he laid the empty bowl aside and walked to the opening of the cave.

A windless dusk was settling over the mountains, its shadows long and dark. He wanted more whiskey but knew he couldn't get drunk. Allister was helpless, and though the scene looked peaceful, it could change fast. Seth had to stay on top of it; that's all he knew. Ride it for the duration because it was too late to get off. Thinking he could catch some sleep if the boy stood guard, he turned around and looked at Burford watching him with shining eyes. Seth figured the best way to repay the boy for his help would be to set him straight about the hell an outlaw's life truly dealt a man. But he needed the boy, so he used him as he was.

In the morning, while he readied to leave, Seth could hear Burford behind him munching the last of the breakfast biscuits. When it was time to load Allister, Burford frisked his palms free of crumbs and offered to help. Seth shook his head and hefted Allister's two hundred pounds into the saddle. He waited a moment to be certain his partner wouldn't fall off, then led the horse outside to where his stood by the open gate.

Seth swung on and his horse surged to a start, but he yanked it back and smiled down at the kid. "Thanks, Burford," he said. "You prob'ly saved me from a hanging."

"Oh no, Mr. Strummar" was the boy's response. "Nobody'll ever hang you!"

"Not if I can get 'em to shoot me first," Seth agreed.

Burford grinned, sharing the joke.

Seth touched his spurs and his horse bolted through the gate, only to be reined down to a skittish lope. He rode twisted in the saddle, making sure Allister stayed put as they crossed the meadow. At the edge of the forest, he looked at the awestruck kid watching from the fence, then at the famous desperado being towed like baggage, and the disparity between the boy's dream and the man's fate made him mad. But when Burford waved in the distance, Seth didn't have the heart not to wave back.

The Making of Jared Dodds
Michael Stotter

Let me tell you from the start that I am going to tell you the truth. Why? Because you asked me to and that should suffice. I've also sworn an oath and placed my hand on the Bible. That should be enough and I've the time to tell you.

You are either going to believe me or not. After all, it's my story and I remember events the way I saw them and can recall. Trouble is, I don't have any evidence or witnesses to call upon to back up my words. You'll have to rely on what I tell you. Are you willing to do that?

I've been called a liar and a cheat so would I lie and cheat you? I can't rightly say. Yes, I've been known to lie, and yes, I've cheated people, many people. Did they deserve the deception? Only fools are deceived, and I must say that at times I got a thrill from the game. And I did consider it a game. A deadly game at times, I must admit, but nevertheless it was a game. I made the rules and I live and will die by them and it is as simple as that, so don't try and read anything else into it.

People have died. Some deserved it, others didn't. How

can I say someone deserves to die? Think about it. Think of what you would do in the same situation. Would you allow some drunkard to slap your ma around? Slap her so hard at times that the finger marks stayed on her face for days afterwards like she'd been branded? And she protected him from others in saying that it was her fault. The first time I can recall was one morning when I walked into the shack and Ma was standing by the stove crying. I went over to her and pulled her hands away from her face and saw her blackened eye.

I asked what happened, and she said that she deserved it because she had broken a jug. His jug. His favorite jug. I was too young to understand it all. Pa did take the belt to us from time to time; it was something we lived with. Then things got worse. He began using his fists. One day Ma had a broken nose, then another time a busted rib, then . . . No, I'm not going to give a list. I don't reckon I'm the first person who's killed their father. He deserved it, wouldn't you say?

So that's when it started, back when I was a skinny runt of thirteen. There was no trouble from the law. We kept in the family. If anyone asked, they were told Pa had gone to some diggings to find a grubstake and he was going to send for us. We buried him beyond the vegetable plot where the pigs couldn't dig him up. I can't rightly say I enjoyed killing him, but I weren't going to sit around and let him beat Ma into a pulp like he did with my older brother, John. He was hurt so bad that he couldn't walk without a stick to help him. He was sixteen when he died.

There were six of us. Three boys and three girls. I was the third eldest but since John was a cripple I was looked on as the eldest boy. With Pa gone, my ma had to struggle to keep things together and looked to me for help. I began working in the kitchen at a hotel for a bit a day. Altogether I spent a half-year there before going on to work for a lumber company. I was just turned fifteen when Emma May died. Emma May was only three.

It was coming up to Christmas and we were excited to

have a family trip into town to collect some dry goods
and Ma was purchasing a bolt of cloth to make the girls
a new dress each. We'd just come out of the mercantile
store and were walking down Main Street when a team-
ster's wagon comes a'rushing down the street. Something
had spooked the horses and there was nothing the driver
could do to control the team. As it came level with us the
tailgate dropped down and a length of chain broke free.
It whipped around and smashed into Emma May's head.
She was only three. She died on the spot. I was holding
her hand.

We buried her three days later—on Christmas Eve. The
driver, J. D. Collins, came to see Ma and offered to pay
for the funeral because he felt so bad. It cost eight dollars.
Not much for a little girl's life was it? But Ma took it
because we didn't have the cash. That's when I decided
it wasn't enough.

A couple of days later I sneaked out and went to see
Collins. He was working in the stable yard. When he saw
me, he stopped working on a wagon jack and sat down.
He was stripped to the waist and the sweat glistened on
his skin. His face was red with labor and it reminded me
of Ma's face after Pa had smacked her.

I came right out and asked if he thought eight dollars
was enough for a child's life. You know what? He
laughed. Said he thought it was plenty.   .

"Your ma should be grateful for one less soul to keep"
was what he actually said.

He put down the hammer he was using to repair the
jack and wiped his hands on his pant's legs, then stood
up asking if I was finished. I remained silent, a little
stunned, and a little shocked at his bluntness. J. D. Collins
shrugged and turned his back and went back to work,
figuring that I'd let it go. I might have done. I should
have done. Should have walked away from there and let
the tears roll down my face. But I couldn't go back home
knowing that Collins thought he could buy us off for eight

dollars. It wasn't right. I knew that, even as young as I was.

"Mister Collins!" I called and he turned around.

"Go away, sonny." He was annoyed.

I carried on. "Mister Collins, one of your horses got to be worth more than eight dollars."

"That's right."

"Iffen it was to die, then you'd be upset, wouldn't you?"

"Damn straight!"

"So all I'm asking you is to give my ma a little more than eight dollars."

He laughed again. "Son, I paid for the funeral. And I'm sorry your sister died but it was an accident. I can't change things. What more do you want from me?"

"To give my ma twenty-five dollars."

I reckoned that twenty-five dollars was a big sum of money. It's the most I'd ever seen at one time. It seemed a fair amount.

J. D. Collins stood there with an amazed look on his face. He looked at me for a half-minute before saying, "I should put you over my knee. You come here again asking for money and I'll teach you a lesson. Now roll your wheels you little croppy!"

I couldn't believe it—Collins was calling me an outlaw! I felt something hot in the pit of my stomach; it was all bunched up like when you get the cramps. All I wanted was a few bucks to help my family. He was responsible for Emma May's death and I figured he should pay. It wasn't my intention to go there and harm him. He brought it on himself.

He turned his back on me and went back to working on the wheel jack. Over to my right there was a broken singletree leaning against the fence. I picked it up and came at him. Used it on him like an ax. Why do you want to know how many times I hit him? He went down and I hit him a couple more times until he stopped twitching. I went through his pockets and found a couple of bits and a quarter, then I went through his room at the side of the stable and found a pouch holding thirty bucks.

I didn't even know that I'd killed him at the time. As far as I was concerned I'd just laid him out. I can't recall being affected by it at all. My main thought was getting the money to give to Ma. It was on my way back home when I realized that I'd just done something awful. I wasn't sorry I done it. No sir, not one bit. But as I walked home I figured that I was going to be in trouble, big trouble. And Ma shouldn't be part of it.

I waited under a cottonwood tree about a half-mile away from our shack until dusk, then I carried on. I scouted around in case the sheriff or his deputy had found out and was waiting for me but it was quiet. There was a late evening breeze that lifted the smell of the pigs my way but other than that it was still. I stayed outside until it was fully dark. One time the door opened and I saw Ma stand in the doorway looking out toward town, looking for me, then she went back inside. The light from the shack went out and I waited until the cold bit into me before I crept in.

Ma was asleep in the chair by the stove, a Bible lay opened in her lap. The grease in the Phoebe lamp had burned out and there was a high smell. My brothers and sisters were asleep in the rope bed in the corner. I took Pa's old revolver, a Navy Six, from the box near the stove, and put it into my jacket pocket. I left the pouch of money on the table. I'd already taken out five dollars for myself.

So does that answer your question of how I got started? Not very colorful was it? But now I suppose you want to hear about my life as a desperado, or, as J. D. Collins called me, a croppy? I know I am making it sound casual, and maybe you're thinking I'm juicing it and what bits have I lied about? But I already told you that you've got to sift out the truth for yourself.

Once I got over the county line I felt safe. I really don't know if the law was after me, and as I couldn't read nor

write I hadn't been able to leave Ma a note to say why
I'd upped and left. She'd probably figured it out for herself. So there I was, a yonkster of fourteen already walking on the wrong side of the tracks. But once out of the
county I told myself to get things straightened out in my
head. I got out of Texas and drifted down into New Mexico by way of various jobs: a cow tracker, a dishwasher
in a grease joint, a laborer in a railyard, and a hand on a
stern-wheeler on the Rio Grande. That's how I got to Las
Cruces, over in Dona Ana County in New Mexico.

❧

IT WAS IN Las Cruces when it all began.

It was July time and hot. The job I had on the stern-
wheeler had come to an end. There was ten dollars of pay
in my back pocket and I had left most of the crew drinking theirs in a saloon. I'd left when they were getting
brave enough to try and down *los gusanos* in one go. I
wasn't that *valiente* or drunk enough to eat those little
worms that were in the bottles of mescal they sold to the
foolish Anglos or the macho hombres. It was around ten
in the evening and I was heading down Amador Street
looking for a room. There were a few people on the street:
men from the local forts, couples walking together, gamblers on their way to the casino in the Amador Hotel on
the corner of Walter and Amador Street. I was happy to
have my feet on solid ground.

I'd been through Las Cruces a few times. Once on a
trail drive that took me to Montana, then a couple more
times with the crew of the *High Tide*, the stern-wheeler
that worked the Rio Grande. Because Las Cruces was a
popular site to cross the river it attracted a fair mix of
people. The population was chiefly Hispanic but many
more Anglos had been drifting in of late. With it being
close to the Organ Mountains off to the east it proved a
regular jumping off point with outlaws.

I don't know whether or not I was thinking about rustlers and the such, but I noticed two men standing in the half-light outside a merchant's store. They were Anglos standing tall and alert. Both wore their rigs high on the hip, the cutaway holsters carrying revolvers. The nearest man to the street carried more weight and looked me over with one casual glance as I passed, then went back looking down Main Street. You could tell that they didn't live here, not townsfolk. They were dressed differently and the way they wore their guns you knew their trade without question. I'd seen hired guns afore up and down the Rio Grande. It was a great temptation to look over my shoulder to see what he found so interesting but I shrugged it off. It was none of my business. I went on my way.

As I neared the mouth of an alley I heard some cursing. The voice was guttural but female at the same time. Curiosity got the better of me and I stopped and looked down the alley. There was a woman who stood no more than five foot high dressed in Levi pants and a white blouse. She was hefting a sack of flour onto the back of a mouse dun that was struggling to get away.

"Do you need some help?" I called.

The woman spun around almost dropping the sack. She had wild brown hair and even in the gloom I could see her steel blue eyes that stood out against the brown of her skin. I'm no good with ages, men or women, but I hazard a guess that she was maybe twenty-five or so.

When she saw I was just a young man she smiled and said, "No, thank you."

Ignoring her, I moved to take the sack away from her. She stopped me by seizing my wrist in a very firm grasp and pulled it away.

"I can manage, señor."

"No offense, ma'am. Just helping."

"Thanks, but I do my own work."

The way she said it gave no room for argument. You only had to look at her to agree that she could take care of herself. She caught me taking a sideways look at her breasts pushing out against the cotton of her *blusa*. She cocked her head to one side.

"Do you have a smoke?"

"Yes, sure," I said. "I only got short sixes."

"Pah! Cheap cigars." She waved the offer away. "How about some chewing tobacco?"

I shook my head. "Don't chaw."

She rattled something off very fast in Spanish. I caught a little of it, something about a little man, didn't get the rest of it.

"Can I buy you a drink?" I asked feeling bold.

She smiled. There was something in her smile that caught me in the throat. Her eyes softened as she thought about the offer for all of a second.

"Sure, why not?" she said.

"My name's Jared Dodds," I said as an introduction.

"I am Maria Conchita Alvarez."

She picked up the sack and used the saddle tie strings to secure it behind the cantle. She noticed me looking at the saddle. It wasn't the normal workaday saddle you'd see a cowboy use but a fancy Mexican stock saddle. The *tapaderos* were decorated with *conchas* and the leather of the skirt was carved with eagles and such.

"You like?" she asked.

"Very much."

"It was a gift."

"Must have been a generous person," I said.

Her laughter was light and mocking. "A gift to myself."

"I see."

"Señor, I am my own person. No one owns me. . . ."

"I wasn't suggesting . . ." Holding up my hands in mock surrender.

She was determined to explain herself. I let her have her head.

"Since I was a little girl my grandmother taught me about plants and poisons and snakes. I make use of herbs to cure illness. My potions are well-known in the country.

For curing people and animals I am paid. That's how it goes."

I don't know why she felt she had to justify owning a fancy saddle to me. I wasn't that interested in the saddle. I would be lying to say I wasn't interested in her. I knew it and she knew it.

∞∾∽

WE WALKED OUT on Main Street heading back the way I had just come. The two gunmen were still positioned outside the merchant's store; the fat one leaned against an awning post picking his nose as the other stared off down the street.

A door opened close by and a voice called good-night. The door slammed shut, cutting off any answer, then the music to a pair of spurs sounded in the night. I took a couple of steps before I realized that Maria had stopped. I looked back.

"Is there a problem?" I asked.

Obviously there was but she shook her head. "Jared, let's go to my cabin. It's up in the mountains, not far." She tugged at my arm. "Let's go."

I saw her look at the two men: There was fear in her eyes.

"Something wrong?" I asked her.

"No."

"Do you know them men?"

"No."

Our voices had dropped to a whisper. My back was to the gunmen and I didn't want to turn around.

"Tell me what they are doing," I said.

"Nothing."

"Just standing there?"

The noise of the spurs was nearer. Strangely loud in the night. Cutting over the noises from around us.

"Mmm. The taller one is undoing his jacket."

"Go on."

"He's pushing it out of the way of his pistol."

"And the other one?"

She took a sharp intake of breath.

"His pistol is out and he is holding it to one side."

The sound of the spurs was louder.

I said to Maria, "Move closer to the dun. Get between it and them."

"But."

"No, no buts. Do it."

She moved so that her horse shielded her from the gunmen. I put my hand into my jacket pocket and gripped the little hideout pistol. It was a double-barreled Remington .41. A good weapon for close-quarter fighting. I kept my hand fisted around the butt.

The spurs were almost on top of us.

"Hardy!"

The voice came from one of the two men.

The spurs stopped.

Now I turned to face the gunmen. The one who had been leaning against the awning stepped to one side and brought up his revolver and fired off a shot before Hardy could reply. Within a split second the other gunman had fired. I couldn't take my eyes off the gunmen. They cocked back the hammers almost as one but Hardy got off a shot that hit the taller gunman in the upper right arm. You could hear the bone crack.

Now Hardy was facing down the one gunman. He wasn't so lucky with this one. A bullet struck Hardy in the stomach and sent him crashing onto his butt. The fat gunman readied himself for a third shot.

Generally the sight of a man sat on his backside in the middle of the street is a funny one. I looked at Hardy and there was no humor to be had. There was a deputy's badge pinned to his waistcoat. Across his stomach there was a spreading dark patch; blood seeped through his fingers as he tried stopping his blood leaking out. His lips were drawn back over his teeth as he brought his revolver up.

The explosions sounded as one.

The fat gunman jumped to one side as if he'd been punched.

Hardy fell backwards.

There was a hole in my jacket pocket.

Maria dropped the reins and ran to Hardy.

"Dave!" she called. "Dave!"

She dropped to her knees and grabbed hold of the lawman's shoulders and shook him. His head rolled from side to side but his body was still twitching.

"Aw, shit!" Maria shouted. "They killed him!"

It's strange when people swear. They do it better in a different language than in their native tongue. Maria was no different. Her heavy Mexican accent dropped for that one word.

The other gunman was almost forgotten. The sound of the hammer being eared back was clear in the silence after the first round of gunplay. I turned to see him bring around the revolver and sight on Maria. I was a couple of feet away and fired my final round. The .41 entered under his ribs and punched its way out of his back. He staggered around for a couple of steps then gently slid down the wall.

A couple of years back I would have been sickened at this sudden violence. No, I haven't forgotten that I'd already killed two men but that seemed a lifetime ago. I'd spent the last three years putting that behind me. Not once, not even drunk, had I used violence and I'd been around some men whose aim in life was to be quarrelsome. But this, this was different. I had control over what I was doing. I could have kept my own counsel and let the gunmen kill the deputy and walk away. But I knew that me and Maria wouldn't be around to see the next sunrise.

Whoever this Dave Hardy had been, he'd meant something to Maria.

I yanked her to her feet and pulled her across to the mouse dun. She didn't put up a struggle and it was easy for me to swing up into the saddle and pull her up behind

me. I raked the dun's ribs with my heels and we were
away.

Behind us came some shouting, some cursing.

By the time the dun had gotten into a gallop all I could
hear was the blood pounding in my ears.

∽∾∾

A FEW MILES out of town we had swapped places and
she rode the dun like the devil was after us. The critter
was near to death when we reached the cabin. Maria
didn't say one word during the journey, and when we
dismounted she disappeared into her cabin and I could
hear her wail. I was left to deal with the horse.

The cabin was little more than a cave cut in the red
rock of the mountainside. A few pinon trees grew in a
clump that protected the front of the cave mouth. A
wooden structure had been built over the entrance some
time back and was in need of repair. The moon gleamed
in a star-studded sky and bathed the area with its blue-
white light. I remember this so well because it was the
first time I'd fallen in love.

When Maria stepped out of the cabin her face was
bloated from crying but she looked lovely. She stood in
the entrance for a heartbeat, then she came to me.

Not that I would tell Maria, but I think she worked it
out that she was the first woman I'd been with and it
didn't bother her. We spent the next couple of days together, eating and drinking most of her stock of bourbon.
There was no mention of Dave Hardy or what he had
meant to her or the killings.

I didn't have any idea if the law were on our trail,
waiting for the chance to catch up and make me pay. One
morning I was sitting on a rock watching the sun rise,
moving like a fire as it turned the sky from pink to azure.
Noises carry far when you're in the hills and the sound
of a horse approaching the cabin gave enough warning. I
moved off the rock and stood guarding the entrance to

the cabin, thinking that this might be the day.

The rider called hello before he came into sight.

He reined in but stayed in the saddle when he saw me. His eyes were alert as he looked me over. I returned the examination. He was a fair bit older than me, and wore a long-handled mustache that ended past his chin. His clothing was no different to anyone else in the area. But like the two gunmen back in Las Cruces he wore his revolvers in the open. There was no badge on show.

Maria came out of the cabin and placed a hand casually on my shoulder.

She said, "Buenos días, James."

He touched the brim of his hat. "Maria."

She waved him down so that we both didn't have to keep looking up at him with the sun behind him. He grunted with a combination of relief and pain.

"The back still hurting?" she asked.

"As ever, as ever."

"James hurt his back when he was thrown," she explained, "but still he rides."

"So what else could I do?"

Maria shrugged.

Now that he was on the ground James stood a little taller than Maria and that made him half a head smaller than me. His face was darkened by the sun and wind, and with a broken nose that was spread across his face it gave him the look of a bronc buster.

He jerked his chin at me. "Who's he?" he asked Maria.

"This is Jared."

If he was waiting for more he wasn't getting it.

Maria looked over at his saddlebags. "No bourbon?"

He shook his head. "Not this time, Maria. We need you to fix up Billy. He took a bullet and it don't look so good for him."

James's request didn't faze Maria. She nodded and went into the cabin. When she was out of sight James turned his eyes on me. For some reason there was a lot of hate there. I held his look the best I could but he had

had more practice than me and I finally looked away.

She came out carrying a satchel over her shoulder and sensed the tension between me and James.

"It is okay," she told James. "Jared can be trusted."

The winter I spent in Montana was warmer than the look I got from him.

"You're vouching for him?" he asked.

"You're questioning me?" Maria replied.

James drew out a heavy sigh and tipped his hat to Maria. He turned and mounted his tan-colored Morgan. Maria managed to squeeze a smile out of him as she saddled the dun. We doubled-up and followed James down the hillside.

∽∾∽

How much do you know about how gangs operate? There are some wild tales to be heard, I can tell you. Some of the meanest came after the war, guerrilla fighters who just kept together because they had nothing to go home for or that civilian life was too quiet. Look at the James-Younger gang who spent a good few years riding around terrorizing small towns, robbing the railroad and overland stagecoaches. There were women involved, too.

If a gang were successful it would naturally gather men to it. Some only operated with a handful of men, others were as large as an army. Outlaws, rustlers, and out-of-work cowhands would join just to have some food and money in their pockets. Some stayed a few weeks, then left to ride the owl hoot trail. Others stayed long enough for the Eastern papers to start writing wild and hairy tales about them. Sometimes rival gangs would pick on each other just to see who was the roughest and toughest. The country was pockmarked with hideouts that were known only to these outlaws.

We were being led to one of those hideouts somewhere east of Las Cruces. It was quiet between us as we kept heading east. James asked Maria if she needed to rest every now and then but she declined. Sometime later, about three hours, James led us into a small ravine. Up ahead it seemed the way was blocked with large rocks, but it wasn't so. There were gaps just wide enough for a mount to get through in single file. That's what we did. The ravine snaked around for a bit until it opened up to a natural circle. This was the camp.

There was a mixture of living quarters: canvas tents, wooden lean-tos, and shacks. Livestock was left to roam around. The whole place looked as if a twister had dumped its load and gone on its way. At the most I counted twenty men. James ordered me to stay with the dun and took Maria to one of the tents. I wasn't going to quarrel with his order because you only had to look around at the outlaws to know that they'd rather shoot you than speak to you.

Despite that, I also felt at ease.

Sometime later Maria came out of the tent wiping her hands on a bloody cloth, followed closely by James and another man. He was tallish, clean-shaven, about one hundred and seventy pounds with dark skin. His nose had been busted once and hooked to the right. They walked over to me.

He said, "We're down a man. Maria here told me about the way you handled yourself in town. Are you looking for work?"

"Sort of."

He shrugged. "Maria here's got nothing but good words for you. I don't know your history but if she says you're jake, that's fine with me."

Maria said, "Sí, Jared." As if she was giving me permission to leave her. She went on: "Take him up on his offer."

I did and I didn't. Torn between the two. Her and the outlaws.

"Look," I said to McCarty, "I don't even have a mount of my own, or a decent weapon."

The smile when it came was a genuine one. He jerked

a thumb over his shoulder toward the tent, saying, "I don't rightly believe that Little Bill will have use for his gear. It's yours iffen you want."

James looked at the ground between his boots. Maria smiled at me so I said, "Yes."

❦

IT WAS LATE afternoon one September morning when Matt Horner came galloping into camp.

"Mike's dead!"

His declaration cut through the noise of the camp.

"I found him down by the creek. His throat cut clear from ear to ear!"

It wasn't unusual to hear about a sudden death; usually it took place on a raid, but Mike Stuart was baby-sitting a few head of cattle a couple of miles away. It shouldn't've happened.

McCarty stood outside his tent, his face suffused with anger.

"Them bastards!"

For just over a month there'd been some friction between our gang and one led by Kid Jack over in Lincoln County. It started with a brawl in which Kid Jack's cousin, Dan Kane, was knifed and killed. Once Jack's gang tried to take our hideout but we easily beat them back. Since then it had been penny-ante stuff: a couple of steers taken, a horse maimed, or a couple of potshots taken at a distance. Nothing to really worry about. Now they had gone and killed Mike Stuart. He happened to be McCarty's brother-in-law. I could see this grow into a revenge raid.

"Saddle up, boys!" McCarty bellowed. "We're riding to hell."

That was McCarty's favorite expression, using it whenever there was bloody business at hand.

Thirty riders left the camp, heading off to where Matt Horner had left Stuart's body. It was still there by the creek. McCarty told Chris Wood, an old trapper, to take the body back to camp, the rest he ordered to follow him. Just as we were about to leave the area I looked at the ground. There was plenty of hoofprints, some made by the cattle and some by shod horses. But the fresher ones were leading away from Kid Jack's camp.

I told McCarty this.

"What does that mean? The Kid had nothing to do with it? Is that what you're telling me?"

"No."

"We know it was his doing."

"We don't."

He wheeled his horse around and rode up to me.

"What the hell you saying?"

I straightened up in the saddle and held his hot gaze. "I'm saying that whoever did this took the cattle and rode off north. I've tracked cows so I know this. These tracks head nowhere near the Kid's place."

McCarty didn't like what I was telling him.

"You're wrong," he said. "We're going after the Kid."

He'd already pinned the murder of his brother-in-law on Kid Jack. He didn't want to talk about it.

I was wrong to say, "I guess you'll do it your way, then."

His Colt Navy cleared leather in a heartbeat and was pointed at me. He made a kind of animal grunt and pulled back the hammer.

All I had time to do was fall out of the saddle.

The bullet thumped into my side.

From the ground I looked up at McCarty looming over me. The Colt was pointing at my head.

"You sonofabitch!" he yelled. "I guess we'll see who's right or wrong."

I waited for the next shot. My breath had caught in my throat and it felt as if I couldn't breathe. I was frightened. Afraid to die.

And then he was gone.

I stayed on the ground listening to the sound of hooves

fade away, and too frightened to get up. The pain in my side burned like a hot ember and I felt the wound. My fingers came away slick with blood. I used my neckerchief to press against the wound and somehow managed to sit up.

Taking a closer look told me that the bullet hadn't gone in but scored a nice bloody furrow over my rib cage. The scar's there if you want to see it. I thought that I had come so close to death I wanted to laugh. A few more moments of feeling sorry for myself and I was ready to mount up and follow those tracks.

I was right. They were heading north. I figured there was no more than a dozen head of cattle and two horsemen. I didn't doubt that this was the work of a couple of cutthroats who'd taken the chance to jump a lone man and steal away the cattle.

I caught up with them about five miles out of San Augustin. The light from their campfire shone bright in the failing light. I guessed they didn't consider that someone would come after them, and they didn't set out to be cautious. I dismounted some way back and ground hobbled my horse. I lit my own fire hidden from sight by the trunk of a fallen cottonwood tree and waited for daybreak.

The bleeding had stopped but it hurt like hell when I moved. I used whatever cover there was to creep up on their camp, listening to the men's snores carry loud in the stillness of the first light of the morning. The cattle didn't stir as I approached. The light of the false dawn covered the ground.

I drew my revolver and kicked at the first man's feet. He came to a spluttering awakening.

I covered him with the weapon and put my finger to my lips, telling him to be silent. Without words I told him to throw out his weapon. He did as he was told. I woke his companion and instructed him to do the same. When their revolvers and knives were at my feet I relaxed a little.

"I got no beef with you gents but back there you killed

a man. Now his kin is pretty pissed about this. But you're in luck. He's got it into his head that someone else did the deed and is off taking care of them."

"So you don't need to point the gun at us anymore," the man on my right said. A bushy red beard covered half his face, his eyes clear and steady, holding no fear.

"Depends on how we deal with this," I replied.

"Well, you've got the jump on us. You tell us."

"Tell me what you was going to do with the cattle."

The men looked at each other. The bearded one shrugged.

"No harm in telling we were taking them to a place we got near Sands Hills."

I said, "And?"

"And add them to the other cattle."

"Then what?"

"Then drive 'em to Fort Selden and sell 'em."

I smiled. It was rich. They were rustling cattle then selling on to the Army.

The other man had pushed himself up into a sitting position and hugged his knees. "What're you going to do with us?" he asked.

"I was going to take the cattle away from you."

"Was?"

"Yeah, but I like the sound of what you're doing. Could you use an extra hand?"

They exchanged puzzled looks mixed with relief.

"Hell, son," the one with the beard and all the talk said, "we'll even cut you in on the deal!"

From one outlaw gang to another all in a day—wasn't bad going, was it? And that's just what we did. The men were Big Nosed John and Doc Colt, or so they called themselves, whether or not they were true names I didn't care to find out, it had nothing to do with me. We sold the herd of cattle to the contractor at the fort for eighteen dollars a head. That added up to a profit of one thousand and eighty dollars.

We'd agreed to divvy up the money once we were a

safe distance from the fort. I killed both of them before they could do the same to me.

∽∘∾

WHAT'S IMPORTANT HERE is that you understand that either one of those men wouldn't have hesitated to kill me. It sounds like they were killed in cold blood. There's truth in that. But if they had their way, then I wouldn't be here talking to you, would I?

For the first time in my life I had some money and as I rode back to camp I worked out a plan. Why should I put myself at risk with a bunch of outlaws, maybe getting killed on some bank or stage holdup? The plan was a simple one, as most good plans are. I'd hang around places where money changed hands, like back at the fort with the contractor. There were plenty of other places where I could ply this trade.

And so I spent the next year drifting around New Mexico, moving from one county to another, using the plan. I'd watch cattlemen, businessmen, and even gamblers come into town, do their business, then follow them and relieve them of their money. I never robbed any bank or stagecoach but I did take a payroll from a railroad paymaster once. I'd gone as far as Socorro and hit some of the mines. Once or twice the law nearly caught up with me but I'd easily lose them.

Being the lone member of my gang had its compensations but toward the end I missed Maria. Oh, she was always on my mind. I don't think a day went by without me thinking of her and our short time together. I figured there'd been time enough gone by and that I could get back down Las Cruces way.

There were no tears of joy when we met up again. I don't really know what I expected. Maria was still living in her cabin in the mountains, and alone. When I arrived she was sat out under the stoop stirring a large pot. She heard my approach and looked up. A little surprised at

first, then she jumped up and ran to me. I dropped out of
the saddle and caught her in my arms.

The first blow struck me above the ear, knocking my
hat off. Then hundreds of blows crashed into my arms,
chest, and neck.

"Bastardo! Bastardo!" She raged at me until her voice
was hoarse. "They told me you were dead. That McCarty
had killed you."

She wiped the trails of snot from her nose with the back
of her hand.

I said, "He would have done but he weren't that good
a shot."

"So where've you been?"

"Oh, here 'n' there."

Her blue eyes glinted again with a familiar hardness.
"So, you come back here now that you've had enough?"

I bent down and picked up my hat, banging the dust
off against my leg and reset it on my head. It gave me a
moment to think. "Maria, I came back because I missed
you."

"Pah!"

"Truly."

She walked slowly back to the pot and carried on stirring. She said, "You don't think that you can ride in here
and begin again, do you?"

I shrugged. *"Por qué no?"*

"Why not? Because things have changed."

"How?"

"I don't need to explain to you."

"I know but . . ."

"Then that's how it is."

"How what is?"

"Idiato! Just go!"

I really didn't understand what she was trying to say.
She wouldn't look up from that damned pot. I went over
and snatched the ladle from her hand and threw it away.

"I *did* come back for you, Maria."

She stood up and pushed me away from her. "Too late,

too late. I spent months mourning you. I loved you, Jared. Yes, don't look so surprised. One of McCarty's men told me that you'd been shot and left for dead. McCarty and most of his men were killed in a gun battle with Kid Jack that day. In one day I had lost my lover and my father! Do you know how hurt I felt?"

"Your father?"

"Why do you think he let you ride with him?"

I shook my head.

"Because I asked him to."

In that moment I knew I loved her, loved her so much it hurt. I had no idea that she had done that for me. McCarty never said. I rubbed my hands over my face but it didn't stop the tears.

"Why didn't he say something?"

"I told him not to."

"But . . ."

"Jared, believe me, anything I asked he would do."

"Then why would he shoot me?" I asked.

It was her turn to shrug.

"There must have been a good reason," she said. "Or did he shoot to wound instead of killing you?"

That stopped me. He had been close enough to put a bullet anywhere in me. There had been a second chance to finish off the job when I was on the deck but he hadn't.

I walked around for a minute, thinking.

"Perhaps he saved me," I said.

"Saved you?"

I thought I had it right in my head. "He knew about us, right?" I said. "The gang was riding out against Kid Jack's tough outlaw band. Mayhaps he didn't want me killed, so he acted like I'd gone up against him and wounded me. That way he didn't have to leave his daughter alone. Mayhaps he had a feeling that he wasn't going to be around to protect you. That he'd leave that task to me."

I stood there, watching her eyes. Waiting as she weighed up what I'd said.

She began to cry. Great sobs racked her body and I went to her. She leaned into me and wailed.

Those moments waiting for her to decide what she was going to do was one of the most fear-filled times of my life. I kissed her through her tears and I smiled. The year I'd spent robbing and killing had worn me out, and coming back here to Maria was what I needed.

"Hold me," she said. "Don't let me go."

❦

THIS IS THE first time I've told anyone any of this. I don't know if you'll understand everything but in time you might. I've forgotten a few things and recalled some events clearly as if they'd happened yesterday. I don't know the future. Who can really tell what's over the next ridge?

I kissed my son on the forehead and pulled the blanket up to his chin. He was sound asleep. A thumb stuck in his mouth. I brushed a stray hank of hair off his forehead.

Maria stood in the doorway and when I drew near, she kissed me on the lips.

"Do you think Thomas understood any of that, Jared?" she asked.

I looked down at our five-year-old boy in his cot. He looked so peaceful. "Can't rightly say," I said, "but next time he asks he might hear some of his pa's other adventures."

I put my arm around Maria's shoulders and said, "Did I ever tell you about the time in Montana when we just finished a cattle drive?"

The Day Lamarr Had a Tall Drink with His Short Daddy

~∞~

Tom Piccirilli

THEY'D TRIED LYNCHING Lamarr again, this time from a goddamn spruce.

There's pine and birch and ash trees all over, and still they strive to hang him off the side of a spindly spruce. Priest could just see it going on: these three little farmhands, all twisted inside from drinking and losing at faro all night, no money left to pay the whores for another go-round, and nothing but the prospect of going home to their mean wives without even two fifty-cent pieces to rub together between the three of them.

So they come stumbling outside at around dawn with sour bellies and they ride two and a half miles out of town and find Lamarr laying on a boulder outside his shack wearing a sombrero. This big black buck topping six two, two hundred and thirty pounds, probably singing one of the slave songs his mother taught him before he strangled the plantation master. And there on his head is this brand-new bright yellow sombrero.

Funny how so many of them thought you could cow a colored man simply by sneering at him and calling him nigger. They get off their horses without even bothering to ground tie them, mosey on up to him, and start in with the insults. Lamarr being who he is, says something to them like, "My good lawd Jesus, these peckerwood sumbitches have come to hassle a poor colored man laying on his property in the beautiful dawn. I think I am so shocked that my eyes may never completely close again, so wide are they in amazement and total surprise."

Priest kept checking all the signs, reading the scene in the sand. This is just about the point when they get one rope and knot it to the goddamn spruce, and Lamarr guffaws until his ass is ready to shake out of his pants. He holds the sombrero and waves it in his face to get some air. The horses know what's coming and get skittish, start backing away. The three yahoos don't cotton to no nigger laughing at them, so somebody runs to get his rifle out of the saddle boot while another sits on the dead log over there finishing off their last bottle of whiskey. The third one does some rope tricks with his lasso. Hoping to toss it nice and easy over Lamarr's neck, yank him along kind as you can be, sir, thank you much, and watch him swing.

Lamarr stands there while this idiot tosses the lasso, and Lamarr is beaming and holding his stomach because he's laughing so hard while the rope falls at his feet, brushes his shoulder, goes flying way off in that direction. He puts the sombrero back on and tells the farmhand, "Here now, aim for the tippytop point. Nice and slow, let it out by the wrist. Come on, now, I know you can handle this sort of pressure we got here."

The guy who went for the rifle finally reaches his horse and starts running back, dragging his boots hard in the dirt and kicking up clots. He slows down to take aim when the lasso finally knocks the sombrero off Lamarr's head. It falls in the dust and spins around before landing rightside up.

Lamarr pulls out his converted Navy .36, which he always keeps at the small of his back, stuck in the bright red sash he wears around his waist all the time. Still smiling and showing every wide white tooth off, he fires three shots and ends the party.

Priest McClaren sighed. It was getting late. Hours had passed but Lamarr was still sitting there on the boulder, the three bodies having been stacked up like cordwood behind the rocks.

"Weren't no cowpokes this time."

"No?" Priest said. "It's what they look like."

"Well, yes, I mean they were, but that's not all."

"What then?"

"Some of Septemus's men."

Priest sighed again, and rubbed his eyes. So maybe this was going to be the final touch that got Septemus's undivided attention.

"Way I figure it, we can do one of two things," Priest said.

"I just hate it when my options are so limited," Lamarr told him. "You sure with all those big thinks of yours you can only come up with an itty-bitty two things we can do?"

"We can ride into town and tell the sheriff what happened . . ."

"Uh-huh."

". . . and you can claim self-defense . . ."

"Uh-huh."

". . . and I can bring you cookies in jail and dig out those nice shiny boots of yours you keep in your closet, just so you look your best when they hang you."

Lamarr whistled and patted his stomach. "I admit before heaven to liking your cookies a'plenty."

"Mama taught me how to sew, too. Second course of action being we ride out to Septemus's place and bring him his fellas back and see what kind of play he makes."

"But you ain't promising to make me no cookies then if we follow that latter course, now are you?"

"No, I'm not. Figure there won't be enough time to do

any baking, seeing as how we'd have to start out about now before these here boys start stinking the valley up."

"Damn." Lamarr seemed to give it considerable thought. "Well, all right. Guess we might as well go see my rich white daddy then." He let out a laugh that didn't end for a while, and by the time it did Priest's chest was layered in sweat and he had chills working up his spine.

∽∾∾

LAMARR HAD BEEN born and grown on a Georgia plantation owned by a man called Thompson, his mother just fifteen years older than him. His daddy was the plantation master's boyhood friend, both of them having attended West Point and serving in the Mexican War together. That's all Lamarr knew of the man except his name, which was Septemus Hart. When Septemus made his annual visit to see his friend he liked to bed the prettiest women on the plantation, whether colored or white. Lamarr figured he had a whole bushel of brothers and sisters on the grounds, but he never tried to find out exactly who was his kin. Only his father mattered.

When Septemus was found in a bath with Thompson's daughter, their long friendship was ended. Septemus had to put some ball shot in Thompson's shoulder just so he could make it out the window without any pants on. Couple years later, when Lamarr strangled Thompson, he sort of thanked his dear old daddy. Thompson couldn't raise that arm much in defense, and Lamarr got to take his time. First choking the master with his left fist, and then his right, making it last a good long while.

It took Lamarr nine years to track Septemus to the town of Patience, Arizona. By then he'd fought with the Yankees against the South even though Union officers weren't much better than men like Thompson, when you got right down to it. Still, he'd killed his fair share of Confederates as part of the Army, and before he deserted he got a chance to kick his white sergeant's teeth out and leave 'em scattered across Chattanooga.

The killing didn't stop there. On his way west, he'd run into rustlers and dry gulchers and plenty of highwaymen of every stripe, including Mexicans and Indians and a band of ex-slaves who liked to think of themselves as hombres when they set fire to any sod house they found on the prairie.

Lamarr found Septemus here in Patience over a year ago, living on a hacienda and owning nearly half the valley, and still taking up with every pretty girl he found, the old bastard. Lamarr introduced himself to Septemus, saying, "Why hello there, Daddy, been a while since you come round visiting your kin, figured I'd pay you a visit." Lamarr, smiling and giving a nice throaty laugh, maybe raising his eyebrows some, then just walking away. He'd been pressing Septemus every chance he got since.

The first time Priest had met Lamarr he'd heard his entire story. Priest was drunk again, having the screaming fits behind the livery, seeing the ghost of his murdered mother flitting all around him. He'd stumbled into a hog pen and would've been stomped to death if Lamarr hadn't gotten him the hell out of there. Priest not only remembered every detail of Lamarr's story, but he also recalled trying to get up from the dirt and clean some of the hog shit off him, Lamarr just standing there and repeatedly shoving him back down in the mud while the tale went on and on. Priest knew the whole account now, except the ending, of course. He couldn't eat pork anymore, either.

Priest draped the bodies over Lamarr's pack mule, and then got back on his sorrel. "You could always just kill him, you know."

"Wouldn't be no fun in that."

"You been nipping at him for a year. Must be getting a bit boring."

"I admit he ain't reacted quite the way I was hoping for," Lamarr said.

"Which is?"

"I'd settle for apoplectic."

"He's too refined for that."

"Didn't seem too refined the day I saw him running without his pants on across the tobacco fields." He eyed the corpses, wondering where they were going to lead him. "After we drop these three stinking boys off on his front step, maybe he'll be a bit more riled."

"If you want him to draw on you, all you have to do is challenge him," Priest said. "He's never backed down yet."

"Figure this is a more private matter than shootin' it out on Main Street with all the womenfolks and children about."

"Just don't expect him to hold still while you throttle him."

"Sure hope not."

∽∾

SEPTEMUS HART OWNED the Home Hearth Theater and could usually be found sitting there in his seat of honor in the balcony, sipping sherry and dressed in a black suit with a purple shirt, a coat with gold epaulets, medals, and tassels on it. He'd been a captain in the Confederate Army and still enjoyed dressing up and showing off the chevrons on his sleeve, using his hanging drawl of an accent when it benefited him as a good ole boy. Septemus owned about half of the rest of Patience, too. He always did his best to appear regal, but Mercer, the left-handed gunny always at his side, sort of ruined the impression. Septemus, forever polished and refined, smiling and chuckling and trying to make eye contact with folks while Mercer gave everyone a dead-cold stare.

Mercer hadn't been on the trail for five years but still looked like he'd just come in from the desert. No matter what happened, he'd never draw unless Septemus was in danger. Someday, Lamarr would push Septemus too far, or vice versa, and Mercer would make a move and then Priest would move, and there'd be bloodshed all over the damn place.

The fact was, Lamarr couldn't kill the old man until Septemus admitted aloud to being Lamarr's daddy, and Septemus just didn't seem like he was going to oblige him.

They rode out to Septemus's hacienda, Lamarr wearing his yellow sombrero the entire way there across the foothills. Even from a quarter mile off you could make out the ornate wrought-iron gate that stood closed before the ranch. A couple of sentries spotted them and ran to the corral to saddle some horses, but they never did ride out. Sweat puddled down into the small of Priest's back, but Lamarr looked like he was almost sleeping in all the shade that sombrero threw.

They drew up to the gate and Cobb, the foreman of the ranch crew, stood on the other side glaring with a little smirk tugging his lips out of shape. He eyed the dead men on the mule and started chewing the inside of his cheek. Cobb's hands didn't stray to his gun belt and Lamarr just kept smiling, not touching the Winchester in the saddle boot close to his fist. Flies swarmed the corpses and the stink was getting worse. Priest didn't exactly like Cobb but he saw no reason for the man to die either.

The moment stretched out. Cobb decided to be smart and relaxed his shoulders. He ignored Lamarr for the time being and said, "McClaren, you have any hand in this?"

"No," Priest said. It sounded a bit cowardly, like he didn't intend to back Lamarr's play when it came to that. Best to make his intentions known right from the start so nobody would be confused when the time came around. "But they were after some killing and that's what they got."

"You side with this nigger buck son of a bitch and you'll be making the worst mistake of your sorry stupid life."

"I appreciate the kind words of advice, Cobb."

"Just listen, you—"

"But the truth of the matter is that I'm partial to that there sombrero and I don't want to see it come to any more harm. I'm planning on borrowing it for the spring dance."

Lamarr perked up. "Borrow this here fine sombrero that resides upon my head at this very second?"

"Yep."

"What makes you think I might readily turn over this hat to you?"

"Well," Priest said. "I was meaning to broach the subject with you a little later on."

"Broach it now, this I'd like to hear, about how you plan to wear my sombrero and sweat it up with all that long hair of yours."

"See, that dance is next week and I was figuring on asking Sarah O'Brien to it and—"

"Sarah O'Brien?" Lamarr frowned and shook his head. "She's too much woman for you."

"I beg to differ on that account."

Seething, Cobb made a guttural sound and growled at Priest, "Why'd I expect a coward like you to listen to reason, what with your dead mama in the ground five years and you never even going after the man who done it. She'd spit in your eye, you drunken—"

Priest pulled and hurled the knife in one fluid motion, winging it sidearm almost absently, so that the blade sort of glided straight on. The pommel struck Cobb in the chin and knocked him on his ass. Chips of his bottom teeth dribbled into his beard stubble but there wasn't any blood. Cobb moaned, shakily got to his feet, and started to clear his Walker Colt from its holster.

Showing off his own perfect white teeth, smiling even wider, Lamarr yanked his rifle from the saddle boot, gripped the lever, and swung it in one hand, cocking it, and let the stock smash Cobb in the chin again. Now there was blood, and plenty of it. Cobb went into a coughing fit, gesturing wildly, while other ranch hands appeared around him. Lamarr held the rifle on them and said, "I'd like to see my daddy now. How's about somebody let us into this damn place?"

They rode toward the hacienda, Cobb groaning while a couple of others fell in beside him and helped him to walk. Priest stopped and picked up his knife. Five men escorted them toward the main house of the ranch. Priest knew Septemus had given orders about Lamarr, but he had no idea what they might be. It was lucky that the three dead hands were new—if they'd been on long enough to have made friends here, things wouldn't have gone as smoothly as they had up to this point.

Caballero music drifted from beyond a few of the outer adobe buildings. Lamarr sort of shook in his saddle like he was dancing along. They were led farther to the center of the headquarters to a building Priest had never seen the likes of before—it took him a minute to realize this was a smaller replica of the Home Hearth Theater.

The aroma of broiling steaks and cooked pork rose over them. Priest's stomach hitched to the left. Women's laughter and a lot of voices, singing and carousing. Sounded like Septemus was throwing a hell of a party.

Priest said, "We might want to rethink this some."

"Today's his birthday," Lamarr told him.

"What? And you knew that already?"

"Course. I got a present I'm just itching to give him."

Priest knew Lamarr had been looking for the right kind of maneuver to get Septemus to acknowledge him, but throwing three dead men at his feet on his birthday in front of a house full of guests might be going a little too far.

But Lamarr cut the pack mule loose and said to the ranch hands, "Here, take these men to town. Tell Doc Laidlaw the mortician to bury 'em for me. He owes me a favor and it'll be paid off with this. You understand? I'm the one doing this, not Septemus."

Nobody much liked taking orders from a colored intruder, but Lamarr wasn't smiling so much now and he had a hard tone of authority. What'd they care who paid the mortician or who didn't? He sounded too much like Septemus to argue.

Priest and Lamarr dismounted at the entrance to the private theater and walked in, covered by even more of Septemus's men, who ringed the place. Priest was surprised so many people could fit in here. Must've been all of two hundred folks having a good time down on the floor and sitting up there in the tiers of seats. He recognized a lot of faces but didn't expect to see so many Mexican officials and their families eating and drinking and dancing, with tiny Mex kids running around holding candy and toys. So, Septemus was making business deals across the border as well.

And there he was, the man of the hour who owned it all, seated at a table near the stage with a pretty Mex girl on his lap, and Mercer the left-handed gunny stationed in the same spot as always.

Septemus stood maybe five eight in his boots, with the firelight glinting off all his brass buttons and medals and the sheath of his Confederate saber. Lamarr had no trouble with walking right up to him, wearing the yellow sombrero, and grinning, waiting patiently.

"What the hell are you doing here?" Septemus asked without the slightest trace of anger. He was actually chuckling.

"I never could resist a big ole grand party like this."

"Should've tried harder."

"Maybe," Lamarr said.

"Heard you took down some of my men."

"Yep."

"I should string you up for that."

"Attempting to string me up is what got them boys in trouble in the first place."

Mercer slipped up behind Priest and said, "Shall I escort these men off your land, Mr. Hart?" Septemus ignored him. Mercer leaned in close and whispered, "One of those men was my cousin."

"You should've watched over him better," Priest said.
"When I settle the score with that nigger bastard I'll make sure to save you some."

Priest had known men who weren't worth a damn at threatening, but he figured Mercer was the worst at it. "Uhm, well, I appreciate that, Mercer. I certainly do."

"You won't be laughing much longer."

Septemus, though, kept chuckling. The air was starting to thicken with tension. "You haven't told me what the hell you want yet."

"I wanted to have a drink with you on your birthday," Lamarr said.

Septemus had as many teeth in his head as Lamarr, and they were all just as big and white. He never dropped the smile for a second, and everything he said had that chortle running through it. "I don't drink with lice-riddled niggers."

"Funny that. Ma said you shared plenty of bottles of whiskey with her, getting her drunk when she was only a child so she'd bed with you. And you never complained once about bedbugs beneath the sheets."

The snickering came on strong then. "Your mama was nothing but a black pig who hardly ever got out of her bed. She liked laying with her masters, don't you think any different."

Priest didn't think anything could rattle Lamarr. He'd just taken care of three men trying to lynch him and none of it had come close to getting under his thick hide. So it was twice as big a shock seeing Lamarr's face tighten up until he didn't look like himself anymore, that big fist slowly rising into the air, swinging out to backhand little Septemus out of his seat and out onto the stage.

Priest said, "Oh shit."

Nearly every gun in the place must've been pulled at once, so that all you heard was one loud slap of leather and a hundred hammers and levers cocking. The Mexican officials had plenty of soldiers along with them to protect their families. Priest figured there was no reason for him to draw his own Colt, so he just stood there forcing himself to breathe.

Septemus rolled for a while, four or five times over and over until he finally came to a stop. When he did he just sat there and shook his head and laughed some more.

Lamarr undid his gun belt, let it drop at his feet, and stepped out onto the stage, the sombrero still high on his head. He'd gotten his calm back but looked a bit guilty that he'd lost it in the first place. Septemus let out a barking guffaw, stood up, and drew his saber.

"Why, Daddy," Lamarr said, "I admit I'm mighty impressed by the length of your sword."

Septemus might've been short but he was solid muscle packed with energy and controlled anger. You didn't build, own, and keep half a city unless you regularly fought for it and always won.

He swung the saber wide, slashing high, expecting Lamarr to dodge low and to the left. Lamarr did exactly that, and Septemus was already in position waiting with the flat of the saber when Lamarr's face showed up in the right place. The pommel crunched against Lamarr's nose and he made a wet growling sound while the blood ran down the back of his throat.

Septemus made a mistake though, just standing there watching and enjoying the sight, expecting the blow to stagger Lamarr. It didn't even slow him. Those fingers came closer. Lamarr had a lot to reach out for—the coat sleeves, the lapels, the epaulets—and his giant fist seized on Septemus's collar and hiked him high into the air. Septemus tried to stab now, no longer playing games, but by the time he tried to thrust down into Lamarr's throat, Lamarr had already punched him clear across the stage again. Septemus rolled some more as Lamarr stomped closer. He kicked out and caught Septemus in the ribs.

The theater was completely silent, even the children. Everyone watched, but only a few of the guns had been put away. Priest kept his arms crossed, away from his pistol and knife. Septemus's orders about Lamarr must've been that if the black buck ever showed up looking for a fight, let Septemus alone with him.

Stabbing out again, Septemus sliced upwards, the blade weaving and landing on Lamarr here and there. Grunting in pain, Lamarr backed off fast. He was suddenly cut in four or five places, the wounds fairly shallow, but leaving him bleeding all over.

Septemus got up smiling and laughing. Priest realized it was all true in that second—Septemus Hart really was Lamarr's daddy, and the old man knew it and even liked Lamarr a little for coming after him. So long as Lamarr didn't kill him they had a chance of getting out of this alive yet.

Dancing forward, Septemus thrust the blade into Lamarr's shoulder. It went in an inch, then another. Lamarr let out something just shy of a scream, a cry that was only partly pain. The rest was roiling hate and rage for all that had gone on beneath the composed exterior. He struggled forward even as the saber twisted in his flesh. Septemus withdrew the blade and tried again.

But Lamarr had had enough. He caught Septemus's wrist and bent it back until the sword went flying. His fist snatched out and clamped onto Septemus's throat, and held him up, way up in the air while Lamarr took his time beating the hell out of the old man. His fist reared back and came driving in again and again, smashing his daddy's face wide open. Septemus didn't give in easily though, and before he fell he got one good blow in himself that rocked Lamarr back and knocked the sombrero soaring.

Mercer had drawn his pistol and stood there just waiting for the chance to use it. Priest figured he could cut his throat pretty easy but some of the Mexicans were bound to get splashed and that wouldn't do any good in making friends.

The sombrero was still tumbling and rolled over to Priest's foot. He picked it up and held it like a prize. He had to gain some height and do this quickly. In two swift steps he hopped up onto the table, kicked Mercer in the face, jumped down, and punched him in the jaw. Mercer's eyes came unfocused but he was still trying to aim. Priest slapped the sombrero onto Mercer's head so hard that he felt the gunny's nose wedge in their nice and snug. Priest aimed for the bulge and smashed Mercer backwards into the first tier of seats.

"You done ruined my hat!" Lamarr cried.

"I apologize for that. I know how close you were to it."

Septemus crawled to his feet and staggered to his chair, huffing hard, with blood running from both nostrils and corners of his mouth. He dropped back some and licked his lips. He grabbed the whiskey bottle and drank, and drank some more like he wasn't ever going to come up for air. When he finally finished he had tears in his eyes.

He shoved the bottle across the table to Lamarr. It was still about half-full. Lamarr filled his lungs, upended the bottle into his mouth, and didn't stop until the last of the whiskey was gone.

By the time they got back to the shack the liquor and loss of blood had caught up to Lamarr and he was too drunk and tired to move much. He just lay there on the bed smiling. Priest figured Septemus was probably doing the same, for different reasons. He hoped that one drink would hold them both over for a while, at least until the next time father and son decided to have a family reunion, when things were bound to end differently.

Hero

Bill Pronzini

THE MOB BOILED upstreet from Saloon Row toward the jailhouse. Some of the men in front carried lanterns and torches made out of rag-wrapped sticks soaked in coal oil; Micah could see the flickering light against the black night sky, the wild quivering shadows. But he couldn't see the men themselves, the hooded and masked leaders, from back here where he was at the rear of the pack. He couldn't see Ike Dall neither. Ike Dall was the one who had the hang rope already shaped out into a noose.

Men surged around Micah, yelling, waving arms and clubs and sixguns. He just couldn't keep up on account of his damn game leg. He kept getting jostled, once almost knocked down. Back there at Hardesty's Gambling Hall he'd been right in the thick of it. He'd been the center of attention, by grab. Now they'd forgot all about him and here he was clumping along on his bad leg, not able to see much, getting bumped and pushed with every dragging step. He could feel the excitement, smell the sweat and the heat and the hunger, but he wasn't a part of it no more.

It wasn't right. Hell damn boy, it just wasn't right. Weren't for him, none of this would be happening. Biggest damn thing ever in Cricklewood, Montana, and all on account of him. He was a hero, wasn't he? Back there at Hardesty's, they'd all said so. Back there at Hardesty's, he'd talked and they'd listened to every word—Ike Dall and Lee Wynkoop and Mack Clausen, all of them, everybody who was somebody in and around Cricklewood. Stood him right up there next to the bar, bought him drinks, looked at him with respect, and listened to every word he said.

"Micah seen it, didn't you, Micah? What that drifter done?"

"Sure I did. Told Marshal Thrall and I'm tellin' you. Weren't for me, he'd of got clean away."

"You're a hero, Micah. By God you are."

"Well, now. Well, I guess I am."

"Tell it again. Tell us how it was."

"Sure. Sure I will. I seen it all."

"What'd you see?"

"I seen that drifter, that Larrabee, hold up the Wells, Fargo stage. I seen him shoot Tom Porter twice, shoot Tom Porter dead as anybody ever was."

"How'd you come to be out by the Helena road?"

"Mr. Coombs sent me out from the livery, to tell Harv Perkins the singletree on his wagon was fixed a day early. I took the shortcut along the river, like I allus do when I'm headin' down the valley. Forded by Fisherman's Bend and went on through that stand of cottonwoods on the other side. That was where I was, in them trees, when I seen it happen."

"Larrabee had the stage stopped right there, did he?"

"Sure. Right there. Had his sixgun out and he was tellin' Tom to throw down the treasure box."

"And Tom throwed it down?"

"Sure he did. He throwed it right down."

"Never made to use his shotgun or his side gun?"

"No sir. Never made no play at all."

"So Larrabee shot him in cold blood."

"Cold blood—sure! Shot Tom twice. Right off the coach box the first time, then when Tom was lyin' there on the ground, rollin' around with that first bullet in him, Larrabee walked up to him cool as you please and put his sixgun agin Tom's head and done it to him proper. Blowed Tom's head half off. Blowed it half off and that's a fact."

"You all heard that. You heard what Micah seen that son of a bitch do to Tom Porter—a decent citizen, a man we all liked and was proud to call friend. I say we don't wait for the circuit judge. What if he lets Larrabee off light? I say we give that murderin' bastard what he deserves here and now, tonight. Now what do you say?"

"Hang him!"

"Stretch his dirty neck!"

"Hang him high!"

Oh, it had been fine back there at Hardesty's. Everybody looking at him the way they done, with respect. Calling him a hero. He'd been somebody then, not just poor crippled-up Micah Hays who done handy work and run errands and shoveled manure down at the Coombs Livery Barn. Oh, it had been fine! But now—now they'd forgot him again, left him behind, left him out of what was going to happen on *his* account. They were all moving upstreet to the jailhouse with their lanterns and their torches and their hunger, leaving him practically alone where he couldn't do or see a damn thing . . .

Micah stopped trying to run on his game leg and limped along slow, watching the mob, wanting to be a part of it but wanting more to see everything that happened after the mob got to the jailhouse. Then he thought: Why, I *can* see it all! Sure I can! I know just where I got to go.

He hobbled ahead to the alley alongside Burley's Feed and Grain, went down it to the staircase built up the side wall. The stairs led to a railed gallery overlooking the street, and to the offices of the town lawyer, Mr. Spivey, that had been built on top of the feedstore roof. Micah stumped up the stairs and went past the dark offices and on down to the far end of the gallery.

Hell damn boy! He sure *could* see from up here, clear as anybody could want. The mob was close to the jail-house now; in the dancy light from the lanterns and torches, he could make out the hooded shape of Ike Dall with his hang-rope noose held high, the shapes of Lee Wynkoop and Mack Clausen and the others who were leading the pack. He could see that big old shade cotton-wood off to one side of the jail, too, with its one gnarly limb that stretched out over the street. That was where they was going to hang the drifter. Ike Dall had said so, back there at Hardesty's. *"We don't have to take him far, by Christ. We'll string him up right there next to the jail."*

The front door of the jailhouse opened and out come Marshal Thrall and his deputy, Ben Dietrich. Micah leaned out over the railing, squinting, feeling the excite-ment scurry up and down inside his chest like a mouse on a wall. Marshal Thrall had a shotgun in his hands and Ben Dietrich held a rifle. The marshal commenced to yell-ing, but whatever it was got lost in the noise from the mob. Mob didn't slow down none, neither, when old Thrall started waving that Greener of his. Marshal wasn't going to shoot nobody, Ike Dall had said. *"Why, we're all Thrall's friends and neighbors. Ben Dietrich's, too. They ain't goin' to shoot up their friends and neighbors, are they? Just to stop the lynching of a murderin' son of a bitch like Larrabee?"*

No, sir, they sure wasn't. That mob didn't slow down none at all. It surged right ahead, right on around Marshal Thrall and Ben Dietrich like floodwaters around a sand-bar, and swallowed them both up and carried them right on into the jailhouse.

A hell of a racket come from inside. Pretty soon the pack parted down the middle and Micah could see four or five men carrying that drifter up in the air, hands tied behind him, the same way you'd carry a side of butchered beef. Hell damn boy! Everybody was whooping it up,

waving torches and lanterns and twirling light around in
the dark like a bunch of kids with pinwheel sparklers. It
put Micah in mind of an Independence Day celebration.
By grab, that was just what it was like. Fireworks on the
Fourth of July.

Well, they carried that murdering Larrabee on over to
the shade cottonwood. He was screaming things, that
drifter was—screaming the whole way. Micah couldn't
hear most of it above the crowd noise, but he caught a
few of the words. And one whole sentence: "I tell you, I
didn't do it!"

"Why, sure you did," Micah said out loud. "Sure you
did. I seen you do it, didn't I?"

Ike Dall throwed his rope over the cottonwood's gnarly
limb, caught the other end and give it to somebody, and
then he put that noose around Larrabee's neck and drew
it tight. Somebody else brung a saddle horse around, held
him steady whilst they hoisted the drifter onto his back.
That Larrabee was screaming like a woman now.

Micah leaned hard against the gallery railing. His
mouth was dry, real dry; he couldn't even work up no
spit to wet it. He'd never seen a lynching before. There'd
been plenty in Montana Territory—more'n a dozen over
in Beaverhead and Madison counties a few years back,
when the vigilantes done for Henry Plummer and his gang
of desperadoes—but never one in Cricklewood nor any
of the other towns Micah had lived in.

The drifter screamed and screamed. Then Micah saw
everybody back off some, away from the horse Larrabee
was on, and Ike Dall raised his arm and brought it down
smack on the cayuse's rump. Horse jumped ahead, frog-
stepping. And Larrabee quit screaming and commenced
to dancing in the air all loosey-goosey, like a puppet on
the end of a string. Before long, though, the dancing
slowed down and then it quit all together. That's done
him, Micah thought. And everybody in the mob knew it,
too, because they all backed off some more and stood

there in a half-circle, staring up at the drifter hanging still
and straight in the smoky light.

Micah stared, too. He leaned against the railing and
stared and stared, and kept on staring long after the mob
started to break up.

Hell damn boy, he thought over and over. Hell damn
boy, if that sure wasn't something to see!

∼∽∾

IT TOOK THE best part of a week for the town to get back
to normal. There was plenty more excitement during that
week—county law coming in, representatives from the
territorial governor's office in Helena, newspaper people,
all kinds of curious strangers. For Micah it was kind of
like the lynching went on and on, a weeklong celebration
like none other he'd ever been part of. Folks kept asking
him questions, interviewing him for newspapers, buying
him drinks, shaking his hand and clapping his back and
calling him a hero the way the men had done that night
at Hardesty's. Oh, it was fine. It was almost as fine as
when he'd been the center of attention before the lynch
mob got started.

But then it all come to an end. The law and the newspaper people and the strangers went away; Cricklewood
settled down to what it had been before the big event, and
Micah settled back into his humdrum job at the Coombs
Livery Barn and his nights on the straw bunk in one corner of the loft. He did his handiwork, ran errands, shoveled manure—and the townsfolk and ranchers and
cowhands stopped buying him drinks, stopped shaking his
hand and clapping his back and calling him hero, stopped
paying much attention to him at all. It was the same as
before, like he was nobody, like he didn't hardly even
exist. Mack Clausen snubbed him on the street no more
than two weeks after the lynching. The one time he tried
to get Ike Dall to talk with him about that night, how it
had felt putting the noose around Larrabee's neck, Ike

wouldn't have none of it. Why, Ike claimed he hadn't even been there that night, hadn't been part of the mob—said that lie right to Micah's face!

Four weeks passed. Five. Micah did his handiwork and ran errands and shoveled manure and now nobody even *mentioned* that night no more, not to him and not to each other. Like it never happened. Like they was ashamed of it or something.

Micah was feeling low the hot Saturday morning he come down the loft ladder and started toward the harness room like he always done first thing. But this wasn't like other mornings because a man was curled up sleeping in one of the stalls near the back doors. Big man, whiskers on his face, dust on his trail clothes. Micah had never seen him before.

Mr. Coombs was up at the other end of the barn, forking hay for the two roan saddle horses he kept for rent. Micah went on up there and said, "Morning, Mr. Coombs."

"Well, Micah. Down late again, eh?"

". . . I reckon so."

"Getting to be a habit lately," Mr. Coombs said. "I don't like it, Micah. See that you start coming down on time from now on, hear?"

"Yes, sir. Mr. Coombs, who's that sleepin' in the back stall?"

"Just some drifter. He didn't say his name."

"Drifter?"

"Came in half-drunk last night, paid me four bits to let him sleep in here. Not the first time I've rented out a stall to a human animal and it won't be the last."

Mr. Coombs turned and started forking some more hay. Micah went away toward the harness room, then stopped after ten paces and stood quiet for a space. And then, moving slow, he hobbled over to where the fire ax hung and pulled it down and limped back behind Mr. Coombs and swung the axe up and shut his eyes and swung the ax down. When he opened his eyes again Mr. Coombs

was lying there with the back of his head cleaved open
and blood and brains spilled out like pulp out of a split
melon.

Hell damn boy, Micah thought.

Then he dropped the ax and run to the front doors and
threw them open and run out onto Main Street yelling at
the top of his voice, "Murder! It's murder! Some damn
drifter killed Mr. Coombs! Split his head wide open with
a fire ax. I seen him do it, I seen it, I seen the whole
thing!"

A Stitch in Time

Riley Froh

CLOSING OUT THE centennial year of 1936 in Texas had a special appeal to me because the Christmas holidays would bring the love of my life home from Baylor University for two glorious weeks. And since Rachel Butler, the daughter of our preacher, was the sister of my best friend, Abner, I would be able to bask in her presence frequently, even though my longing was still done at a distance. My joy was compounded by anticipation of release from my own studies at the local high school. Those were good days.

Or so I thought, for I mistakenly assumed that Abner would take a seasonal break from the usual wrong, wicked, and immoral processes by which he strove to acquire someone else's property for our use. Abner was affected with a high degree of intellectual independence when it came to conforming to the statutes set forth by the criminal justice system of Texas. Although I was generally inclined to obey the law, my own weakness allowed him to con me into pulling another foolish stunt with him,

one that proved costly but an episode that showed me a
view of Rachel I would not soon forget.

"Trust me. This one's foolproof," he said.

"You know your daddy's gonna make us stay in the
church house to ring in the New Year," I said. I was
referring to the Baptist custom known as watch night.
"We ain't gonna have no time to rob no one."

"He'll let us out if the ox is in the ditch," Abner pre-
dicted. "And I can see to that."

"You ain't gonna push the ox in there are you, Abner?"
I asked, knowing he was.

"See, here's the deal," he explained, his eyes bright
with his scheming. "I'll run Old Man Clancy's herd up in
that trap next to the woods. Then I'll tell him his cattle is
scattered in the place over this way. He'll have a hissy
and want Daddy to have us pen his cattle. Which we'll
do, of course, 'cause there won't be nothin' to it. What
we'll really do with our time is rob the cash box at the
New Year's dance at String Prairie."

"The cattle part's easy," I said. "Now, liftin' the cash
box is somethin' else. But even if it'd work, which it
won't, I ain't gonna do it."

"You ain't never gonna get to court Rachel neither," he
said matter-of-factly, "unless you get some real money.
You seen that big present she has under the tree from that
Baylor big shot. I'll bet it's a set of dishes for her hope
chest or maybe even a fur coat. And I seen that little
knickknack you bought her. There ain't gonna be no comparison. Now you know that the way to a woman's heart
is through her purse. Why do you think their eyes look
like dollar signs when they blink?"

"You're on," I said unwisely, for even though money
is a passport to polite society, I should have known that
Rachel was above the vices and follies that guided her
wild and worldly brother.

My family opened its presents on Christmas morning,
so it was customary for me to join the Butlers on the night
before for their exchange of gifts. We gathered in the

preacher's expansive country home for just such an evening that December 24th in 1936.

Rachel glowed in her place by the sparkling tree. Even though incredibly feminine, she was large and strong and powerful like her father. Abner, slight and wiry, took after his mother's side. Talk ran to the ministerial student of very good family with substantial means she was dating at Baylor. My blood boiled, but when she opened my small package to her, she came over to me and kissed me on the cheek with those rich, full lips I hungered after and squeezed the back of my neck with an exquisite touch that left an electric throb for some time where she had brushed me with her expressive fingers. So I fully resolved to go ahead and help her brother pull the job he had planned for the end of the year.

Abner's New Year's Eve scenario worked perfectly, except that Old Man Clancy had more than a hissy: He threw a regular walleyed fit, virtually demanding that Brother Butler have us pen his cattle before the blue norther hit, which his rheumatism—the malady that kept him from rounding up his stock himself—was telling him was on its way from the North Pole.

"Abner," the Right Reverend Dr. Anthony Butler commanded his able and willing son, "I hate to disappoint you about the celebration tonight, but one of our church members has need of your services. You boys get your horses and round up Brother Archibald's cattle. And remember always, boys, the parable of the lost sheep as you do your duty. There are twenty-one head that must be accounted for. Stay with it as long as you need to, but recover every one of them even if it takes all night."

When Abner's father gave orders, they frequently rang with the pomp and flourish of a ceremony. And they always bore the stamp of the authority that he carried in the community. It didn't do to cross that man, whether you were a church member or not. He would admonish one of his flock with stern words, but he would beat the hell out of anybody else that got in his way, regardless of the size or number of his opponents. "They don't come too big for Anthony Butler," the sages of the county said correctly about our formidable, old-time preacher.

It was already dark when we cut across country toward String Prairie. Unless you've lived in Texas, it's hard to understand those mild days in the dead of winter just before a blue norther hits. Sometimes there's only been one or two killing frosts by Thanksgiving, and most of the leaves are still on the trees. Then conditions start indicating that a frigid blast is on its way from the North Pole. There really is a calm before the storm. Old folks start feeling aches and pains in certain joints. Birds and animals, both wild and domestic, become restless and stay on the move. A peculiar strangeness fills the air. We were riding that night in just such a warm and muggy atmosphere, probably in the same mood as the deer we spooked and the rabbits we jumped.

Abner and I had cashed in on this sort of spell many times, for we had better luck in our poaching operations in just such atmospheric conditions. You see, Texas does not really possess a climate; rather, it can only boast of having weather, and the only thing constant about that is change. What marks the Texas norther and distinguishes it from the cold front that attacks our northern neighbors is the suddenness of the icy north wind driving the extreme warmth ahead of it.

These winds sweep southward in unobstructed fury across the plains of the northwest and they heighten their velocity with every state they pass. By the time these cold air currents reach Texas, they are in no mood to slow down and are fraught with portentous meaning and chilling intent, particularly when accompanied by rain or sleet.

One of the most striking aspects of these storms is that they really are blue in color. You can actually stand in the middle of Highway 183 in south-central Texas and watch them rolling down the road as azure as the ice of the northern lights until they swoop down on you with the passion of their arctic kiss. Riding through the woods only hours before such a drastic cold front was due to arrive is an enchanting experience, especially when one seemed to be moving in a time frame that depicted an historic past when bandits robbed the romantic way—on horseback.

Even today, the hitching racks still stand in front of that old saloon at String Prairie, giving it the look of authenticity you would expect of a bar that once counted John Wesley Hardin among its customers. The dance hall in back where cowboys and ranchers swung or staggered across the floor with arms around their neighbors' wives or daughters has long since fallen into ruin. The night we robbed the place, it was all in pretty good shape considering it had been standing in the woods for over a half-century. We had been listening to the music for some time as we approached through the trees. At last we sat our horses on the edge of the clearing and surveyed the merriment of the swirling couples in the rosy glow of the kerosene lamps. I had half a mind just to go on and attend the dance, but Abner was adamant about pulling the job. He had what you might call real focus when his intentions were dishonest and he sincerely wanted to consummate a crime.

"Here's the deal, see," he explained patiently. "Oscar takes the money at the dance hall door. Puts it in the cash box. Then he goes over to the office in back of the bar to count the take. Ain't no security or even thought of needin' it this far out in the brush. Eventually he'll go back into the bar to get another drink—you know how he loves the stuff—and then we'll make our move. Grab the box and run."

"Sounds too easy to work," I muttered as we moved forward on foot.

We clung to the shadows along the back of the saloon and peeked through the solitary dirty window on the other side of the office from which we had ridden. There slumped Oscar in his chair, fast asleep in front of the black container on his desk, a bottle cradled in his arms.

"I'm gonna get that money while the gittin's good," Abner whispered. "You keep a lookout." He pulled his bandanna over his face and was gone before I could say anything.

He tiptoed into the room, lifted the box, but then the door from the bar briskly opened. "Hey," yelled the lanky bartender, as he leapt to block the rear exit. Since the desk was to the side of the cluttered room, he had the angle on Abner, and he cut him off. While Oscar looked around stupidly, still half-asleep or drunk or both, Abner lit out for the door to the saloon.

I guess years of practice had honed the barkeep's skills. With surprising speed, he drew a pocket knife while at the same time clicking it open by sliding it across his trouser leg. He took a giant stride toward my partner and flashed a swipe at him with the knife. I saw Abner's shirt tail pop out of his pants with the jerk of the blade against the cloth as his assailant bounced back against the door my friend slammed in his face.

"Look out, he's got a gun," I yelled as I lobbed a good-sized rock through the windowpane. Oscar and his employee hit the floor under shards of window glass and didn't see me legging it past the still open back door and into the woods after Abner, who had come out the front running in stride.

When we reached the horses, we flinched at the blast of a twelve-gauge shotgun. Looking back, we saw the flash of the second barrel. They were firing at the woods the other way, assuming we had beat it that direction from the side of the broken window. We eased off quietly as the dance hall emptied behind us and the excited voices shrilly pronounced various accounts of what happened or what they thought had taken place. The description of the robber they were bandying about fit Goliath, whereas Abner matched David in size. This was all to our advantage, of course, in the follow-up investigation by the authorities.

"Did he cut you?" I asked, when we got deeper into the timber.

"Yeah, but I think it's just a scratch. It ain't bleedin' too much."

"If it's bleedin' at all, it ain't no scratch."

"Well, when we get to the bottom of this hill, we'll take a smoke and check it out. After we see how much money we got first."

We lit our Chesterfields and puffed a moment to calm our nerves. Then I struck another match while Abner lifted the lid on our treasure. It was as empty as a bureaucrat's head.

"I reckon Oscar had done stuck the loot in the safe," I said.

"Either that or else they had a free dance," Abner mused sarcastically. "All we got out of the deal is this here knife wound."

"I thought you said it was just a scratch."

"That's 'fore it began to smart so. You better take a look at it."

I rode my pony around to where I was facing the other way from Abner, struck a match, and peered at the place while Abner held up his shirt. The knife had made the kind of slice a sharp blade makes, clean and neat. The bad part was that it was a pretty deep cut. The good thing was that it was in the fleshy part of the side right above the hip bone. It really wasn't bleeding much, but it was going to require professional treatment. It needed some stitches.

"We're caught now," I said, " 'cause this is goin' to have to be tended to by Doc Nugent. And there's goin' to be questions, and . . ."

"Not necessarily," Abner said, immediately taking charge of the situation.

"You remember when we sewed up Ol' Bill here when he got hung up in that bobwire." He patted his horse's shoulder. "Well, we bought an extra horse repair kit from the vet that day, and it's still in the barn right alongside that whole animal first-aid chest. There's alcohol and everything. You can fix it up."

"I can't," I said weakly, swallowing the sudden lump in my throat.

"You can 'cause you got to," Abner said, pushing his horse forward. I followed on my mare, but I needed a drink badly.

We rode in silence, making good time, and stopping only once to drop the cash box in an old well at an abandoned homestead. We knew that the New Year had come, for we could hear the country folk firing shotguns, rifles, and pistols into the air all around us as we approached our tiny community. I was steeling my nerves to practice medicine without a license, but I was needing that drink worse and worse. Fortunately, we had a jug hidden under the corn sheller.

Entering the barn through the back door, we surveyed the darkened Butler place in the distance. All was quiet. While Abner lit the lantern, I got that drink I craved. Then I took another. I sat down on the milking stool, arranging my tools around me while Abner took a snort out of the bottle. He was amazingly calm, as usual, when the going got tough.

I disinfected my hands and cleaned the wound thoroughly. Abner took a little gasp when I splashed the alcohol on liberally as I worked, but I used enough to kill every germ clear to his other side. Next I almost gulped a drink of the fatal rubbing alcohol before he stopped me. I reached for the other jug, and he wisely stopped me from taking another hit from that also. With the directions for sewing up a horse spread out before me, I grasped the needle and suture fastenings and stuck Abner once. Then I passed out.

When I came around, Abner was staring at me intently. "It's like when we become blood brothers after that picture show. You done the exact same thing that day," he said in a curiously humorous tone for such a trying situation. "Now go get Rachel," he commanded in his firm voice of leadership.

"Gladly," I said, stumbling off toward the house.

I could hear Brother Butler's snores long before I got to Rachel's back bedroom window. Abner's mother was also a sound sleeper or else she would have never got a wink of rest with all that racket. Of course, they each had a clear conscience, and they slept the sleep of those with peace of mind. They were good people. So was their daughter. Now the other offspring in the barn. Well, you know about him.

I dwelt visually on the love of my life for some time before scratching on the screen and whispering her name. I had never seen anything more beautiful than that gorgeous creature, slumbering soundly and spread diagonally across the whiteness of that rumpled bed in a room trimmed in lace the color of pure snow that caught every particle of moon- and starlight through the window panes. At last she opened her eyes, focused on my face at the window for a moment, uncurled herself, and slipped to the floor. There was something profoundly elegant in the way she moved, the shimmering gown a thin veil on her ample figure. The whole family possessed a strange grace in their manner of getting around.

"What's he done now?" she asked.

"Better come take a look at him," I answered.

She threw a feminine robe over her shoulders, unlatched the screen, and baled out into my arms before I was really ready. I was still growing in those days, and those full-figured, full-grown country girls were pretty solid. I staggered backward under her weight, and she caught me to keep me from falling when her feet hit the ground. I had to hurry to catch up with her, for she was already beating it toward the lantern glow through the cracks in the barn. Rachel had that same take-charge personality her brother sported, and she did so after one glance at the situation.

"I don't know what you've been up to," she said sternly, "but I'm getting Dr. Nugent."

"Best you don't know nothin' about this," Abner said just as firmly, "but if you call Doc Nugent we're liable to be getting over this in a jail cell. You got to take care of it, Rachel."

She took a deep breath and moved over to my stool. She took another, deeper breath and began to give orders.

"Go back to my room and get the hand mirror from my dressing table," she commanded. "Now hurry!"

She was disinfecting her hands as I took off. The house was alive with Brother Butler's hoarse and harsh roars, so I bounded into the pearly iridescence of my beloved's room without caution, but before I could grab the mirror I was frozen in place upon viewing Rachel's underthings lying on the chair next to her dresser. They took on an added interest to me in the realization that she had so recently worn them and removed them in that amazingly provocative way women have of coming out of their lingerie, had only just peeled them off that wonderfully womanish form I had seen outlined in negligee only moments before. The feminineness of the surroundings overwhelmed me. I wanted to reach out and touch those personal garments, to clutch them to my heart. I forced myself to leave the comfort of my enchanted circumstances and return to the barn.

"Hurry up. Get over here," Rachel said. "Where in the world have you been!"

"I, I . . ."

"Never mind. Now hold this lantern. Here. Right. Now reflect more light from the mirror directly on the place. Good. Okay. Hold it right there. Be still now," she concluded her orders. "All right, baby, here I go," she said to Abner.

She began to stitch with an intensity while at the same time biting her tongue, her exquisitely lovely face tense with concentration and the moist beginnings of a light film of perspiration. As she sewed, her robe fell off her shoulders and the front of her gown gravitated forward, gradually exposing her breasts to my view.

"Hold that light still!" the sharp voice of the object of my affections commanded, but it was a good thing that she was almost finished because I simply could not direct my attention to the business at hand. She bandaged Abner elaborately around the waist with a support going up over his shoulder.

"There," she exclaimed with relief. "I've got a feeling that this is going to be all right, but I'm going to have another look at it tomorrow, and if it doesn't look good, I'll call Dr. Nugent myself."

Abner was in no shape to argue. He sat down on a hay bale and leaned back against a stall, but I could see the color returning to his pale face. Rachel leaned over and placed a motherly kiss on his cheek, patted him gently on the head, and led the way back toward the house.

No longer preoccupied with her brother's needs, she became her modest self again, demurely hiding her charms by holding her robe around her shoulders and clutching her gown to her neck. I gave her a boost through the window, becoming conscious again of her firm, muscular, and athletic figure. Before ducking under the screen, which was hinged at the top, she suddenly and impulsively reached out and grasped the back of my head, forcefully pulled my face toward hers, and kissed me fiercely on the mouth.

"Take care of him," she whispered fervently.

I had desperately wanted to kiss her like that ever since I had prematurely entered puberty, and when it happened it was such a surprise that I was taken aback. Before I could recover and answer, she closed the screen and then glided over to her bed, where she fell on her knees and clasped her hands together with her elbows on the covers. I knew she was earnestly praying for her wild and reckless brother.

I'm sure she thought that I was gone, but I lingered for some time, drawn by the feminine and alluring curve of her nightgown stretched tightly across her hips. But I had taken advantage of her vulnerability long enough for one evening. I forced myself away from the windowsill and hustled back to the barn.

I had been in love with Rachel for as long as I could remember, and now I was even more enthralled and infatuated than usual with her. It is strange that novelists, playwrights, and movie directors invariably base their most sensuous characters on loose females. How little they know of real emotional individuals. The most passionate women in the world are the intensely religious and spiritual creatures like the one I had been witnessing, but even though this is the truth, it will forever remain obscured by the myth of the erotic joys the jaded woman of easy virtue is supposed to be capable of providing.

Abner was a tough customer, but he was in low spirits when I got back to him. Still, he tried to keep up his leadership role.

"You're goin' to have to finish this one up alone, pardner," he said. "I'm goin' to bed. Just be sure to fix the gate back and brush out the tracks around the spot as well as you can. Better hurry. That norther's fixin' to hit.

"Let me help you to the house," I said.

"No, I can make it. If you'll just take care of my horse before you go."

I watched him make up his mind to move, get up, and walk unsteadily out of the barn. I kept my eye on him until I saw him enter his kitchen door as though we were just getting in from rounding up the cattle, not that either one of his parents would be awake to notice, but it helped to keep up appearances just in case.

I put out the lantern, unsaddled Abner's horse, turned him in the lot, and rode off toward the high end of the neighbor's property. My mare was throwing her head, smelling the unsettled air. The cattle were milling in the pen where Abner had driven them. They were surging out against the gate before I could really get it opened as I leaned down from the saddle to do so. I closed it again and hit the ground a few licks with a post oak branch.

Then I swung into the saddle, feeling that same tingle in the air that the animals were sensing. I saw the trees toward Lockhart start to bend and twist, heard the wind doing its work, noted the first cool advance breeze, then caught the full brunt of the norther as I gave my pony her head. The temperature dropped noticeably, then began to fall rapidly. A real Texas norther was upon the land with nothing between me and the North Pole but a barbed wire fence. By morning it would be freezing, and there was the odor of the rain in the whirling air currents. All our tracks to and from String Prairie would be erased by dawn.

My whole being experienced that flow of excitement that sudden changes in climate always bring to Texans. And to me, the whole violent night, including both the knife thrust and the cutting weather, was a sign for the Texas centennial year, symbolic of the time period Abner and I brought a veritable crime wave to our county by writing a memorable chapter in the history of the Lone Star State with our capers.

The Angel of Santa Sofia
Loren D. Estleman

THE PINKERTON WAS a lean kid with a rusty fringe along his upper lip and a passion for plaid vests and tequila taken without salt and buxom, dark-eyed *señoritas* twice his age. He was working on one at his table now who he claimed was involved with a case, but her bedroom eyes and the fierce glances the couple was drawing from a mustachioed Mexican at the bar said different. Well, he was old enough to take care of himself.

"I hate to keep interrupting," I told him patiently, "but I've come six hundred miles, and I'd sort of like to be reassured that it wasn't for nothing."

"Who'd you say you were again?" He sipped his tequila without taking his eyes from the handsome *mujer*.

I laid the badge, which I never wear, atop the warrant I'd been carrying since Montana. "Page Murdock, U.S. Deputy Marshal. Ten days ago you wired Judge Blackthorne in Helena that you had Dale Sykes under surveillance here in Santa Sofia. Where is he?"

"In a mission down by the river." He had scarcely glanced at either of the items. "You can't miss him. He fits the description on that dodger you had out on him."

Some persuasion seemed in order. I was muddy with dust and perspiration and exhausted from eighteen straight hours in the saddle, not counting the other one hundred and sixty I had spent there over the past ten days. I drew my English revolver from its holster and clanked it down in front of him. "Show me."

He gave the weapon rather more attention than he had my other credentials. Then he sighed, kissed his disappointed companion's hand, and snatched his plug hat from the table.

A short ride from town found us on a rise overlooking an adobe chapel awash in the old gold rays of the setting sun. The only things stirring in the yard were a tobacco-colored dog yawning and stretching from a day spent dozing in whatever shade was available and a couple of Yaqui Indians busy rehanging the building's arched oaken door. You could see the same thing in pueblos all over that part of Arizona. We had been watching for about ten minutes when a figure in a brown hooded robe came out past them carrying a bucket in the direction of the river. The Pinkerton, whose name was Walsh, pointed at him.

"You're joking," I said.

He shook his head. "He's Sykes, down to the stiff elbow and strawberry mark on his left cheek. Around here he's known as Brother Dale. The locals know who he is and what he's done and don't care."

"It's wonderful what a little money can do. The conductor he shot in that mail train robbery two years ago is still chained to a bed. He'll be there the rest of his life."

"As I understand it," said Walsh, "there's no money involved. According to the townspeople I questioned, a local farmer found him lying beside the road a mile north of here about two weeks after the robbery. He had four bullets in him. There isn't a doctor for a hundred miles, so he was taken to the old padre. He was delirious by that time, and it wasn't long before everyone knew his life history. The padre calls his recovery a miracle. The Ya-

quis think tequila had more to do with it. At any rate,
instead of heading down across the border as expected
when he was strong enough, Sykes paid for his keep by
doing odd jobs around the mission, fixing things up,
things like that. Claimed he had seen the light. Last year
he was at the river washing that brown robe the padre
gave him when a little girl playing along the bank fell in.
He jumped in and saved her from drowning. Since then
he's been something of a folk hero hereabouts."

I squinted through the failing light at the man kneeling
on the riverbank. His stiffened right elbow was made obvious by the way he manipulated the bucket while filling
it. The bone had been shattered by a bullet during a shoot-
out at a botched-up bank robbery five years before. "This
is going to be easier than I thought," I said.

"That's what you think," snorted the Pinkerton. "As far
as the people of Santa Sofia are concerned, he's an angel."

"Angels fall."

⌐◦~◦⌐

THE SHERIFF, A dark, thickset Mexican who shooed his
wife and daughters away from the dinner table while he
spoke with us, had a habit of waving both arms over his
head when agitated, which appeared to be his normal
state. He became even more so when I requested his as-
sistance in arresting Dale Sykes.

"*Lo siento, señores!*" he cried, narrowly missing the
coal-oil lamp suspended from the ceiling with a flying
right hand. "This is something I cannot do. The election,
she is but *tres semanas*—three weeks—away. To help
apprehend the most popular man since Miguel Hidalgo
would be to commit what you *norteamericanos* would call
political suicide. I will let you house him in my jail, as
no peace officer can refuse another the use of his facilities,
but I dare not go further."

I could have persuaded him to cooperate, but it was
obvious that he would have been worse than no support

at all. I did get him to lend me a pair of horses from the string of three he kept in a corral behind his home, left my own exhausted mount to the care of his son-in-law, and with Walsh riding beside me and the third horse in tow I returned to the mission.

No guards were posted out front, and the door was unlocked. Inside the chapel was a cavern saved from absolute blackness by a hundred tiny flames that danced wildly in the disturbed air. One of the flames at the far end was moving, propelled by the hands of an old man standing behind the altar, who was busy lighting candles with a long taper. He wore a robe like the one we had seen on Sykes with the hood thrown back to reveal a head of colorless hair curling over a black skullcap and a face like ancient oilcloth. Bright eyes observed our approach.

"I am Father Mendoza. May I help you?" As he spoke his wasted features leapt into sudden prominence as if illumined by his holy spirit, but it was only the reflected glow of the flaming taper as he brought it to his lips. He blew it out.

I showed the badge. He nodded sadly.

"He told me you would come."

"God?" asked Walsh.

"Brother Dale. He said that someday men would come to take him back to atone for his sins."

"Where is he?" I demanded. Piety brings out my bad side.

"In the back. Firearms will not be necessary."

I ignored him, drawing my gun as I strode toward the arch dimly outlined in the back wall. A tremendous bulk blocked my path. I looked up into the stern features of one of the Yaquis I had seen at work in the yard earlier. "Call him off," I told Mendoza. "Before his blood defiles the sanctity of the church."

"For God's sake, Murdock!" breathed the Pinkerton.

"Let him pass, Diego," Mendoza said.

The Indian stepped aside with a grunt, and I pushed past, Walsh at my heels. We were in a dank corridor, heavy with mildew and lit only by a pale glow beyond a half-open door to the right. There were two others, both closed. I chose the open one.

Dale Sykes, looking much as he had in the old roto-gravure Judge Blackthorne had distributed among the marshals only heavier and more sinister with the straw-berry mark on his cheek an angry red blaze, was seated on the edge of a stone pallet strewn not too generously with straw, reading a worn Bible in the light of a candle guttering on a rickety table at his elbow. He, too, had peeled back his hood, exposing a skullcap and a wealth of ill-kept black hair. He looked up as we entered and made a move toward the book with his clumsy right arm.

"Stop!" My bellow rang off the walls of the cramped cell. "Get that Bible."

Walsh glanced at me strangely but stepped forward and wrenched the black-bound volume from Sykes's hand.

"I was only marking my place," said the man on the pallet.

I accepted the Bible and riffled through it while Walsh covered Sykes with a baby Remington he had taken from a special pocket beneath his left arm. The book had no hollow where a gun could be hidden. I tossed it onto the pallet. "Keep him covered while I search him," I told the Pinkerton.

There was nothing on him but a small belt purse con-taining a few coins. "Who shot you?" I asked him.

"My partners." His tone was low, apologetic. "We ar-gued about how to divide the money from the mail-train job. I lost, and they left me for dead."

"The same way you left that conductor," I said.

"He didn't die? Each night I pray that he did not."

"I'm sure he prays every night that he did. Get going." I moved away from the door and waved him toward it with my gun.

The sheriff, who lived across the alley from the jail, muttered a string of gentle blasphemies in Spanish as he unlocked the door to the only cell. The key grated. Jails don't get a lot of use in border towns. When it was open I shoved the prisoner stumbling over the iron cot in the corner.

"There's no call to be so rough," the Pinkerton protested.

"We'll keep an eye on him tonight if it's all right with you," I told the sheriff. "If that son-in-law of yours is any good with horses we'll be able to pull out in the morning."

"What do you mean, 'we'?" Walsh's embryonic mustache bristled.

"The Great Northern Pacific has placed a thousand dollars on Sykes's head. I thought you might want to split it."

He made no reply.

We were interrupted only once during our vigil when someone rapped on the front door. I came up out of a sound sleep on the sheriff's cot, drawing my gun. Walsh, who was standing first watch, was at the door with his Remington in hand. "Who is it?"

There was a muffled response. The Pinkerton opened the door and stepped back, displaying the gun. A short Mexican with a drawn, tragic face, attired in the sandals and shapeless white cotton shirt and trousers that comprise the male uniform down there, moved inside timidly, sombrero clutched in both hands. Just before Walsh closed the door behind him I caught a glimpse of a crowd of men in similar costumes and drably clad women gathered in front of the building.

In a voice scarcely above a whisper, our visitor said, "I have come, good *señores*, to petition for Brother Dale's release."

Walsh snorted. I said, "Who are you?"

"Francisco Vargas, *Señor* Marshal. I am the man whose little daughter Brother Dale rescued from the river last year. Because of this it was decided that I speak for the citizens of Santa Sofia."

"The whole town's with you on this?" I was standing over him now. He was trembling. He was old enough to remember Maximilian and the days when all authority was considered evil.

"Go home, Francisco." Sykes had both hands on the bars of his cell. "I have sinned and must accept my punishment. Go home, and tell everyone else to do the same."

"*Hermano* Dale!" Vargas stepped toward the prisoner. Their hands were almost touching, when I lunged and sent the Mexican reeling with a backhand slash across his face.

"Murdock!" cried Walsh, outraged. He thrust his revolver at me. I leveled mine. He stopped.

"Search him!" I snapped, indicating the Mexican cowering across the room. "That sombrero alone could hide an arsenal."

Somewhat subdued, the Pinkerton put away his gun and turned to the task. When he was finished he fixed me with an accusing glare. "He's not carrying so much as a nail file."

A stone crashed through the barred window in the door. Angry shouts drifted in through the jagged aperture.

"Now you've done it!" Walsh barked.

I flung an arm around Vargas's neck and dragged him into the center of the room. "Tell them if they aren't gone in five minutes, I'll scatter your brains!" I placed the muzzle of my revolver against his right temple.

He did as directed. I remembered enough Spanish from my cowpunching days to know that nothing slipped past me. Walsh, watching at the window, told me when the last of the spectators had left. I let the Mexican go with the assurance that further incidents would mean Sykes's life and took the next watch without comment. That seemed to suit the Pinkerton.

Dawn found the sheriff conspicuously absent, which was more than I could say for the rest of the town. It was out in force as we marched our prisoner out to where the son-in-law waited with our horses and the one I had bought from the sheriff the night before. I tossed the young man a five-dollar gold piece for their care and was ordering Sykes to mount up when a Mexican girl of about ten stepped out of the crowd bearing flowers *"por el Her-mano Dale."* I saw Francisco Vargas standing nearby and knew who she was.

"No gifts," I said, stepping between her and Sykes.

An angry murmuring arose from the crowd.

"Please," said Sykes, "may I speak to her?"

"Don't you have a heart?" Walsh demanded. "Let him."

I looked the girl over. "Just a second," I said, and tore the flowers from her grasp. I pulled apart the paper wrapping. Flowers fluttered to the ground, nothing more. The crowd laughed nastily. "Make it quick," I snapped.

The girl was crying. Bending over her, Sykes said a few soothing words in Spanish and raised a hand to tuck a stray tendril of hair inside her scarf. He fanned his fingers, made a fist beside her ear, and asked her to hold out her hand. When she did so, four coins dropped into it from his fist. She laughed delightedly. He kissed her and turned toward his horse.

"Where'd you pick that up?" I demanded.

"My father taught it to me. The children love it."

We left Santa Sofia at a trot, Sykes in the middle. Walsh reined in after half a mile.

"What's the matter?" I drew rein. "Are we being fol-lowed?"

"No, and we're not likely to be. I'm going back."

"Meaning?"

"Meaning I don't like your kind of law, Murdock." His face was flushed. "This isn't the same man who robbed that mail train two years ago. His name may be Sykes, and it may have been his finger that pulled the trigger on that conductor, but he isn't the same. But that doesn't make any difference to you, does it?"

"Is it supposed to?"

He looked at me sadly. "If you don't know the answer to that, you're beyond help."

"Suit yourself. Casa Grande is full of good men with guns who'll be willing to help collect that reward."

He wheeled and cantered off without another word.

∽◦∾

A HANDFUL OF lights were still burning in Santa Sofia as I rode ploddingly down its only street, leading the second horse with its burden slung across the saddle. As I neared the sheriff's home, a fresh yellow glow spread from one of the windows. The lawman emerged carrying a shotgun and struggling to tug his suspenders up over his red-flanneled shoulders. "*Señor* Deputy!" he called. I kept going.

Another figure came trotting out the door of the cantina. This proved to be Walsh. "Murdock, what is it?" He took hold of my bridle. "What are you doing back? You just left this morning."

A crowd was gathering. A lantern was produced, and the dead man on the other horse was examined. "It is Brother Dale!" someone exclaimed. There was an ominous rumbling.

"You killed him!" Walsh looked horrified.

"He pulled a gun," I said. "Ten miles north of here. He got off a shot. So did I. I didn't miss."

"He has been shot in the back!" said the sheriff.

"His horse panicked. He was turning to rein it back around when I plugged him." I had to shout to be heard above the furious babble of voices.

The Pinkerton was livid. "You're not only a murderer, but a liar as well! Where would he get a gun?"

"I wondered about that, too. I think Vargas passed it to him last night just before I jumped him. You saw Sykes's sleight-of-hand trick with the coins. He could have plucked it out of the sombrero just as easily without us seeing him and hidden it out until it would do him the most good."

"Hogwash! You hated him and took advantage of the first opportunity to kill him. You'll hang for this, Murdock, badge or no badge!"

"Then why did I come back?" While he was puzzling

that one out I drew my revolver. "Let go of that bridle."

He obeyed. "Where are you going?"

"To the mission."

The whole town had turned out by the time I reached the chapel, shouting *"Asesino!"* and brandishing machetes and pitchforks. The padre and the two Yaquis were standing in front. I had to back inside, rotating the gun right and left. I don't remember if I had cleared the threshold before I collapsed.

Later Father Mendoza told me he'd taken twenty-seven stitches in the gash Brother Dale's bullet had carved along the right side of my rib cage.

The Authors

Louis L'Amour (1908–1988) was the most successful Western writer of all time, selling fifteen to twenty thousand books a day at the height of his popularity. He wrote the kind of action fiction beloved by so many generations of Americans, with strong heroes, evil villains, proud, energetic heroines, and all of the excitement and danger that the West represented. His novels include such masterpieces as *Hondo, Shalako, Down the Long Hills, The Cherokee Trail*, and *Last of the Breed*. His most famous series was the Sacketts saga, later made into several excellent television movies. And yet, often overlooked in all his success, was the philosophic side of L'Amour, as demonstrated in this wonderful story.

Trey Barker grew up in Texas but currently lives in Colorado, where he writes fiction and stage plays in a number of genres. His first novel, *The Dark House*, was published in September 2000 by Blue Murder Press.

In a full-time writing career that has spanned a couple of decades, **James M. Reasoner** has written in virtually every category of commercial fiction. His novel *Texas Wind* is a true cult classic and his gritty crime stories about contemporary Texas are in the first rank of today's suspense fiction. He has written many books in ongoing Western series, including the *Faraday*, *Stagecoach*, and *Abilene* novel series. Fortunately for Western readers, his Westerns are just as good as his crime work.

C. Hall Thompson is best known for his novel *A Gun for Billy Reo*, a classic study of a boy's rite of passage to manhood in the West. He wrote two other novels during his career, *Under the Badge* and *Montana*, but neither lived up to the impressive writing in his second novel. "Posse" is a short story featuring Billy Reo, with a markedly different ending than the book.

Marcus Pelegrimas is an author who lives and writes in St. Louis, Missouri.

Bill Gulick was born in Missouri in 1916. He notes, in a biographical sketch, "I write books that are set in the West—not Westerns." In such fully realized novels as *Bend of the Snake* and *Liveliest Town in the West*, one sees the distinction Gulick makes. His books are character studies as well as plot-driven stories, and his take on frontier America is almost always as exciting as his story lines. Gulick has continued to write, and write well, into the present day. He is one of those writers whose love of the craft is apparent in each and every sentence.

Ed Gorman is a Midwesterner. He was born in Iowa in 1941; grew up in Minneapolis, Minnesota, and Marion, Iowa; and finally settled down in Cedar Rapids, Iowa. While primarily a suspense novelist, he has written half a dozen Western novels and published a collection of Western stories. His novel *Wolf Moon* was a Spur nominee for

Best Paperback Original. About his Western novels, *Publishers Weekly* said, "Gorman writes Westerns for grownups," which the author says he took as a high compliment, and was indeed his goal in writing his books.

Morris Hershman lives in New York City and has published a wide variety of fiction in several genres. Other work by him appears in *Murder Most Irish, Santa Clues*, and *Crimes of Passion*.

Frank Gruber (1904–1969) wrote more than fifty novels during his thirty-plus years as a writer, turning to fiction writing after stints as a trade journal editor and correspondence school teacher. Besides Westerns, he also wrote screenplays and several mysteries. His books captured the essence of the Western frontiersman, often men and women coming from the East during the Civil War to begin new lives in the West. Notable novels include *Fighting Man, This Gun Is Still, Quantrell's Raiders*, and *Town Tamer*.

Al Sarrantonio's writing covers a wide range of territory that includes horror, mystery, Western, and science fiction. His short tales of horror, which have appeared in *Whispers, The Horror Show*, and the *Shadows* anthologies, helped to define contemporary dark fantasy. His novels include *West Texas, Campbell Wood, October, House Haunted*, and the science-fiction werewolf story *Moonbane*. He co-edited the anthology *100 Hair-Raising Little Horror Stories*.

Daniel Ransom's science-fiction novel *Zone Soldiers* explores a future United States weakened by the collapse of society and sectioned off into different areas where humans are sent to live. He has also written another science-fiction novel, *The Fugitive Stars*. Other stories by him appear in *Monster Brigade 3000, Future Net*, and *Dracula: Prince of Darkness*. Besides writing science fiction and western fiction, he's also a successful horror writer, as evidenced by his novels *The Serpent's Kiss* and *The Long Midnight*.

Elizabeth Fackler is an acclaimed author of historical fiction, including the critically praised *Billy the Kid: The Legend of El Chivato* and *Texas Lily*. Her series featuring the outlaw Seth Strummar includes *Blood Kin, Backtrail, Road from Betrayal, Badlands*, and *Breaking Even*. Her latest mystery, *Patricide*, is a gritty tale of murder set in modern El Paso. Another Seth story, *Backlash*, will be published in the anthology *Weird Trails* later this year.

Michael Stotter has worked at various jobs in publishing, one of which was helping George Gilman (whose violent books about the mythic West became bestsellers in the 1970s) produce a fanzine that kept his readers abreast of the author's forthcoming new books. Stotter is now involved in the British crime scene, in particular with the fine magazine *A Shot in the Dark*, and has turned to writing his own Westerns. His novels include the well-reviewed *McKinney's Revenge* and *Tombstone Showdown*.

Tom Piccirilli is the author of eight novels, including *Hexes, Shards, The Night Class, The Deceased*, and his Felicity's Crown mystery series consisting of *The Dead Past* and *Sorrow's Crown*. He's sold more than one hundred stories to various anthologies, including *Future Crimes, Bad News, The Conspiracy Files, Star Colonies, Best of the American West II, New Mythos Legends*, and the magazines *Cemetery Dance, Carpe Noctem, The Third Alternative, CrimeWave, Lore*, and *Hardboiled*, among many others. He lives in Estes Park, Colorado, where he's currently working on a Western novel.

Bill Pronzini has worked in virtually every genre of popular fiction. Though he's best known as the creator of the

Nameless mystery novels, he has written several first-rate Westerns, as well as a half dozen remarkable novels of dark suspense. This is not to slight his Western stories at all, with novels such as *Starvation Camp, Quincannon*, and *Firewind*, establishing him as a master of the Western. In addition to his novels, Pronzini is an especially gifted short story writer, several of his pieces winning prestigious awards, including the Shamus.

Riley Froh was born in Luling, Texas, where he grew up around ranch people similar to the ones in his short story. He is descended from the town's original settlers. His great-great grandfather drove cattle and his great-great-great grandfather was a noted Texas ranger. He holds a Bachelor's and a Master's degree from Southwest Texas State University and a Ph.D. from Texas A&M University. He is the author of *Wildcatter Extraordinary, Edgar B. Davis and Sequences in Business Capitalism*, and several scholarly articles on Texas themes.

Loren D. Estleman is generally considered the best Western writer of his generation. Such novels as *Aces & Eights, The Stranglers*, and *Bloody Season* rank with the very best Western novels ever written. As will be seen here, Estleman brings high style to his writing, the sentences things of beauty in and of themselves. Few writers of prose can claim that. He has brought poetry, historical truth and great wisdom to the genre. His finest short Western fiction was collected in *The Best Western Stories of Loren D. Estleman*.

Copyrights and Permissions

8. Since we may never attain union with the Divine beloved, let us be content with the dust of His threshold.

AJA translates 1 2 3 4 5 6 7 8.
Another verse-translation by JP.

35

MQ 376, B 393, RS 28, P 344.

Metre: رمل مثمّن مخبون مقصور ∪∪−−|∪∪−−|∪∪−−|$\overline{∪∪}$−.

Order of lines: B + RS as MQ. P 1 2 3 5 4 6 7.

1. For اهل دلست این و B + RS + P read پیر مغانست.

2. Cf. 1⁴.

4. JN has misunderstood; HB is less elegant but more accurate:

"Heaven's organist, that robber, superior men waylays:
   At this how check my sorrow, nor clamorous tumult raise?"

5. JN is again inaccurate; HB again pedestrian but correct:

"No wine we poured to water the rose's boiling glow;
   And so we boil from yearning in flames of hopeless woe."

He glosses: "When the summer came we drank no wine."

6. JN omits; HB is incorrect:

"A fiery dew ideal from tulips' cups we drain:
   Hence evil eye! this rapture from wine nor song we gain."

But wine and music make up Ḥāfiẓ' specific for rapture, cf. 3⁸, 13¹⁰, 22²; and it is the lack of them (cf. lines 2, 5) that has made the poet distraught: the "imaginary" wine of the tulip's cup is better than none at all.

7. The poet says the very opposite of what JN translates; so RS:

> "Wem, Hafis, kann man das Wunder
> Jemals mitzutheilen wagen,
> Dass wir Sprosser sei'n und schweigen
> In der Rose Wonnetagen?"

JN translates 1 2 3 4 5 7.

Other verse-translations by JP, HB.

36

MQ 387, B 457, RS 15, P 407.

Metre: رمل مثمّن مخبون مقصور $\cup\cup--|\cup\cup--|\cup\cup--|\overline{\cup\cup}-$.

Order of lines: B + RS 1 2 3 4 5 6 8 9 7. P 1 2 3 4 5 7 6 8 9.

2. For اى B + RS read كاى.

4. The comparison of the mystic with a mote dancing in the sunbeam is common in Persian poetry; the appropriateness of the image چرخ زنان to the whirling Mevlevi dance is obvious.

5. For ور B reads در (misprint).

6. For من B + RS read ما. Note the pun پيمان—پيمانه.

7. For وز B + RS read ز. Ahriman was the spirit of evil and darkness in the Zoroastrian religion; his name is then extended to signify "seducer", "devil". The poet gives a remarkable picture of the conflict between profane and sacred love.

8. For با صبا B + RS read بصبا. 'Umar Khaiyām has a variation (how less perfect!) of this theme:

در هر دشتى كه لاله‌زارى بودست   آن لاله ز خون شهريارى بودست
هر برگ بنفشه كز زمين مى‌رويد   خاليست كه بر رخ نگارى بودست

FitzGerald:

> "I sometimes think that never blows so red
> The Rose as where some buried Caesar bled;
> That every Hyacinth the Garden wears
> Dropt in her Lap from some once lovely Head."

9. For شیرین دهنان B + RS read سیمین ذقنان.

AJA translates 1 2 3 4 5 6 7 8 9.

Other verse-translations by JP, HB, RG.

37

MQ 392, B 453, RS 11, P 392.

Metre: مضارع مثمّن اخرب

$--\cup|-\cup--|--\cup|-\cup-\underline{\cup}.$

Order of lines unvaried.

1. For کوی MQ reads گوی (misprint).

2. For توان P reads بود.

5. An elegant play on words that defies adequate translation.

6. See 8[4] and note.

7. For یحیی B + RS + P read منصور. Shāh Manṣūr is identical
with Shujā' al-Dīn, son of Sharaf al-Dīn Muẓaffar, son of Mubāriz
al-Dīn Muḥammad, and was a nephew of Shāh Shujā' (for whom
see note on 11[5]); after a troubled reign he was put to death by
Tīmūr in 795/1393. Shāh Yaḥyā (Nuṣrat al-Dīn) his brother had
an equally turbulent career. Both rulers are mentioned several
times by Ḥāfiẓ. For the history of the ill-fated Muẓaffarid house,
see *Encyclopaedia of Islam*, vol. III, pp. 798–9.

WL translates 1 2 3 4 5 6 7.

Other verse-translations by JP, HB, RG.

38

MQ 396, B 459, RS 17, P 405.

Metre: مضارع مثمّن اخرب مکفوف محذوف

$--\cup|-\cup-\cup|\cup--\cup|-\cup-.$

Order of lines: P 1 2 5 * 4 6. B + RS as MQ.

1. This poem is in the same metre and rhyme as another by Ḥāfiẓ (MQ 395) beginning:

گلبرگ را ز سنبل مشکین نقاب کن

یعنی که رخ بپوش و جهانی خراب کن

4. For the conceit, cf. 13⁴ and note; Ḥāfiẓ says elsewhere:

خیز و در کاسهٔ زر آب طربناک انداز

پیشتر زانکه شود کاسهٔ سر خاک انداز

5. After this line P adds (taking the verse out of MQ 395):

همچون حباب دیده بروی قدح گشای

وین خانه را قیاس اساس از حباب کن

6. For روی عزم B + RS read عزم جزم.

AJA translates 1 2 3 4 5 6.

Other verse-translations by JP, HB.

39

MQ 407, B 477, RS 10, P 413.

Metre: رمل مثمّن مخبون محذوف ∪∪−−|∪∪−−|∪∪−−|∪̄∪−.

Order of lines: B + RS 1 2 3 4 7 5 6 8. P 1 2 7 3 4 5 6 8.

1. A splendid meditation on a vision of the crescent moon.

2. For بخفتیدی B + RS read بخسبیدی. RG's version of this poem is rather free; for a closer translation, though less poetical, see HB.

3. Sc. if you cut all material ties; cf. 6². P reads روی و (misprint).

4. For شب دزد P reads شبگرد.

6. For عرصهٔ B reads عرضهٔ (misprint).

8. For زهد B + RS read زرق. The woollen robe is the mark of the Ṣūfī; cf. 42⁵.

RG translates 1 2 7 4 6 5.

Other verse-translations by JP, HB.

40

MQ 417, B 489, RS 11, P 428.

Metre: متقارب مثمّن اثلم ‏ .–– ∪ | ––(∪) | ––∪ | ––∪.

Order of lines: B+RS 1 2 3 4 5 6 * § ‡ ∥ 7. P as MQ.

1. Ḥāfiẓ has another poem in the same rare metre and rhyme:

گردن نهادیم الحکم لله ‏ ‏ گر تیغ بارد در کوی آن ماه

Note the play on the two meanings of *mudām*.

2. See note on 33²; for the internal rhyming (rather uncommon
in Ḥāfiẓ) cf. 3²˒⁹.

3. For برندی B+RS read بمستی.

4. For دست B+RS+P read قول.

6. After this line B+RS add:

صبر از خدا خواه صبر از خدا خواه	از صبر عاشق خوشتر نباشد
صوفی بینداز این رسم و این راه	دلق ملمّع زنّار راهست
از وصل جانان صد لوحش الله	وقتی برویش خوش بود وقتم
سر بر ندارم از خاك درگاه	رخ بر نتابم از راه خدمت

7. B+RS reverse درس and ورد.

AJA translates 1 2 3 4 5 6 7.

Another verse-translation by JP.

41

MQ 428, B 487, RS 9, P 432.

Metre: هزج مسدّس محذوف ‏ .––∪ | ‏ –––∪ | –––∪.

Order of lines: B+RS 1 2 3 4 5 6 8 9 7 10. P as MQ.

2. For هستیش ز شهر B+RS read بشهر هستیش. A splendid
epitome of the poet's philosophy of unreason!

3. For عشوهٔ P reads جرعهٔ. RG has misunderstood this and the following line; RS is better:

> "Der schöne Weinverkäufer sah
> Mich dann gar freundlich an,
> So dass ich, vor des Schicksals List
> Nun sicher, leben kann.
>
> Vom Schenken mit den Bogenbrau'n
> Vernahm, was folgt, mein Ohr:
> 'O du, den sich des Tadels Pfeil
> Zum Ziele auserkohr!'"

6. Cf. 47^{13-15}. The Anca is a fabulous bird, hence its nesting-place is unattainable.

7. For وصل B reads حسن. For حسن B reads وصل; P reads عشق. The literal meaning is, "What man profits of union with that royal beauty who is ever playing at self-love?" This and the lines following contain the essence of the Ṣūfī doctrine of Divine love: God created the world to be an image of Himself; how can the image aspire to the love of its Creator? All things, in so far as they have any meaning at all, are reflections of the Divine beauty, and do not exist apart from God. This then is the riddle of life: that we are by our very being impelled to seek the love of Him who is utterly self-sufficient and has no need of us or our love.

9. For برانيم B + RS read برانٖم. For this and the following line, cf. 3^8 and note.

RG translates 1 2 3 4 5 6 8 9 7 10.

Other verse-translations by JP, HB (four verses):

42

MQ 447, B 518, RS 24, P 470.

Metre: هزج مسدّس محذوف $\cup - - - | \cup - - - | \cup - -$.

Order of lines: B + RS 1 2 6 3 4 5 7. P as MQ.

1. Cf. 47⁷⁻⁸.

2. Presumably the *naṣīḥat* is the poet's customary warning that material beauty is transient, the only course is to drink the wine of unreason; cf. 37⁷⁻⁸.

4. For حکم B + RS read مهر. The sentiment is similar to that expressed by Ḥāfiẓ elsewhere:

در کوی نیکنامی مارا گذر ندادند   گر تو نمی‌پسندی تغییر کن قضا را

7. The poet, as his name indicates, knew the Qur'ān by heart (ḥāfiẓ): in a double sense therefore he had the Scriptures in his breast!

AJA translates 1 2 3 4 5 6 7.

Another verse-translation by JP.

43

MQ 452, B 503, RS 9, P 492.

Metre: خفیف مخبون محذوف ‿‿ – – | ∪ – ∪ – | ‿‿ – •.

Order of lines: B + RS 1 2 3 4 * § 5. P as MQ.

1. An excellent meditation on the true and false Ṣūfī.

2. The word عقیله properly signifies "noble veiled woman", and is then applied by extension to anything noble and precious. The poet is of course being sarcastic: noble reason—the religion of self-love and pride—has nothing to do with his philosophy of unreasoning love.

3. What better text than this to explain Ḥāfiẓ' use of the terms "wine" and "drunkenness" to mean the denial of reason and the annihilation of self?

4. For دوای B + RS + P read گواه. After this line B + RS add:

نبود باغ خلدرا رونق   بی می راوق و لب حوری

مهر آن ماه بایدت ورزید   گر چه چون آفتاب مشهوری

Two singularly inept verses!

WL translates 1 2 3 § 4 5.

Another verse-translation by JP.

44

MQ 465, B 528, RS 34, P 490.

Metre: مضارع مثمّن اخرب مكفوف محذوف

$$- - \cup \, | - \cup - \cup \, | \cup - - \cup \, | - \cup -.$$

Order of lines: P 1 2 5 3 4 6 7. B + RS as P.

1. RS reads رفتم بباغ تا که بچینم سحر گلی.

2. غلغل as well as meaning "clamour" also signifies the sound made by a liquid being poured out of a long-necked flagon.

3. B + RS read چمن باغ.

4. For حسن B + RS read خار. For the second hemistich B + RS read اینرا تغیّری نه و آنرا تبدّلی.

7. For فرج B + RS + P read فرح. For از B + RS read زین. For چرخ B + RS read کون.

AJA translates 1 2 3 4 5 6 7.

Other verse-translations by JP, GB, HB.

45

MQ 476, B 566, RS 72, P 445.

Metre: مجتثّ مثمّن مخبون $\cup - \cup - \, | \cup \cup - - \, | \cup - \cup - \, | \cup \cup - -.$

Order of lines: B + RS 1 2 3 4 6 5 7. P as MQ.

2. For راهت B + RS read راهست. RS translates: "Mein Aug' ruht auf der Strasse Rand". The phrase is omitted by RG.

3. For عزیزم B + RS read ضعیفم. For فزایش B + RS + P read فزایت; MQ defends the reading فزایش by referring the enclitic pronoun to جان. For ببخشش B + RS read ببخش.

6. For بیندم B + RS read نبندم and so RG translates.

7. For بدان B + RS read بهر. Perhaps we are to conclude from this last line that the poem was addressed to an Arab friend, Ḥāfiẓ intending a pun on the double meaning of *Turkī*.

RG translates 1 2 3 6 5 4 7.

Another verse-translation by JP.

MQ p. 356, B 686, RS 2 (p. 464), F 11, P 863.

Metre: متقارب مثمّن محذوف | •-∪ | --∪ | --∪ | --∪ •.

Order of lines highly irregular.

1. This fine poem in *mathnawī* verse has suffered from wholesale interpolations. I have followed the text established by F which restores perfect symmetry to an otherwise shapeless agglomeration and disembarrasses the poet of many weak lines.

2. "Both parts", i.e. grace and perfection.

3. See notes on 11⁶, 12⁷, 15⁵. For یا MQ + P read بده.

4. For تمام B + RS read مدام.

5. The original has "the treasure of Qārūn" (i.e. Korah). For the story of Korah, Moses' wealthy kinsman, his oppression and his overthrow, see Qur'ān, Sūra XXVIII, 76–82.

7. With this catalogue of the ancient kings of Persia cf. 13⁴.

9. The Persian poets often compare the world with an ancient convent, in which men lodge for their little time.

10. This and the following three lines are not in B + RS.

12. For رفت MQ + P read رای. Shīda was the son of Afrāsiyāb.

13. For کاخش MQ + P read قصرش. For هم دخمه‌اش MQ reads دخمه‌اش نیز, P reads دخمه نیزش.

14. The "virgin chastely veiled" is the wine, often so called by the Persian poets.

17. For بر درم B + RS + MQ + P read بر زنم. The word شیر گیر has the double meaning (both intended here) of "lion-taming" and "tipsy". The "old wolf" is, as often in Persian poetry, the world, cunning and full of treachery.

18. MQ reads در آن میسرشت P; در آن مَیْ سرشت.

19. For دماغ MQ + P read مشام. For یا MQ + P read بده.

20. For سر از به من ده میم ده B + RS + MQ + P read. For
.شوم ایمن از فکرت هولناک B + RS read سری, MQ + P read ز

23. For the ruin and the treasure, see 9[7] and note.

25. For دم از پارسائی MQ reads دم پادشاهی (breaking the rhyme), P دم پادشائی, B + RS در پارسائی. For در خسروی B + RS + MQ + P read دم خسروی.

26. For رود زهره دورد MQ + P read رود آواز زهره. Cf.:

در آسمان نه عجب گر بگفتهٔ حافظ   سرود زهره برقص آورد مسیحا را

Other verse-translations by JP, HB.

47

MQ p. 354, B 685, RS 1 (p. 454), F 8, P 861.

Metre: هزج مسدّس محذوف ∪ – – – | ∪ – – – | ∪ – –.
Order of lines irregular.

1. I have adopted the edition of F which largely reconstructs the poem. For بسیار MQ + P read چندین.

2. For تنها رو MQ + P read و تنها. For یکس B + RS + MQ + P read دو یکس. For و دد و دام و RS, دد و دم در B reads دو راه است و. For و داست MQ + P دد و.

3. P reads 4 here and then 3.

4. For که P reads چو. For میبینم P reads میبینی. For ایمن B + RS + MQ + P read خرّم.

5. For حبیبان B + RS + MQ + P read رفیقان.

6. For کاری بر آید B + RS, کاری گشاید MQ + P read این ره سرآید. For Khiḍr see note on 187.

7. B + RS + MQ + P here run on to the section 11–15; this line is l. 20 in B + RS + MQ, l. 19 in P.

8. This line is l. 15 in B + RS, l. 19 in MQ, l. 18 in P. For زخم B + RS + MQ + P read تیغ.

9. This line is l. 14 in B + RS, l. 30 in P; it is not given in MQ.

10. This line is l. 22 in B + RS, l. 21 in MQ, l. 20 in P.

11. This line and the four following are ll. 7–11 in B + RS + P, ll. 7, 9–12 in MQ. For عطا MQ + P read وفا. The poet quotes Qur'ān, Sūra 21[89] (Zachariah crying to God for a child to succeed him). After this line MQ adds:

چنینم هست یاد از پیر دانا   فراموشم نشد هرگز همانا

But this is a very feeble verse.

12. For رند MQ reads رندی.

14. For و گفتا MQ + P read گفتا. For the significance of the simurgh, see note on 41[6].

16. This line is l. 16 in MQ + P + B + RS. For نیاز B + RS read نثار. For ما B + RS + MQ + P read من.

17. This line is l. 13 in B + RS + MQ, l. 12 in P. For سهی MQ + P read روان. For ز بال B + RS read ز شاخ, MQ, چو شاخ ز, and P ز تاک و. If بال is correct, it must signify "top".

18. This line is l. 15 in MQ, l. 14 in P, l. 17 in B + RS. B + RS read کفت و کوئی. B + RS + MQ read سر چشمه و یک طرف.

19. This line is l. 17 in MQ + P, l. 18 in B + RS.

20. This line is l. 19 in MQ + B + RS, l. 15 in P. For آیدت MQ + P read آمدت.

21. This line is l. 14 in MQ, l. 13 in P, l. 12 in B + RS. For سرمست MQ + P read بدمست.

22. This line is l. 28 in MQ, l. 27 in P, l. 32 in B + RS. For مخوانید MQ + P read بخوانید.

23. This line is l. 29 in MQ, l. 28 in P, l. 33 in B + RS. For سنگ انداز MQ + P read حکم انداز.

24. This line and the four following are ll. 23–7 in MQ, ll. 22–6 in P, ll. 31, 34–7 in B + RS. For به تقریر B + RS + MQ + P read بتحریر. The poet refers to Qur'ān, Sūra LXVIII, 1 and puns on the

word *nūn* which the commentators interpret as "fish"; he implies
that his poetry is as divinely inspired as the Qur'ān, cf. 6¹¹.

25. B+RS read كشتيم...سرشتيم. For بود B+RS read گشت.

26. For مغز شعر نغزش MQ reads نغز شعر و مغز, B+RS+P
و اجزاست. For مغز شعر و مغز B+RS read read.

27. For بيا وز P reads بياور.

28. For چين P reads جين (misprint). For نه زآن MQ+P read
نه آن. For آهو P reads حورى. See 333³ and note: the poet repeats
his claim that his poetry has a celestial origin.

Another verse-translation by JP.

48

F 10.

Metre: متقارب مثمّن مقصور ∪ – – | ∪ – – | ∪ – – | ∪ –.

1. F has reconstructed this poem out of lines excluded by him
from the *Sāqī-nāma* (46); these lines are found in other editions
of that composition (MQ, P).

2. For هميدارم MQ+P read همى بينم.

3. For وگر MQ reads دگر. For رند P reads زند.

4. The idea is evidently proverbial. Cf. Fakhr al-Dīn Gurgānī,
Vīs u Rāmīn (ed. Minovi), p. 440:

شنيدستى كه شب آبستن آيد   نداند كس كه فردا زو چه زايد

For other parallels, see 'Alī Akbar Dihkhudā, *Amthāl u ḥikam*,
pp. 947–8.

5. For و ساغر MQ+P read به ساغر.

49

MQ p. 367, B 268, RS 154, P 680.

Metre: رمل مثمّن مقصور – ∪ – – | – ∪ – – | – ∪ – – | – ∪ –.
Order of lines unvaried.

1. The older editors (B + RS) printed this poem among the ghazals, but modern Persian editors place it among the *muqaṭṭaʿāt*. For رندی B + RS read جانان .

3. For برد و شد B + RS + P read می.برد .

5. B + RS read تلخ و تیز و گلرنگست .Cf. 31⁶ دختری شبگرد و for the description.

Other verse-translations by JP, RG.

50

MQ p. 369, B 604, RS 31, P 692.

Metre: رمل مثمّن مخبون مقصور ᴗᴗ– –|ᴗᴗ– –|ᴗᴗ– –|‾ᴗᴗ–.
Order of lines unvaried.

1. B + RS read سرور سلطان .

2. For کاف و الف B + RS read پنج و سه روز .کاف و الف = 20 +
1 = 21. For نظم B + RS read وضع .

3. For او B + RS read وی . The phrase رحمت حق is a chronogram; the numerical value of the constituent letters is

$$200 + 8 + 40 + 400 + 8 + 100 = 756.$$

Another verse-translation by JP.

LIST OF TRANSLATORS

INDEX OF FIRST LINES

INDEX OF FIRST LINES